# BOOKS BY JIM HARRISON

## NOVELS

*Wolf*
*A Good Day to Die*
*Farmer*
*Legends of the Fall*
*Warlock*
*Sundog*
*Dalva*

## POETRY

*Plain Song*
*Locations*
*Outlyer*
*Letters to Yesenin*
*Returning to Earth*
*Selected & New Poems*
*The Theory & Practice of Rivers & Other Poems*

# DALVA

## JIM HARRISON

E. P. Dutton/Seymour Lawrence • New York

*Publisher's Note:* This novel is a work of fiction. Names, characters, places, and incidents either are the product of the author's imagination or are used fictitiously, and any resemblance to actual persons, living or dead, events, or locales is entirely coincidental.

No part of this publication may be reproduced or transmitted in any form or by any means, electronic or mechanical, including photocopy, recording, or any information storage and retrieval system now known or to be invented, without permission in writing from the publisher, except by a reviewer who wishes to quote brief passages in connection with a review written for inclusion in a magazine, newspaper, or broadcast.

Published in the United States by E. P. Dutton / Seymour Lawrence, a division of NAL Penguin Inc., 2 Park Avenue, New York, N.Y. 10016.

Published simultaneously in Canada by
Fitzhenry and Whiteside, Limited, Toronto.

Library of Congress Cataloging-in-Publication Data

Harrison, Jim, 1937–
Dalva.

I. Title.
PS3558.A67D35   1988      813'.54      87-24442
ISBN: 0-525-24624-X

DESIGNED BY EARL TIDWELL

1 3 5 7 9 10 8 6 4 2

First Edition

Excerpt from "Gacela of the Dark Death" from *Selected Poems* by Federico García Lorca reprinted with permission. Copyright © 1955 by New Directions Publishing Corporation. Translated by Stephen Spender and G. L. Gill.

Lyric from "Heart of Gold" by Neil Young used by permission. Copyright © 1971 by Silver Fiddle. All rights reserved.

*for Linda King Harrison*

# ACKNOWLEDGMENTS

Any and all misrepresentations of historical fact in this book are intentional. In Book II I poke fun at a tradition of scholarship, mindful of the fact that without this tradition we are at the mercy of the renditions of political forces which are always self-serving and dead wrong. I have used dozens of source books and monographs too numerous to mention here. However, I want to thank Douglas Peacock and Michael and Nancy Rothenberg for their research efforts. Also Peter Matthiessen, Tamara Plakins Thornton of Yale University and Cooperstown, John Harrison of the University of Arkansas, Bernard Fontana of the University of Arizona, Mick Harris of the University of Kentucky, and Bernie Rink of Northwestern Michigan College.

# CONTENTS

We loved the earth but could not stay.

—OLD SAYING

# BOOK I

# DALVA

# DALVA

*Santa Monica—April 7, 1986, 4:00 A.M.*

It was today—rather yesterday I think—that he told me it was important not to accept life as a brutal approximation. I said people don't talk like that in this neighborhood. The fly that flies around me now in the dark is every fly that ever flew around me. I am on the couch, and when I awoke I thought I heard voices down by the river, a branch of the Niobrara River where with my sister I was baptized in a white dress. A boy yelled *water snake* and the preacher said *get thee out of here snake* and we all laughed. The snake drifted off in the current and the singing began. There are no rivers around here. Turning on the lamp above the couch I see he's not here either. I can hear a car screeching on the coast highway even at this hour. There are always cars. The girl in the green bathing suit was hit seven times before the last car tossed her in a ditch. The autopsy said California speedball. Her suit was the color of winter wheat as I remember it, almost unnaturally green when the snow melted. It was so nice to have another color on earth other than brown grass, white snow, and black trees. Now between the cars I hear the ocean and the breeze lifts the pale-blue curtains with a sea odor the same as my skin. I'm quite happy though I may have to move after all these years, seven, actually. There is an abrasion, almost like a slight burn, from his mustache on my thigh. He asked if I wanted him to shave his mustache and I said You'd be lost without it. That made him somewhat angry as if his vanity depended solely on something so fragile as a mustache. Of course he wasn't listening to what I said but to all of his imagined resonances of what I said. When I laughed he became angrier and marched very dramatically around the room in his jockey shorts which were baggy in the rear. It was somehow warm and amusing but when he tried to grab my shoulders and shake me I told him to go back to his hotel and screw himself in front of the mirror until he felt he wanted to actually be with me again. So he left.

○

I thought I was writing this to my son in case I never get to see him, and in case something should happen to me, what I have written would tell him about his mother. My friend of last evening said, What if he isn't worth the effort? That hadn't occurred to me. I don't know where he is and I have never seen him except for a moment after his birth. I can't go to him because I'm not sure he knows I exist. Perhaps his adoptive parents never told him he was adopted. This is all less sentimental than it is unfinished business, a longing to know someone I have no particular right to know. But to know this son would complete the freedom men of my acquaintance seem to consider their birthright. And then, perhaps, my son is looking for me?

○

My name is Dalva. This is a rather strange name for someone from the upper Midwest but the explanation is simple. My father's older brother was a victim of rebellion and adventure magazines, and was at odd times a merchant seaman, a prospector for gold and precious metals, and finally a geologist. Late in the Great Depression Paul was somewhere in the interior of Brazil from which he returned, after squandering most of his earnings in Rio, to the farm with some presents including a 78 rpm record of the sambas of that period. One of the sambas—in Portuguese of course—was "Estrella Dalva," or "Morning Star," and my parents loved the song. Naomi, my mother, told me that on warm summer evenings she and my father would put the record on the Victrola and dance up and down the big front porch of the farmhouse. My uncle Paul had taught them what he said was the samba before he disappeared again.

I just now thought that you can only meet a man at the level of his intentions. When my father and mother met and courted in the thirties the intentions were clear; they were both from fourth-generation farm families and the point was to marry and to continue traditions that had made their predecessors reasonably happy. This is not to say that they were simple-minded people in bib overalls and flour-sack gingham dress. There were several thousand acres of corn and wheat, Herefords, hogs, even a small slaughterhouse that at one time supplied prime beef to certain restaurants in faraway Chicago, Saint Louis, and Kansas City. From scrapbooks Mother has stored there are records of their trips to Chicago, New Orleans, Miami, and once to New York City which was my mother's favorite. From World War II, when my father was a fighter pilot stationed in England, there is a photo of him with three gentlemen in front of the Hereford Registry in Hereford, England. He is in a jaunty hat and looks rather like one of the early photos of Howard Hughes. As Naomi would say, or prate, "Blood will tell," and his unstable streak came out in his passion for airplanes. He was not called up but reenlisted for the Korean War because he wanted to learn to fly jet fighters. So between the ages of five and nine I knew my father, and I have still not exhausted the memories of those years. Beryl Markham said that when she stopped in Tunis on the way back to Europe in her small plane she met a prostitute who wanted to go home, but didn't know where home was because she had been taken from her parents at age seven. She only knew that in her homeland there were tall trees and it was occasionally cold.

But I'm not one to live or subsist on memory, treating it as most do, the past and future as an encapsulated space or nodule we walked into, and then out of, rather than a continuum of the life we have already lived and will live. What was my father, really? Genes provide the fragilest of continuities.

On the farm we had a small plane called a Stinson Voyager. We'd go for Sunday rides when the weather was right. If I had been sick and out of school my father would tell me I'd feel better or be well by the time we landed and I believed him. I liked seeing the water birds on sandbars in the Missouri River, the way they flew up in clouds, then landed again when our immense shadow passed.

○

What upsets me is the terrifying and inconsolable bitterness of life; at close range in certain friends, and particularly in my sister who regards her mid-life as an arctic prison though she lives in Tucson. She's never been given much to going out of doors. She lives in a fine home with a gray-and-white interior backed up against the Catalinas though she has never walked in these mountains. I thought of her yesterday at daylight when I walked the beach. Someone had spray-painted the word MENACE on the benches in Palisades Park, and on the steps going down to the beach, and somehow on a highway overpass. I stopped counting at twenty. Fortunately most lunatics don't have the vigor of Charles Manson. I was interested in someone who spent a whole night spray-painting MENACE virtually in the face of the Pacific Ocean. Perhaps this vandal is the flip side of my sister. It is somewhat a mystery to me how the rich can feel so utterly fatigued and victimized. She drifts back and forth without specific density across the line of what she thinks is the unbearable present, but then she surprised me this March, during Easter, when my mother and I visited. I asked her how it was possible to live so thoroughly without nouns. At that moment she was waiting for the single drink she allowed herself each day at six.

"Why don't you save up for six days and have seven drinks on Sunday?" Naomi asked. My mother does not stand back from any of the forms life takes. "You could have yourself a party."

But my sister just sat there looking at the martini she would make last an hour, thinking about nouns as if on the lip of speaking the sentence my mother and I knew wouldn't come. Ruth went to the piano and played a Mozart exercise my mother favored which also served as a signal for me to begin fixing dinner.

"Nouns are a burden to people these days," Mother said. "Maybe they always were. Tell me about your latest fellow."

"Michael is in the history department at Stanford. He heard about our journals years ago and last fall in Nebraska traced me back to Santa Monica. He's about twenty pounds overweight and self-important. He tends to lecture at you and might talk about the history of food over dinner, the history of rain when it's raining. He's an expert at everything awful that ever happened in the history of the world. He's brilliant without being very conscious. He's a bad lover but I like being around him."

"I think he sounds just wonderful. I've always preferred men to be a little goofy. If they're trying to be men in the movies they get tiresome. I had this little fling with an ornithologist because I liked the way he climbed trees, waded up creeks, or into stock ponds to take photos. . . ." My mother is sixty-five.

We hadn't heard the music stop and Ruth was right behind us at the kitchen door. Grandfather, who was half Oglala Sioux, called her Shy Bird Who Flies Away. Though Ruth is only one-eighth Sioux she had assumed certain Sioux qualities as she grew older, a kind of stillness that she forced to surround her.

"I think you're right about nouns. Think of 'car,' 'house,' 'piano,' 'food,' 'priest.' " We were prepared for the rush of words that came not more than once a day when we visited. "We have always been lapsed Methodists but I met this priest and we talk about love and death, art and God, which are all nouns of a sort I believe. He's not a priest in a church but works with a charity for Indians and I know he sees me partly as a contributor. He loves to drive the car Ted sent me for Christmas." Ted is her husband from whom she had been separated for fifteen years, the father of her son, a man who at twenty-eight discovered he was conclusively a homosexual. Ruth was born four years before Father died in Korea, losing the two central men in her life to quirks of history and sexuality. Ted and Ruth met at the Eastman School of Music where they intended to become famous in the music world, she as a pianist and he as a composer. Instead, she raised her child who apparently doesn't care for her, blaming her specifically for the loss of his father. From my distance the arts always have seemed brutal, with the chances of the work being durable far less likely than had the aspirant tried to become an astronaut. And the failures I know are filled with an indefinable longing and melancholy for a flowering that was stunted in preparation for any number of reasons.

I was studying a Chinese recipe and ignoring Ruth until I heard the word "boyfriend." It was akin to touching an electric fence as a child. I turned to notice that Mother was equally shocked, reaching nervously for the cigarettes she had abandoned years ago.

"Yes, I have a boyfriend. A lover. He's my only lover in fifteen years. The priest is my lover. He's really quite homely. He even told me that one reason he became a priest was because he was so homely. Singly, the features wouldn't be that bad but arranged together as they are, the result is homeliness. Remember our cow dog, the mongrel we had when we were little called Sam who was so ugly? Anyway, Ted sent me some scarves from Paris, then an expensive car from a local dealer a few days later to go with the scarves. I had read about an Indian charity and checked it out with my neighbor who runs the newspaper. So I drove the car down there and met the priest. I gave him the signed title and the keys and asked him to call a cab for me, but he insisted on driving me home. I made him iced tea and he loved all the paintings and prints Ted and I had collected. Then he asked if I'd like to take a ride to the Papago Reservation the next day. He said the head of the diocese was in Los Angeles for a few days and he had never driven such a wonderful car. I was unsure and said I had never met any Indians in Arizona but I grew up around some of the Sioux and they frightened me. That's because Granddad told me he was really a ghost who had never been born and would never die. I didn't realize he probably was kidding. The priest wondered why I'd give a forty-thousand-dollar brand-new car to people who frightened me. I said Because I can read. Remember Grandpa's Edward Curtis books? We had to wash our hands before we looked at them. So the next morning I made a picnic basket and he picked me up. He was originally from near Indianapolis and grew up loving fast cars as boys must do around there. It is a mystery how anyone could be that thrilled by a car. We took the long way, driving down toward Nogales, then across the Arivaca Canyon road through the Tumacori Mountains. It's a narrow dirt road with many curves and my priest loved the trip, though I thought he drove alarmingly. Nothing would have happened if there hadn't been a sudden, brief thunderstorm. The clay on the road turned to butter and we were caught in a big dip in the mountain road. He said we would be OK when it dried out so we had a picnic in the car and drank a bottle of white wine. Then the rain stopped and the sun came out and it was hot and clear again. I got out of the car, crawled through a fence, and walked down a hill to a spring-fed stock pond. You know I'm not very enthused about nature so it was quite an adventure. The priest was frightened because there were cattle in the pines near the pond, one of them a bull, but I said that Hereford bulls aren't dangerous so he joined me. He said it would take an hour for the road to dry off. I took off my shoes and waded in the pond, washing my face in the spring. I was terribly excited for no particular reason. Maybe I was feeling desire without admitting it. I don't think so. It was just that I was doing something different. Then the priest said I should take a swim and that he had four sisters and bare skin didn't bother him a bit. So I took off my skirt and blouse and dove in the water in my bra and panties. He stripped to his shorts and followed. It was absolutely perfect swimming though he was intensely nervous. I said that God was busy in cancer wards, Africa, and Central America, and wasn't watching him. I got out to sun on a warm rock but he stayed in the water. Finally he said I guess I have an erection. I said You can't stay in the water the rest of your life. He said Don't look, and got out of the water and sat beside me staring straight ahead. I thought I am not going to let him get away so I stood up and took off my bra and panties hanging them on a bush to dry. Then I told him rather sternly to lay on his back on the grass and to close his eyes if he wished. He was shaking so hard I thought he'd fall apart like an old car. So I made love to him."

Ruth began to laugh, then to cry and laugh at the same

time. We hugged and patted her, praising her for breaking her drought of affection in such a unique way.

"A splendid story," Naomi said.

"It's a beautiful thing to happen. I'm proud of you," I said. "I couldn't have done a better job myself."

Ruth thought this was very funny because she always has chided me by letter and on the phone for what she calls "promiscuity," while I am lightly critical about her abstinence.

"The trouble was he wouldn't stop crying and that reminded me of Ted and the night he told me about his problems, so I wanted to cry too but knew it was somehow unthinkable. He cried so hard I had to drive back to Tucson. He'd grind his teeth, say prayers in Latin, then weep again. He asked me to pray with him but I said I didn't know how because, not being Catholic, I didn't know the prayers. This at the same time shocked and calmed him. Why did I donate a car to the Catholics if I was a Protestant? I donated the car so it could be sold and the money would be used to help the Indians. But the Indians are Catholics he said. The Indians are Indians before they are Catholics I replied. He said he had felt his soul come out of him and into me and then he began crying again because he had betrayed Mary and ruined his life. Oh for God's sake you fucking ninny, I yelled at him, and he became silent until we got to the house. For some reason I told him to come in and I'd give him a tranquilizer but all I had was aspirin which he took. Within minutes he said the tranquilizer was making him feel very strange. We had a drink and I made a snack tray with the pâté recipe you sent me, Dalva. He quoted me some poems and told me about the missions he had worked at in Brazil and Mexico. Now he was in his thirties and wanted to leave the country again. Brazil was difficult for him because you couldn't avoid seeing all those beautiful bottoms in Rio. He poured himself another drink and said that one night he paid a girl to come to his hotel room so he could kiss her bottom. The tranquilizer is making me say this he said. So he kissed her bottom but she laughed because it tickled and that ruined everything. His eyes brimmed with tears again so I thought fast because I didn't want to lose him. That's what you want to do to me, isn't it? Admit it. He nodded and stared out the window. I think that's a good idea and that's what you should do. He said it was still daylight and maybe it wouldn't hurt because he had already sinned that day which wouldn't be over until midnight. He's quite a thinker. I stood up and started to take off my clothes. He got down on the floor. We really went to town all evening and I sent him home before midnight."

Now we began laughing again, and Ruth decided to have another martini. I went back to the stove and began chopping garlic and fresh jalapeños.

"What in God's name are you going to do about him?" Naomi asked. "Maybe you should look for a normal person now that you've got started again."

"I never met a normal person and neither have you. I think he's going to be sent away by his bishop. Naturally he confessed his sins though he waited two weeks until it became unbearable. You said Dad loved us but he went back to war anyway. There's another funny part. The priest showed up rather early the next morning while I was weeding my herb garden. He had some books for me on Catholicism as if a light bulb had told him that the situation would improve if he could convert me. He wanted us to pray together but first I had to put something on more appropriate than shorts. So we asked God's forgiveness for our bestial ways. He used the word 'bestial,' then we drove down to the Papago Reservation. Most of the Papagos are quite fat because we changed their diet and over half of them have diabetes. I held a Papago baby which made me want another one but age forty-three is borderline. Perhaps I'm making him sound stupid but he knows a great deal about Indians, South America, and a grab bag that he calls the 'mystery of the cosmos,' including astronomy, mythology, anthropology. On the way home we stopped to get out of the car to look at the sunset. He gave me a hug and managed to get excited after being so high-minded. I said No, not if you're going to make me ask forgiveness for being bestial. So we did it up against a boulder and some Papagos beeped their pickup horn and yelled *Padre* when they passed. To my surprise he sat down with his bare butt on the rocky desert floor and began laughing so I laughed too."

○

A week after I returned to Santa Monica she called to say that her priest was being sent to Costa Rica with all due speed. She hoped she was pregnant but her best chances were the last few days before his departure and he wasn't cooperating due to a nervous collapse. His movements were also being monitored by an old priest who was a recovering alcoholic. She said the two of them together reminded her of the "Mutt & Jeff" comic strip. She sounded untypically merry on the phone, enjoying the rare whorish feeling she was sure would pass. One of her blind students had also done particularly well in a piano competition. I told her to call the day he left because I was sure she would need someone to talk to.

○

All of us work. My mother has an involved theory of work that she claims comes from my father, uncles, grandparents, and on into the past: people have an instinct to be useful and can't handle the relentless *everydayness* of life unless they work hard. It is sheer idleness that deadens the soul and causes neuroses. The flavor of what she meant is not as Calvinist as it might sound. Work could be anything that aroused your curiosity: the natural world, music, anthropology, the stars, or even sewing or gardening. When we were little girls we would invent dresses the Queen of Egypt might wear, or have a special garden where we ordered seeds for vegetables or flowers we had never heard of. We grew collard greens which we didn't like but our horses did. The horses wouldn't eat the Chinese cabbage called "bok choy" but the cattle loved it. We got some seeds from New Mexico and grew Indian corn that had blue ears. Mother got a book from the university in Lincoln to find out what the Indians did with blue corn and we spent all day making tortillas out of it. It is difficult to eat blue food so we sat there in the Nebraska kitchen just staring at the pale-blue tortillas on the platter. "Some things take getting used to," Naomi said. Then she told us a story we already knew how her grandfather would fry grasshoppers in bacon grease until they were crispy and eat them while listening to Fritz Kreisler play the violin on the Victrola. She rather liked the grasshoppers, but after he died she never fixed them for herself.

○

Ruth was better at horses though I was two years older. Horses were our obsession. Childhood is an often violent Eden and after Ruth was thrown, breaking her wrist when her horse tripped in a gopher hole, she never rode again. She was twelve at the time and missed a piano competition in Omaha that was important to her. This is a small item except to the little girl to whom it happens. We were maddened by her one-hand practice, until Mother bought some one-hand sheet music. Our closest neighbors were three miles away, a childless older couple, so I rode alone after that.

○

Dear Son! I am being honest but not honest enough. Once up in Minnesota I saw a three-legged bobcat, a not quite whole bobcat with one leg lost to a trap. There is the saw about cutting the horse's legs off to get him in a box. The year it happened to me the moon was never quite full. Is the story always how we tried to continue our lives as if we had once lived in Eden? Eden is the childhood still in the garden, or at least the part of it we try to keep there. Maybe childhood is a myth of survival for us. I was a child until fifteen, but most others are far more truncated.

Last winter I worked at a clinic for teenagers who "abused" drugs and alcohol. It was a public mixture of poor whites and Latinos from the barrio close by in El Segundo. A little boy—he was thirteen but small for his age—told me he needed to go to the doctor very badly. We were talking in my small windowless office and I made a note of the pain he was in which I misinterpreted as being mental. I speak Spanish but was still getting nowhere on the doctor question. I got up from the desk and sat beside him on the couch. I hugged him and sang a little song children sing in Sonora. He broke down and said he had a crazy uncle who had been fucking him and it had made him sick. This wasn't shocking in itself as I had dealt with the problem, though it almost always concerned girls and their fathers or relatives. Franco (I'll call him) began to pale and tremble. I checked his pulse and drew him to his feet. The blood was beginning to soak through the paper towels he had stuffed into the back of his pants. I didn't want to chance a long wait in emergency at the public hospital so I rushed him to the office of a gynecologist friend. The anal injuries turned out to be too severe to be handled in the office, so the gynecologist, who is a compassionate soul, checked the boy into a private hospital where he immediately underwent surgery for repairs. The doctor and I went for a drink and decided to split the costs on the boy. The doctor is an ex-lover and lectured me on the way that I had jumped over all the rules of the case.

"First you call the county medical examiner. . . ."

"Then I call the police, suspecting a felony. . . ."

"Then you wait for a doctor from Bombay who got his degree in Bologna, Italy. He's been awake all night sewing up some kids after a gang fight. The doc is probably wired on speed."

"And the police will need the boy's middle name, proof of citizenship, photos of his ruptured ass. They'll want to know if he's absolutely sure his uncle did this to him."

And so on. The doctor stood at the sound of a Japanese alarm clock that was his beeper. He went to the phone and I hoped it wasn't bad news about the boy. He returned and said no, it was just another baby about to be born backward into the world. The couple was rich and he would charge extra to help make up for his misbegotten generosity to the boy. I had another drink, a margarita because it was a hot day. I looked through the sugar gums and the palms across Ocean Avenue to the Pacific. How could all this happen when there was an ocean? For a long time I thought of every boy I saw as possibly my own son, but I never could properly adjust the ages. I am forty-five now so my son would be twenty-nine, an incomprehensible figure for the small, shriveled red creature I only saw for a few minutes. When I was in college the child was always a kindergartner. When I graduated the child was actually nine, but to me he was still five, one of a group tethered together with yarn on a cold morning waiting for the Minneapolis museum to open. When they got tangled I helped a patient schoolteacher straighten out the line and wipe some noses. I worked in a day-care center one day for a few hours but I couldn't bear it.

Two modest drinks made me simple-minded. I walked out into the bright sunlight, got in my car, and checked for an address in the boy's file which I brought along for hospital information. I thought I'd reason with the mother in the probability that she was ignorant of the rape. It was the beginning of rush hour on the Santa Monica Freeway, and if you are to leave Santa Monica itself you must become a nickel-ante Buddhist. Usually I established a minimal serenity by playing the radio or tapes, but the music didn't work that day.

Now there's a specific banality to rage as a reaction, an unearned sense of cleansing virtue. And what kind of rage led the uncle to abuse the boy? I would do my best to see him locked up but my own rage came from within, from another source, while it was the boy who was sinned against. Only the purest of heart can become murderous for others.

I parked on a crowded street in front of the barrio address. A group of boys were loitering against a stucco fence in front of the small bungalow. They taunted me in Spanish.

"Did you come to fuck me, beautiful gringo?"

"You have some growing to do, you miserable little goat turd."

"I am already big. Do you want to see?"

"I forgot my glasses. How could you be my lover when you spend your days playing with yourself? Is this the house of Franco? Where is his mother?"

The boys, all in their early teens, were delighted with my unexpected gutter Spanish.

"His mother went away with a pimp. Where is our friend?"

The boys shrank back and I turned to see a man striding toward me with implausibly cruel eyes. The eyes startled me because they belonged to someone long dead whom I had loved. I tried to move away but his eyes slowed me and he grabbed my wrist.

"What do you want, bitch?"

"If the mother isn't here I want to speak to the uncle of

Franco." Now he was twisting my wrist painfully. "I want to stop this man from fucking his nephew to death."

Still holding my wrist he vaulted the fence and began slapping me. I turned to the boys and said "Please." At first they were frightened but then the one who had teased me pulled out a collapsed car aerial, stretched it to its full length, and whipped it across the uncle's face. The uncle screamed and let go of my wrist. He turned to attack the boys but they had all taken out their aerials and flailed at the man who ran in circles trying to cover his eyes. The aerials whistled through the air tearing the man's skin and clothing to shreds. He was a bloody, god-awful mess and now I tried to stop the boys but only a police car careening down the street toward us stopped them. The boys ran, one of them slowing to throw a rock at the squad car which broke the windshield. The uncle disappeared into the house and, evidently, out the back door since the police never found him.

The aftermath was predictably unpleasant. I was suspended, then offered a clerkish job, and refusing that, was fired. The dreadful thing to me was that my impulsiveness allowed the uncle to escape, not the number of infractions of social-work rules I had violated. The police made a cursory attempt at a follow-up the next afternoon at the hospital. I went along as a translator but the boy refused to answer any of the questions, telling me it was a private matter. I was puzzled by this until in the corridor the police told me that such offenses among country people from Mexico are considered unsuitable for the law. It's something that has to be dealt with individually or by a family member. I said that the boy was far too young to begin to deal with his uncle. The police replied the boy might wait for years until he felt capable.

At dawn a few days later Franco called to say he had sneaked out of the hospital. He insisted that he was fine and would pay me back some day. I was terribly upset because I had visited him the day before and we had had a wonderful time talking, though he still looked very ill. I was frantic and insisted that he call me collect every week, or write me letters. In case he returned to Mexico I told him to contact my old uncle Paul, the geologist and mining engineer, who lived in Mulege on Baja when he wasn't visiting a girlfriend at Bahia

Kino on the mainland. The boy said he didn't have a pencil and paper but perhaps he would remember. And that was all.

I made coffee and took it out to my small balcony. It was barely light and there was a warm stiff breeze mixed with the odor of salt water, juniper, eucalyptus, oleander, palm. The ocean was rumpled and gray. I think I stayed here this long because of the trees and the ocean. One year when I was having particularly intense problems I sat here for an hour at daylight and an hour at twilight. The landscape helped me to let the problems float out through the top of my head, through my skin, and into the air. I thought at the time of a college professor who told me that Santayana had said that we have religion so as to have another life to run concurrently with the actual world. It seemed my problem was refusing this dualism and trying to make my life my religion.

The wind off the Pacific cooled and the clarity of the air brought on a dim memory, a blurred outline of sensations similar to *déjà-vu*. It was a year or so after World War II, I think. I must have been six or seven and Ruth was three. My father liked to go camping for pleasure and to get away from the farm. The four of us flew up to the Missouri River in the Stinson, landing on a farmer's grass strip. The farmer was an improbably tall Norwegian and helped Dad load the gear on a horse-drawn wagon. We sat on the gear and bedding with Naomi holding Ruth. There was the smell of ripe wheat, the sweating horses, and tobacco from Dad and the farmer. Under the wagon seat I could see manure on the farmer's boots, and through a crack on the wagon floor the ground was moving beneath us. After miles of a trail beside the wheat the wagon moved down a steep hill along a creek bordered by cotton-woods; the creek flowed into the Missouri which was broad, slow, and flat. The grass was deep and there were deer, pheasants, and prairie chickens, flushed by our wagon. Mother started a fire and made coffee while Dad and the farmer set up camp. Then they had coffee with sugar and strong, pungent-smelling whiskey. The farmer left with the wagon and horses. Dad put shells in his shotgun and we walked back up the hill and along the edge of the wheat field where he shot a pheasant and a prairie chicken. I got to carry the birds for a while but they were heavy so I rode on his back. At the camp we all plucked the feathers off the birds except baby Ruth who put feathers in her mouth. Dad cut up the birds and they browned them, put in carrots, onions, and potatoes. They put the pot over the fire and we all went down to the creek mouth and went swimming. After dinner the setting sun turned the river orange. At night there was an orange moon and I heard coyotes. At first light I watched my parents sleep. Little Ruth opened her eyes, smiled at me, and went back to sleep. I walked alone down to the river. The wind came up strongly and the water smelled raw and fresh. A large eddy and sandbar were full of water birds. There was a bird taller than myself which I recognized from Naomi's Audubon cards as a great blue heron. I walked farther up the bank of the river until I heard them calling "Dalva." I saw Father walking toward me with a smile. I pointed to the heron and he nodded and picked me up. I let my cheek rub against his unshaven face. Soon after that trip we drove him to the train one October afternoon. They told us his plane was shot down outside of Inchon. We did not get a body back, but buried an empty coffin as a gesture.

○

Ruth called again this morning with good but tentative news. Sex has returned her sense of playfulness. Her voice is no longer dry and fatigued, though I worry a bit that this is a vaguely manic phase that the family is susceptible to. What she did is have the priest in for dinner, along with his "bodyguard" or chaperone, the older priest with the drinking problem. It was a well-planned campaign to win her last chance to get pregnant: she poached Maine lobsters, chilled them, and served them as an appetizer with a Montrachet. Ted is an oenophile and sends her additions to the cellar they began together. Next was some quail she had marinated, then grilled, and finally a rough-cut filet covered with garlic and pepper, with a Grand-Eschezaux and her last bottle of Romaneé Conti. The old priest was a delightful talker and had studied in France in the thirties. He had always been poor and had never drunk such wines, though he had read of them, and he'd be damned if at age seventy-one he'd miss the chance to drink

them. I teased Ruth then about her somber and pious comments on prostitutes when she had served over a thousand
dollars' worth of wine in order to make love. She said the old
man never did fall asleep, so she had to settle for a quick act
standing in the bathroom over the sink looking at each other
in the mirror. Now all she had to do was wait and see if she was
pregnant while the father went off to work among the poor in
Costa Rica.

○

Here is how it happened to me, how I had my child early in
my sixteenth year. It has often occurred to me that I may be
a grandmother at forty-five. I tried it out in front of the mirror,
whispering *grandma* at myself softly but it was all too unknow-
able to be effective. But now I am drifting away from it again.
Naomi and Ruth feel wordlessly upset that the land will go to
Ruth's son, there being no other heirs in the prospect, another
reason for the priest mating. None of us mind the name
Northridge disappearing, but it would be a shame to see the
land leave the family, and Ruth's son professes to hate it and
has not visited since his early teens. Enough!

○

His name was Duane, though he was half Sioux and he gave
me many versions of his Sioux name depending on how he felt
that day. Grandfather's place, which is the original homestead,
is three miles north of the farm. The homestead was a full
section, six hundred and forty acres, onto which the other land
had been added since 1876, to form a total of some thirty-five
hundred acres, which is not that much higher than average for
this part of the country. Our good fortune was that the land is
bisected by two creeks that form a small river, so that the land
was low and particularly fertile, and could easily be irrigated.
The central grace note, though, is that my great-grandfather
studied botany and agriculture for two years at Cornell College before he entered the Civil War. In fact, an accidental
traveler down the county gravel road near Grandfather's

would think he was passing a forest, but this is a little far-fetched since the farm is so far from the state highway that there are no accidental travelers. All the trees were planted by Great-grandfather to form shelter belts and windbreaks from the violent weather of the plains, and to provide fuel and lumber in an area where it was scarce and expensive. There are irregular rows of bull pine and ponderosa, and the density of the deciduous caragana, buffalo berry, russian olive, wild cherry, juneberry, wild plum, thornapple, and willow. The final inside rows are the larger green ash, white elm, silver maple, black walnut, european larch, hackberry, wild black cherry. About a decade ago Naomi, through the state conservationists, made the area a designated bird sanctuary in order to keep out hunters. Scarcely anyone visits except for a few ornithologists from universities in the spring and fall. Inside the borders of trees are fields, and ponds, a creek, and inside the most central forty, the original farmhouse. Enough!

○

Duane arrived one hot late August afternoon in 1956. I found him walking up the long driveway, his feet shuffling in the soft dust. I rode up behind him and he never turned around. I said, *May I help you?* but he only said his own and Grandfather's names. He was about my age I thought, fourteen, scarred and windburned in soiled old clothes, carrying his belongings in a knotted burlap potato sack. I could smell him above the lathered horse, and told him he better jump on my horse because Grandpa had a pack of Airedales who wouldn't take warmly to a stranger. He only shook his head no, so I rode ahead at a gallop to get Grandpa. He was sitting on his porch as usual and at first was puzzled, then intensely excited though noncommittal. He had to wait at the pickup as I patted each of the half-dozen Airedales on the head before they jumped in the back of the truck. If I didn't pat each one in turn they would become nasty to each other. I loved these uniquely cranky dogs partly for the way they welcomed me, and how wildly excited they became when I went riding and invited them along. I never took them when I rode into coyote country because the dogs once dug up and ate a litter of coyote pups despite my efforts to fight them off with my riding crop. After they gobbled up the pups the dogs pretended to be ashamed and embarrassed. Enough!

○

We found Duane sitting cross-legged in the dust. The dogs set up a fearsome howl but never dared jump out of the truck without Grandpa's permission. We got out and Grandpa knelt beside Duane who wasn't moving. They spoke in Sioux and Grandpa helped Duane to his feet and embraced him tightly. When we got back to the house Grandpa said I should leave, and to tell no one at our place of the visitor. Despite the passage of seven years or so he still partly blamed Naomi for letting father go back to war, and they were frequently at odds.

○

I'm sure I loved Duane, at least at the beginning, because he so pointedly ignored me. He came from up near Parmelee on the Rosebud Indian Reservation, and though his looks were predominantly Sioux his eyes were Caucasian, cold and green like green stones in cold flowing water. Technically he was a cowboy—it was all he knew how to do and he did it well. He refused to live in Grandpa's house but took up residence in a shed that was once a bunkhouse. Two of the Airedales decided to live with him of their own accord. Duane refused to go to school; he told Grandpa that he could read and write and that was as far as he needed to go in that area. He spent his time looking after the remaining Herefords, repairing farm buildings, cutting wood, with the largest chore being the irrigating. The only other hired hand was Lundquist, an old Swede bachelor friend of Grandpa's. He taught Duane irrigating and jabbered all day on the matter of his own Swedenborgian version of Christianity. Lundquist daily forgave Duane for the death of a distant relative in Minnesota who was murdered during the Sioux uprising in the mid-nineteenth century. The actual farmwork wasn't that onerous since Grandpa mostly grew two crops of alfalfa a year within his forest borders, and the bulk of the rest of our land was leased on shares to neighbors.

On New Year's Day of that first year Duane received a fine buckskin quarter horse from a cutting-horse strain, plus a handmade saddle from Agua Prieta on the Arizona border. Normally the gift would have come on Christmas but Grandfather had lost his religion during World War I in Europe and didn't observe Christmas. The day stands out clearly: it was a warmish, clear winter morning with the thawing mud in the barnyard a little slippery. I had gone way over to Chadron with Grandpa the day before to fetch the horse, and the saddle had come by mail. Duane came riding in on the Appaloosa from feeding the cattle and saw me standing there holding the reins of the buckskin. He nodded at me as coolly as usual, then walked over and studied the horse. He looked at Grandpa who stood back in the sunlight against the barn. "Guess that's the best-looking animal I ever saw," Duane said. Grandpa nodded at me, so I said, "It's for you, Duane." He turned his back to us for a full ten minutes, or what seemed an unimaginably long time given the situation. Finally I came up behind him and ran my hand with the reins along his arm to his hand. I whispered "I love you" against his neck for no reason. I didn't know I was going to say it.

That was the first day Duane let me go riding with him. We rode until twilight with the two dogs until I heard Naomi ring the dinner bell in the distance. Duane rode across the wheat stubble until he turned around within a hundred yards of our farmhouse. It was the most romantic day of my life and we never spoke or touched except when I handed him the reins.

○

One of the main sadnesses of my life at that time, and on occasions since, is that I matured early and was thought by others to be overly attractive. It isn't the usual thing to be complained about but it unfairly, I thought, set me aside, brought notice when none was desired. It made me shy, and I tended to withdraw at the first mention of what I looked like. It wasn't so bad in country school where Naomi was the sole teacher and there were only four of us in the seventh grade, but for eighth grade I had to take the school bus to the nearest town of any size which, for certain reasons, will be unnamed. There the attention was constant from the older town boys and I was at a loss what to do. I was thirteen and refused all dates, saying my mother wouldn't let me go out. I also refused the invitation to become a cheerleader because I wanted to take the school bus home to be with my horses. I trusted one senior boy because he was the son of our doctor and seemed quite pleasant. He gave me a ride home in his convertible one late-April day, full of himself because he had been accepted by far-off Dartmouth. He tried very hard to rape me but I was quite strong from taking care of horses and actually broke one of his fingers, though not before he forced my face close to his penis which erupted all over me. I was so shocked I laughed. He held his broken finger and began crying for forgiveness. It was stupid and profoundly unpleasant. Naturally he spread it around school that I had given him a great blow-job, but school was almost out for the year, and I hoped people would forget.

If anything ninth grade was worse. Mother insisted I dress well, but I hid some sloppy clothes to wear in my school locker. I played basketball for a month or so but quit after another unpleasant incident. The coach kept me very late, well after everyone had left, to practice free throws, and to play one on one. While I was drying off after a shower he simply walked right into the girls' locker room. He said he wouldn't hurt me or even touch me but he wanted to see me naked. I was quite frightened when he came closer saying *Please* over and over again. I didn't know what to do so I dropped the towel and turned all the way around. He said *Once more* so I did it again and then he left. When I got in the car I almost told Naomi but I knew that the coach had three children and I didn't want to make trouble for him.

○

In contrast to other males Duane hadn't shown a trace of affection in the year and a half since his arrival. All that we shared was the love of horses but that drew us together suffi-ciently to give me enough solace to keep going. At one point I had become so depressed I thought of maiming myself, burn-ing my face, or ending my life. Naomi wanted to take me to a psychiatrist in the state capital but I refused. One evening she gave me my first glass of wine and sent Ruth out of the room. I told her much of what was bothering me and she held me and wept with me. She said that what was happening to me was the condition of life, and that I had to behave with pride and honor so that I could respect myself. When I found someone to love who loved me it would all make more sense and become much better. I didn't tell her I loved Duane because she thought him so rude as to be mentally diseased.

One Saturday I was hazing some young steers for Duane so he could practice his buckskin on cutting, which is when the rider allows the horse to enter the herd, select a steer, and "cut" him out of the herd. My job was to keep the steers from dispersing and running off in every direction. The oldest Airedale understood the game and helped me to turn back especially recalcitrant steers. I think the dog stuck it out merely for the outside chance of getting to bite a steer.

That day it began to sleet so we went in the barn and practiced roping on some old steer horns perched on a pole. We practiced team roping together when the weather was good. I was the "header," that is, I lassoed the horns while Duane was the "heeler," which was much harder because you have to lasso the back hoofs of a running steer. Duane seemed especially cold and removed that day so I tried to tease him about a necklace he wore. He wouldn't tell me what the necklace meant no matter how I badgered him.

"I heard two footballers down at the feed store say you were the best-looking girl in school," he said, knowing how much it bothered me. "They also said you were the best fuck in the county."

"That's not true, Duane." I had broken into tears. "You know that's not true."

"Why would they say it if it wasn't true?" he asked, grabbing my arm and making me face him. "You never offered it to me because I'm an Indian."

"I would do it with you because I love you, Duane."

"I'd never fuck a white girl anyway. Not one who'd fuck those farmers."

"I'm a little bit Indian and I didn't fuck those farmers."

"There's no way you can prove it," he yelled.

"Make love to me and then you can tell I'm a virgin." I began to take off my clothes. "Come ahead you big-mouth coward." He only glanced at me; then his face became knotty with rage. He ran out of the barn and I could hear the pickup starting.

When I rode home I couldn't stop crying. I wanted to die but couldn't decide how to go about it. I stopped along a big hole in the creek, now covered with ice, that we used for swimming in the summer. I thought of drowning myself but I didn't want to upset Naomi and Ruth. Also I was suddenly very tired, cold, and hungry. It was still sleeting and I hoped the ice would break the power line so we could light the oil lamps. After dinner we'd play cards on the dining-room table beneath portraits of Great-grandfather, Grandfather, and Father. I would think, Why did he leave us alone to go to Korea?

After dinner Grandpa pulled into the yard in his old sedan, which startled us because he always drove the pickup. Naomi and I had to go into town with him because Duane was in jail and they needed my part of the story. In the sheriff's office I said I had never had anything to do with the bruised and severely battered football players. Grandfather was enraged and the sheriff cowered before him. The parents of the football players were frightened, perhaps unfairly, because Grandfather is rich and we are the oldest family in the county. When they brought Duane out of the cell he was unmarked. The football players tried to sneer, but Duane looked through them as if they weren't there. The sheriff said that if anyone slandered me again there would be trouble. Grandpa said, "One more word and I'll run all of you filth straight back to Omaha." The parents begged forgiveness but he ignored them. I could see he was enjoying his righteous indignation. Out in the parking lot of the county building I said thank you to Duane. He squeezed my arm and said "It's fine, partner." I almost fell apart when he called me "partner."

I was not bothered by the boys at school after that, though I was lonely and I was given the behind-the-back nickname of "Squaw." I didn't mind the nickname; in fact, I was proud of it, because it meant in the minds of others that I belonged to Duane. When he found out, however, he laughed and said I could never be a squaw because there was so little Indian in

me as to be unnoticeable. This made me quarrelsome and I
said, Where did you get those hazel-green eyes if you're so
pure? His anger seemed to make him want to tell me something, but he only said he was over half Sioux and in the eyes
of the law that made him Sioux.

After that we didn't have anything to do with each other
for a month. One summer evening when Grandpa was over for
dinner he took me aside and told me it was a terrible mistake
to fall in love with an Indian boy. I was embarrassed but had
the presence to ask him why his own father had married a
Sioux girl. "Who knows why anybody marries anybody." His
own wife, whom I never saw and who was long dead, had been
a rich girl from Omaha who drank herself into an early grave.
"What I'm saying is they aren't like us, and if you don't behave
and stop chasing Duane I'll send him away." It was the first
time I stood up to him. "Does that mean you're not like us?"
He hugged me and said, "You know and I know I'm not like
anybody. You show the same signs."

I felt it was all unnecessary since Duane showed not the
slightest sign of being anything more than minimally my "partner." I tried becoming less pushy and doe-eyed which did
serve to make him friendlier. He took me to some Indian burial
mounds in a dense thicket in the farthest corner of the property. I didn't tell him that my father had taken me there soon
after I was given my first pony. Not far from the burial mounds
Duane had erected a small tipi out of poles, canvas, and hides.
He told me he slept there often and "communed" with dead
warriors. I asked him where he got the word "commune" and
he admitted he had taken to reading some of the books in
Grandfather's library. It was the first cool evening in September and the air was clearer than it had been all summer, with
a slight but steady breeze from the north. I mention the breeze
because Duane asked me if I ever noticed that the wind in the
thickets made a different sound depending on which direction
the wind came from. The reason was that the trees rubbed
against each other differently. I admitted I had never noticed
this and he said, "Of course, you're not an Indian." I was a bit
downcast at the reminder so he gave my arm a squeeze, then
gave me my first real hope by saying there might just be a
ceremony to make me a bona-fide Sioux. He'd check if he ever

got back to Parmelee. I hated to leave but my mother insisted I be home before dark when I was with Duane. I went to my tethered horse and Duane said, "If I asked you to stay all night, would you?" I nodded that I would and he came up to me, his face so close that I thought we were going to have our first kiss. The last of the sun was over my shoulder and on his face, but he suddenly turned away.

That summer I became friends with a girl named Charlene who at seventeen was two years older than me. She lived in a small apartment in town above a café that her mother managed. Her father had died in World War II and this misfortune of war helped bring us together. I barely knew her at school where she had a bad reputation. It was rumored that when rich pheasant-hunters from the East appeared in late October and November Charlene made love with them for money. Charlene was very pretty but an outcast; she didn't belong to a church or any school groups. The only time she had spoken to me at school was when I was in the eighth grade— she told me to "be tough" when the older boys were bothering me. We didn't get to know each other until we began talking in the town library.

On Saturday afternoons Naomi would drive to town to shop for groceries and do errands. Ruth would tag along with me to the saddle-and-harness shop, and then we'd have a soda and all meet at the library. We never saw Duane in town because he would do farm errands on weekdays, claiming it was too crowded on Saturday. The town was the county seat but barely had a population of a thousand. I had been reading *Of Human Bondage, Look Homeward, Angel,* also *Raintree County* by Ross Lockridge. They were wonderful books and I was puzzled when I read in the paper that Mr. Lockridge had committed suicide. Charlene saw me with the books and we began talking. She was in her waitress uniform and said she came in on Saturdays after work to get something to read in order to forget her awful life. We met and talked on a half-dozen Saturdays, and I asked her to come to dinner on Sunday because I knew the café would be closed. She said thank you but she wasn't our kind of people, but then Naomi showed up and talked her into it.

Charlene began spending every Sunday with us. Grandpa

liked her a great deal when I brought her over. It was her first time on a horse, which thrilled her. Duane made himself scarce—it was always difficult for him to deal with more than one person at once. Naomi gave Charlene lessons in sewing and made some clothes for her that couldn't be bought short of a long drive to Omaha. Naomi told me in private that she hoped Charlene wouldn't sell herself to pheasant-hunters again in the fall. She said more than one upstanding woman in the area had done so, so it wasn't an item on which a woman should be judged unfairly.

One night when she was staying over Charlene told me the rumors were true. She said she was saving up to leave town and go to college. I asked her what all the men did to her, but she said if I didn't know already she wasn't going to tell me. I said I did know but was interested in the details. She said she got to be very picky because they all wanted her, and one man from Detroit paid her a hundred dollars, which was what she made in the café in an entire month. The only embarrassing quality of her visits was the degree to which she was impressed by our house and Grandpa's. It was natural of her but it upset me. We had few visitors and I certainly knew that we were what was called "fortunate," but one tended to take it all for granted. Furniture and paintings in both houses had been accumulated on travels beginning with Great-grandfather, but mostly by Grandfather around World War I in Paris and London, and later by his wife, and also by my parents. It was the time in life when you wanted to be like everyone else, even though you had begun to understand there was no *everyone else,* and there never had been.

○

My bad luck, innocently enough, started with religion. We had always gone to a small Wesleyan Methodist church a few miles down the road. Everyone did for miles around except the Scandinavians who had a similarly small church that was Lutheran. Once a year, in July, the churches held a joint barbecue and picnic. It was all quite friendly and social, our religion, and our preacher, though very old and quite ineffectual, was admired by all. On this particular Sunday we had to get to church a little early because Ruth served as the pianist. Charlene was with us—she had never been to church until she began coming to our house for Saturday night and Sunday, and found it interesting though peculiar.

I remember it was the first Sunday after Labor Day and it was very hot after the brief cool spell when I was out at Duane's tipi. Our regular minister was away on vacation in Minneapolis, and his replacement was a young, handsome preacher from theological school who was a fireball and aimed, according to the mimeographed announcement, to be an evangelist. We were accustomed to restrained homilies on the tamer aspects of the New Testament, and the substitute preacher swept everyone in the congregation off their feet, except Naomi who was quietly tolerant. He thundered, roared, strutted up and down the aisle, physically grabbed us; in short, he gave us drama and we were unused to drama. The gist is that many of the inventors of the atom bomb and hydrogen bomb were Jews, or "children of Israel." God had called upon his Chosen People to be his tool to invent the destruction of the world, which would call forth the Second Coming of Christ. All those who were truly saved would be drawn up in the Rapture before the Conflagration. Everyone else, no matter how sincere, would endure unbelievable torture with millions and billions of radiation-crazed zombies devouring each other's flesh, and the animal and sea world going berserk, and primitive tribes, including Indians, rising up to slaughter the whites. I remember thinking for a moment that Duane would save me. For the time being, the church moaned and wept. When the sermon neared its end and the wringing-wet preacher gave the invitation to come forward, there was a general rush to the front to give our lives to Jesus, including me, Ruth, Charlene, and more than two dozen others, including all the younger people.

In the confused but saner aftermath it was decided that we all should be baptized just in case hydrogen bombs were actually aimed at our part of the country. In the upper Midwest, no doubt due to the weather, many things are considered chores—including funerals, weddings, baptisms—that need to be accomplished with a certain dispatch. The plan was to meet at the swimming hole on our farm as soon as a picnic could be gathered (food is never neglected) and the proper clothing found, which was anything close to white.

We reassembled by midafternoon and the ceremony went well except for the appearance of a water snake. The weather was so hot that the water felt especially cool and sweet. Naomi looked at Ruth, Charlene, and me in our wet white dresses and said it couldn't have done us any harm. While I was wiping my face with a towel I heard a bird whistle that I knew had to be Duane. The others went off to eat so I snuck through a grove of trees to where I saw Duane sitting on his buckskin.

"What were you goddamned monkeys doing in the river?" he asked.

"Well, we were getting baptized in case the war comes and the world ends." I felt a little stupid and naked in my white wet dress. I tried to cover myself and gave up.

He told me to jump on the horse with him, which surprised me because I had never been asked to do so. He smelled of alcohol which also surprised me because he said alcohol was a poison that was killing the Sioux. At the tipi he put his hand on my bare bottom where my wet clothes hiked up as I slid off the horse. He offered me a bottle full of wild-plum wine from Lundquist. I drank quite deeply and he put his arms around me.

"I don't like the idea of you getting baptized. How can you be my girl if you're getting baptized and singing those songs?"

His lips were close to mine so I kissed them for the first time. I couldn't help myself. He peeled the dress up over my head and threw it in the grass. He stood back, looked at me, then let out a cry or yell. We went into his tent and made love and it was the strangest feeling of my life, as if I were walking up the sun-warmed boards of a cellar door and my feet couldn't keep my body balanced. I looked into his half-closed eyes but I knew he somehow couldn't see me, and there was a little humor in the awkward posture because my knees were bent and so far back. I didn't think I went in that far but he managed and I thought, whatever this is, I like it very much with my hands on his sweat slippery back slipping down to his bottom. When he was finishing he wrenched me around as if he were trying to drag and crush me into his body, and when he rolled off he was breathing like a horse after a hard run.

Then he fell asleep in the hot tent and far off I heard Naomi ringing the bell. I went out into the late afternoon and slipped into my damp dress. I ran all the way, except for stopping to take a quick swim. I wondered if I would look different to everyone. That was the last time I saw Duane for fifteen years.

○

I've stayed in Santa Monica this long partly because of the trees. When we were young Ruth had the notion from books of photographs that the cities of the coasts, now thought of as our dream coasts, looked fragile and delicate. It was an interesting idea to us that in our lifetimes these huge buildings would very probably fall over. The idea is peculiar to the northern Midwest—anything too tall tips over. Stick your head out and you might get it cut off. Only the grain elevators are allowed to emerge, offering a stolid and comforting grandeur to the untraveled.

○

I didn't tell Mother until November that I was pregnant. I told her I only had missed one period when it was actually two. That was so she wouldn't think it was Duane, who had disappeared. I told her it was a pheasant-hunter. Her first reaction was a rage that I had never seen before, not against me—I was her "poor baby"—but against the perverted man. I had to add one lie to another because Naomi immediately called Charlene who swore innocence in the matter. I invented a tale of being out riding and meeting a handsome man who was looking for a lost English setter. I helped him find the dog and he seduced me, which wasn't difficult because I was tired of being a virgin. Naomi took me in her arms and consoled me, saying it wasn't the end of the world I had lived in so innocently. She withdrew me from school in November during Thanksgiving break, telling the superintendent that she intended to send me to school in the East. The only people who knew were a doctor in Lincoln, Ruth, Charlene—whose contempt for the world was so great she could share in any secret—and Grandpa.

It was hardest on Grandpa, perhaps harder on him than

on me because I had the resilience of my age and he had none. A poet, I can't remember who, said there is a point beyond which the exposed heart cannot recover. I was fifteen, nearly sixteen, and he was seventy-three. I was the "apple of his eye," perhaps the feminine counterpart of my father.

From the time that Duane disappeared in late September until I was taken away the day after Thanksgiving, I rode over to Grandpa's every day to see if there was any news from Duane. I never asked directly for news and he never mentioned directly that Naomi had told him I was pregnant. He was considered extremely eccentric well beyond the confines of our county, though never to me. In many ways he had been my substitute father for the nearly ten years since Dad died in Korea, the point in time in which he had ceased active life and retreated behind his successive walls of trees. He had had "too much life" he said, and wanted to think it over before he died. Not that there was grimness on my nearly daily visits—I had at least ten routes to ride over and back, and each of them were well-worn paths. He was grave if I was unhappy, and either went to the heart of the problem with subtlety, or sought to divert me with talk of books, travel, or horses. Naomi felt that he spent far too much on horses for me, but then he had been a horseman all of his life. Even in those days he thought nothing of spending ten thousand dollars on a horse, while a car was nothing more than a vulgar convenience.

His quarrel with Naomi was much deeper than I suspected at the time, because the bits and snatches of it I had heard were not totally comprehensible. As an instance, a few years after Dad died, I was reading in her upstairs bedroom to five-year-old Ruth who had the flu. I stopped because through a floor heating-register I heard Grandpa's angry voice talking to Naomi. I knelt down and Ruth jumped out of bed and we both put our ears to the register. Grandpa used words and phrases that were tinny and muffled in the vent: *You are being a martyr you shouldn't raise the girls here he's dead and you shouldn't stay here as a goddamn monument to his memory the dead are the last people who want us to be unhappy find a gentleman friend a father please for his sake you are barely thirty you are a lovely woman. . . .* I can still see Ruth's face, smiling but flushed with fever.

I knew from Sunday school that a martyr was someone who died for others. Naomi said years later that growing up in a poor family in the Depression and marrying a man so prosperous and dashing as Father was a shock to the system, so that when he died in Korea she wanted to hold on to what they had had together. Strangely enough, it was my pregnancy that forced her into what she thought of as the outside world.

○

It is nearly thirty years ago and I still feel the pain of that October and November so that my heart aches, my skin tightens, and I can barely swallow. There was a stretch of Indian summer when I would sit with Grandpa on the porch swing watching autumn, then squeeze my eyes as if Duane were walking up the driveway back to me. There was nothing left of him, not a trace, in the bunkhouse except the two Airedales who dozed on his cot as if waiting. I groomed his buckskin but hadn't the heart to ride the horse.

One afternoon, the day before Thanksgiving when I cleaned out my locker and said a tearful goodbye to Charlene, I rode over to Grandpa's against Naomi's wishes in a gathering snowstorm. I asked him to light the soft oil lamps because they cast a yellow light around the room, but the light made him look old and quite sad. Behind his head on the den wall was a folio print from Edward Curtis of the warrior chief Two Whistles with a crow perched on his head. Outside the sky was gray and full of snow with the wind buffeting the windowpanes. He put his favorite Paganini violin solo on the Victrola. He rejected more modern record players, having grown fond of and used to the bad sound reproduction. He repeated one of my favorite stories of seeing War Admiral win the 1937 Kentucky Derby, then drifted off into the splendor of the Dublin Horse Show. When he finished I was looking out the window, thinking I would have to stay the night, and happy at the prospect. I said something idle to the effect of "I could just shoot myself if Duane doesn't come back."

"Dalva, goddamnit!" he roared. Then for the first time I'd ever seen it, he began to cry. I rushed to him, begging him to forgive me for saying something stupid. You must never say that, he said. He repeated himself. He poured us each some whiskey, a full glass for himself and a little bit for me.

In the next hour I was to become old before my time. He told me that my grandmother had been somewhat insane and had committed suicide with whiskey and sleeping pills. She had been a lovely and kind soul but had left him to raise the boys. Now that my father was dead, and my uncle estranged, wasting his life wandering the world, I had to live, and he had deeded me this strange corner of the farm. They all could have their goddamn wheat and corn. Then his face darkened and he held my hand. Just before the war my uncle Paul had come home from Brazil, and he and my father, Wesley, had gotten along well, so Grandpa had taken them to a hunting cabin he kept out in the Black Hills. They had a fine drive out though they drank too much and Lundquist had followed in a truck with the horses and bird dogs. Grandpa and Wesley had had a good time hunting but Paul had disappeared for two days, returning with a lovely Sioux girl "to clean the cabin" he said. The girl didn't care for Paul at all, but fell in love with your father and he with her. Naomi knows nothing of this. Paul and Wesley fought over the girl and I gave her some money and I sent her away while your father had taken a horse to town to be shod. I liked her a great deal and told her to get in touch with me if there ever was a problem. Actually I sent her away because I was taken with her also. It was all a goddamn mess and I was relieved when we got back home. She wrote me a note with the help of a missionary saying she was pregnant. I sent a man out there to check and it was true. So I sent her money on a monthly basis for ten years or so, until I thought she disappeared or died of drink as many Sioux do; then I supported the child through a mission school. When Duane showed up here he didn't know who you were. Then he came back the day you were baptized and said he wanted to marry you and I told him he couldn't legally because you were his half-sister. He ran away. I know there is no pheasant-hunter. Naomi couldn't bear to hear this. We're the only ones who must ever know this. You have done nothing wrong except to love someone. I would have told him earlier who you were except I thought you were helping to keep him here.

Grandpa embraced me. I told him I loved him and I meant to stay alive.

○

I've seen Franco's uncle twice in the past week, once from the balcony through my binoculars, and once face to face under a theatre marquee when I was with my ex–gentleman friend the gynecologist. I have no solid reason to believe he is seeking me. Outside the theatre he merely glanced at me, his face swollen from the recently healed scars. He is an unlikely new resident of Santa Monica, though I'm wondering why, if he is looking for me, he doesn't simply knock on my door. He obviously had no difficulty finding out my address from the clinic.

So I called Ted and arranged a meeting. I wanted to avoid the police and knew that Ted with his peripheral business connections would have a way of checking on the boy's uncle. Ted lives in the Malibu Colony in one of those houses you see featured in *Architectural Digest:* normal mortals think How beautiful but I wouldn't care to live there. In addition to the gatekeeper and a private police force in the Colony, Ted has a houseman who also serves as a bodyguard. This houseman doesn't seem to belong to California—he is happily married with two small children, an ex–homicide detective from Albany, New York. He is hyperenergetic, a first-rate cook, wine connoisseur, and gardener, household accountant. He very quickly took the place of three other employees, excepting a Salvadoran maid. I mention this man, Andrew, because such a level of competence and wit is so rare. Ted told me that Andrew retired from police work because he shot a girl during an attempted robbery and found the experience unendurable. The girl was black and Andrew is mulatto. He is married to a schoolteacher who is also an accomplished cellist. Ruth introduced them before she left Los Angeles for Tucson some years ago.

I was a little startled when I reached Ted's to find my professor of the baggy undies there. It had been a week or so since I had seen him, and he had apparently contacted Ted through Ruth, in hopes that more pressure could be applied from another direction. What the professor, Michael, wanted was access to the family papers and journals, particularly those of my great-grandfather dealing with his "astounding" ideas on what was termed the "Indian problem" in the nineteenth century. Ruth, Mother, and I (and earlier, Grandfather) had decided to keep all the material sequestered after the release of one essay in 1965 to the Nebraska Historical Society, which had caused some not very dramatic publicity and problems. Before he had begun what turned out to be an enormous tree-nursery business to provide root stock to mostly North and South Dakota and Nebraska farmers, Great-grandfather had served as an agricultural missionary to the Oglala Sioux. In the 1880s he had published two articles in *Harper's Monthly*, and several in *McClure's*. He retired to the farm, from the political controversy of what to do with the Sioux, after 1890, when Wounded Knee occurred, though he continued to know Joe White Coyote, Henry Horse, Daniel Blue Horse, Kills a Hundred, and the Minneconjous, Jackson He-Crow, Philip Black Moon, Edward Owl King. He was the closest to He Dog, the friend of Crazy Horse, but tended to be intensely secretive about He Dog. Grandfather had discussed his own father with Edward Curtis, George Bird Grinnell, Mari Sandoz, David Humphreys Miller, and a few others, but then decided in the late forties to put an end to such discussions. We still feel we made an error of honor in allowing part of the journal to be published in 1965. When I returned that spring without my baby I was told by Grandfather a number of specifics that I promised to keep secret, though they have no value except to the very few who care about such matters.

I'm only bringing this up at an unsuitable time because it made inroads toward ruining a fine dinner (bouillabaisse) and raised a kind of anger in me similar to that I felt over the violated boy. Before dinner I had a few private words with Ted and he quickly decided to have Andrew look into the scarred uncle who was apparently shadowing me. But at dinner Ted openly spoke of Ruth before Professor Michael, which upset me and I chided him. Ted likes to imitate the acerbic wit of Gore Vidal, which can be raw, amusing, even revealing, but ultimately of limited use. A certain nasty aspect of Michael's otherwise delightful character arose halfway through the main course. It came in an oddly circuitous manner through a com-

ment on the movie *Amadeus,* which Ted loathed as inaccurate
and insulting. Michael spoke of the uses of history at length,
larding his talk with enough of the anecdotal to keep the layman (sic!) interested. I spotted the gist well before he got to it:
to wit, I was in defiance of a grand tradition of scholarship by
not turning over the goods to a lover but virtual stranger. I
gulped my Meursault and was guilty of a barely controlled
explosion: history in his terms was utterly self-serving and no
one had a right to know what he was looking for. Everyone was
dead, and everything that followed in political terms was the
equivalent of spitting on the memory of the dead. I said, You
seem to think that if you don't tell someone, nothing has happened. I won't allow you to paw over these people for historical novelty or whatever. You will put a dress of your own
designing on them like a circus poodle.

"That's ethical mandarinism," said Michael, a term at
which Ted gave a gasp of pleasure. "You think you're the
keeper of the Grail and no one deserves to know what and why
the Grail is."

"Not at all," I said. "We are no longer the same people
who could have made critical decisions. We have become a
totally different people, a different country. What you call history avoids any valuable concern for people. The essence is the
mythology that allows us to conquer the native populations—
actually over a hundred small civilizations—and then to make
sure that their destiny becomes one of humiliation, a day-by-
day shame and defeat, and what's more, we can feel right
about it because they are drunken Indians."

"But I want to show how the myth worked." He was getting irate now. "And you're preventing me."

"We all know how it worked. You're merely the boy who
wants to take the back off the clock. You don't even want to
be a mechanic, you just want to watch."

"You're reaching a bit, my dear." He was trying to slow
me down. "If I'm the mere voyeur, who are these supposed
mechanics?"

"I mean Congress, Washington as a whole. My uncle Paul
used to say that they ought to run an open sewer in thousand-
yard pig troughs through the Senate, House, and White House
to remind these folks what and who they are."

"Amusing, but what does it mean? Before you get too folksy why don't you admit your position is essentially feminist? You're a woman, and by some sort of dull-witted extension you identify your womanhood with these defeated people. . . ."

"That's what I mean!" I interrupted so loudly I heard Andrew stumble in the kitchen. "You sit there scratching your dick under the table in a state of total unwitting identification with the victors. Your weapon is your doctorate in history which you suppose entitles you to open all doors. I don't identify with anyone. Indians are Indians. Blacks are blacks. Women are women."

Now Ted was desperate to enter what he probably thought was sheer fun, at least an alternative to record-business talk. "Teddy Roosevelt invited Sitting Bull, American Horse, and Geronimo to his inauguration. All of Washington was miffed when these chiefs weren't the least bit impressed. Politicians can't bear the knowledge that people care more for food, sex, love, their families and jobs, than they care for political machinations. . . ."

Michael waved Ted's comment away with a flap of his hand. He finished an eight-ounce hit of wine he had poured in his empty brandy glass. He was clearly pissed off to some nether edge but was so resolutely an academician, even while drunk, that he was summoning up an additional vicious clunker.

"I've often found it amusing that people with a negotiable amount of inherited wealth"—they always get you for this!—"hold a charmed, remote outlook toward minorities. As a simple, wandering scholar I'm far closer to their nature than you are."

"You should drive out to Black Mesa in your BMW and tell that one to the Hopis."

"You fucking bitch!" he screamed. "You miserable bitch!"

Andrew ran out of the kitchen to prevent any possible violence, but Michael had calmly taken another drink between "bitch"es. Ted had meanwhile collapsed off his chair with laughter. "Ruth was trying to be nice. I bet she said, 'I'll consent to give you the papers if Dalva and Naomi will.'"

Michael shook his head and in the process decided to be

charming again. After all, he probably thought, there's no point in needlessly cutting off contact. With a sequence of not very probing questions he got Ted started on the sexual habits of rock stars, which turned out to be somewhat limited by drug ingestion.

I said good night and Ted showed me to the door with regret. I hugged him, feeling how his tall, gaunt body retained its boyishness.

"I'm sorry I talked about Ruth. He presented himself as a close friend. You slept with him, didn't you? But then in my circles that doesn't mean a great deal. It was a wonderful night, you know, like in a Russian novel where Pyotr Stepanovich steps into the parlor and announces that he's been brooding on the recent problem of infant suicide. *En passant* the tykes see news photos of the president or attorney general and hurl themselves out windows onto cobblestones and windswept snow."

○

Ruth called to say she wasn't pregnant. Oh my God, I'm sorry, I said, but then she said she wasn't particularly sorry. The letters from the priest in Costa Rica had been full of the vilest sort of recriminations, the intent being to somehow prove that she had managed the whole thing herself. There was the suggestion that she had bewitched him and that thankfully God had sent him to Costa Rica well out of her sphere of influence. She wondered what he was doing with the suggestive photos he had begged for, taken with a discount-store Polaroid. She had viewed the photos session, she admitted it with some embarrassment, as the single silliest event of her life, but was reassured by my laughter. Then she told me she had gone out twice with a Mexican grocer, a widower and the father of one of her piano students. All of Ruth's students are physically handicapped, the largest proportion being blind. She thinks of her teaching as "music for solace" and works very hard at it. The grocer's blind daughter was seven years old, a lovely little girl who showed a great deal of promise. The grocer himself was haunted by the fact that he hadn't insisted that his wife go to the doctor earlier even though she had died of fallopian cancer which is nearly always undetectable in its early stages and consequently fatal. The first date had been so courtly and somber, dinner and a movie, that she had doubted she'd see him again. He had called her the next morning to ask her to a fiesta dance in honor of a saint. She had accepted because no one had asked her to a dance since she had met Ted at Eastman. In a panic she had spent a week learning to dance Mexican polka style from her cleaning woman who was overweight but agile. Then at the fiesta they had merely sat at a front table with his well-heeled but stuffy relatives until she bribed his twelve-year-old nephew to dance with her. After that it had been wonderful though the leavetaking at her door had been a subdued embrace.

My breath shortened and I was holding the phone tightly because I knew what she was going to say. She began with the anticipated "Remember when . . ." And I did remember, in itself a harmless memory of an event that followed an intensely difficult time. She was referring to the County Fair and how three months after I returned from having my baby I won a dance contest with Charlene as a partner. It was a communal effort to break through the aftereffects of the birth, a kind of lassitude or somnolence where I would sit at my upstairs window at first light trying to balance out what my life had been. It began in early August, a few weeks before the fair. Normally I would have been working with the horses to enter several classes at the fair but I couldn't bear to look at a horse because Duane had come in late May to pick up the buckskin a week before I came home and I had missed him. What happened was that Charlene's mother, Lena, brought her out to see me on a Sunday afternoon. Charlene's mother was thin and sharp-featured, shy, an unsuccessful lover of garage mechanics, a clothing-store salesman, the constable, a farm-implement dealer. She had come to Nebraska from Chicago with her husband and the infant Charlene to make a "fresh start." That day she had told me her husband missed the city but she had refused to go back. Mother persuaded her to stay for dinner. Ruth was just finishing her piano practice in the music room and Lena was curious. She said she used to play the piano in a polka band in Chicago while her husband drank and played accordion. It took some effort to persuade her, including a gin

and tonic, but Ruth dragged her to the grand piano whose use
had been limited to the classics. It became a strange sight that
hot August afternoon with two mothers and three daughters
jumping around the house, the mothers drinking gin and the
daughters lemonade with a little gin snuck into it. Ruth took
over the easy, raucous melodies at the piano and Lena showed
us the steps. We rolled up the Persian rug in the parlor for
extra room. No one wanted to stop so we didn't. Everyone
seemed to be dancing out their own loneliness, and when that
was over, we danced together, separating when the urge took
us. I danced before the portrait of my father, and I danced into
the kitchen when I began to weep because I didn't want to
upset the others. I danced right through my weeping. I began
to see others for the first time in three months. We watched
each other as we danced with sweat beginning to moisten our
Sunday dresses, then soak them. Lena and Ruth would trade
off at the piano, then continue moving at the kitchen sink as
they ran cold water on their sore fingers. Naomi tripped and
fell, springing back up and nearly falling again as I caught her.
Ruth jumped straight up and down, her eyes on some distant
imaginary object. Charlene's steps were intricate and we held
on to each other as I tried to imitate them.

Suddenly we were too tired to go on. We laughed for a
while then became strangely silent. Naomi led us out to the car
and we drove to the swimming hole where three of us had
been baptized the year before. We all lazed nudely in the
river, paddling in circles, utterly quiet. I forced out air and
sank down to the bottom thinking of Duane's whistle that had
led me away. I stayed down so long that Charlene swam down
past me and grabbed my arm, drawing me back to the surface.

We continued to practice the next three weeks under
Lena's tutelage. Naomi altered Father's tuxedo for Charlene to
wear, because we were supposed to be a couple and thought
the sham might pass muster. In the northeast corner of the
county there was a big concentration of Polish and Slovakian
farm families and they always won the contest. Naomi thought
the dress Lena designed for me was rather too short, but Lena
pointed out that all the judges were male and there was no
point in "fighting reality."

We won handily before a crowd of a thousand or so cowboys, yokels, bumpkins, big farmers, marginal farmers, wives, children, 4-H Club members, schoolboys in blue FFA (Future Farmers of America) jackets. Grandfather told me that there was no question that we were the best, not forgetting Ruth at the piano, but my legs didn't hurt our chances. Curiously, I was no longer upset at a reference to my body, and the fact that a group of town boys cheered for "Squaw" pleased me. Away from the others, out behind the grandstand in the dark, Charlene and I sat on the grass and watched the gaudy lights of the Ferris wheel and the yellow square that was the entrance to the horse barn. I felt a sharp pain at the thought that I might have competed with Duane at calf roping. Grandfather had assured me that Duane had asked about me when he had retrieved the buckskin. Suddenly Charlene put an arm around me and kissed me deeply on the lips. I pulled away and she apologized and said she hoped she hadn't ruined our friendship. I said of course not. I had been through enough that so direct a gesture failed to shock me, and besides, I knew that Charlene hated men. She cried so I reassured her over and over that we would be friends forever. We still are, though she lives in Paris now with a third husband and we haven't seen each other in several years. At the time the experience reminded me of the novels I was reading, and Charlene's lips on mine were merely part of a chapter.

○

Andrew stopped by this afternoon to say I may have to move. The boy's uncle, Guillermo Sandoval by name, can't be reliably controlled except by a bullet, and unless I would agree to that measure, moving was the only option. I wouldn't agree. Andrew expected that, and went to some lengths to describe what kind of man we were dealing with: a barrio drug enforcer, a U. S. citizen out of McAllen, Texas, so he couldn't be deported; an intelligent psychopath who claimed that he and his nephew were in love (!), a man who claimed he didn't hate me for causing his aerial whipping though God would surely cause me to have an accident at some point. Meanwhile Ted had had the man put under twenty-four-hour surveillance, which might prompt rash behavior if discovered. I asked Andrew how he found all of this out. He said he "held a gun to the sucker's head."

When Andrew left I sat at my balcony and stared at the summery Pacific and thought how deeply irrational the situation had become, that just beneath the ordinary skin of ordinary life—the life that looked so comforting and normal from the balcony—something uncontrollable was whirling with all the indirection of the Brownian movement. The posture of writing it down is after the fact; the event recorded in tranquillity has a larger sense of tranquillity than it has earned.

○

But I am getting ahead of myself. It was some time before I realized that it was my uncle Paul who saved my weary soul that summer. I had come to him in Patagonia, Arizona, actually south of a point between Patagonia and Sonoita, by a circuitous route. The Monday after Thanksgiving Mother drove me northeast toward Marquette, Michigan, on Lake Superior where I was to live with her cousin and his wife and have my baby. It was a two-day trip that was stretched into five by snowstorms. We spent nights in Sioux Falls, South Dakota; Blue Earth, Minnesota; Minneapolis; and two nights in Duluth, before reaching Marquette on the kind of brilliant, cloudless day that signals the passing of an Arctic front. Lake Superior, surely our most inhospitable body of water, was roaring under a glittery sky only a few blocks from the house. I hadn't minded the delay, because beneath my breastbone I knew that this would be the first time I had spent more than a night away from my mother. It all seemed a mistake because it was barely three months and the baby hadn't made its presence felt. I wanted to be either home or back in Duluth, in the hotel where we could see all of the harbor during the few hours the blizzard let up. We had had a wonderful room-service dinner sitting by the window; then Mother began to cry and I comforted her with more strength than I owned. I liked the snow-laden forest and hills, so unlike Nebraska, on the road between Duluth and Marquette.

Mother's cousin, Warren, was in his early forties and a game biologist for the Department of the Interior, and his wife, Maureen, a plump vigorous woman, taught drama at the local college. Warren was slender, quiet, contemplative, obsessed with birds and mammals, while Maureen was loud, hearty, profane, the first woman I ever met who swore a lot. In fact, the first thing she said at the door was "Jesus H. Christ, what a beauty!" For some reason I laughed, and she embraced me. But I cried for an hour or so when Mother left the next morning, so Maureen insisted I go to a play rehearsal with her. I was abashed sitting in a small auditorium watching the students speak their parts in Garcia Lorca's *Blood Wedding.* It had never occurred to me that people could speak that passionately out loud. Grandfather had read Shakespeare to me but this was raw and direct. Several of the men sat down next to me during a break but I was too shy to say much. One of the men, a graduate student from Chicago, was unbelievably handsome and this made me nervous. He was dressed in the fashion of the bohemians I had seen in a photo essay in *Life* magazine. Maureen waved the men away, whispering to me, "No wonder you're pregnant."

The time passed quickly because I was given so much schoolwork to do and on a level beyond my capacity. Warren tossed my schoolbooks aside and put me on a science program of his own devising. Maureen did the same in the humanities, screeching "Puppy shit" as she threw my textbook on English and American literature into the fireplace. She taught me what she called "living literature" rather than the writers she loathed in the text—Pope, Dryden, Tennyson, William Cullen Bryant, Howells Markham. Her favorites were Keats and Yeats, Dickens, Twain, Melville, Whitman, and William Faulkner, who was difficult at first, though I identified closely with *Light in August.* Maureen also started me on a rigorous study of Spanish which I hated at the time but have been grateful for ever since. They both strongly disapproved of the country-Western music station I listened to all day but decided I must need the music in order to endure it. The music made me homesick but had the familiarity of old and favorite clothes. Duane's favorite singer was Hank Williams, who Maureen admitted had a certain quality she called *duende,* a Spanish gypsy term for "ghost" or "soul."

Once Maureen came home from work early. I was in the

shower and didn't hear her and she found me standing nude in front of my bedroom mirror looking for signs of rumored baby. I was a little embarrassed after I dressed and sat down to review my schoolwork. She had a large tumbler of imported sherry and poured me a small glass. The Jerez sherry was an indulgence she had learned during the two years she had lived in Barcelona and Ibiza. She pushed the schoolwork aside and started to talk, more a slangish monologue than a lecture: "I certainly don't believe that story about you screwing a pheasant-hunter but that's your business, and right now it should matter to no one except you. You're going to have a hard time, because you are lovely and your body is as fine as I've seen." I objected to this as ugly and irrelevant but she went on: "You have to study extremely hard and find some subject or profession you're obsessed with because in our culture it has been very hard on the attractive women I know. They are leered at, teased, abused, set on a pedestal, and no one takes them seriously, so you have to use all your energies to develop the kind of character that can withstand this bullshit. You don't want to waste your life reacting to it. Don't waste your time on men who talk and stare but don't listen to you. They just want to fuck you. Women I've known in your position get easily depressed because they are valued for something, their looks, which they had nothing to do with, you get it? It's all genetic. And there's a lot of envy from other women. I wouldn't mind looking like you for a few weeks just to bowl the assholes over for a change."

"Aren't you happy with Warren?" I asked.

"Of course. He's the best man I ever had and I tried quite a few, though most of them weren't top-drawer. I met him when I was twenty-eight and it took two years to get him to marry me. I hiked every goddamn hill and swamp in the Upper Peninsula with him during that time. I quit that on our honeymoon which was a week of more camping on Isle Royale. Warren thought it was very funny when I quit because he knew I never liked it in the first place and I was just acting. Then he sent me off to New York City for a week of theatre as a present. I also know you're thinking of ways to keep your baby but you can forget it because no one's going to let you."

Unfortunately, the week before Naomi, Ruth, and Grandfather were to arrive for Christmas vacation I became ill with a particularly virulent form of flu. At the tail end of the flu came a serious case of pneumonia which put me in the local hospital. I did not become better and the holidays were an uncomfortable dream of visits from Naomi and Ruth. For a stretch of time my fever made me somewhat delirious and the regular doctors were joined by a specialist Grandfather had flown up from Omaha. The pregnancy complicated matters and there was fear for both of our lives. One late night after the fever had begun to subside Grandfather came in against the wishes of the nurses. He said he had made a mistake that he wanted to correct. He had hoped so badly that I would forget Duane that he hadn't given me the necklace that Duane had left behind for me. I grasped the necklace, seeing immediately it was the one Duane wore with a plain small stone in a copperish setting. There was also an envelope that had come more recently in the mail. It was a Christmas card with a Rapid City postmark. The card was a crèche scene and Duane had printed "This here card is a joke. You sing one of your songs for me and I'll sing one of mine for you, your friend Duane." There was no return address. I kissed Grandfather's hand and rolled over to face the wall, holding the necklace to my lips. When he left, a nurse who had become a friend came in and asked me what was in my hand.

"My boyfriend sent me his good-luck necklace." She helped me put it on and brought a hand mirror so I could see myself. It was one of the happiest moments of my life. That night I dreamed of riding with Duane on horses that ran through the air, under the ground through the soil, under the surface of lakes and rivers. I awoke the next morning feeling much better. I hid the necklace from Naomi and Ruth because they would recognize it.

The doctor from Omaha had insisted before he left that I be moved away from the cold damp climate of the Upper Peninsula. It was the kind of suggestion that put Grandfather into his "umbrage" mood, as Naomi called it. He had been staying at the only good hotel in town and Maureen had seen him at a restaurant with an attractive woman. He was also wearing elegant but old-fashioned suits that had the vaguely foreign touch of New York or London.

It was confusing when I got out of the hospital and learned that I was only to be at Maureen and Warren's for another day, or until the weather let up. Warren and Grandfather got me from the hospital in an old Dodge power wagon borrowed from Warren's job. The streets were partly drifted over and no one was around though it was noon. The wind blew so hard the whole world became blinding white, and Warren would stop the truck until it cleared a bit. I could sense their nervousness but thought it was all quite wonderful because I was out of the hospital.

Back at Warren's I ate my promised hamburger in the kitchen with Ruth sitting beside me, the sort of silly relief you want from hospital food, and listened to the quarrel in the living room. Naomi wanted to take me home and Grandfather insisted that it was the doctor's second choice to a drier climate. I could hear the anger in his voice as he repeated charges of how Naomi was suffocating us in our Nebraska "nest" and, in this case, my health was at stake. Naomi's voice was a little quavery in protest though on our way to Michigan, in the hotel in Duluth, she admitted we all ought to get "out and around" more often. She had said she tended to think of the world as something that had killed her husband and the farm as their beloved and safe place. Grandfather made a speech to the effect that everything was arranged. A friend of his from Chicago was going to pick them up in his plane and fly me to Tucson. My uncle Paul whom I had only seen at my dad's funeral would take me to his ranch house near Patagonia, where there would be a registered nurse who was also a teacher. All the calls had been made and the plan was final.

And that's what happened. The weather cleared in the night, the plane from Chicago arrived, and off we went, arriving in Tucson in the evening. It was someone's corporate plane so there were nice chairs to sit on, also a small bed where I could rest. I played gin rummy with Ruth who must have been twelve or so. Ruth whispered to me that she had thanked God I was pregnant because she at last had gotten to go places and ride on an airplane. She was sorry to say it but it was true. We met Uncle Paul at the airport along with a dark-skinned woman who called herself Emilia. Ruth and I sat and watched television—Naomi disapproved of it so we had none at home—

while Grandfather, Naomi, Paul, and Emilia had a meeting in an office. Ruth was angry because she had learned we weren't going to keep the baby. She was unsure about my abilities but she knew she could handle the job. They came out of the office and we said goodbye.

Paul put his arm around me when we watched out the window as the plane took off for Grand Island. "You look like your dad and my mother. I was always sort of homely myself. Emilia here knows everything worth knowing. You'll like her."

At the Desert Inn there were two bedrooms for us and a parlor where we ate dinner. I was so quiet that Paul asked me what I was thinking about. I admitted that I always had heard that he was a wild-eyed and crazy treasure-hunter who lived with different women without being married. I also told him that when I went to see the movie *The Treasure of the Sierra Madre* with Naomi she said Humphrey Bogart was just like my uncle Paul. He thought this was very funny and told me he had been surprised and happy when my father had the sense to marry a farm girl.

Like many men who wander the world and live far from their native culture, Paul had evolved elaborate and private theories about many things. The same thing seems to happen with all solitary people, hermits, country bachelors, trappers. The moment we reached his ranch house the next morning we went on as long a walk as my health could bear. His notion was that hard-working Mexican women of the peasant class had an easier time in childbirth because of their enforced exercise. Therefore, at least a two-hour walk was in order every day before I began my studies. In his frequent absences, Emilia was to take me, or make sure one of the two hired hands took me. I went for these walks right through the winter until I reached my seventh month of pregnancy, when I still waddled slowly around the outbuildings. Paul approved of the books I brought from Warren and Maureen, adding his own prejudices in favor of Spanish and Italian culture. He said if I ever visited Spain, or Florence in Italy, I would understand to what depths of greed and stupidity the United States had sunk.

There were two Tennessee walking horses Paul used for hunting but I still could not look at a horse without thinking of Duane. Hunting was Paul's main passion along with geology, and women, to whom he was courtly. I saw the bills on his desk from sending flowers to a half-dozen or so women around the United States. He had a kennel where he kept English setters and pointers for hunting quail, and a Labrador for ducks that was allowed to wander around except at night. His one concession to Grandfather was a large male Airedale kept to look after things. The idea of a guard dog wasn't a popular notion then, though many rural people owned a dog who performed the function. I asked Emilia why one of the hired hands carried a large pistol and she said he was a retired *bandito*. His name was Tino and his son—Tito, of all things—wasn't allowed to carry a gun unless he was walking with me. He used the occasions to exercise the bird dogs, and when they pointed a covey of quail Tito would shoot in the air to keep the dogs interested.

When Paul was home from Mexico we would drive with several of the dogs to new areas within a hundred miles or so. He would point out geological formations, flora, and fauna, but not much of it registered on me. This didn't disturb him. He told me when he first came to southern Arizona it all looked like moonscape to him, and probably more so to me what with being pregnant.

"Should I want to shoot the young man?" he asked one morning. We were sitting near a beautiful spring far up Sycamore Canyon off the Arivaca road, oddly enough the same area where Ruth seduced her priest so many years later. I shook my head no and he hugged me. He smelled like my father had up on the Missouri when I was a child.

"Your father would have. He was a violent man at times. Dad bought us sixteen-ounce boxing gloves so we wouldn't hurt each other. Your father was a great fighter whenever it was called for but he gave it up when he got married. He liked machines. I liked books and rocks. I take after my mother except for the drinking. I don't like to drink very much."

I asked him why the hired man had a gun. He said the border country was always a little bit risky. The drug heroin was smuggled across the boundary; also, people sneaked into the U. S. and he had a few business enemies in Mexico.

Once when Emilia and I were plucking quail for dinner I asked her if she was Paul's lover. "Sometimes," she said. I continued the line of questioning until she became embar-

rassed and changed the subject by saying the doctor was coming in the morning. I disliked the doctor who was puffy white
and wore too much cologne. "Who was the lucky boy?" he
asked during the first examination when I lay with my legs up.
I told him I didn't know because I had been drunk and there
were several. A wave of disgust passed across his face and
further examinations were without conversation.

○

I had my son April 27 in a Tucson hospital. Mother was there
with me, and Uncle Paul acted the nervous father. I hugged
the baby for just a moment and kissed it goodbye. I wanted to
give it Duane's necklace but I knew this would be lost or the
gesture misunderstood. Somehow, when I was supposed to be
sleeping, I overheard talk in the hall that the baby was going
to be adopted by a couple in Minneapolis. I think they were
out in the hall waiting to see the baby.

When Mother took me home to Nebraska, Ruth embraced
me mightily, then became angry and rushed to her room because I didn't have a photo of the baby. "What's his name,
goddamn you?" she screamed. I was too tired to cry. Grandfather embraced me and stared out the window. For some reason I wanted to work in the garden. I walked with Naomi and
Grandfather out into the garden, and then slowly around the
house as if we had a purpose.

The summer passed a little like a mixture of dreaming and
sleepwalking until the afternoon of our polka party. It was
Uncle Paul's theory of walking that helped a great deal. I found
my father's World War II canteen in the attic and sometimes
I would pack a sandwich, or double back to Grandfather's to
have lunch and to take some dogs along. I wasn't particularly
more observant than I had been in Arizona though later my
memory was sharper than I would have expected. Nowadays
there are all sorts of technical explanations for such times—I
know them because I studied them at the university and in
graduate school. For a girl of my age at the time, experiencing
what I had, the emotional "burnout," as it is rather glibly
called, was actually a vital emptiness, a time when life was
so poignant, and full of what is understood as suffering but

is really only life herself making us unavoidably unique. I still reread a letter Uncle Paul sent me soon after I arrived home.

My Beloved Dalva!
It was a delight to have you here. It made me love my brother more in retrospect because he had a part in your being alive. You are at an age when you are not to yourself what you are to others. You were spreading good feeling from your prison, joking about your tummy, singing while you brushed the dogs, making us Nebraska desserts, telling stories about my father so I actually wanted to see him again. When I got home from the airport Tino and Tito imitated your fine lisping Castilian and we laughed, then fell silent because you were gone. Emilia wouldn't come out of her room, and the Labrador wandered around the property looking for you. In a childish way I was angry that you were gone. I don't wish you any trouble because I love you, but you must know that I am always here if you need a refuge, or want to get away. I haven't been to church since I was fourteen but I pray that things will get better for you. I have never met a girl who made everyone she met feel more strongly that they liked to live, a fuzzy notion but true.
What follows are some notes I made for you about our walks and trips. I felt that later on you might want to know just what it was you saw. I began walking at your age just because the natural world seemed to absorb the poison in me. Then I gradually wanted to understand why this was so and I suspect you will too. Strange, but we started on the same place, the same farm, and I knew some of the same anguish at your age, which is not to say that I fully comprehend what you are going through.
What you saw from Patagonia is much like the entire SE corner of Arizona—a 5,000-foot-high rolling plateau with grassy benches falling off into broad valleys with cienegas of sycamore, cottonwood, and live oak, a cooler, breezier, and slightly wetter place to live than up in Tucson (which is out of the question anyway because of all the realtors!). Sonoita Creek, along with Aravaipa and Madera,

is one of the few remaining Sonoran Desert creeks with
native fishes. In that bosque along Sonoita Creek west of
Patagonia where you had morning sickness, there are a
vast number of pugnacious, iridescent-throated hum-
mingbirds, impossible to identify except the males hover-
ing close to us. The fabled coppery-tailed trogon sometimes nests here but I've only seen him once in the area,
and several times up in Madera Canyon where we picked
those wild hot peppers, the chilatepines. I take these on
airplane and train trips to make the food palatable.

You see juniper and scrub oak on the north-facing
terraces at 5,000 feet. Looking north, the grasslands are
mixed with low, scrubby mesquite, a sure sign of overgrazing, just as overgrazing destroyed much of the Sand Hills
back home. There are also colonies of Huachuca agave,
rising toward the Santa Ritas where a forest of several
species of oak, juniper, and piñon pine climbs toward the
ponderosa zone at about 7,000 feet. It can be nice and cool
up there when the valley is blistering.

In the bosque, under black walnut and big hackberry
trees, you see the blunted tracks of javelina (the strong-
tasting wild pig that Tino and Tito love to eat), a Mohave
rattler in a thicket of wolfberry rustling among fallen
leaves of ash and Arizona holly. You liked these usually dry
creek bottoms where we saw tracks of deer, coyote, coati-
mundi, gray fox, bobcat, and ringtail cat. Occasionally I've
seen the tracks of mountain lion, the scent of which upsets
the bird dogs. Wolves and grizzlies were here into the
early part of the twentieth century and the Yaquis still
have two words for "coyote": "coyote" and "big coyote."
I still think that huge coyote we saw that morning down
on the slope of the Huachucas was a Mexican lobo. That
was the area, the San Rafael Valley, where you asked me
why I didn't buy a huge ranch, and I said that was what
was wrong with my father. He wanted to own every goddamn acre he looked at. When we were supposed to be
hunting he was always looking at ranches and farms. Of
course when he got tired of it all, and everything else, he
turned quite a dollar selling the land off.

West, the Pajaritos stretch into Mexico and run, under

different names, south toward Caborca and west to Sonoita. The upper Sonoran country is rugged, little known, and remarkably well watered. Remember Sycamore Canyon, where you cooled your feet in the spring and the dogs swam around in circles, their eyes bright with pleasure? Harlequin or Mearn's quail are here. Velvet mesquite grows all the way up to 5,500 feet, the much-frosted zone.

Farther west across the valley there are scailed quail where it's not overgrazed. For some reason you found this area scary, the way the sacred Papago mountain, Babaquivari, dominates the landscape. It is and should be scary. The Papagos are scary, so are the Yaquis and the different branches of the Apache. What grand people! We minimize these people now so we don't have to feel bad about what we did to them. An English author who was otherwise quite daffy said that the only aristocracy is that of consciousness. Some day you must study the hundred or so tribes, the civilizations, that we annihilated.

This is enough for now. Emilia is helping me pack for a trip to Chiapas. Some day we should climb up Babaquivari together, up through the prickly pear, the different chollas, the two acacias, catclaw and whitehorn, jojoba, white rhatany, and Mexican tea; higher is sangre de drago, juniper, piñon and Ajo oak, alligator juniper. Together we can look into I'itoi's cave, the Papago God! You won't see a sorry bunch of Methodists sitting around praying for a fast buck. Please write me. I love you. Uncle Paul.

I'm not sure why the letter meant so much to me because my memories of the area seemed a dullish welter broken only by an occasional sharp image. But the letter served as a totem that, along with the long walks, got me through the summer until the day we all danced together. Of course there is something absurdly nonunique in a sixteen-year-old girl wandering around the fields, windbreaks, and creeks thinking about God, sex, and love, the vacuum of the baby.

On the night of a full moon my breasts hurt from unused milk though I had been given a pill for the condition. I sat at the window all night watching the moon until it set just before dawn. It arose red, turned pink, then white, then pink, then red as it returned to earth, a summer moon. The moon drew me far away from myself and I imagined that my dead father and Duane saw the moon from a different angle. Before I went up to bed Ruth played me Beethoven's *Moonlight Sonata* on the piano. She could play it in the dark. I could also hear the squeak of the porch swing where Naomi sat every summer evening in what she called a "pointless reverie." Ruth was embarrassed by the beauty of the mood and told me that my breasts were so big as to look truly silly.

At daylight I dressed in my walking clothes and put a thermos of coffee, something to eat, and two books on local birds and fauna in my day pack. I never looked at the books but carried them along at Naomi's insistence that I do something useful. Suddenly she was standing at the kitchen door in her nightgown as if wanting to say something. I was angry at the intrusion, and wouldn't face her, staring at the rows of tomatoes she had canned the day before. The tomatoes looked as if they were suffocating in the glass jars, livid red and suffering. "Are you OK?" she asked. "I'm just walking off the baby," I said, going out the door without turning to her, something I regretted halfway to Grandfather's when the rhythm of walking had already taken over and I felt soothed.

The smallest of the bitch Airedales was waiting out where the path neared a cattail-choked pond. She waited there every morning in hopes that she would get to go along. Grandfather liked me to take her because she was a first-rate snake dog; that is, she smelled a rattler before the snake was even alarmed, and if we gave permission, would kill it, and if she was hungry, eat it. Since rattlers meant no harm I never let her kill them except around the outbuildings. The other dogs would merely bark but Sonia—Ruth named her that after a doll—would go in for the kill, first letting the snake tire itself with repetitive strikes. Killing a snake made her very proud and she would march around stiff and bouncy at the same time like a gaited horse. She was also good at chasing away angry range cows who were protecting calves.

Behind Grandfather's, where the county road stopped, the land became hillier and was ill-suited for corn, wheat, or alfalfa. This land was the back end of a twenty-section ranch which, though it sounds large, barely made its owners a living because all the water was ours. We had all the property on both sides of the bordering creek.

I crossed the almost dry creek, then the fence, and followed a contour of eroded hills and gulches toward the west. I turned north after a mile or so, took off my shoes, and crossed the Niobrara which was sandy and less than knee-deep in summer, then moved farther north along the neighbor's fence line which came short of the water. The large trees, ash, linden, elm, with hanging wild grapevines, were left behind on the floodplain as I climbed up through a gully into the rugged caprock. Sonia smelled a snake but I hurried her along, wanting to reach the upper end of a small box canyon. I had been there with Duane and there was a seep he had dug out to water the horses. There were small trees for shade, a large flat rock on which we had eaten a roast chicken Grandfather had sent along, also a Ball jar of lemonade in which the ice had melted. Duane was reading Edward Curtis at the time and announced that this was a holy place. I said How do you know, and he answered that any fool could tell. To prove it he found several arrowheads, and sat on the flat rock for a full hour in silence, facing the east. It made me feel sort of religious at the time, and that's why I returned there with Sonia.

I was somewhat confused because several days before our Methodist minister had stopped by to visit me. He had sent Naomi and Ruth out of the parlor so we could talk and pray. He asked me to beg for forgiveness for having a baby out of wedlock. I asked him how he knew and he said he had heard through Mrs. Lundquist who worked for Grandfather. I refused to ask forgiveness and he pleaded with me. I looked up at the portrait of my dad and he seemed to say I didn't have to beg for anything. Later at dinner Ruth did a wonderful imitation of the minister—"Oh Gawd, Gawd, saaave wayward Dalva!" Naomi was cross at first but ended up laughing. In any event, it was the end of my churchgoing.

So I sat on the rock waiting for something to happen. I wasn't sure what it would be but I was hopeful. Sonia flopped down in the cool grass by the seep and watched me, then drifted off into a world of dog snores and dreams. When I sat down I checked the railroad watch in my day pack. It was just short of 8:00 A.M. and I would still be there at 5:00 P.M. when I would leave in order to be home by dark.

My only outward accomplishment was a sunburn on top of my tan and a desperate hunger because I had given Sonia my sandwich. I let my coffee cool so that it would be a substitute for water. There was a spring a mile or so away but I stuck to my rock—the seep water was too discolored to trust. I saw a prairie falcon that flew over the canyon edge, then wheeled away shrieking with surprise when she saw me. I saw a doe and a fawn but Sonia chased them away, roaring as if they meant us harm. I rehearsed my entire life and I heard my heart for the first time. In the morning I had fantasies of love and laughter, even creating the image of Duane and my father riding horseback up the draw toward me. In the afternoon I nursed my baby and flew with a crow overhead. Mostly I had a very long and intensely restful "nothing." I had the odd sensation that I was understanding the earth. This is all very simpleminded and I mention it only because I still do much the same thing when troubled.

Later in the afternoon Sonia leapt up with a maddened howl and raced down the draw only to be met by Grandfather's other dogs. They all came at me at a dead, noisy run and I felt like prey. Grandfather followed on his big sorrel, leading another horse.

"I hope I'm not intruding. Your mother was worried."

"I was just thinking things over." I reached up for the canteen he offered as he got off the horse.

"You look like a sorry Indian even if you're just a trace. I used to come to this spot and so did the boys. When he was a boy your uncle Paul dug out the spring and stayed here a whole week when he hated me the most."

"Why did he hate you? He doesn't seem to anymore."

"He thinks I killed his mother in one way or another. When you're a boy you don't understand your mother is crazy because she's your mother. She babied Paul and neglected your dad because he was too much like me."

"I think Paul is a fine person."

"He doubtless is. You learn finally that some things aren't meant to heal. But you already know that. That's probably why you're up here."

I nodded and reached out for his hand which for the first time seemed a little frail. I felt a pang as if acknowledging that this old man I loved so much would die some day. He read my thoughts.

"If I live seven more months will you go to the Dublin Horse Show with me? I'll show you the right way to spend some money. I haven't been since 1937 and I miss it."

"I'd love to but I don't think I could miss school."

"Goddamn your school. It's a worthless piece of cowshit taught by flies."

I laughed and we mounted the horses despite the memory of Duane. He's probably riding a horse right now, I thought, somewhere out in Dakota.

○

Andrew came over early this morning, just after I picked up my mail which included letters from Naomi, Ruth, and one from Professor Michael postmarked Palo Alto. Everyone in the history of my family was a letter writer, a diary keeper. It's as if they thought they'd disappear if they didn't put themselves on paper. For a while in my twenties I stopped the habit but it made my thinking boringly recurrent. I resumed the practice so I could get rid of the thoughts and information, leaving room for something new. You make a topographical map of contours, then move on. Of course it's a great deal easier when you never write for publication. The professor gave me several of his books and articles and I made the error of commenting that he sure did screw the lid on tight. This idle quip caused a fourteen-hour (by actual count) defense of his methods.

Andrew had good news. Our sociopath friend, Guillermo, took an Air West flight to Houston with a connection to McAllen. The police in McAllen said the man paid two weeks of rent in advance at a medium-priced motel. They believed the DEA was shadowing the man though they wouldn't offer any specifics.

"How many days would it take you to pack this place up?" he asked, looking around as if to estimate.

"An afternoon. I've been here seven years but most of my stuff is in Nebraska."

Andrew went to the stove where I was warming up some leftover *posole,* a Mexican pork, hot-chile, yellow-hominy stew. I learned this dish, among dozens of others, when I was with a young man who wanted to live a simple, Third World existence, which turned out to be amazingly complicated for me—I did the shopping, tended the garden, cooked the natural food, kept the house, while he meditated. When he stopped making love in order to achieve yet another "level" I moved out. The sixties were like that. He now owns a Mercedes dealership in Florida he bought by wholesaling cocaine. The seventies!

"Can I have some of this? I'm fucking tired of cooking French and northern Italian for Ted. Last year it was Szechuan, then Hunanese. Next year it'll be watermelon and flan."

"What if you wanted to find a baby put up for adoption twenty-nine years ago?"

"A real cold track but possible. You'd want a pure white guy to do the job out in farm country. The idea is also ill-advised. You better get another job."

I didn't ask him why it was ill-advised because I already knew. If there's any seeking to do it should be instigated by the child who was given up, or away, abandoned, perhaps taken from its mother.

"Why don't you begin by asking your mother who the child was given to?" He was eating his *posole* with gusto and caught me off guard—an ex-detective is apparently never off duty.

"I wouldn't want her to know I was looking."

"I can find somebody to do the job but I think it's a bad idea. And expensive, but I understand you can afford it."

"Does that make it doubly bad?"

"You won't get that shit off me. Leave it to the professor. Look at this half-colored boy. My dad was a schoolteacher in Roxbury, in Boston, before we moved to Albany. Son, he says, don't waste your time worrying about parity on earth. Jesus said, To them that has, much is given. I'm not religious but what the hell does that mean?"

"I never understood it," I said. "I like to work and I've never been much of a spender. A man I know says I've always got a return ticket. But then he likes to spend money."

"What you're saying is that it's not your fault. Of course not. Look at Ted. He loves to piss away money. He serves great wine to these dipshit, drugged-up musicians when Mogen David would be appropriate. He loves you people, you know? You and Ruth and your mother. He thinks you're the class act. Maybe you just thought spending was hard, pointless work. Ted said that if anyone's ancestors put five grand in a good bank in 1871 and it did a modest five percent for a hundred and ten years you would have a million and a half. I bet a lot of fortunes are built just because some folks never got around to spending money. I'm such a pain in the ass about it I let my wife handle everything. It's easier."

When Andrew left I felt a specific desire for him that I had recognized before. I remembered a quote from Ortega y Gasset that Uncle Paul had framed on his study wall in Patagonia from a text he had laboriously translated: "If you don't have standards *nothing* can have any merit. Man uses even sublimity to degrade himself." No matter how many times Andrew had given me an appraising eye, which I returned, we both knew it wasn't a good idea. I have long ago given up trying to figure out the components of sexual desire. Ted teased me about how I could sleep with the professor whom he referred to as a "witty toad." I answered that I got to sleep with the man's brain too, which was an advantage over certain of his friends I had met who had been obviously purchased from a Beverly Hills butcher shop. "The best meat rack is in West Hollywood, dear, down on Melrose." I apologized for beginning this minor tiff, but he said he enjoyed it. He reminded me of the evening we had spent with Andrew drinking a bottle of old Calvados. It was a semi-gay parlor game where we were supposed to admit our worst sexual behavior, or at least our most outrageous. Ted started innocently with a tale on how he had let an old Viennese musicologist at Eastman fuck him for an A grade on an unwritten term paper.

Andrew and I booed the tale as banal. Andrew countered with a tale of screwing a very fat rich woman while he was a student at Boston University. What was so terrible about that? Well, it had gone on for a year while he worked part-time at an expensive food-and-wine shop where there was no opportunity for more than a slight taste of what they sold. He had literally fucked this tremendously unpleasant woman for caviar, truffles, foie gras, confit d'oie, good Bordeauxs. Piffle, Ted said, any German or French girl would have done the same thing in 1946. I admitted that I had slept with my old friend Charlene when I was a student at the University of Minnesota. This was treated with bored indulgence by both of them. Ted bragged that he had fucked his secretary's husband for five hundred dollars' worth of cocaine. This was getting closer. Andrew moved on with a blush to an underage shoplifter. Ted and I looked at each other and confessed a near miss years ago. I had come home from graduate school at Christmas with my Third World meditator while Ruth had brought Ted home from Eastman for the first time. My meditator, George by name, had been difficult from the moment we had arrived. Was the cow manure returned to the soil where it belonged? Of course, steers are nondirectional shitters while dairy cattle, of which we had none, are more specific because of fences, corrals, paddocks, but the manure from the steers' wintering sheds is spread every March. Good, George said. On Christmas Eve we had turkey and George said turkey has been denatured by chemicals. Naomi replied that it was a barnyard turkey bought from a neighbor at which point George overate. On Christmas Day we had a roast from a prime steer Lundquist would butcher for us every fall, hanging the roasts in the cooler for a month or so of aging. George lectured us on how three ounces of lean meat a day was adequate. Naomi was nonplussed at this gratuitous impoliteness. George was actually a pleasant man except in the company of strangers, when he couldn't stop lecturing. Ted teased him on how with all these nutritional theories he managed to be thirty pounds overweight. George huffed off to my room though he later returned for a quiet sandwich. After dinner Ruth and I took turns dancing with Ted to rock-and-roll records. Naomi had gone to bed, and then Ruth followed. We continued dancing to Sam

Cooke, Buddy Holly, Little Richard, B. B. King, and so on. Ted was the best dancer I had ever known. I told him to turn around so I could slip off my panty hose which were too warm. He didn't turn around but we were drinking and it didn't seem to matter. We danced close then and he had a very obvious hard-on beneath his trousers which he pressed against me. I sat down and said I wouldn't continue. He was standing right in front of my face and I couldn't help reaching out and rubbing my hand against it. He unzipped his fly and I put the head of it in my mouth for just a second, then ran upstairs to my room. I managed to wake up my angry meditator enough to make love to me.

Andrew thought this was a major-league story. He asked Ted why, if I excited him so much, he had become homosexual? Ted was unnaturally thoughtful for a few minutes, then said, "It's not what turns one on, but what turns one on the most strongly."

○

My three letters were all rather startling. Ruth wrote that her grocer had presented his financial statement, then asked her to marry him. He wanted her to see the statement so she wouldn't think he wanted her money. She was a little confused and wanted us to visit either in Santa Monica, Tucson, or wherever. Mother's note was an abrupt proposal which required a phone call. She had to know within a few days if I was interested in coming back and teaching for a year at the country school from which she was retiring. The members of the county schoolboard, all in their sixties like Naomi, had kept the school open for years due to her persistence. Otherwise most of the children would have spent a full hour each way on the school bus. The enrollment was down to seventeen in grades one through eight, but she had wangled one more year just in case I cared to come home. Between the lines this meant that Ted had told Ruth, who told Naomi, that my life might be in some danger. She didn't expect me to live with her. My own place, which had been Grandfather's, had been "house-sat" for over twenty years by a finicky Norwegian bachelor cousin of the Lundquists. He was supposedly retranslating Rölvaag's

*Giants in the Earth* though no one saw any of the evidence. On my visits he moved into Duane's bunkhouse which had been nicely redone by a traveling hippie couple Naomi had befriended.

Part of Naomi's peculiar, hard-won sanity is that she doesn't think of her private quarrels as acts of heroism. Her strategies are quiet, her suggestions tentative. My first impulse was "Why not?" Her note ended with the tease that while I wouldn't find any drug problems, there were two seventh-grade twins who were potential drunks. One of them was sexually precocious and she was busy saving the virtue of three of the girls, also saving the boys from irate Lutheran parents.

Professor Michael's letter permanently changed my idea about the man. I was a little suspicious after the first para-graph—when someone pulls off a mask you are left wondering if the new face is yet another mask. The prose owned none of the acerbic, contentious quality of his scholarly articles or his public personality. The letter was a half-dozen pages, begin-ning with an ingenious biographical sketch. There was an occa-sional call for violins but the attempt was at naked honesty, albeit lyrical: born in the Ohio Valley to marginal farm-factory parents and relatives, fundamentalist Protestant, fair-haired student winning a scholarship to Notre Dame which caused a break with his family (a Catholic college!), factory work in summers, a year in a writing program at Northwestern with a failed, awful novel to show for it, long and arduous graduate work at the University of Wisconsin and Yale, ending with a Ph.D. in American studies, a couple of nonscholarly books, marriage and divorce, daughter in private school which cost him a full third of his take-home pay, six years of teaching at Stanford but still without tenure.

The bottom line was on the last page, in the form of a supplication and an offer. He had just returned from Loreto on Baja to meet with my uncle Paul in the hopes that my denial to see family papers could be circumvented. Uncle Paul, whom he "adored," said it was still up to me. The problem was his sabbatical, for which he had been given a large additional foundation grant, would begin in the summer. Tenure de-pended on the book he would write during his sabbatical. The center of the difficulty was that a professor from the University of Wisconsin on the grants committee had previously been denied access to our papers and had demanded proof of Michael's access as a contingency to the grant. He had to deliver this permission in a week's time to his own chairman at Stanford. At this point, if he couldn't do so, he would lose his grant, sabbatical, and very probably his job due to "moral turpitude"—i.e., lying—no matter that the students had voted him teacher of the year for his lecturing techniques, his wonderfully amusing oratory. If he lost his job his daughter would have to be withdrawn from private school which would break her heart. He rented an apartment and there was a loan on his BMW exceeding its current value due to a minor collision with his mailbox. In other words, his fate was entirely in my hands.

It was such a sorry mess I began to laugh, reminding me as it did of a more grotesque version of parts of my own life, and the lives of many of those I knew. His offer, however, brought me to despair; I lost my breath and wandered out to the balcony but my tears blurred the Pacific. "Remember that night," he wrote, "when you ridiculed my mustache, or at least teased me about it? I grabbed your arm and you became justifiably angry. I don't think I have any violence in me or perhaps it all comes out my mouth, or is subdued in drinking! My ex-wife used to slap me and I never defended myself. Coleridge said somewhere that we are like spiders who spin webs of deceit out of our asses. Perhaps along with my scholarly bent I have the temperament of an unsuccessful horse-player, a binge gambler. My frantic quarreling with you over at Ted's was a signal of the depth of trouble I was in. Anyway, the night at your place you mentioned that you wanted to find your son, or you were going to write something to explain yourself and your background. You could monitor my project which would cover the background. And I could find your son. I know I could because I am trained as a researcher and have a great deal of credibility. This is all I have to offer and perhaps you would rather do it without me. I beg, I implore you to consider my situation. To be sure, I have lied repeatedly to my collective profession thinking I could bend your will. I truly care for you, but that's another matter. Frankly, I have wondered why you bothered with me in the first place, traveling in the circles that you do. Ted spends more than my salary in wine every year. Finding your son is all I have to offer. Please call me the minute you finish this letter. I have given serious consideration to suicide but couldn't do it because of my daughter. Otherwise I would threaten you with it."

Out on the balcony I thought that certain kinds of suffering are altogether too ambitious. I remembered childhood stories of abandoned dogs who found their way, after numberless torments of weather, bridges, highways, dogcatchers, a thousand miles back home. Their compass evidently was their longing to be there. It's a nice story but what of all the young people I've worked with who have run away from some impossible situation, then return to find the door closed? It is difficult to help someone who feels discarded. They think of themselves, finally, as garbage and are willing prey to all those who victimize them sexually, and later on, emotionally. Somehow the fact that there is no home doesn't decrease the longing. I'm not sure why. Of necessity we can create layers of activities to cover this longing but it is always felt beneath the surface. To become inert has always been to me the worst of survival tactics. The professor says that time is the most natural of artificialities, and that no one but a nitwit lives within its mechanistic specifics. An event of a few moments dominates years. Just now I was thinking of the precise moment I had to give up Duane's necklace.

○

On my seventeenth birthday, on October 10, my grandfather, with the grudging permission of Naomi, gave me my first car. It was a new turquoise-colored Ford convertible with a white top and looked desperately inappropriate in the Nebraska landscape, especially parked next to Mother's drab and muddy Plymouth. I stood embarrassed in the yard in front of everyone—Charlene and Lena were out from town—until I took my cue from Ruth who was jumping around wildly. We went for a ride, with me driving and Charlene and Ruth on the seat beside me. It was sunny though cool for October but we put the top down anyway and drove into town, stopping at the single drive-in which was a meeting place for young people. Everyone was friendly, even one of the boys that Duane had beaten up. There is a haphazard resilience in young people that is not shared by adults, an ability to forget bitterness. Something as stupid and vulgar as a pretty car can be a tonic to all, at least for an afternoon.

I think the car hastened the death of my grandfather though he tried to absolve me of this notion on his deathbed. What happened is that the car equaled freedom to me, and naturally a longer-range freedom than that of walking or horseback. Perhaps this is less true of women than men, but in my upbringing the differentiation wasn't emphasized. On sleepless nights I would go downstairs, flick on the yard light, and look out at the car. Sometimes I would take an old road atlas and touring guide out of the parlor desk and study the possibilities. I began to slowly draw small amounts of money out of my savings account before I had a definite plan. For the first time in several years I counted my collection of silver dollars I had started as a little girl. There was also a stack of ten twenty-dollar gold pieces that Grandfather had found behind some books in his library in the summer. He had said "Spend these on a gewgaw or whatever." It occurred to me that it would look suspicious if I tried to buy gas or a motel room with a twenty-dollar gold piece. I was on the verge of jumping into one of those holes in life out of which we emerge a bit tattered and bloody though we remain nonetheless sure that we had to make the jump.

One evening a few weeks after my birthday, when our part of Nebraska had entered a warm Indian summer, I was out in the driveway wiping the car windows with a chamois cloth. The insides of the car windows were covered with the nose prints of Grandfather's Airedales. That day, when I had driven to his house after school, he had suggested we take the dogs for a spin with the top down. The dogs sat in the backseat rather grave and self-important as we drove down mile after mile of gravel roads. Grandfather had bronchitis and sipped whiskey from a flask, talking about how in the fine, early years of his marriage he and his wife (this was in the late thirties) would jump in their car and drive all the way to Chicago in less than three days just to eat in a bona-fide French restaurant. At a crossroads he permitted the frantic dogs to jump out and chase a coyote—in a lifetime of chasing coyotes they had never

caught one save the pups in the den. This coyote had a sense
of humor and ran in great circles, passing the car several times
with the dogs kept at a consistent hundred yards behind him.
When the dogs flopped in exhaustion beside the car the coyote
sat down in the exact place the chase had begun, and continued to watch us until we left.

So in the evening while I was cleaning the car and the
dusk disappeared into dark I heard a coyote. I walked out into
the pasture into the warm darkness beyond the sound of Ruth's
piano practice. My skin tingled and my stomach hollowed because I somehow thought it might be Duane who could imitate
coyotes to the point they would answer him. Duane said the
coyotes didn't believe his call, they were only curious and
amused. But out there in the pasture I admitted to myself I was
going to try to find Duane.

Mother had been cautious with me after the baby on the
advice of something she had read, not to pry, not to submit my
every moment and mood to scrutiny, and in exchange I offered
as much honesty as I could muster. I slipped out of bed the next
morning at 5:00 A.M. and left a note saying not to worry, but
that I was going to visit my old friend Duane. To make sure I
wouldn't be stopped I woke up Ruth, gave her the note, and
told her to give it to Mother after school. Ruth was reading
*Wuthering Heights* at the time and thought my search for a
lost love was "utterly thrilling."

○

I reached Route 12, then drove west until I arrived at Valentine
at daylight where I stopped for breakfast, but my butterflies
were so bad I couldn't eat the meal. The waitress, who reminded me of a spindlier version of Lena, expressed concern.
I said I was worried about my grandmother who was quite sick
in Rapid City. The waitress sat down with a cup of coffee and
chatted for a while. She admired my sheepskin coat and Paul
Bond boots. She said, "Don't talk to no cowboys. They just
want to get in your pants." She said this rather loudly, glancing
at a table of cowboys eating their eggs. I felt my face redden
and stared out the window at a stock semi full of steers probably headed to the feedlots of Sioux City and eventual slaughter.

I paid my bill, thanked her for the advice, and left. What is so wrong with loving a half-brother? I thought.

I took Route 83 north toward Murdo, turning off on 18 in the Rosebud Indian Reservation on the road to Parmelee. I didn't have much hope that Duane would be there as if waiting for me but I hoped to at least cold-track him as the local hunters called it. White people have a hard time understanding why Indians live the way they do, identifying it with the manner our own peculiar "white trash" live; I mean the bare-ground lawns, broken fences, discarded, picked-over cars, ramshackle houses. Grandfather said you don't want to understand someone if you are stealing, or have stolen, all their property. It might make you feel bad about what you did if you understood them.

Parmelee was indeed a sorry-looking place. Indian summer had suddenly disappeared and a cold wind out of the north blew icy dust in my eyes as I knocked on doors which quickly closed in my face. Some kids and barking dogs began to follow me at a polite distance. The kids laughed and shrieked when I spoke to them in a few words of rudimentary Sioux. I did see an old man working under the upraised hood of a junk car. He poked out, smiled, and said, "May I help you, daughter," in Sioux. When questioned, he said that he had heard that both Duane and his mother were down in Pine Ridge.

Pine Ridge was another hundred miles down the road but my heart was light as I drove with the wild and blustery north wind rocking the car. I even sang along to the country songs on the radio from a Rapid City station—thinking that Duane might be listening to the same station. It was easiest to sing with Patsy Cline because that was how I felt.

Pine Ridge was terribly unfriendly but again my rather clumsy attempts at the Sioux language got me the unpleasant information. Duane had been drunk and had beaten up a cop down in Chadron a month or so before and was in jail there. If he wasn't in jail he had left the area because you were a dead duck if you beat up a cop. This was told me by a tall, skinny young man in tattered clothes who coughed so hard he wobbled. He added that Duane's mother was supported by a rich man up in Buffalo Gap.

On the way to Chadron I lost my confidence and began weeping. It was now midafternoon and the world seemed a cold and violent place. I was ashamed and began to despise my fancy car which looked so garish in Indian territory. A few weeks before, in our county, a Norwegian farmer had died from general exhaustion. He was in his late forties, his parents had lost their farm in the Depression, and he was afraid of losing the farm he had secured through marriage. I knew his children at school, a half-dozen of them, and they were always exhausted, sunburned, wind-chaffed, and gaunt. If their corn picker broke down they picked by hand until well after dark. The newspaper quoted the bank as saying the man was paid up but was working for a·down payment for more land.

I lost all my courage when I drove past the jail in Chadron. I circled the jail three times without stopping. It somehow seemed unimaginable that Duane was in there, or that, if he was, the authorities would let me see him. I started shaking so hard I pulled off near a park and looked at my map. I decided to drive the twenty miles out to Fort Robinson to regather my composure. Duane said his mother had taken him to Fort Robinson when he was a little boy because it was the location of the murder of Crazy Horse. That afternoon with the clear cold wind and empty parking lot the cavalry barns were ghostly and the fort and officer quarters didn't look like they belonged in the beauty of the rolling, sparsely forested landscape. Across the road at the location of the stockade, where the actual murder took place, a ranger said I had to leave because it was five and they were closing for the day. The ranger was obnoxious and wondered why a "pretty girl" like myself cared about Crazy Horse in the first place. For some reason I said I was an extremely distant relative and was trying to get the guts to kill some white folks. The ranger snorted and laughed and told me to get on my way.

Back in Chadron I walked directly into the sheriff's office in front of the jail and was just as directly arrested. My car keys were taken and I was seated next to the sheriff's desk as he made some phone calls in a whispery, noncommittal voice. He was a small, kindly man. He brought me a cup of coffee and told me my boyfriend, who was a "mean sucker," had been bailed out and was long gone. Soon the local rancher who had sold us Duane's buckskin two years before arrived and picked me up. I spent the night with him and his family. I didn't feel bad by then because I had given up. I helped the rancher's daughter who was my age do chores. Out of earshot of her father she said her dad would whip her ass if she went out with an Indian boy.

Next morning I slept late and Grandfather arrived at breakfast red-faced and jubilant in his old otter-skin coat and a hunting hat. Our doctor had flown him over in his Stearman biplane and the trip had been wonderful if a bit chilly. He was coughing and sipped whiskey as he ate. The rancher took us to the sheriff's office where pleasantries were exchanged. The sheriff looked at me oddly and said that everyone should be in love at least once. This is the kind of inexplicable comment one remembers forever.

When we were alone in my car Grandfather asked me why, knowing what I knew, I had gone to look for Duane. I said I couldn't help myself. He said that was a good answer and directed me north out of Chadron instead of east toward home. Just south of Hot Springs, an hour or so out of Chadron, we turned off toward Buffalo Gap, then off again on a narrow gravel road going into the mountains. We had been talking about nothing in particular but the history of the landscape. He knew the area and its history well because we were on the way to his hunting cabin. Some of the very last buffalo had hidden out in this area. He said General Sherman brought the South to its knees by burning crops and destroying all the livestock. The Indians were starved into submission by the destruction of the buffalo as government policy. The South recovered its crops, cows, and pigs but the buffalo were gone forever except as isolated novelties. He liked in these moments of anger to quote General Philip Sheridan who had said, "To destroy the Indian, you must destroy the Indian's commissary. For the sake of lasting peace let us kill, skin and sell until we have exterminated the buffalo. Then your prairies will be covered with speckled cattle and the festive cowboy."

From what the Sioux boy had told me in Pine Ridge I pretty much expected to see Duane's mother at Grandfather's hunting cabin. He showed no hesitation in sharing this secret with me though he waited until the last moment to do so. He'd had her traced to Denver after Duane showed up at the farm, and had settled her in the cabin where he'd first met her along with my father and Uncle Paul.

There were the remains of a well-ordered garden outside a door protected by a not very angry black Labrador. The log cabin was much larger than I had expected with a big screened porch facing down-valley to the south. Out beside a shed and small corral I could see Duane's buckskin staring at us and whinnying. When I turned around she was standing in the open door, tall and thin, almost handsome, but with the somewhat dead eyes I would later recognize as those of a recovered serious alcoholic. She smiled and held her hand out to me. Her hand was strong but had the feeling of a hand that had been crushed and healed improperly. Later Grandfather said she had been run over by a car in Alliance when she fell asleep drunk on a side road. Her name in Sioux meant "kestrel," or "sparrow hawk."

Inside the cabin I was drawn naturally to the fireplace, and the startling photographs on the mantel. There was a photo of Paul and my father with Sparrow Hawk between them. Behind me they were talking in Sioux and I picked up little of it except numerous terms of endearment. There was also a photo of me with the Airedales, several of Duane, including a recent one on his buckskin. When I turned back to the room she was right behind me and asked me to call her by her American name which was Rachel. Then she asked me to return the necklace Duane had given me. She said she could see I was as strong as my father and Grandfather but Duane was a lunatic and needed the necklace. She pronounced "lunatic" in three distinct syllables as if there was no doubt that this word was a precise description of Duane's character. I took off the necklace without hesitation and she fondled the unremarkable stone in her palm. She turned and said something mournful to Grandfather, who got up from the sofa and embraced her. Then she wailed, and I rushed from the cabin grabbing Duane's old aviator jacket instead of my own. The jacket had been my father's before Naomi gave it to Duane because she said he never looked warm enough.

My ears were ringing from Rachel's wail so I saddled up

the buckskin. I swore long and loudly to block out the wail. The black Labrador barked with excitement which helped. It was my first hard ride in over a year and I rode like a crazy woman. The buckskin was rank and willful so I put it through figure eights until it lathered, then took off up the valley with the dog laboring to keep up. I rode the horse as hard as I dared, then cooled him off with a long walk. I could still see the cabin a half-dozen miles down-valley and imagined the wails coming up through the chimney. I found a stock tank and let the horse drink, then tethered it and lifted the dog over the edge and watched it swim in happy circles. I got pretty wet lifting the dog out of the tank but didn't care—there is something about doing a favor for a dog that calms you down. I stood there as if a statue, my hand against the buckskin's neck feeling his slowing pulse. I had a feeling of dreamlike clarity and perhaps undeserved strength when I remembered something Grandfather had said when he found me after my walk in the hills on the far side of the Niobrara: how each of us must live with a full measure of loneliness that is inescapable, and we must not destroy ourselves with our passion to escape this aloneness. Leaning against that stock tank in the high neck of the valley I could hear the wind and the breathing of the dog and horse. Everyone I had ever known drifted through my mind and out into the air along with the sense that the resonance of their voices resembled the voices of birds and animals. I was somewhat surprised finally to look up and see the sun.

When I reached the cabin I found I had been gone three hours. Rachel warmed up my dinner while Grandfather slept on the couch. His breathing was coarse and his face looked feverish. She said she had hoped we would spend the night but he felt sick and wanted to go home.

○

A fine May morning on the balcony: my dawn walk was a bit melancholy, the heat I could feel coming signaling the advent of the beach season and its crowds. I took the phone out on the balcony and talked to Mother. We arranged to meet with Ruth in San Francisco the day after Naomi's country school finished its season which was only a few days off. It would be the first time, she said, that she would miss the Memorial Day service at the country cemetery for the war dead in thirty-seven years, but she knew her daughters needed her and it was certain her husband didn't. Then Andrew called somewhat anxiously to say that the authorities had lost track of Guillermo Sandoval in McAllen, Texas, and that Ted had insisted a man be put on my track full-time for protection. I explained my schedule and the fact I'd probably move back to Nebraska in June. He said it was safer if I didn't know who this guard was since the psychopath in question was devious. Ted came on the phone and insisted on lunch. I rejected his elegant choices, picking instead a café a few blocks away from my apartment that was favored by all the Australians in Santa Monica. He agreed with his patented sigh.

The hour or so on the phone helped make me decide to accept Naomi's teaching offer: barely a month out of work and I felt less than useful, though I had done a great deal of reading and writing. Perhaps it's because the phone is a close tie to the government as the greatest source of enervation in our time. Actually teaching youngsters to read and write would be a wonderful tonic to the phone and California. Out of kindness, though, I quickly called Michael and told him I was leaning in his direction, and would probably see him on Tuesday. His voice quavered and he began speaking as fast as possible short of incoherence. I cut him off by saying I missed him and good-bye.

When I showered and dressed for lunch I felt a tremor of loneliness that I recognized as mostly sexual. This passed and was displaced by the vertiginous notion that another section, a largish piece of my life was coming to an end. The professor's convoluted notions of time were not all that inaccurate though they owned too many sharp corners. Maybe that *is* an essential difference between male and female—I see my life abstractly in terms of interlocking spirals, circles, gyres, while the professor is more linear and geometric. I intended to talk to him about this again after I exhausted him in bed which, to be frank, didn't take that long.

As I walked to the restaurant I felt a sharp pang beneath my breastbone that I was bent on leaving the place that had been a relatively happy home. All my moves had been so radical—New York City and Los Angeles had alternated with remote regions of Montana, Minnesota, Michigan, and Nebraska. There had been short, unsuccessful attempts to live in foreign countries—France, England, Mexico, Brazil—but I was so thoroughly an American that my homesickness led to a premature return; out of forty-five years well over forty-three had been spent in New York or Los Angeles, or in areas so remote that my friends in those cities found them laughable.

I was in the pub part of the restaurant and standing near the window when Ted's car pulled up. As everyone knows, Californians tend to be car snobs with a sharp eye out for such small items as a limousine with rental licenses. Ted's was his own, a silver 600 Mercedes with the back set up as an ambulatory and convertible office. He spent so much time between Malibu and Beverly Hills and the airport it was easy to justify the extravagance, and the IRS cooperated. I had ridden in the car only a few times before I decided the silliness was overwhelming. There was the additional idea that envy along with self-pity serve as our most repulsive emotions, and it was no fun getting out of the car only to be stared at by people to whom such things mean a great deal. Ted, however, dismissed this as bogus Midwestern modesty.

"You look awful," I said. And he did as he smiled out from a pale and fatigued puffiness.

"I was celebrating. I passed the antibodies test. I'm clean, and now I'm going to be careful."

I reached across the table and took his hand. To moralists the scene would be ludicrous, perhaps disgusting, but I'm not a moralist and he was a dear friend. He had refused to take the test out of fear but I had helped him into it. If an act of love spreads a fatal disease, I argued, then you give up the act of love. His happiness was tempered by the fact that one of his closest friends had flunked the test.

"That's it for him. Kaput. No more love. The odds are he won't even get it himself. But what I want now is for you to talk Ruth out of marrying this Mexican grocer. He's much more dangerous than the batty priest."

"Behind every ex-artiste is a snot," I countered, misquoting Auden.

"That's true but you'll admit Latin men are all sweetness,

*mi corazón* and that sort of thing, until she says yes; then they become bullies."

"That's true generally but Ruth is smart enough to know if he's different."

"No, she's not, for Christ's sake. She's full of vague longings. She's pre the last three or four fucking wars. She's Emily Dickinson and Virginia Woolf. She's half goddamn nitwit every day and a hundred percent nitwit when it comes to men. I still love her but she won't listen to me."

"Of course you love her," I said without irony, "but that doesn't make you worth listening to on the subject. Some of your choices for me when I came to town weren't quite on the money."

"I agree. I thought you were different. Just promise me you won't let her make the move until you look the guy over."

I weakened and made the promise. We were interrupted by a young Australian graduate student from Darwin who said hello with a blush and slipped me an envelope. He said he was going home for a few months, then hurried off.

"I'll give you a C-note if I can read it."

"Where's the money?" I said.

Ted handed over the bill, and took the envelope with pleasure. "What a disappointment! 'My dearest Dalva, Here is the fifty I owe you. Thanks, Harold.' Jesus, tell him to change his name. Harolds go nowhere. Harold Stassen. Name me another. I bet you slept with the poor boy."

"Of course. One afternoon in here he was reading Doris Lessing and I like Doris Lessing. Now I've tripled my money."

"Doubled! Ruth says you're going back home. You're going to have to down-shift to farmers."

"There're a few cowboys left. Besides I'm going back to work, buy some horses and dogs, and grow old."

"I'd like to organize a large bet on your return here or to New York. You need neutral territory to live in. Ghosts make you old. You never heard from the boy again, did you?"

"No. I'm hoping he'll contact Uncle Paul, who's looking for him."

"Good. Nothing shakes my faith like queer crimes. They're terribly embarrassing."

"Sex crimes always are. I took a whole graduate course in

crimes of a sexual nature. It's much worse than the newspapers print." Suddenly in my mind it was winter in Minneapolis and I could hear the professor's cold, passionless monotone, really the only sort of voice appropriate to the subject. There were too many photos, some in color.

"Are you listening? I said Why don't you go to San Francisco a day or two early? Andrew said that creep might be back in town."

"Of course. Why not." I tried to regather myself from Minneapolis.

The food at lunch was so unremarkable as to be soothing— "bangers and mash" the English call it. Ted treated it as an adventure. He had the very rare ability to find life interesting in its most minimalist details. His early admission that he couldn't create anything had served to broaden his energies rather than narrow them. Absolute self-acceptance isn't all that common. He wanted to cancel his appointments so we could drive up to Trankas and take a beach walk. He had become active in a land syndicate composed of moguls anticipating growth to the north. Now he considered it all a "healthy pursuit" and wanted to show me part of the land. I begged off, saying the moving company had sent over cartons and I wanted to start packing. To prolong the meeting he tried to start a quarrel over my intention to drive my old '81 Subaru all the way to Nebraska.

○

Back at my apartment I decided to have a few drinks while packing, something I've always done when moving, to savor the full banality of the process. I would pack a box, I decided, then mix a drink and write in this journal, then pack another box, and so on, until I fell asleep. It seemed a delightful plan so I changed into my Levis and a "Fuck Hate" T-shirt that one of Ted's musician friends had given me. There was a nagging desire to try to call my Australian graduate-student friend but I subdued it. I poured a few fingers of Herradura tequila and began by packing some precious objects while I was still totally sober: an alabaster peach given to me by a Brazilian; a stuffed crow, rather tattered, inherited from my father; a boar-hoof

Yaqui rattle; a true pearl necklace that was my grandmother's; a glass-encased Peruvian butterfly; a moon-white coyote skull found on a walk with Grandfather; my father's high-school class ring. I remember at the time that Grandfather told me the coyote had died very old because the teeth were worn down, the incisors chipped. Two of the teeth were loose so we had glued them back securely into the jaw. Lastly, there was Duane's necklace, which I had gotten back during a nightmare.

○

Tequila and a skull. Pearls and a butterfly, a stone-hard peach. We didn't leave Buffalo Gap that day until late in the afternoon, because Rachel wanted Grandfather to sleep as long as possible. I called Mother, who kindly pretended nothing had happened. I said we should be home by midnight. The fire in the fireplace drew evenly and I noticed the wind had stopped. I went outside, sat on the ground in the afternoon sun, and petted the dog, who dashed off and retrieved his largest filthy bone. I didn't hear Rachel come up behind me until she spoke.

"I'm sorry what my son did to you."

"I'm not. Anyway, he didn't do it to me, we did it together."

"I hope you're as strong as you talk."

"I better be," I said, laughing. "Or I'm really up shit creek."

She sat down beside me on the ground and said something in Sioux to the dog, who immediately played dead. Then she pulled his ear and he came back to life.

"I look old because I was drunk as I could be for over ten years. I was a whore in Denver until I lost my looks. Then your grandfather found me. You know that Duane is no good for you."

"That's what I'm told. I guess we're related and that makes it wrong." Now my face burned and there were tears in my throat.

She put her arm around me. "Don't blame your dad. We were after each other the moment we met. I was cleaning the cabin and washing dishes when your dad came in from hunting with your grandfather. Paul says, Look who I found to help us out in the cabin. Paul saw me in Buffalo Gap and gave my dad fifty bucks to get me to come help. That was more cash than we had ever seen. So I helped your dad cook dinner and I thought, This is the man in the world I want. Then your grandfather says to me in Sioux, which shocked me because I thought they were pure white, I better get you out of here before my sons get in a fight. Wesley is married and Paul isn't so pick on Paul. Or me. That's what he said. I think it was 1942. But next day I went off on horseback with your dad and that evening everyone got drunk and your dad and Paul got in a fight over me. The next day your granddad took me back to town. . . ."

Rachel stopped herself and turned around, hearing Grandfather close the door. He stood there with his otter-skin coat buttoned to the neck despite the freshet of south wind. He beamed feverishly at us and said "My girlfriends," then was overcome and couldn't continue as he looked out over the valley. I'm sure he was saying goodbye to this retreat he had discovered soon after World War I. Rachel rose and they embraced. She walked with him to my car which he patted, then laughed as if sharing the knowledge with us of how absurd the aqua convertible looked in the landscape.

The first stop was for whiskey to quell his cough. The late-October twilight was abrupt and soon we were driving straight into the moon which had emerged unrecognizably at the end of the road. This enormous moon delighted him and as the moon lifted the landscape brightened, the outlines of the Sand Hills against the sky were dulcet and blurred. When we hit a dip in the road where a creek crossed, the yellow cottonwood leaves swirled around the car. He fiddled with the radio and swore when he found nothing classical, then found a country station playing Bob Wills and the Texas Playboys. He told me he had danced to this band with a pretty *señorita* on a horse-buying trip to Fort Worth before World War II. Then he asked me to pull over so we could put the top down. I said we shouldn't because it was getting colder and he was sick but he insisted.

Later we stopped at a roadhouse owned by an old crony of his and ate fried steaks and looked at a scrapbook full of pictures of hunting, bird dogs, and horses. "So this is Wesley's daughter. You don't say," said the old man. Back in the car it seemed colder but still he wanted the top down. He didn't seem drunk, and I remembered that Naomi said in the old days you would have thought Grandfather was Lord Byron himself. Now we were only an hour or so from home and he told me to sing him asleep. I said I wasn't too musical but sang Jim Reeves, Patsy Cline, awful renditions of Sam Cooke, and Elvis Presley's "Heartbreak Hotel." He couldn't sleep and chanted something in Sioux several times and I asked him what it meant. He said it meant "Take courage, the earth is all that lasts." He seemed a little embarrassed by how somber the words sounded, so he sang a dirty song from World War I, which he copied down for me the next day:

> Here's to the Kaiser, he's on his last hitch.
> We're after his ass the damned son of a bitch.
> We'll enter his palace, and shit on the floor,
> And hang Old Glory right over the door.

> Then out of the palace and up the brick street,
> We'll piss on all Germans we happen to meet.
> We'll eat all his sauerkraut, and drink all his gin
> And kick his damned ass right out of Berlin.

> And when all is over
> We'll go home en masse
> And tell all our friends
> That old Bill kissed our ass.

○

I'm pouring another drink. The song has a strangeness now that I never noticed before. Great-grandfather caught the nasty tail end of the Civil War, and was on the periphery of the Indian Wars. Grandfather tried to sign up at age twelve to fight in Cuba after the *Maine* was blown up and was rejected, then later survived three years in France in World War I. My father, of course, was a willing participant in World War II and Korea. And there was Duane in Vietnam. What a neat bundle, no doubt repeated in hundreds of thousands of family histories.

What an irony if my son were an "adviser" in Central America. Ruth said her son, Ted, Jr., couldn't wait to get out of the Air Force Academy and see some real action.

I just called Bill, the Australian graduate student, instead of pouring another drink. He also was packing and I offered to take him out to Guido's for a goodbye dinner which he accepted with enthusiasm. Actually he acts more English than Australian—Australians often seem helpless parodies of gusto. I lay down for a nap to sleep off the drinks. I began to think of Grandfather's last three weeks—he died on Thanksgiving morning—but I pushed it all away. I was the nurse and I don't feel nurselike now. I'm nearly twenty years older than Bill, while my perpetual five-year-old is only a little his senior.

Once when I thought I needed therapy, in my early thirties, I went to an analyst in New York. After a half-dozen meetings the analyst said I didn't need any help despite the fact that he needed patients. I had gone to him to check if I wasn't being a little promiscuous. He said most people drink merely because they began drinking, and some people are especially attuned physically and mentally to making love. I thought this was simple-minded and told him so, though without venom. He said most truths are utterly unremarkable. This stopped me cold and I immediately tried to think of something perverse and terribly complicated to say. I blurted out that I had made love to two men at once. He replied that I no doubt did this out of curiosity and affection. I was stopped again. He said he thought of himself as merely a "balancer" and the impulse behind his practice was mainly to stop people from destroying their "selves" in the thousand or so manners available to all of us. He said I came to see him because I thought I might be fucking too much and his initial impression was that I didn't seem to be. If I wished, we could have a number of sessions to be absolutely sure. Meanwhile, and this is what I'm getting at, he asked me to talk to him about my family history which I did over a number of weeks. He made an observation that didn't seem particularly noteworthy at the time: the entire history of my family was tenuous, hanging by the single thread of parenthood from a great-grandfather to a grandfather, to a father with two daughters. Both Great-grandfather and Grandfather were relatively old before they were parents. The lesson here was how tentative, how evanescent my arrival was. I had told him that I was without a specific talent, other than that of curiosity, and he saw that as a large item. It is terrible to assume life is one thing, he said, only to discover it is another. A highly mobile curiosity gives you the option of looking into alternatives. His was the lightest shade of melancholy I ever witnessed, making me permanently suspicious of those self-improvement projects, the flip soul-tinkering our age is afflicted with. He didn't bill me for the last fifty-minute session which we spent asking each other questions. As a Polish (Warsaw) émigré to the U. S. in the mid-thirties he had never been west of the Mississippi except for two flyover professional visits to California. He and his wife were thinking seriously of moving to Israel and they wanted to see the Western states first. I outlined an itinerary including, at his insistence, Route 20 in northern Nebraska so he could drive the same route I had taken with Grandfather on our night ride. I was going to ask him if he had any living relatives but veered away from the question because I suspected strongly that he didn't. On the wall was a print of Hokusai's painting of a group of blind men fording a stream. This was the year after Duane died. When we said goodbye he advised me that grief is an often fatal but treatable disease.

○

Up bright and early at 6:00 A.M. in order to make a few notes before I take Bill to LAX for his long flight to Darwin, and me for my PSA hop to San Francisco. Like the baby itself I am avoiding what happened to Duane. I awoke in the middle of the night after eating too much cioppino and some nonstrenuous lovemaking. I was sure I heard someone fiddling with the door. I took the .38 Andrew gave me out of the dresser, stood at the door, and said "Go away" in an even voice. I heard footsteps moving away, then stood there for a minute or so to regain composure thinking how awful it would be to shoot him. I had seen the blue, protuberant wounds of a gunshot victim years ago in the emergency room of a Minneapolis hospital.

○

Professor Michael standing there at the airport baggage curb looked as battered as the front end of his car. We embraced lightly and he smelled vinegarish, his aura dense with tobacco, alcohol through the pores, a ruddiness from the flush of illness rather than health. His appearance was so appalling that I paused overlong getting in the car. He read my thoughts.

"I've been out of sorts."

"Perhaps we can drive straight to the bridge so you can get it over with."

"That's not funny, dear." And behind the wheel he began to shake.

I kissed his cheek and said I'd drive. When I got out to trade places a cab behind us began beeping and I found myself at the driver's window screaming "You asshole." The cabbie was a large black man who thought this was very funny. "It can't be that bad, sweetheart," he said.

Back in the car I smiled though Michael was still shaking. I waved at the cabdriver and moved off, thinking of all the exacerbated adrenals at airports, the neutral fetor in the air that is worse than a dead skunk in the path.

"I haven't been able to keep down food," Michael began, "unless I have a few drinks; then I can keep down soup. Also I can't sleep so I have headaches. One of my students gave me a Percodan but I fell asleep across my desk which was rather embarrassing. I was worried you'd change your mind and not show up. I didn't want to call you again so I called Ruth who said she and your mother were due tomorrow. But I couldn't believe anything until I saw you. Now I'll be OK."

"After a few months in a clinic you might be OK." It had occurred to me that this destructive behavior was a male substitute for the weeping used by women. "You could have gotten the same results by beating yourself with a hammer. I'd say you were up to a fifth a day plus three packs of cigarettes. And whatever else. Probably a bottle of wine with dinner. Is that all?"

"A line of coke or two from rich graduate students. This is scarcely the time to kick me in the balls. The heroine arrives.

With salvation comes punishment. The weak man needs to be thrashed. That sort of thing."

"Given all the evidence it's hard to see myself as a bully."

"I'm sorry. I'm clearly deranged. You came here out of pity and kindness."

○

It was a difficult afternoon. At the hotel he insisted he had to go back to the university but was so wobbly I took him up to the room. While I was in the bathroom he located the small fridge in the closet that held soft drinks, bottled water, wine, and liquor. By the time I caught him he had already finished two of the two-ounce bottles of whiskey. Out of guilt he went on the offensive, complaining about my "pricey, piss-elegant" quarters. I took out a piece of hotel stationery and drew up a one-paragraph contract, stating that his habits were by my permission during the period of our work together, or the papers would be withdrawn. That did the job. He gave up then and began crying. I brought him a sedative from a first-aid kit I always carry in case I want to go hiking. I helped him undress, put him to bed, then waited beside the bed holding his hand until he slept. When he began to snore I unpacked, freshened up, then went out to buy him some clothes that didn't smell. At the last moment I called his chairman at Stanford and explained we were busy ironing out details and Michael wouldn't be in today. After shopping for the clothes I walked long and briskly, thinking of Naomi and Ruth, Pawnees, Chippewas, and how at age forty-five my tolerance for cities was waning. It was a beautiful day and San Francisco was a beautiful city, but my heart wasn't moved as it used to be except by the sight of Alcatraz, which looked pure and Mediterranean in the middle of the bay. There was a tinge of regret that I had relented with Michael to save his neck, but then I have tried to keep my tendency toward escape within manageable bounds. When Ted warned me that if I wasn't careful I would become a lonely old woman, the notion sounded very attractive. Some poet whose name escapes me had written, "The days are stacked against what we think we are."

Back in the hotel room I tried to read but found myself

watching Michael sleep. He was sweating and odorous and the sheet had slipped from his body. He lay curled with one hand cupping his penis and the other on the furze of hair between his breasts. Of all the naked men I had seen in my life he was the least appealing in the usual terms of judgment. His head was too large for his neck, his chest and arms too small for his belly; only his legs were normal and reasonably well formed. At one point he hummed in his sleep and his penis grew erect in his hand for a few minutes before receding. The support system wasn't very promising for so large a brain.

I went back out into the living room that he had complained about as being "pricey." My grandfather had included a joke in his will meant to occasionally shove Naomi, Ruth, and myself out of our Nebraska nest. He had left an assortment of stocks in a fund administered by a bank in Omaha, the dividends of which had to be spent yearly on travel or the dividends would be sent to the National Rifle Association, Naomi's *bête noire.* She never minded Father's bird-hunting but as a girl growing up on a farm near O'Neill someone had shot her pet deer and she was relentless on the subject of hunting mammals. The fund hadn't been that large in the beginning but had grown over the years to the point where in 1983 Naomi had taken three schoolteacher friends on a Lindblad tour up the Amazon. One year when a trip had to be canceled due to a bout with pneumonia the NRA had sent a thank-you letter, to her disgust, for the ample contribution. Ruth was a homebody and I wasn't much help, preferring travel in recent years to areas where accommodations were cheap. We had recently sought legal advice to break the terms of the trust in order to split it between the Audubon Society and the Indian school in Sante Fe, New Mexico. It had served its purpose.

I fell asleep in my slip in a chair beside the window. The light always seems autumnal in San Francisco, whether in May or October, and I watched the sky darken while drifting in and out of sleep, conscious that I was listening to Michael's breathing as I had my grandfather's so many years before. There was a natural impulse not to nurse Michael to health but to grab him by the hair and shake him. One evening he had talked in elegant paragraphs about alcoholism—there was nothing new to me in the data but the presentation was beautiful. From alcohol he went on to the specific neuroses of history, the different masks of God in our waking and sleeping lives that are extended into our public, collective life. Nothing was amiss except that he seemed unaware that his head was connected in any meaningful way to his body. He told me he once nearly drowned because he simply forgot he was swimming. Only a month before when his head was in my lap he had fainted because he forgot to breathe. Rather than a cliché or a parody he was a throwback—contemporary professors tend to resemble M. B. A.'s embarked on no-nonsense careers.

When the bellhop rang with the altered clothes Michael answered the phone. Out of curiosity I listened to him talk to the operator before I went into the bedroom.

"The day went away. It's dark outside," he said.

I knew he might begin talking about other days when this had happened so I sent him off for a bath, then called housekeeping to change the bed. While his bathwater thundered I poured myself a drink and speculated about his secret life, his concealed ideas about himself. I'm sure this is equally true of most women—it is certainly true of myself—but I've only really studied the phenomenon in a half-dozen or so lovers. The secret life can be based in the childhood mythology of cowboys and Indians, the outlaw, and rambling gambler, or more recently, in the popular culture of detectives, rock music, sports, gurus, religious and political leaders. The roots seem always connected to sex and power, and how free they felt as children to enact feelings that ran counter to the behavior they were taught. It is usually deeply comic but also poignant: thus an outwardly loutish executive is inwardly a Southern gentleman who should have been a medical missionary (he thinks) to Africa, and is helpful to a fault in the kitchen; the defrocked Episcopalian intellectual becomes an inept Robert Ryan on a camping trip and the lovemaking, which was too polite in Santa Monica, becomes rowdy and wordless in a sleeping bag; the young cowboy becomes a stern father at dawn in the Wyoming motel room. Even the voice patterns change. He calls out from the tub for a glass of white wine, which is reasonable. I discover him covered to the eyes in bubbles.

"I found the packet in the cabinet. I'm thirty-nine and this is the first bubble bath in my life. I'm doing something truly different! I feel pretty good but I'm hungry. Join me darling!"

○

Three A.M. by the travel clock. He became rather manic from raw nerves so I gave him another sedative about an hour ago. I can't sleep because he's holding my hand rather tightly and grinding his teeth. He smells like bubble bath and the Chinese food we had for a late dinner. I limited him to one bottle of Pouilly-Fumé at dinner and he found it impossible to sleep on such short rations; thus the sedative. Just before he slept he said he could see the entirety of the United States topographically against the ceiling, and everything that happened throughout every area and state in history was whirling right before his eyes: with his arm he pointed out Duluth as a permanent settlement in 1852; how Fort Lewis became Fort Benton between 1846 and 1850; Yankton when it lost its title as capital of the Dakota Territory; he saw some friends of Cochise strangle themselves in jail; Wovovka dancing his ghost dance frightened him, and he turned on his pillow to face me.

"It's sort of like three-dimensional television only larger. That's why I usually sleep with the lights on. I drink because I'm excitable."

"I understand the lights part but I'm not sure about the whiskey volume."

"I'm going to ask you a personal question. Why didn't you ever have another baby?"

"My illness in the hospital when I was pregnant made me barren."

"I'm very sorry. Perhaps you have more reason to drink than I do, and that's a hard thing for an alkie to say."

"I know it is. I like a drink once in a while when I'm sure it's going to be a pleasure. Usually I prefer undiminished consciousness."

"Dostoevsky said that to be too acutely conscious is to be diseased. It's troublesome statements like that that got me out of literature and into history. It's a mystery to me why white wine and Chinese food give me a hard-on. Maybe you have something to do with it." He turned around and squirmed under the sheet. "I hope so." I was left with part of a very ample penis in my mouth when the sedative kicked in and his nuzzling turned into a snore. I moved a leg to avoid a repeat of the suffocation problem. I turned on the light and rearranged my one-hundred-eighty-pound hairy baby. I couldn't help laughing.

It actually had been a wonderful evening, starting with the bubble bath, during which we made love for almost ten seconds on the edge of the tub. "I must have overrevved," he had said apologetically. He was stunned by his new clothes, then became dreadful in front of the mirror about paying me back. I stopped him short of prating about his lower-class upbringing by saying that in equivalent terms to his salary the clothes had cost me only a hundred dollars, and that if he continued I'd pitch them out the seventh-story window. He put on a Misoni sweater and some soft wool trousers, then said his first expensive clothes were giving him a hard-on. Since I was dressed for dinner I said that right now I'd prefer something to eat over another run at his hard-on. "It will only take a minute," he said, with more than a trace of sarcasm. I knelt on the couch and he lifted my skirt. I admit it went on forever and was quite nice.

Before we could have dinner we had to find some vitamins for him. Luckily, our young cabdriver was a fitness type who worked nights in order to exercise all day, and knew of a nutrition center that was open late. The cabbie and Michael talked excitedly about decidedly Off Broadway vitamins and minerals with miraculous recuperative powers. "With apologies to the lady with you I can ball all night on three capsules of Nigerian Yohimbe," the cabbie said. I remembered Michael lecturing Ted and Andrew on the wonders of trace minerals with a Calvados in one hand and a cigarette in the other, forcing himself to put one down so he could snort a line of cocaine.

At dinner Michael passed himself off at the expensive Chinese restaurant as a food critic probing the establishment's abilities with duck. He ordered a whole Peking duck; as an afterthought I slipped in a fish for myself. When the maître d' inquired what magazine he worked for Michael faked a huff, saying he worked "anonymously" and paid his own bills. The intent of the ruse was solely to get carefully prepared food.

"You're basically dishonest about everything, aren't you?"

"I think 'playful' is a better word. Obviously I get my ass in a sling once in a while. That's what you're doing in San Francisco isn't it? I feel unworthy but grateful."

"Why would I want you to lose everything you haven't worked very hard for?"

"What an awful thing to say. You farm girls aren't very romantic, for God's sake. I think I'm owed a double whiskey for that insult."

"No. Maybe tomorrow afternoon. I want to see if you have the D.T.'s in front of your chairman."

"I was totally dry for ten, or seven, or five days when I had my appendix out. Also when I had the flu. Raymond Chandler said when he quit drinking the world lost its Technicolor. God created color to be seen. I will not blaspheme Him by ignoring the wonders of His handiwork." And so on.

Now in bed I'm wondering if sleeping with him isn't more reality than I need, akin to a night in a dentist's chair. When we work on the papers he'll stay in Duane's quarters and absorb Rölvaag's spirit, whatever it might be. *He likes to say, We are in hell. Hell is our culture and its flood of trash, it's almost total inundation by trash. That's part of his greed theory, and I am somehow a little guilty for having enough money to stay out of the trash flood. I said What about the work I've done, especially the last three years with those children? I didn't have to, he said. But I did. Now I'm thinking of the legs of that Yaqui deer dancer at the Pascua in Tucson at Easter who danced three days and three nights so the Lord could arise again. Dancing seventy-two hours on legs with antlers on his head and a blindfold, at my age he was with legs made of cables and wires of flesh. What was that word in high-school physics? Specific density, I think. How much of him there was in one place so if he wasn't dancing he would fall into the earth. Dancing under the overpass of Route 10 between L. A. and Texas with a thousand trucks per hour, he was from down in Mexico, they said, where he lived on a mesa getting ready to dance three days and three nights once a year.*

*I can smell the red dust raised by his feet, the Pharisees in black robes swirling up the dust around him. He jumped so far sideways my stomach hurt and there was a dizziness in the air as if there wasn't enough air to breathe. He was a deer.*

○

Awake at bare first light because I thought Michael's rasping breath was Grandfather's and I had become a bird floating earthward above the south, the sunny side of the barn where we sat with the dogs out of the Nebraska wind. After he retrieved me from Chadron it took him only a week to die. The next morning the doctor told us to get Paul to come home, his father was dying. It took Paul two days to get there from Chiapas, by which time the quarter-horse friend had brought Rachel from Buffalo Gap. Naomi and Rachel liked each other a great deal which made me nervous, though only Grandfather, Rachel, and I knew the entire story. Rachel and Paul tried to track down Duane but he had disappeared from the place Grandfather had sent him. One morning a few days before he died Grandfather told me he had seen Duane in his sleep near a river town up in Oregon. They had talked and Duane was fine. Rachel was taking turns with me sitting beside his bed so I called her in because Grandfather wanted to tell her about seeing Duane. They spoke in Sioux and she became quite happy.

The usual late-November weather held off and every day was clear, sunny, but very cold. An ex-governor was there visiting Grandfather when Paul showed up. I don't remember ever being quite so happy to see someone. Paul hadn't been home since my father Wesley's funeral, and after he arrived Grandfather asked us to post a sign out on the gate for no more visitors. Paul was a strong person in every respect and it made us all feel much better that he was there. The governor said goodbye and Paul went in with Grandfather and closed the door. I helped Naomi and Rachel make dinner. That morning Grandfather said he wanted to eat his last pheasant, but a half-hour later he added that he thought he should eat his last venison stew and Bordeaux wine. I sent Lundquist off for both a deer and a few pheasants, not a difficult chore on the prop-

erty. An awkward moment came at lunch when Mrs. Lundquist, who had become quite crazy, showed up with the same
Methodist minister who had been so unpleasant to me. Rachel
and Naomi turned them away but they wouldn't go willingly.
The preacher and Mrs. Lundquist knelt on the cold ground
outside Grandfather's window—Lundquist made himself
scarce out of embarrassment. I could see the kind old man
peeking around the corner of the barn at the spectacle. Grandfather had been sleeping but when we reached him he was
propped up by the window watching them pray with amusement. He gestured and I opened the window. "Thank you for
your concern but I am going into the earth which is the best
place I can think of." That's what he told them.

The last morning of his life Grandfather was expansive,
nearly ebullient, though he was so weak Paul had to carry him
out to our seats on the hay bales behind the barn.

"I carried him and now he's carrying me. Isn't that the
goddamnedest thing! Wesley was the fighter but Paul was the
strongest. When Paul was angry he would start digging another irrigation ditch, or go way back to Omaha and sit in the
library. Isn't that right, Paul?"

"You're right, Father. I'd do anything to keep off a horse."

"You own any horses now, son?"

"As a matter of fact I got a half-dozen down in Sonoita. I
bet Dalva told you. I like them because they're simple-minded
and unreliable, like politicians. It's like owning a stable full of
politicians that can't talk."

"Dalva here can ride better than either of you boys could.
Certain things skip a generation, though I've never been sure
what they meant by that."

Paul sat on one side of him and I sat on the other. He
hadn't been drinking much but the doctor said it no longer
mattered so I helped steady the flask at his lips.

"I got things set up pretty well for everyone but that's
been so for years. I don't regret what I did in life. I wish I had
done more of it. More of everything. It never occurred to me
I wouldn't read all the books I owned. That's a funny thought,
isn't it? I can see a hundred books right before my eyes I want
to read right now. I never finished Bernard De Voto or H. L.
Mencken. Son of a bitch. Dalva, I said to Paul I'm sorry I didn't

get down to see him, and he said I'm sorry I didn't get up here more often. Don't get angry with Naomi and run off forever."

I said I wouldn't. The dogs were lying half in a pile in the sun. Only Sonia, the oldest female, realized with her chin on Grandfather's knee that something was wrong. He kept rubbing the top of her nose; then he fell asleep against Paul's shoulder for a while. Naomi and Rachel came out with sandwiches and a thermos of coffee. For a moment it was so still all you could hear was the slight gurgle of the creek, nearly dry from the fall drought. Then a heifer bawled out for company over near Duane's bunkhouse. Rachel knelt down by Grandfather's knee and petted Sonia. Naomi could tell the end was near and said she was going over to the school to get Ruth so she could say goodbye. We could hear her car all the way out to the section road with the stones cracking under the fenders and the gravel-road dust filtering through the windbreaks. Far off to the east where the yellowed alfalfa seemed to seep into the woods I could see a coyote trotting along. I was going to say something but Rachel and Paul had also noticed the coyote which I had often seen along that hedgerow. Rachel was alarmed and said the coyote might have come to get the soul of Grandfather.

"I hope so." Awake, he startled us. "I always liked coyotes but then I never raised any sheep. Before Wesley died I had a fine bird dog that got into the pen one day and killed all the chickens. And stacked them in a mound. Coyotes would only take a chicken or two now and then. This barn is getting too warm." He loosened the collar of the otter coat. The barn reflected the sun's warmth but the air was quite chilly. Rachel thought we should go in, with her eye on the distant coyote, but Grandfather said no. He made a strange humming sound. My hands were clenched because in my heart I wanted him to pray to God so he would go to heaven. I knew very little about the Sioux religion but I wanted to see him again. All he said of World War I when he lost his faith was that there were horrors that went beyond religion and banished it. We could hear Naomi's car pulling back into the barnyard.

"My own father said this was a great sea of grass. I only saw it that way in a few places when I was a child. If there had been enough water the place would have been crowded with people. There's lots of water where Duane is in Oregon where the trees are like huge grass."

Ruth and Naomi approached. Ruth was tearful. "I'm sorry you're dying, Grandfather," she said in her matter-of-fact way. "I love you." And he said something that frightened her: "I'm not going to die. No one ever dies." Then he said in a whisper, "Jesus, the world is upside down and I'm falling through the sky." And he died.

There was no funeral service but a home burial the next morning out in the middle of a huge grove of lilacs, planted for that purpose more than a half-century before. Other than the family there was Rachel, the Lundquists, and three of Grandfather's old bird-hunting cronies from town, the doctor, a lawyer, and the undertaker who brought out a pine box. I suspect a home burial is against the law now but in 1958 either it was legal or no one would have dared question it. Paul and Lundquist had dug the grave and you could see Lundquist was proud of the trimness of the hole. Mrs. Lundquist was calm, partly I suspect because the lawyer told her that Grandfather had willed them a pleasant farm down the road from our place. Paul told me later that Rachel sat up all night with the body and he could hear her singing from his upstairs bedroom. After respects were made—no words were said—we ate the venison stew and the pheasant and drank a great deal of fine wine from the thirties that Paul selected from the cellar.

So Grandfather was buried there on the farm with his mother and father, his father's first wife, his son Wesley—his wife is buried in Omaha with her own people. After lunch Paul and I saddled up two horses and took the dogs for a long run. I let him take the lead and wasn't all that surprised when we ended up near the thicket and burial mound along the creek. For some reason I rode around the exact spot Duane's tipi had been, not that it was sacred or anything but my heart had begun pounding. From a nearby tree there was a rope with bleached white coyote and deer skulls that Duane had hung in the thicket to scare any interlopers away. Paul looked at me and for some reason at that moment I knew he had figured out the whole secret. To this day he has never mentioned it.

"You know until Wesley died your grandfather could be a real hard son of a bitch. You got the best part of him. Now you have lost two fathers; I'll have to pass for the third. But maybe you're old enough at sixteen so you won't need one too often. Everyone's different this way. Your sister Ruth seems sure of herself."

"She wants one thing, to be a pianist. I don't have any idea what I want to be. My friend Charlene says my dreams will tell me what I should do but that doesn't seem very reliable."

Paul began laughing and we rode north at a gallop toward the Niobrara River, a different route to the box canyon favored by both of us. At the river we watered the dogs and horses, then forded easily where the river was wide and shallow. We sat on the flat rock in the canyon for a half-hour or so.

"What do you dream about?" Paul asked.

"A lot of sexual stuff. Also about animals—wolves, bears, coyotes, deer, songbirds, and hawks." A pair of migrating rough-legged hawks swooped past us headed downriver, probably waiting for the warmer afternoon air to make their way farther south.

"Sounds pretty good to me. I read where dreams are supposed to help the brain catch up with the life, sort of a Rube Goldberg machine to ease the pressure. I'm not sure. I used to dream a lot about being in bed with my mother. Maybe that's why I stick to Mexican women."

"Do you believe in heaven and hell?"

"Holy Christ, Dalva, I've been your dad for less than twenty-four hours. Let's start with easier questions."

"How about one from a popular song. Will my lover come back to me?" And that's when I began weeping. I hadn't wept at the burial service but all that I had already lost in life, two fathers, a son, and a lover, swirled in my brain, and in the air in the canyon, out over the river and up into the sky. I thought my chest and head would crack open like a melon. Paul hugged me and said a sentence or two in Spanish. A week or so later he sent a translation up from Sonoita, a few lines from a Lorca "Gacela" that he loved.

> I want to sleep the dream of the apples,
> to withdraw from the tumult of cemeteries,
> I want to sleep the dream of that child
> who wanted to cut his heart on the high seas.

○

I woke up Michael a full hour before we had to leave for the airport to pick up Naomi and Ruth. He fairly sprang around the room, assuring me he hadn't felt better in years. Along with an ample breakfast we had to ask room service for a popular stomach remedy so that Michael could counteract his duck feast and put yet more in his belly (sausage, eggs, potatoes). He began to bargain for future drinks—say, between the airport and the meeting.

"I thought you hadn't felt better in years."

"I'm talking about precautionary measures, insurance, like two aspirin before an event that will cause a headache."

"I'll put one of those little bottles in my purse just in case." This satisfied him for the time being.

We picked Naomi and Ruth up at the airport and drove directly, if somewhat erratically, down to Palo Alto. Like many drivers Michael felt you must look at someone you're talking to and Naomi and Ruth were in the backseat. For reasons lacking clarity the talk jumped from the farm crisis, to the potential exhaustion of the Oglala aquifer, to marriage, on which subject Michael was manic and captious to the point where Naomi and Ruth interpreted his comments as part of a comic routine.

"I doubt if any of you know what it feels like to wake up from a sound sleep only to find that someone is beating you. My wife, to be exact."

"You're fortunate she wasn't using a gun or a knife. In our county last year a woman shot her sleeping husband at close range with a shotgun." Naomi said this though I doubted it was true because she sends me the county newspaper every week. She's always been capable of inventing an anecdote to prove a point.

"Is what you're telling me another tale of woeful spouse abuse where after two decades of beating Martha slaughters the jerk and is exonerated? I've never touched a woman in anger."

"Not at all. We were quite surprised. The husband was an elder in the Swedish Lutheran church and ran the grain elevator. The local gossip was that he drove her insane with boredom."

"Jesus! How wonderful." Michael swerved on the freeway but the traffic was light.

"That must have been the man that changed his socks three or four times a day, wasn't it?" Ruth asked. "Dalva, can you still do your marriage speech?"

"I haven't used it in years but I could give it a try." Ruth was referring to a passage from C. G. Jung I had cribbed as a patented response to everyone who asked me why I wasn't married yet, beginning in my mid-twenties, through my thirties and early forties. I've always felt the question preposterously impolite though I respond in a quiet, conversational tone. "I think women nowadays feel there's no real security in marriage. What does her husband's faithfulness mean when she knows his feelings and thoughts are running after others, and that he's too calculating or too much of a chicken-shit to follow them? And what's the point in her being faithful when she knows she's simply using it to exploit her legal right of possession, and warping her own soul? Most women have intimations of a higher fidelity to the spirit and to a love beyond human weakness and imperfection."

Naomi and Ruth clapped. "I can't handle that without a drink," Michael said, and I handed him his miniature bottle. He was flushed and edgy as we entered the Stanford campus but, nevertheless, slipped the bottle in his sport jacket as a show of something.

The actual content of the meeting was perfunctory: the three of us signed a document giving Michael full access to our family papers for the duration of his sabbatical year. In attendance were the chairman, the dean of science and arts, a rare-book librarian, and a museum curator who inquired, in barely more than a whisper, what had happened to the collection of Plains Indian artifacts begun by my great-grandfather. I was the only one who knew, but fibbed by saying that they had been sold to a private collector in Sweden. The dean and chairman were subtly impressed by Michael's new tailoring— men are as critical on this matter as any woman—which must have seemed a contrast to the usual bleary, cheapish tweeds. Everyone was pleased that a sensitive matter had been cleared up, the challenges from other, perhaps less qualified institutions put to rest. The rare-book librarian offered free storage for the papers under the notion that a bank vault in Nebraska probably wasn't temperature- and humidity-controlled. Ruth pointed out rather sharply that we had taken care of that matter. We all had an amicable cup of tea, had our hands shaken, and Michael's back patted.

"It's painful how some folks treat you when they think you're rich," Naomi said, when we were back in the car with a parking ticket on the window.

"The major problem in the modern university is parking, just as the major problem in modern Christianity is evidently bare asses in magazines." He uncapped his miniature, sighed, finished it in a single swallow.

We spent the next three days in what Naomi called utter "frivolity," a word not used much anymore in a frivolous society. The hotel concierge found us a cancellation up at a bed-and-breakfast in Napa Valley—a difficult thing on Memorial Day weekend. The three of us drove up and Michael joined us with his daughter, Laurel by name, the next day. She was a shy, pretty girl, the soul of neatness. The first moment she could get me aside she begged me to intercede with her father to allow her to go back to public school the coming year. At the private boarding school Michael had sent her to nearly all the girls were rich and she felt lonely and out of place. I meant to keep track of his relentless fibbing. Laurel spent time with Ruth and myself while Naomi went off with Michael and a map to test the wine at all the vineyards in the area. One morning she woke him at 5:00 A.M. on his boozy promise to take her bird-watching. While he was stumbling around the room it was interesting to note how his new clothes had disintegrated in appearance in a mere three days.

Ruth had decided not to marry her grocer, making the decision on the flight up from Tucson. We were walking down the main street of Saint Helena when she told me this; we had paused before a shopwindow that distorted our images in the manner of a funhouse mirror. While we talked we waved, mugged, flapped, and moved to change our reflections. Sleeping with the grocer wasn't erotic like sleeping with the "dip-shit" priest who continued writing from Costa Rica. She had recently reread Emily Dickinson, which had reminded her to take another look at Emily Brontë. What was the point of marrying if her soul wasn't stirred? I wasn't much help because the question made me think of Duane. *I was wet from the creek and he was hot and dry, the almost spoiled fruit smell of the wild-plum wine sour on his breath, dirt and twigs sticking to us, the small circle of light in my eyes from the top of the tipi. I didn't think I went in that far.* I returned to earth when a courtly old gentleman stopped on the street and asked us if we were sisters. Ruth smiled, and nodded yes. He did a Chaplin glance up and down the street, saying "Where are the lucky fellows?" Then did a little dance step as he walked away. I felt suddenly sad for I wanted more of this attitude in life. I teased Ruth about her girlhood crush on Robert Ryan. She brought me up short when she said she had loved Robert Ryan because she somehow imagined he acted like the father she was too young to remember.

The finale was a meal in Yountville at Mustard's where Michael ordered all ten entrées for the five of us. He was a little manic but Mother was happy from a day of wine-tasting and bird-watching, so it was hard to be cross with him. It was a place favored by locals, and a number of people from the wineries waved or nodded at Naomi and Michael. He seemed to know a good deal about wine but he doubtless also could pass himself off as an astrophysicist. I was unnerved by the sight of an older man from Pacific Palisades in the far corner of the restaurant. He was renowned for his sexual cruelty to women in the film colony. I found myself wondering how there could still be pathology when pathology had begun to approach the norm.

The change of mood followed me back to Santa Monica the next afternoon. I began to regret what training I had had in psychiatric social work. Enthusiasms can stretch one into remote corners, from comparative literature (three-day-old bread), to game biology (biometric fatuities), the Peace Corps (kindness regimented into banality), to social work (torn anuses, and the very real boot heel of the late twentieth century grinding the bottom ten percent into very real dust). In short, I was ready for Nebraska.

When I reached the parking garage under my apartment

building from the airport there was a quarrel in process between a professional football player who lived in the building
and two women. Someone had swiped his cocaine. The building superintendent was watching and greeted me with a wink
and a shrug. There was another man waxing his car and ignoring the fuss. In the elevator it occurred to me that every man,
woman, and dog in America was tethered on too short a lead
or chain, and that's how they begin the training of guard
dogs—a three-foot lead to an iron post and the dog was permanently pissed off within a few weeks.

About an hour later, just before Andrew called, I remembered I had seen a movement in the far corner of the garage
beyond my immediate attention span. Andrew was calling
from the basement asking me to come right down and sign a
complaint against Guillermo Sandoval to add to a dozen others. How could this be? I thought. It's not even dark yet.

The police were the same two who had handled the original problem with the boy and greeted me by name. "We got
the fucker," they said. Andrew was talking to the man who had
been waxing a car. He turned out to be the bodyguard Ted had
hired. The two women had disappeared and the football
player and the building superintendent were eagerly talking
to a reporter. A TV mobile unit swerved up to the garage
entrance, then stopped and checked for clearance. I noticed
the bodyguard's shirt was torn in one place and he had a
handkerchief wrapped around a hand with some blood coming
through it. Sandoval was handcuffed to an iron support pole,
and leaning against a car fender; the healed scars gave his face
a rumpled look. We looked at each other long and hard and I
refused to avert my glance. Not very deep in my heart I admitted I could have shot him like a rabid dog. What had happened
is the two women in the cocaine quarrel had begun screaming
and Sandoval, fearing a problem he hadn't bargained for,
slipped from his hiding place and had been seen by the bodyguard. The bodyguard couldn't subdue Sandoval by himself, in
fact was losing the struggle, when the football player in a fit of
rage over his lost cocaine decided to help. Meanwhile the
building super notified the police and the relieved bodyguard
called Andrew. I was a bit numb from it all and was unwittingly
shown in the late TV news, and morning newspapers, as the

damsel in distress saved by the linebacker. All the other details were neglected. Around such violence there is always a smell in the air like tire smoke. Sandoval was carrying a sharpened car aerial, a piece of rope, and a .38 Ruger. Among this evidence the rope disturbed me the most.

Two hours later, after a half-dozen drinks, a lot of trembling, and some stories, I was in bed with Andrew. We decided not to feel bad about it because we had been thinking about making love for several years. Except we felt a little bit bad anyway. It was far beyond talk and any immediate effort to clear up the situation, as people say. Instead, we decided to feel merely compromised and made a late dinner out of my freezer, an assortment of recipes my uncle Paul had taught me in Mexico. Violence, sex, food, death. I showed Andrew a letter from a social-worker friend who had moved to Detroit. Her first assignment was to counsel the children of two men whose heads had been cut off in a dope execution. She said she had never had to handle a dismemberment case before.

Curiously, I didn't feel bleak at dawn. I've always had a rather masculine, perhaps naïve, sense of recovery—so many men believe a morning can mean a fresh start, while women suspect a night's sleep scarcely changes the terms of life. With Andrew it was only a matter of comfort; adult lovers can pretend nothing has really happened because it hasn't. There is an obvious trace of melancholy in this freedom.

I took my habitual beach walk, the pleasure of which was tempered by the city crews cleaning up the detritus of the first big summer weekend. I gave up and climbed the embankment stairs, heading east on San Vincente. I smiled, remembering Naomi's first visit years before. Armed with George Hasting's *Trees of Santa Monica* she attacked the hundreds of botanical introductions as if she were Rommel invading North Africa. It was a two-week campaign with a city map on my living-room wall streaked with multicolored crayon marks. Many mornings I hiked along with her, though somewhat inattentive to the details she found fascinating. "My God, a yellow oleander from the dogbane family, *Thevetia peruviana,* native to Mexico, Central and South America, the West Indies, and it's right here in front of us." I suppose I'm a romantic and the sight of a specific bird or tree reminds me of the other times I've seen the bird or tree, and there's no urge, despite my training in the area, to run to a book for a name.

I spent the afternoon with the movers and had an early farewell dinner with Ted and Andrew. I had seen them at the most once a month but leavetaking proved difficult for all of us. It was as if precise language was just beyond our reach and the clumsiness wasn't obvious enough to be humorous. Andrew was uncommonly moody and drank too much, baking a fish too long for the first time ever. His eyes were moist as he dumped it into the trash. Ted gulped his drink as we watched a big dog chase a little one down the beach, tumbling the smaller animal repeatedly in the surf. He became sullen and wanted Andrew to shoot the larger dog. At first he was happy that Ruth had given up the idea of the grocer, then became morose over his lack of family. His son had decided not to visit the coming summer. During his third consecutive drink he tried to pin me down on a possible date for a return visit, and my inability to give him one hurt his feelings. It was still well before dark when we simply gave up, hugged each other, and said goodbye.

I left an hour before daylight, getting on U.S. 10 in the middle of Santa Monica—if you cared to you could drive straight through to Jacksonville, Florida, on this same highway, but I got off in Indio and took 86 down to U.S. 8. I had driven home in three days when in a hurry but this time I was giving myself a week to ten days or more if I chose. There was also the barely admissible thought that I wouldn't pass this way again, that the vertigo of leaving L. A. was mostly that of relief. I numbered the things, the people, and the locations that I would miss but none of them tugged at the heart as much as the trees and most of all, the Pacific, which I had listened to so many days and nights that I often thought we could speak a common language: perhaps a verbless language just short of madness, a sound of flowing blood and water, but nevertheless a language.

By early evening I had reached the dirt road a dozen miles short of Ajo, Arizona, that was my immediate destination. I turned off back west into the desert toward the mountains for a dozen miles, downshifting into four-wheel drive in the loose sand. The road disappeared and I turned up a dry wash at the bottom of an arroyo, parked under a paloverde tree. I stood for a moment in the nearly absolute silence, the car engine ticking away its heat, then covered the car with a lightweight camouflage tarp, a promise of concealment to the two men who had introduced me to the area. I didn't feel silly at this paramilitary gesture, only thankful that the enormous bare spot on the map that I faced was still reasonably intact in 1986. I took out my summer sleeping bag and a gallon canteen of water, then leaned against the car and put on my hiking boots.

I still had over an hour of light when I set off up the wash toward the Growler Mountains. It was a twenty-minute walk to where we had cached a collapsible army cot years before, in deference to my waking up one morning with a rattlesnake nestled on my sleeping bag. One of the men thought this was very funny but that same evening he had been bitten in the calf by a sidewinder while gathering firewood. Luckily the snake hadn't injected any venom—not an uncommon thing. I pulled a fang out of his calf with tweezers and we had a few unpleasant hours waiting to see if an emergency move was going to be necessary.

I found the cot inside a cairn we had built, set up my simple camp, and went to gather some firewood. The air had finally begun to cool, and the trickle of sweat between my breasts dried into an itch. I wandered carefully among the cholla, octillo, the bright-green agave from which tequila is made, and the greasewood, picking up ironwood sticks for my fire.

Back at my camp I stacked the wood, then took off all my clothes and sat on the cot naked to watch the dark descend over the mountains. The Cabeza Prieta, a huge area just above the Arizona-Mexico border, doubles as a wildlife refuge and an Air Force gunnery range, which must certainly send a double message to desert creatures. I had given up trying to worry about such matters. Not a mile from the cot we had discovered a footpath over a thousand years old littered occasionally with shards of pottery from ancient water jars, and the brighter glint of seashells. The Hohokam Indians, a tribe that had disappeared a thousand years ago, used the path to travel south from the Gila River to the Sea of Cortez to gather seashells for jewelry. What was it called before the Sea of Cortez? Cortez

was a latecomer like ourselves. I could see them walking in a
file through the desert in the moonlight when it was cooler,
down to the sea to camp and gather shells. Now the darkness
did not seem to descend but swept slowly up the mountains as
if the dark came out of the earth herself. I felt the slightest
tremor of fear hearing the first call of the elf owl, who lives in
the holes it burrows into the saguaro cactus. I had camped here
several times before and each time this tremor had arrived
when I sensed the vast foreignness of the landscape. I had
never seen anyone here before. The assortment that was me
was totally alone, except for the desert, a slip of moon, and the
summer constellations slowly emerging above me.

I had all night to watch the stars so I got off the cot to light
the fire. A scorpion, a less friendly relative of the shrimp, skittered away from the flame. I stopped short of saying hello to
him, or to the coyote I heard miles away south of me. I was
hungry but never ate when I slept here, wanting to stay awake
as long as possible to look at the stars. Uncle Paul had introduced me to the two men who first brought me here. I looked
upward from the gathering fire and thought of a line in an
essay by Lorca, "the enormous night straining her waist
against the Milky Way." I looked down at my body, my arms
and belly and thighs turned golden by the fire. I liked living
a great deal but there was nothing in me that regretted growing older. I lay back down on the cot in a state of intense
physical excitement for reasons I couldn't understand. I felt an
almost imperceptible breeze touch my feet and move up my
body. It was my incapacity to admit what laying there on a
June night at that latitude would cause—the curious way our
emotions withhold information from us.

It was the first of June in 1972 when Naomi called me in
New York where I worked as an assistant to a ragtag film
documentarian who was obsessed with the poor. We worked
and lived together, along with an English sound man, making
cinéma-vérité short films for Public Broadcasting. The afternoon Naomi called we were packing the van for a trip to West
Virginia for some footage on a coal-mine strike. "I looked at
this postcard for two days without calling," she said. "It's from
Duane in the Florida Keys and says for you to come down
quick, I don't feel too good." She added a phone number and

the fact that I would be in her prayers. I called the number but there was no answer. I called Delta, made a reservation, and packed an overnight bag. I tried to explain myself to the director and lover but was summarily fired from an affair and a job.

I reached Key West before midnight, rented a car, and drove to a motel recommended by a Cuban girl on the plane who wore lots of jewelry. No one at the number had answered at either La Guardia or the Miami airport. The air smelled like dead fish and rotten fruit and even at that late hour was sodden with humidity. Oddly, the airport bar doubled as a strip club and through the open door I could see a girl grabbing her ankles and bending over as far as possible. This was 1972, well before Key West cleaned itself up and became a tourist mecca.

At the motel I drove the desk operator crazy by calling the number every ten minutes for the next hour and a half. Finally he suggested that I direct-dial from the bar. It was the Pier House bar, crowded and nightmarish with what I thought was a convention. There were at least two dozen men and women around my age, thirty, who wore blue shirts that had "Club Mandible" printed on them. They were getting quite drunk and some of them were smoking huge marijuana cigarettes out on the patio. I bought a drink and stood outside in the hall by the pay phone, watching the activity in the bar. It reminded me of some sort of party in a private insane asylum. Then a woman answered the phone. Her name was Grace Pindar and she sounded black. Yes, Duane expected me, and no he wasn't there, he was out fishing until at least noon tomorrow. How can he fish at night? That's when they catch the fish, she said. Duane and Grace's husband were commercial fishermen. Bobby was the captain and Duane was the mate. She gave me directions to where they lived on Big Pine Key.

Now I was trembling and walked out the door, across the patio beside the pool, and down to the water. A slight breeze had come up and the palm fronds were rattling. Two burly men were standing in the water in their clothes flycasting to tarpon that were rolling under a light attached to a dock. One of the men screamed "Holy shit" as he hooked a huge tarpon, which jumped in the dark several times before it broke off. He waded back to the beach where I was standing and tied on another fly. "You want to have some fun?" he asked. He had a big twisted nose but a kind face. Now the other fisherman, with one eye and a brown moonface, waded toward me and I felt a decided urge to go to my room. I asked them where Big Pine Key was and they offered to drive me there. I got the directions, thanked them, and went to my room. I must have awakened and fallen back to sleep a hundred times that night, listening to the wind rattle the palm fronds, the party noise of people jumping in the pool, the slurred shouts that the humidity and walls softened until all the words and dreams in the world became round.

I know in my heart there was nothing that I could have done for him. In the fourteen years since I had seen or heard from him he had punished himself and had been punished, as much as any human could and still be alive. There was the question of to what degree, and in what parts of his soul and body he was still alive: *I can see the house and clearing and trailer in a bare pine grove with dead stacked brush, a salt-water channel, and a pool hedged by mangroves. There was no one there I thought but a dog who became friendly, the house no more than a shack with the TV on but no one around. Gray chickens and three piglets in a pen. I went down to the tidal creek and there in a corral in the pines was the buckskin, and I jumped and the dog barked at me. I thought a ghost horse, but he was sixteen, not all that old for a horse but missing a hind hoof up to the pastern. I slid through the corral bars and looked. It was healed, a nubbin hide-covered, the horse sun-bleached but looked well brushed. The tidal creek was full and moving as a small river and there were egrets. A voice said, "He want a swim, that's all he want to do is swim." Grace was brown-black, Bahamian. They'll be home soon. She took me to Duane's old Airstream trailer which was implausibly neat inside, with dozens of bottles of prescription medicine and pictures on the wall of me; his mother, Rachel; and an old one of Grandfather on a horse. You're pretty Duane is good with ladies but now he's sick, you could take him to a good hospital not the VA hospital. Grace was hard to understand. We heard the boat coming up the creek. I ran down and Bobby Pindar who was about forty but you couldn't tell really yelled for Grace who caught the lines and tied off to the dock. Duane got up from where he was lying down on the cooler covered with*

*canvas, shirtless, and I could see holes, indentations in him,
also in his cheek and neck because they were whiter than his
skin. Scar tissue doesn't tan well. He hugged me, smelling like
sun, fish, and salt. I got you down here because I want you to
have my benefits. They said I'm dying. Rachel said you had to
give the kid away. Maybe you can find him and give him some
of my benefits from the army. They unloaded the fish with
Duane telling me the names of different fish. I couldn't quite
talk. He hugged me again and I started to cry but he told me
to stop. We're getting married so you can have my service
benefits he said shaking from sickness. Grace set up a table in
a grove of trees near the creek and started a fire. Bobby Pindar
carried a tub of ice filled with beer. Grace had a bottle of rum,
a bottle of hot peppers, Cuban bread, and the chickens she was
going to cook. Duane got the buckskin who was excited. Bobby
said that horse is the champion swimming horse of the world
and should be on TV. Duane got on with just a halter and the
horse jumped off the dock. Duane gave a big rodeo hoot and
the horse swam up the tidal creek into the mangroves, then
back to us and up a path. You try it he said. I took off my skirt
and blouse. It was wonderful, jumping through the air with
a huge splash. Duane dove in the water and we swam with the
horse up and down the clear, deep creek. We caught three
hundred pounds of shrimp with a net across this creek he told
me. We got out of the creek and drank rum and beer. Bobby
Pindar came down and said we got to have the wedding before
we eat. Duane said he's looking at your tits and ass so I put my
clothes on. They had a license. What if I'm already married?
I teased, but that only stopped them for a moment until I
shook my head no. I am the full-fledged captain of a boat I
marry you said Pindar. Duane took off his necklace and put
it around my neck. Kiss her Duane you asshole Grace said. He
kissed me. I never been married how do I know? Duane said,
I only know about war and horses. We ate some shrimp and
drank a lot. Duane went off to pee and Bobby said Duane had
the record for the most time spent in combat, almost four years
before they shipped him home as good as dead. He has a sack
full of medals for you. It don't look good for ole Duane he said.
We ate shrimp and chicken and drank more, then went swimming again without the horse. I was drunker than he was and*

*I asked what all was wrong. Kidneys liver pancreas stomach—
he would have to be hooked to a machine at the VA hospital
to stay alive. I'll take care of you I said. It was nearly dark and
Grace who was quite drunk yelled at us to start our honeymoon so we went to Duane's trailer to please her. He poured
us big glasses of rum, I know now to get rid of me. We clicked
glasses. How's it with you little sister? he said. Then I fell
asleep or passed out with his arms around me and my face
against his neck. Even in my sleep I could feel his arms around
me. I'm with my lover and we'll take the horse back to the
country I thought. Doctors will make him better and we'll live
up in the cabin in Buffalo Gap with the horse. On the way
we'll stop at the Missouri River, then the Niobrara, and let the
horse swim, and we'll dam the small spring in Buffalo Gap
and let the horse swim there. In the middle of the night there
was a loud banging and a flashlight in my face. It was Bobby
yelling that Duane and the buckskin were gone. He dragged
me to the boat. Another fisherman called and said he saw
Duane and the horse swimming out Bow Channel past Logger-
head Key toward open water in the dark and when he pulled
alongside Duane pointed a gun at him. Bobby took the boat
out the creek and into the channel. These same stars wavered
and I rinsed my face and shivered. At a buoy we met the other
fisherman who had called the Coast Guard. I heard the man
whisper that he followed Duane and the horse at a distance out
toward American Shoals and the Gulf Stream. He heard two
shots and guessed that the first was for the horse and the
second was for Duane. Bobby started to cry, then stopped, and
both boats steered toward the oncoming lights of the Coast
Guard launch. I looked up at the stars which had never seemed
so huge. I sat on my father's lap in a blanket to watch the
shooting stars. Naomi said there is the archer the crow and
whale and lion shining in the black sky. Should I have been
with Duane plunging in these waves that make the stars waver
and sway, over the phosphorescent crests and down through
troughs and up again? The three boats searched all night but
we never found the horse or Duane. The Coast Guard said
sharks and blood. I was not well after that and Uncle Paul
came from Arizona to get me. Months later, in October, with
the permission of Naomi and Ruth who saw no harm, I buried*

*an empty coffin like my father's in our cemetery in the middle*
*of the lilac grove.*

○

Now it is first light in the desert and I've watched the stars fade
and disappear. There's only enough dew to moisten the skin.
A little while ago I turned in the sleeping bag, hearing the
coyote, but I didn't see him. It was pleasurable to be there and
think where and how far I'd drive that day.

# BOOK II

# MICHAEL

# MICHAEL'S WORKBOOK

## *June 6, 1986—Nebraska*

I was shaken awake at 6:00 A.M. by a very large woman who wore the sort of baggy flower-print housedress my mother favored when I was a child. She said her name was Frieda and that my breakfast was ready. Dalva had told her over the phone that I liked my breakfast just after dawn. What humor! Frieda stood directly behind my chair while I ate, as if critiquing my performance. I knew this was the way old-fashioned Scandinavian women fed their families, but it made me bolt my food. She was disturbed when I only ate two of the three pork chops, half the potatoes and eggs. Then she brought a worn denim jacket and fairly pushed me out the door for the long morning walk she had been advised was my habit.

I stood in the backyard, not more than vaguely conscious, yet full of relief and a little fear. Dalva's arrival had been delayed in order to meet her uncle Paul in Sonoita, Arizona. Dalva is punctual on a nominal level but never seems to know the date or year of anything within the nearest decade. She says she sees events, the past itself, in terms of "clumps" of years, which is a blithe evasion indeed. I told her that the study of history can't afford such messiness, and that by the age of sixteen I knew the birthdates of all the kings and queens of

England. She thought this quite funny, and described the amusement of the Indians when they were first exposed to calendars, also to the cartographers and surveyors who were measuring with exactitude the heights of mountains. Her high school history teacher had also been her basketball coach, and it had been his practice to hand out sheets of paper with raw historical dates, and the trick was to figure out what happened on them. Sad to say, this man seemed to turn her away from the only precision aspect history offers.

My precious BMW had shitcanned outside of Denver, blowing its engine and faltering to a noisy halt on the downside of a mountain pass. The dealership told me the car wasn't designed to function on filthy oil, or to pull a U-Haul trailer laden with heavy cartons of books over the Rocky Mountains. I told them to fix it and issued a deposit check I couldn't cover. They were kind enough, though, to help me find a moving company, and I spent a morning arranging this and that, then boarded a Greyhound bus for Nebraska, arriving at midnight aided by a pint of whiskey. The desolate little village was closed up tight, but Naomi was there waiting in her car. She had volunteered to drive the three hours to the closest airport when I had called, but I told her I was far too unstable to get on one of those cramped metal tubes used by feeder airlines.

Now I was trying to locate the precise nature of the vertigo that tugged strongly at my stomach and limbs, making me feel spongy, hollow-headed. I had escaped, for the time being, the academic firing squad and was on the loose: a year in which to prove myself worthy of tenure, of permanent employment, a small matter entailing close to an additional million dollars during a professional lifetime at one of the "top ten" institutions. When I left the house the back steps seemed three feet high—that was it—and the steps tried to recall the time I had stumbled walking out of the Moscow airport. During my divorce negotiations I had wangled a free vacation by escorting a student group to Russia. For this, I had sprinted to the bookstore, spent an hour devouring a Fodor guide, and won the job over a lumpy woman from the Russian department and a black linguist who actually spoke the language. My fibs about the wonders of Tashkent and the fleshpots of Kiev convinced the student committee. Naturally, the trip was not made less miserable by my ignorance, though it certainly was an eye-opener for this fading leftist. The following year, on a similar boondoggle, I found it was easier to be a Marxist in Florence and Rome.

In this barnyard I was emotionally back at the Moscow airport, though without student charges puking out Aeroflot vodka on the curb. Naomi had invited me to stay overnight at her place, but I said it would be better to wake up at the homestead headquarters. The fact of the matter was that I had been frightened. After showing me to a downstairs master bedroom slept in by the succession of John Wesley Northridges, she left and I headed for an old horsehair couch in the den. I looked out the window and watched Naomi's red taillights heading down the drive. It was too quiet. There was no TV or radio to be found. I finally located the phone in a kitchen cupboard but couldn't think of anyone to call. I sipped sparingly at my few remaining ounces of whiskey left over from the bus trip, then looked unsuccessfully for more. I was sweating, but when I took off my sport coat I felt less strong, so put it back on. I turned on every light and paced around, mostly to hear the reassuring sound of my own footsteps. My first survey told me that I could have called in a semi truck and packed the contents off to Sotheby's or Christie's, retiring on the proceeds. I don't know much about china, silver, furniture, but the library and paintings were splendid (Remington, Charley Russell, a Sargent landscape, Burchfield, Sheeler, Eakins, Marsden Hartley, a smallish Hopper, Stuart Davis, some Modigliani drawings of the usual long-necked ladies), and a glass case held the entire Edward Sheriff Curtis folio, the current worth I knew to be over a hundred grand. A lucky probe of a cabinet revealed an assortment of brandy bottles, some of which were thirty years old back in the fifties. A judicious, concealed amount from each bottle would bring sleep. I fetched a glass from the kitchen, bowed at a portrait of the deceased owner, avoided a portrait of Dalva, and poured. I looked for a more contemporary book and selected a volume on the sorry life of Monet. There was a Yankee spareness about the house that didn't baffle my night fears.

Now, in the dawn barnyard, I approached a small flock of geese strutting along a creek, but they proved unfriendly and I nearly had to boot some sense into their apparent leader. I looked back at the big farmhouse, weathered but still grand, that reminded me of New England, from which the man who had it built had arrived via Andersonville and the Civil War. I was a little alarmed to see Frieda staring back from the kitchen window as if urging me on my walk. It seemed curious that she drove a large, gleaming pickup truck with RAM lettered on the tailgate in bold letters. A land of big women and big pickups.

I walked out past the barn to the bunkhouse that was to serve as my home and study. The door was locked but it looked pleasantly rustic through a window. I could see a radio and a record player but no television, and the roof was without an aerial. I glanced back at the main house and could still see the outline of Frieda in the kitchen. I strolled off at a pace I didn't intend to maintain, toward the first wall of trees in the west and away from the sun. Dalva was supposed to call at midmorning, and the present need was to find a good place to snooze until that time.

The night before, on our ride from town, I had told Naomi that the soul of history could not be approached with the cautious servility of the scholar. She said that sounded fine but wasn't sure what I meant. What it really meant was that I wanted her to think well of my high calling, but I certainly couldn't say that directly. Naomi is less intimidating than Dalva, perhaps because of her age and because she lacks that edge of fierceness occasionally seen in her daughter. Sadly enough, I've never met a woman around my own age as companionable as Naomi. Our day of bird-watching and wine-drinking in the Napa Valley was perhaps the finest I've ever spent with anyone. Her high-mindedness is so gentle and forgiving that it was impossible for me to pull any of my captious, asshole moves.

The first wall of trees that constituted a windbreak was as thick as I imagined a jungle to be, but I made my way through to the other side, pausing after I was frightened witless by a flushed deer. There was an element of disappointment to find a forty-acre-or-so field of alfalfa which clung to my legs and soaked my pants with dew, surrounded by another windbreak. The symmetry became irritating and the deepness of the June green in the field and trees seemed something to struggle with.

Passing through another windbreak, this one thicker than the last, yielded the same thing, with the single unique quality of a rock pile in the center of the field. I made my way to it as if it were a pile of diamonds, took off my jacket in the gathering heat, and sat down. For lack of a better place, I could doze sitting on a rock.

It was partly the overwhelming substance of the place that bothered me: a wealth that was so subdued and hidden that it was invisible to the outside world. When I was in grade school a steel-mill foreman who lived down the street bought a new Cadillac. Everyone in the neighborhood knew he was thick with some crooks in the union, but this fact didn't dampen our admiration for the car. One Saturday afternoon when he was drinking beer he let us help wash the car, though no one was allowed to sit in it. This house and farm dredged up some of those childhood memories of envious awe, not that I wanted a farm, but more what it all seemed to represent: the paintings and furniture, a dozen bottles of barely touched great brandy. And this was the factor that made Dalva forever out of reach except on some nominal sexual level. Sitting on this rock pile I could see her life so totally shorn of bric-a-brac, *bibelots,* as the French call them, living her life without much confusion, surrounded by beloved objects, and incapable of a graceless move. Why should this fire my anger? We often find out we are not quite what we thought we are. The boy sticks his head in the window of a brand-new Cadillac car and the man he becomes can't quite get over it. The man rather glibly describes himself as a historian, that is, he studies the records of the large-scale habits of mankind, war, famine, politics, the fuel that is greed. What we are, what we have done, what we have made, weighs as heavily and usually as unnoticeably as gravity weighs upon us. It is the historian's job to study this unseeable gravity, to take core samples from the past and bring them to the quasi-light of the present. Since those old outworn enormities like Arnold Toynbee have passed on, we have become minimalists. I chose the Nebraska area several years ago for a book, because I drove through the state and it seemed charmingly simpleminded. More specifically, I chose the advent of farming in the Great Plains and the final solution of the Indian question. Through good luck, chicanery, perhaps laziness, I further limited the field to the history of a single dominant family and its relation to the advent of farming and the Indian question. You can imagine scholars pillaging the attics of old farmhouses, the records of local historical societies. But in such material there is no concept of what was really going on at the time, just a brutal mishmash of everyday life, the Great Plains as a nineteenth-century gulag, where the leading cause of death was exhaustion. Professor Lesy's *Wisconsin Death Trip* is a model sourcebook of this sort of thing. It is hard for a layman to imagine my excitement when I came across the only public material on the Northridge family in the *Proceedings of the Nebraska Historical Society.* Of course I'm not really interested in the Sioux but in how the first John Wesley Northridge looked at the Sioux, who are anyway as intractable as the African Masai. Only a few pages of his journal were allowed to be published, along with a dozen or so pages of the usual dreary commentary. Over the years there must have been dozens of scholars competing for the material, all receiving the form-letter rejection I first received from a trust officer in Omaha. Here is part of the printed sample in J. W. Northridge's pungent style:

**May 3, 1865**
**To see the countryside it is better to be on foot. Marching is good training for this, if for nothing else to a civilized man: in fact, absolutely nothing else. To march is to bear the Mark of the Beast. In Andersonville I did not march but starved, but then my time was mercifully short compared to others, and so I spent, was ordered to spend, my time burying the less fortunate than I with camphor in my nose to temper the stench of the dead. The depth of their graves depended on my waning energies. I must add that I much preferred burying the dead to writing letters for the dying—so arduous to make the final genuflection to the beloved for someone else. "My dearest Martha, My sight grows dim now and my hands that once held you strongly to my breast cannot bear the weight of a pen. I speak this letter to my friend named John Wesley, a godly soul who is from our native New England, a botanist & preacher conscripted by error in Boston. He has promised to deliver this letter, among others—perhaps too many to carry—should this terrible war ever end. Remember how we**

marched away thinking it a fortnight's lark? Please tell little Robert and Susanah that their father who loves them with all of his heart died for the Republic. It is my prayer and trust that your youth, grace, and beauty will find you another to take my place, and the Lord will grant that I see you in Paradise someday."

A man who writes a hundred or so such letters finds himself well shut of Heaven and Hell. This horror has returned me close to Earth and I would not trade a fragrant thistle along this road to the North for a warehouse of Bibles. Before I made my trade with the Devil which I cannot admit yet to paper I was bound for the Plains as a Missionary and Botanist to help the native population, the Indians, to make the inevitable transition from warriors to tillers of the soil, an occupation toward which I am advised they have no predisposition. I shall hide the preacher and show them how to feed themselves without buffalo. I was a captive of war, and they are captive of the Void that befalls a conquered people, their conqueror having emerged from Bedlam to slay millions in this Civil War. And so released by Victory I chose to avoid the stink of trains, the freight of living and dead, and walk north into summer, to give what knowledge I may to these Sioux Indians.

I had lain back on the rock pile like a desert father, fatigued by breakfast, walking, my almost portentous thoughts, with the jacket balled up for a pillow, and had my first dream ever about Indians, who (in the dream) were apparently buried under the rock pile with their spirits rising upward as invisible smoke. There was something moving under my chin and I awoke screaming, surrounded by snakes. I somehow propelled myself forward like a launching rocket, turning to see that the rock pile was covered by black snakes sunning themselves. There was a loud noise that turned out to be my yelling, which I managed to do while running backward. Son of a bitch, but I was so frightened I almost dumped in my pants! I am not by inclination a nature buff, and this experience cinched my dislike of its tooth-and-claw world. I stood there soothing my frantic heart—I am under medication for high blood pressure—thinking that, were I a well-equipped soldier, I would lob a grenade in the middle of the bastards, Indian ghosts and all.

I set off for the sun, the direction of the house, at a sturdy pace, plunging through two more windbreak barriers before it occurred to me that the sun moves, or the earth moves, I had forgotten which, and I had lost my bearings. I came upon a creek and recalled that the aggressive geese of the morning were dithering along a creek, but was it the same one? This was becoming a problem that a dozen years of graduate school hadn't prepared me for. My stomach was growling and my mouth was parched, but I doubted the purity of the creek water. The stomach growl meant unreliably that it might be noon, but this was a situation where the time of day wasn't very helpful. I made an almost successful leap across the creek and discovered a faint trail, which I followed for several hundred yards: here and there were piles of scattered brown pellets the size of marbles, a mystery until I picked one up, smelled it, and deduced it was animal poop, and that the tiny sharp footprints were probably those of deer or goats. Goat tracks would lead me to a farm but deer tracks wouldn't. There are deductive limits. I remembered from boyhood stories that there was moss on the north sides of trees, but the local trees had arranged their moss haphazardly. I stepped near a pheasant and was met by a bowel-shaking squawk. I knelt, discovering I had stepped on one of a dozen or so eggs she had laid. I mentally noted the location in case I should end up having to eat the eggs. The creek emptied into a larger creek and I became mired to my knees in the muddy bank for a few moments, losing one of the handmade brogans purchased in London years before. I loved these shoes and now I had only a shoe, so I stuck a fallen tree limb in the bank to mark the spot. My skin crawled when I remembered Dalva telling me how cows got fatally stuck in quicksand. A comforting plane passed far overhead, but between the plane and myself large birds, perhaps buzzards, were circling, without doubt waiting for me to lose my will to live. There was a visibly larger trail on the far side of the creek, so I plunged across, only to find that the water clarity was deceptive, the creek deep, and I had to swim. I gulped a little water, damning the bacterial consequences. I followed the creek downstream until I found a sandy, scrubby area at the edge of the woods I refused to enter, fearing either more woods or yet another damnable alfalfa field on the other side. I sat down on a pile of sand, noting the remnants of charred wood where some Indian must have built a fire. Just inside the thicket were large mounds covered with a tangle of vines, shrubs, and small trees. Hanging from a tree limb and attached to a thong was a bleached animal skull. I felt a helpless anger. This is 1986—June 6, to be exact—and this fucking place is disturbing me. I would have left immediately but the sandy area offered a little comfort and a glimmer of memory of myself as an infant in a sandbox and, later, amusing my daughter in a sandbox. I turned away from the white skull that swayed in the breeze, curled up, and took another nap.

○

Rather than snakes, this time I awoke to church bells—oh, blessed Angelus! Actually the bells were a surrealistic kick in the balls. What were bells doing in this half-tilled wilderness? It appeared to be early evening, and as a backdrop to the bells there was an incessant whine of mosquitoes, many of which had fed on me during my sleep. My body was tight and sore from the day's exertion but I felt curiously well rested (not surprising after circa five hours of outdoor naps). I would have given anything for a couple of fingers of Paddy whiskey and a pint of Guinness stout, which was my reward for a longish walk on Saint Stephen's Green during my months in Dublin. Added to the thirst was the wildest hunger I have ever known. I'm a bit of a food snob, but the places my daughter dragged me off to when she was a child—Burger Chef, McDonald's, Kentucky Fried Chicken—now seemed wonderful. I'd take her off to Golden Gate Park on Saturday with a bucket o' chicken, some Pepsi, and the newspaper.

I walked as fast as possible on one shoe toward the far-off tintinnabulation of the bells. When the bells paused for a few moments I desperately sped up in the direction of the echo's source. I fairly popped through a row of trees, bruising my foot on a log. There in the distance, seemingly miles away, was a farmhouse from which the bell sound came. Now I was in a waist-high wheat field and I readily admit there were copious tears of relief in my eyes. The relief was leavened somewhat when I saw a group of a dozen horsemen bearing down on me from the left at top speed. Jesus Christ, I am to be hanged for trespass, I thought. They thundered to a halt in a circle around me, a mixture of mounted cowboys and farmers in bib overalls. One huge fellow jumped off his horse and lifted me as if a big feather to the back of another's saddle. He said they all thought I had "got nailed by a rattler," the idea of which filled me with nausea. No one had advised me there were rattlesnakes in the area.

The upshot was that the farmhouse was Naomi's and when I had stayed away so long she had assembled this ragtag posse to find me. There were additional men leaning against pickups and four-wheel-drive vehicles in her yard. Some were drinking beer. The big fellow lifted me off the horse and into the embrace of Naomi.

"Beer," I croaked, and I was handed a cold, opened can, which I quaffed in a single long draft, and was handed another. Frieda was there and asked—inappropriately, I thought— what had happened to the jacket she had given me. I felt called upon to deliver a speech of thanks to the crowd, but my throat was quavery, so Naomi filled in. Then she led me to the house, though I couldn't help waving and bowing from the porch, which elicited a cheer.

Naomi drew me a bath and fixed me a giant drink. Lying in the tub I imagined Dalva in the same tub as a girl, soaking off a day on horseback out on the range. This brought on a hard-on, which disappeared when I rehearsed my god-awful adventure, which I knew would bring Dalva a great deal of amusement, the bitch. In high school I had worked as a busboy at the local country club, which, in addition to the usual golf course, included a horse barn and an arena for equitation and an outdoor course for jumpers. I noted at the time that riding had a fine effect on the girls' fannies in their riding habits, as if jouncing and bouncing on the saddles kneaded their bottoms into graceful proportions, made their thighs strong and supple. That was certainly true of Dalva. After so many lumpy, petulant college girls, she was a piece of almost unendurable good luck. She was so nonchalant and withdrawn about my efforts to impress her that it was a shock when she asked me to stay the night. The hard-on rearrives. It is curious, though, that her descriptions of her mother and grandfather's farm were so

modest, almost childish. I suspect this is because the way anyone grows up becomes quite ordinary to them, their senses
adapted to a child's-eye view of physical surroundings. I grew
up in a cramped row house, lived in cramped dormitories and
small rooms in America and foreign cities, married and lived
in a tiny apartment, then moved on to a small duplex, to a
dollhouse with two ten-by-twelve bedrooms. This bathroom is
larger and better furnished than any living room I've belonged
to, but, then, the bath and drink are too good for this to occasion a snit.

Naomi rapped at the door and said that dinner would be
ready in fifteen minutes. As I dried myself and put on a robe
left for me I thought of my sorest point with Dalva, which was
her effervescent streak of irrationality. Academic reality tends
to be shared, consensual, perhaps a little closed, cloistered to
what is thought of as the outside world. One pleasant evening
on the balcony in Santa Monica she wondered at the extremely
low incidence of cancer among schizophrenics. I said bullshit,
but she found the documentation in a reliable book. This is the
sort of thing that nags at the mind. To further bait me she said
there was a Menninger Clinic researcher who knew a Shoshoni
medicine man who could cause lightning and thunder. After
I vented my rage she smiled and said it really didn't matter if
either of us believed it. Then she said that being with me was
like riding a bicycle where moment by moment I was trying
to maintain balance, consciously or not.

Naomi helped me out to the porch—my left foot was so
sore as to be inoperative—where she had set up dinner on this
warm June evening. She had assumed I would be hungry, so
had roasted a barnyard chicken with a fine sauce that had a
hint of fresh tarragon, potatoes, a salad of new greens from the
garden, and two bottles of chilled Freemark Abbey Chardon-
nay. She had turned off the porch lights and lit an old oil lamp
with a white flowered globe. She had a slice of breast and a
single glass of wine, and I polished off the rest of everything,
down to the last drop and morsel, accompanied by the sort of
light chitchat that works with good food. There was a slightly
errant note in the enormous quantity of bugs that had collected on the porch screen as if trying to get in after human
prey, but Naomi assured me that the bugs, some of them big,

were benign. And thus went my first day on the job. I was
tucked into sleep in Dalva's room and bed; the last memory the
poster of James Dean in a red jacket, smoking a cigarette,
staring listlessly from the wall.

○

Lilacs, and coffee, and a cowgirl with her back turned. Dalva
in jeans, boots, a checked shirt, the sprig of lilac on the tray
with the coffee. No newspaper. She held an aerial map, then
looked down at my exposed and swollen foot. I wiggled my
toes and she looked at me. She pointed to a chair on which
rested my loaned jacket and lost brogan, now polished, plus
some of my clothes from the other house.

"You made quite a first-day splash. I didn't know you were
a hiker. Here's where you were." She sat on the edge of the
bed and traced her finger across the map, pushing away my
hand on her leg. "It actually was quite a walk. Here's the rock
pile and over here is where you lost your shoe. Old Lundquist
took out his little terrier this morning and found the jacket and
shoe. Never give him more than one drink in a day. He's
eighty-seven and can't handle it." She again brushed the hand
away that I placed against her bottom. "Not in this room. I'm
going to teach you to ride a horse. Horses always know the way
home."

I dressed and hobbled down the stairs, unable to get my
shoe laced up. I was confused by the resurgence of a dream of
an Indian college student I knew in San Francisco sitting on
my snake-covered rock pile. He was a Nez Percé from up in
Washington, the only bona-fide Indian I have ever met. My
wife had been badgering me about doing some nasty yard
work, mowing the lawn, trimming the shrubs. As a youth I had
been forced into such work for pocket change and vowed
never to do it again. On the bulletin board of the Student
Union I found a three-by-five card that said "Native American,
Clean and Industrious, Will Perform Inane Chores for Much
Needed Cash." I should have been tipped off by the word
"Inane"; he was a wild-eyed poli-sci major, a Kropotkin anar-
chist who was doing his senior paper on the Nechaev Affair and

the roots of the Russian Revolution. He was the most contrary bastard I'd ever met but possessed an intricate and goofy wit, so that I actually helped all day with the yard work. I had awakened a few moments at dawn wondering what he was doing on the rock pile. While we were raking he said, "You can't feel like an Indian in the Bay Area without getting real drunk."

○

After a marvelous breakfast, accompanied by a four-day-old copy of the Sunday *New York Times,* Dalva took me off to the bank for a first look at the family papers. Rather than using her dusty and mud-spattered Subaru in the driveway, we went out to the barn and drove off in an ancient aqua-colored convertible. The top was down because there was no top left, but the car appeared to be in fine mechanical shape and the engine had recently been replaced. I was a little appalled to discover it was considerably faster than my BMW—because of the distances they are heavy-footed in Nebraska. We slowed down passing her Wesleyan Methodist church, then stopped at the country school where she intended to teach the coming year. It all reminded me of an America I had supposed to be vanished. Through the window the single room glistened with recent varnish, and the spirit of McGuffey hovered over the oak wainscoting. Near the back door was an iron railing for tethering horses. She said some of the children still chose to ride cross-country to school. I wondered aloud if there was an irony involved, whether children did this naturally, or if they had learned from television that it was admirable to be picturesque.

"Try to consider how much time your mind wastes figuring out how to make such asshole comments," she responded.

"I just thought it was a valid consideration."

"A lot of them love rock music, go to the movies, and some grow their own dope. They also feed the stock, help butcher pigs, join the 4-H, and ride horses. Where's the irony? I know rodeo cowboys who blow half their winnings on cocaine but they still love horses."

I blushed. All I was trying to do was be witty, but, then, academic wit is by nature derisive. I didn't, in any event, like being looked at as if I were a dead frog in the middle of the road. There was the additional nervousness of going to town and being in public view after yesterday's dismal fuck-up. She read the nature of my moroseness.

"Don't worry about getting lost yesterday. They're all quite pleased and they'll talk about it for years. They think that's what happens to brilliant professors. There might be a small item in the weekly newspaper, 'Scholar Loses Shoe.' We got a call from town this morning asking you to speak at Rotary Club lunch next Wednesday."

"Should I do it?" I had an image of ample drinks and joints of rare beef.

"Of course you should," she said with a twinkle that I wish I had recorded.

She suddenly looked so lovely that I wanted to suggest a trip out into the weeds but didn't dare. For some reason I mentioned the Nez Percé student on the rock pile in my dream. I suppose I wanted to make her less intimidating. In these semi-angry moods or after she had a few drinks she owned the edge of a predator. It must have come down through her father, because Naomi had none of these qualities.

"That's an interesting dream," she said. "Maybe dreams are in the nature of the landscape? When I was in England and France I dreamt of knights and warhorses and I never do in America. In Arizona I dreamt of melon patches trailing all the way from Orabai down the Sierra Madre in Mexico, which is where they think the Hopis came from. Here I dream a lot about animals and Indians, and I never did in Santa Monica."

This threatened my scholarly integrity so I made a speech right there in the hot, muggy schoolyard, beginning with Freud's *Interpretation of Dreams,* with sidetracks into Otto Rank and Karen Horney. In the interest of winning the point I overlooked those irrational mushmouths Carl Jung and his contemporary camp follower, James Hillman. She laughed when I began to pound an imaginary lectern. Then she hugged and kissed me.

"You're an absolute living, fucking bookcase. What a marvel."

○

The wind in the topless car was too loud for talk the rest of the
way to town, so I had time to refuel my intellectual grudges.
Our very first quarrel had taken place near the end, fortunately, of a fine meal she had treated me to at the puckish
Chinois on Main in Santa Monica. To be kind I'll call it "Dalva's
airplane theory." The upshot was that from an airliner the
entirety of the United States, except for a few spotty wilderness areas, looks raked over, tracked up, skinned, scalped—in
short, abused. I said, I see human history with a dignity, albeit
tentative, and your vision is infected with a girlish infatuation
with Wordsworth and Shelley. She said, Let me finish. What I
mean, she said, is that in out-of-the-way places there's still a
certain spirit, I mean in gullies, off-the-road ditches, neglected
creek banks and bottoms, places that have only been tilled
once, then neglected, or not at all, like the Sand Hills, parts of
northern Wisconsin, the Upper Peninsula of Michigan, or the
untillable but grazed plains of Wyoming, Montana, Nevada,
the desert, even the ocean in the middle of the night. She was
excited to the point of breathlessness about this matter. Just
where did you get your degrees? I asked. She was stunned and
simply got up and walked out of the restaurant. I sat there a
little upset with myself for being so acerbic and wondering
how I was going to pay a big check with thirty bucks and an
expired credit card. I left my wallet with the waitress and went
outside looking for her. She was leaning against the car and I
couldn't see her expression in the darkness. I got down on my
knees and begged her forgiveness, telling her the semi-fib that
I had read something similar to her notion in Gaston Bache-
lard's *Poetics of Space.* I buried my face, snuffling, in her skirt.
Two passing teenagers yelled, "Go for it."
    At the bank we were escorted, after Dalva was fawned
over by everyone in sight, back to a cool room that was an
extension of the main vault. I had kept my composure when
I thought I heard some titters in the background—without
doubt my sorry story had spread to the farthest reaches of the
county. I had expected a jumble of boxes and cartons whose
contents would take months to log: instead there were five

modest wood sea chests with bright brass fittings sitting on a table. Our guide, who was the oldest banker in existence and a near albino, begged his leave, and I looked at Dalva rather nervously.

"I expected more. . . . I mean I expected a mess. May we look at something?"

"In the early seventies I had a breakdown and spent the winter sorting everything out. I did a bibliography on the contents. The first two are Great-grandfather's which, for now, are the only ones you can look at, and these two are Grandfather's. The last one is shared by Wesley and Paul."

She opened the first, revealing a researcher's dream of tidiness, with her typed list of contents resting on neat stacks of bound ledgers, and packets of letters. I lifted out a ledger in the middle of a stack and opened it at the center, reading it at a bookmarked place.

**May 13, 1871: Rode hard our third day down from near Fort Randall with He Dog who was of bad humor & feverish he said from bad beef. We camped on the north fork of the Loup in fine weather & he made an emetic from a root he dug up (blue cornflower), retching half the night but woke in fine health. I studied the river bottom with a hopeless map and made several new specimen entries. He Dog trapped two marsh rats and made a fine stew which increased our strength. He questioned my statement on politics yet again, wherein I insist it is the process by which one man's rights are made more than another's. He is amused by this. Then I repeated on request more tales of the War where he is often less interested in men than the number of horses. It is curious that my given Sioux name which means "earthdiver" is never used in concourse, and the direct use of names is considered impolite, an attempt to thieve power, in fact. I was called thus because I am forever digging holes and inspecting the root systems of trees to determine their hardiness in certain soils. We napped in the heat of mid-day so as to explore until dark. It is somewhat disturbing but He Dog, ever alert to danger, naps upright & with his eyes wide open.**

My heart beat wildly—this little passage alone meant that J. W. Northridge was truly in the thick of things. To offer a brief

gloss: The Sioux warrior He Dog was a crony, a close friend of
the seminal war chief, Crazy Horse ("Crazy" is a vulgarism in
contemporary terms; his true name meant "enchanted" or
"magic," really something more than all three). The north
branch of the Loup was on the verge (in three years) of being
overrun by settlers, in defiance of a treaty made with the Sioux,
the area being in proximity to the Black Hills, the most sacred
place of the Sioux (interesting to note that we never kept a
single treaty with the Indians—beware, the rest of the world!).
A traveler from the British Isles at the time, Lord Bryce, ridiculed our immoral capitulation to the railroads, land swindlers,
and greedy settlers who rushed willy-nilly into legal Indian
Territory, then bleated for God and the U. S. Cavalry to save
their necks. Another point is Northridge as horticulturist and
botanist, an agricultural missionary. As T. P. Thorton points out
in her significant study "Cultivating the American Character:
Horticulture as Moral Reform in the Antebellum Era," the
cultivation of fruit and other trees before the Civil War in New
England and New York was considered to be morally uplifting,
an antidote to the rapacity of greed that was consuming the
nation. As an orphan and a bastard child Northridge worked
at Wodenethe, the enormous fruit garden of Henry Winthrop
Sargent in Dutchess County, New York. I could go on with
animal husbandry, the care and breeding of horses among the
Sioux, quite as intricate as in present-day Lexington, Kentucky, or among the former-day Cossacks and Mongols of the
fabled steppes of Asia. And all of this, historically speaking, is
in the recent past. Three hundred Sioux, mostly women and
children, were butchered at Wounded Knee while, back in the
Midwest, Henry Ford was tinkering with the idea of spare
parts for his first auto. For those of us who are adults, most of
our grandparents were alive in 1890!

In short, I was in a whirl, breathless, nearly faint. When
Dalva helped me tote the first trunk out to her topless car I
scanned the sky for rain clouds. I began to hyperventilate and
the sorry street wobbled a bit. At my feet I imagined the street
to be mud and Northridge tethering his horse before this very
bank, avoided by the burghers, so Dalva tells me, because of
his madness. She came to my aid and sat me in the car. She
wondered if I needed to breathe in a paper bag, which is the

way to ameliorate a hyperventilation attack. I lowered my head into my shirt like a turtle for a few minutes, which did the job. Under my shirt I could see He Dog napping with his eyes open under a cottonwood, the flies circling around the leftovers of the marsh-rat (muskrat) stew, the grama grass responsive to the slightest breeze. Outside my shirt Dalva was talking to someone. I debated whether or not to poke my enturtled head back into the world. There was the notion that my behavior might be misunderstood. I emerged to be introduced to Lena, a café proprietress, a pinkish, slight old woman who reminded me of a crow. This unlikely woman had recently been to Paris, France, to visit her daughter, a somehow startling idea—Nebraska strikes one as a place where it never occurs to the citizens to leave.

On the way home we stopped at an uninspired-looking grocery store, but it was the only game in town, as it were. Dalva assured me that Mrs. Lundquist did the shopping, but my nervous nature requires snacks, and the refrigerator lacked a certain junkiness I enjoyed. I asked Dalva to guard the trunk, a request she thought amusing since the area is without thieves, or so she said.

There wasn't a single interesting item in the store except a jar of pickled "beefalo tongue" (!) from a herd raised by a local rancher and crossbred with cattle, the idea of which seemed a perversion of nature. When I got back outside Dalva was nowhere to be seen, and I rushed toward the Ford to make sure the chest was there. She waved from a pay phone at the service station next door. There is a question why a rich woman would own such a shabby car, the sun-blasted seat so hot on my ass that I barely could sit down. I opened the jar of pickled tongue and took a few bites, wishing I had a cold beer. It turned out she had been talking to a Mexican private detective in Ensenada, still on the unsuccessful track of the abused boy. There is something embarrassing about what the "Modern Living" pages of newspapers refer to as sexual abuse: the rampant id, murderous and nondirectional. The year before I had allowed my daughter to have three of her friends over for a pajama party. When I returned from the cinema and bar they were on the couch eating popcorn and watching a VHS horror film, the sharp odor of cannabis in the air. One of the little chicklettes, a Nordic type named Kristin, wore a nightie that sent me hastily to my room with sweating hair roots. Until that moment I hadn't considered anyone that age since I was fourteen myself. I did penance by reading Wittgenstein, a pre-Nazi pederast cruising the Berlin and Oxford meat racks for sallow butcher boys, albeit one of the great minds of the century.

Dalva helped me unload my treasure at the bunkhouse, then went off to make some lunch. To my amazement the moving van had arrived and Frieda Lundquist had unpacked my clothing and books. There was a small refrigerator in the corner with a six-pack of beer and I sipped one slowly, not wanting to blur my senses as I began to turn the pages of one of the journals. The study of history is hard on the system; there is a continual struggle against the infantile wish to have control at least in retrospect. My Ph.D. dissertation, *Bitter Ore: The Life and Death of an Ohio Valley Steeltown,* passed muster with flying colors, though in fact the work was shot through with fraudulent detail, faked if plausible interviews. *Bitter Ore* was published by a university press and was well reviewed in academic circles, but there is this notion that I, like a tax cheater, might be found out some day. I had written the whole mess under the influence of booze and Dexedrine, with my blurred and electric peripheries avoiding any hard work. My travel grant back to the Ohio Valley was dissipated on Chicago high life. The point is that I have resolved to play this one straight, or as straight as possible. I am not capable of writing an etiology of the tribes of the Great Plains. To be flip, I can't believe God created history only in order to keep track of human suffering: any intelligent amateur might perceive that the Sioux and other tribes were poor agrarians because they were swindled into receiving the very worst farmland in a political situation not unlike that of contemporary South Africa—"apartheid" may be a Dutch word but it is a universal idea.

Dalva called me to lunch and away from my morose vision. I couldn't help babbling about all of this as I ate my *salade niçoise* and drank my lunch ration of four ounces of white wine. Most of us continue under the ready assumption that we are being understood, and that we understand others, forgetting that the human level of attention isn't very reliable. Dalva had an uncommon level of attentiveness, which put almost too much pressure on me when I talked, since I have the habit of doing my mental exploring out loud. She listened carefully, paused, then responded. If she smiled there was a good chance I was going to take cannon fire amidships. When I spoke about Indian reservations and apartheid she answered by saying that her social-worker friend in Detroit had joked that local murders had kept pace with those in the entire country of South Africa. I asked her what that had to do with it.

"Dead is dead, wherever it is. You might as well have given a hoe to a Martian as given a hoe to a Sioux. They were nomadic hunters and gatherers, not farmers. The Ponca and Shawnee were pretty good at crops, but not the Sioux." She heard something and went to the window above the sink. My heart stirred at her leaning bottom in the tight jeans. I suggested what is lightly known as a "nooner," and it was then that I got the appalling news that she couldn't make love to me in this house or the bunkhouse. I was stunned into stuttering.

"Why the fuck not? How childish."

"I just couldn't do it. We can go for a walk or a ride. There's a motel down the road."

"I didn't see any motel."

"It's actually about fifty miles away."

A large horse trailer pulled into the yard, towed by a pickup. We walked outside and helped a sprightly old man unload four horses; rather, I watched, then was handed ropes attached to two of the horses while Dalva and the old man went inside the trailer to get the others. I knew from my reading that it was important to show these beasts mastery, and to exude no odor of fear, or they would take advantage of it, which they did immediately. One yanked mightily at the rope, which gave my shoulder a harsh jolt, while the other, I hoped playfully, bit my shirt sleeve and began to back away with the shirt in his or her mouth. It was a medievalist's vision of torture, and the shirt began to give way. I let off with a shout, which seemed to further anger and excite both of them. Dalva and the old man leapt out of the trailer and rescued me, but not my favorite linen shirt. The old man cuffed the bejesus out of the horses, which offered me minimal satisfaction. Dalva laughed hard and I told her to go fuck herself. I walked to the bunkhouse, regretting that I had been so excited in town about the papers that I had forgotten to buy whiskey. If Dalva went off for a ride I intended to sneak in the house for a few hits of her precious brandy, a small recompense for my tattered shirt.

Back at my desk I picked another Northridge ledger at random. I would not become systematic until I read through them at least once. I could see that much of the material was of a tendentious religious nature, and many of the notes would be of interest only to a botanist. His spleen warmed me for I had not calmed from my brush with horses.

### Sept. 3, 1874

It should not surprise us that swine are swinish and they are everywhere the Captains of our realm, and that everywhere down to the merest lad Greed thrives. My horse, poor soul drew up lame short of Yankton, and I was given a ride by a family of bone pickers who drew nine dollars per ton at the railhead for buffalo bones. They advised me that in west Kansas the same bones brought twelve dollars a ton. They were so wrathful on this subject that I finally chose to walk overland leading my horse. They had been driven out of Kansas by a gang who, so they said, picked five thousand tons of buffalo bones in a summer's work. These men shot Comanches on sight for fear of being murdered in their sleep. The bones in the fields block the coulters & moldboards of the steam plows. The bones are used for combs, knife handles, the refining of sugar, and ground for fertilizer. It is indeed a melancholy use for these grand beasts.

I checked my maps as I read further, noting that Northridge covered over twenty-seven miles in one day, leading his lame horse. Dalva said I walked four miles during my day in the wilds. I rechecked the figures in other passages, discovering that on the summer solstice in 1873 Northridge walked thirty-seven miles between dawn and dark in order to purchase a new horse. These were offered as navigational statements without a tinge of bragging. I intended to call a friend in the athletic department at Stanford who, though he enters Ironmen contests, drinks a great deal of beer. He would be able to verify if these figures were in the realm of probability. I have my own opinion that rigorous exercise packs us far too tightly within our skin, and makes for an unhealthy old age.

It is interesting to note that in an approximately fifteen-year period up until 1883 an estimated twenty thousand buffalo hunters slaughtered between five and seven million of the animals, pretty much the continent's entire population. In 1883 Sitting Bull organized the slaughter of a remaining herd of a thousand buffalo by a thousand Sioux braves to prevent the white men from getting them.

## May 29, 1875

On the fairest day of Spring came upon a family of Swede home-steaders quite lost in the tall prairie grass and had been so they said for two days. This is a common enough occurrence and I guided them south for three days as they were in Treaty land and I feared for their safety. These are a dour though handsome people, and I found them a creek bottom with several springs to build their sod houses, instructing them as best I could on their survival. A land manipulator had taken much of their money, a frequent story, so they had pressed on into empty territory from their unhappiness further East. I warned them sternly away from a hill far to the West as I had surprised a sow grizzly and her cub there, and it was only the quickness of my horse that saved the bear's life. I am loathe to shoot them as they are revered by all Tribes and only killed under the most special circumstances. Grizzlies are the Leviathans of our land as surely as the great whales own the sea, and the elephant is Lord of Africa. I moved on after a day as I saw the daughter of sixteen bathing in the creek and this sorely distressed my sleep. Not having consorted with harlots or been married I have never seen a woman of my own race completely devoid of clothing. I have vowed not to marry until I complete my work though St. Paul advises it is better to marry than burn. The sting of such threats was lost at Andersonville & I will content myself with women I know among the Sioux. I wondered why I fathered no children among them and a squaw told me they have herbs to prevent parentage until the proper time. I helped the Swedes make out their papers and assured them I would give them to the Gov't Land Agent of my acquaintance as they are fearful of another swindle. I reassured the father, telling him how to find me and that though I was a

man of the cloth I had proven good at correcting injustice. I
would as soon thrash a grafter as eat my lunch. You cannot roll
over as a plump southern possum to the evil of the frontier. I
confess I gave a large Black Hills gold nugget to the aforemen-
tioned girl, Aase by name, saying it would provide a dowry, or a
winter's food if the first crop failed.

I read and made markers until five, barely remembering
to smoke and forgetting altogether to drink the beer in the
refrigerator. My neck and eyes were sore, so I popped a can
and went outdoors. Dalva's car was gone and the horses were
in the corral. There was the childish wish to throw a few stones
at the horses out of vengeance, but the two culprits weren't
identifiable from the other two. I walked up to the corral and
the four of them charged the fence, so I leapt back. They stood
there staring at me intensely, and I couldn't help thinking they
wanted to make friends. I told them we were going to have to
work this thing out.

Back at the bunkhouse I opened another beer—my circadian rhythms demand a little alcohol late in the afternoon.
I was weary for change, so opened my first packet of letters,
which were for the year 1879. Much of the correspondence was
of a horticultural nature with a firm called Lake Country Nurseries, which was centered in Chicago but had branch offices in
La Crosse, Wisconsin; Minneapolis; Sioux Falls; Sioux City; and
Council Bluffs. It was evident that each office had an agent who
was responding to a series of questions from Northridge. The
responses were generally of an apologetic nature and it didn't
take long to determine that Northridge actually owned the
nursery business. This fact became specific in the bank correspondence from Chicago, which showed Northridge to have a
balance of some thirty-seven thousand dollars in August of
1879, not much in our day, but it must be multiplied by at least
a factor of seven to bring it to current terms of buying power.
I was astounded that a purported orphan and missionary to the
Indians could acquire this much money, despite the enormous
market for seeds, plants, root stock, and cuttings for the westward movement of settlers. I was too tired to look for clues and
waited impatiently for the arrival of Dalva to ask where the
capital came from. It was curious that none of the journal

passages mentioned this other life, as if it were a somewhat schizophrenic secret he was trying to keep from himself, though this was fragile speculation on my part.

Now it was six and I felt a pang of hunger. I was in somewhat of a huff as I walked to the house, bent on a sip of brandy. I gazed at the paintings for a few moments, touching their surfaces under the naïve idea they might be prints. I took a swig of a Hine that was bottled in the thirties, then one of a Calvados put away hastily on hearing Dalva roar down the long drive and into the yard. Passing through the kitchen, I quickly washed my mouth out with orange juice, then went outside.

"I peeked in your window but you were hard at work. These are sort of presents. I'm not trying to change your life overnight, just increase the braking power."

It took a few moments for me to determine that the UPS and air-freight cartons stacked in the backseat were from purveyors of food and wine in New York and California. I was overcome and felt my face redden. I had a rather meager childhood, but, then, so did everyone in our neighborhood. Christmas usually meant bedroom slippers, a horn for my third-hand bike, my first alarm clock, a fishing reel for a dirty river with no fish, a rubberoid football. The simplest gift tends to knock me for a loop. She came around the side of the car and gave me a squeeze and a kiss.

"Brandy. Or is that Calvados?" she asked after a whiff of my breath.

"I couldn't find any whiskey. I just took a tad." I was far too happy to pule and whine excuses.

○

Our first homestead evening went well, with a single discordant note: she wouldn't tell me where her great-grandfather got the capital to establish his nursery business. She thought it was important that I do my own detective work and arrive at conclusions that would gradually evolve. I verged on starting a quarrel, but she looked too good in a cotton summer skirt and pale-blue blouse, and the meal had been wonderful (a roasted, rough-cut filet of prime local well-hung beef, with a sauce made of dried morels and wild leeks sent from her mother's cousin in Michigan). As a joke I was served my cabernet in a sixteen-ounce Texas wineglass some fool had sent her. At the end of dinner I began a speech I had been rehearsing, an attempt to change the possible locations of lovemaking into something more comfortable. She listened with the usual attentiveness, then stood and suggested a drive, making my speech for nought.

It was a strange drive, a sense that you could see the June heat lifting off the earth, the greenness darkening as the twilight waned. Far off to the west there were thunderheads that caught the sun we could no longer see and made the air yellowish. We took a gravel road north that dead-ended at the Niobrara River, the wind around the speeding car too loud for talk. Dalva adapted her habit of alertness to her driving, and I felt reasonably safe as she swerved to a halt along the riverbank. There was a breeze being pushed by the distant storm that kept the mosquitoes away. I pointed out a rather alarming light in the east that turned out to be the moon. She said as a girl she had driven here a lot when the car was brand-new, and one August night she had seen three flying saucers. I began to mutter about this, but then she passed me a bottle of brandy she had been kind enough to bring along in her purse. A swallow of it made me quiver, and I felt a nonspecific eeriness about being out in nature in the dark, and tried to think of another time, short of the few camping trips of my youth. When I turned back from the moon and my general prattle, Dalva had taken off her clothes and was stepping into the river. I declined the invitation to join her, though a very small part of me wanted to do so; stepping willy-nilly into a black, flowing river is not in my repertoire. She swam away and I could see the sheen of the moon on her back and bottom. Then she stood up where the water was shallow, shook her hair, and let off with a blood-curdling howl. This jellied my bowels for an instant, but she quickly called to me that she was fine. Her howl put a stop to the night birds and insects. I saw bats flitting around but that was OK, since flying creatures are a positive category. A full minute later there was a yodel of some sort from the hills on the far side of the river, which I thought at first was an echo. Dalva, still out in the river, made another howl, in a much lower key, and the creature responded, or several of them did up and down the hills, and one of them downriver on our side. At first I supposed they were farm dogs, but there didn't seem to be any farms in the immediate area. She came out of the river and stood beside me, saying, Aren't coyotes wonderful? Instead of being a little frightened, I agreed—the year before I had helped my daughter with her science term paper on coyotes and thought of them as astounding, though it never occurred to me I would ever be in the middle of them. She shivered and I put my arms around her, moving her body around to dry her with my clothes. She laughed and kissed me; then we made love in the backseat of the car with an energy I could barely remember. We were both surprised by the lightning and thunder and had only made it halfway home when the rain came down in sheets of water. I know that when we got home, dried off and built a fire in the fireplace, and poured a brandy, she wanted to continue but felt she couldn't in the farmhouse. For a change, I said nothing on the matter.

○

I was startled awake at first light by the feeling that someone was looking in the window at me. I rushed outside in my shorts in an act of uncommon valor but no one was there except the horses staring from the corral. Don't they ever sleep? The geese along the creek set up a nasalated racket, and the red sky in the east gave the entire landscape a slightly pinkish cast. I could hear the excitable thud of my heart and a bird I recognized as a whippoorwill. I wondered idly if the Indians always got up at dawn or, if bored, they simply slept in like normal folks. It was probable that old Northridge never missed the first crack of day. One passage indicated that he was forever walking or riding his horse around when the moon was large. Different strokes, I thought, but, then, the mind is forever making comments the voice is wise enough not to speak.

Back in the bunkhouse I put a pot of coffee on the hot plate and took a shower. Certain thoughts had jolted my brain far too awake for me to go back to bed. One of them was the need for scholarly distance, which is far easier to manage in a carrel in a research library. We are not in business to lick the wounds of history but to describe them. While it is a truism that man has not learned much more than the sexual act, and that fire burns when you stick your hand into it, it behooves the scholar to immerse himself in the analyses of the problem, rather than the problem itself. One has to guard himself relentlessly against sentiment, mere opinion, speculation not based on fact. In the early seventies, when some of my fellow graduate students were involved in the American Indian Movement's occupation of Alcatraz, I chided them for being unprofessional: How can you study the nineteenth century when you become so emotionally involved with its sorriest descendants? And that was a question that stared back at me from my coffee, not that Dalva was sorry, but I was beginning to see that she was somehow a spiritual heir of those who were. My uneasiness was so intense that I jumped out of my skin when there was a knock at the door.

She was bringing my breakfast tray and the explanation that she would be gone throughout the day and perhaps half the evening at a horse function called a "cutting." I was instantly resentful enough not to inquire what a "cutting" was, though I had to admire her trim Western outfit. I peeked under the breakfast napkin and saw some bagels with cream cheese, and an ample pile of lox and raw onion. I had been so grotesquely involved in my work I had forgotten the food packages of the day before! Anyone who has known me would find this unbelievable. The moment she left I'd go inside and check the booty. I stood and hugged her, feeling her buttocks under the twill riding trousers, my wiener beginning to point through my parted robe. She gave it a friendly squeeze and asked if I'd mind going to town with old Lundquist, whom I hadn't met, at noon to pick up horse feed at the grain elevator. She added to please not let Lundquist go in the bar because Saturday afternoons tended to get out of hand. I assured her that I would keep the old geezer in check. We turned to see a rather garish Lincoln entering the yard towing a horse trailer, and off she went.

I would have settled for any tripish newsprint to go with my breakfast. I couldn't imagine a household without newspapers, magazines, or television, and here I was imprisoned within one, and my car in far-off Denver. We had meant to pick up Dalva's other car over at Naomi's. Maybe I'd call and fix her dinner: something incautious and Italian to counter this somewhat dismal outback. I begin to eat my lox and picked a later journal, from November.

## Aug. 25, 1877

At my camp on the Loup in the gravest melancholy the first anniversary of her death. [?] I have tried mightily to commune with her spirit and those of my dead friends among the Sioux but with only the very slightest of success. I have heard that there is a medicine man with the Cheyenne up in Lame Deer in Montana Territory that may help me in this matter, though my friend Grinnell says the most powerful men of this sort are to be found far to the southwest in Arizona. He counsels me to return to the strength of our own faith for solace. I said I do not sense the God of Israel alive in this land. Word was brought to me this morning that my friend and brother by his adoption, the brave White Tree, was clubbed to death at Fort Robinson for spitting on a soldier's saddle. He was dragged from his tipi at night by the soldiers so they could murder him in secret. His wife hid and witnessed this and sent me word. I feel an urge to murder the murderers deep in my gullet.

In my dreams my dead wife told me to leave this place of ours and so I will. In the dream there was a profusion barely short of horror and she was thin as on her deathbed, but her voice was sweet and melodic. We were in the canyon where we found the wolf cubs and took care not to disturb them. They were the merest pups but the largest, perhaps ten pounds in weight, made bold to frighten us away. In the dream the canyon was full of her favorite birds: the purple martin *(Progne subis),* the killdeer plover *(Aegialitis vociferus),* the least sandpiper *(Tringa minutillia),* also curlews & heron-shaped birds beyond my familiarity. We sat on a rock amid choke cherry, wild black currant, red osier dogwood, wolfberry, all in densest bloom. Her breath was close to my ear but she spoke not. I embraced her and she went into my body, the canyon disappeared, and I was transported alone to the summit of Harney's Butte. I suppose this to mean she is forever in my heart & blood.

Needless to say, this wasn't the sort of breakfast reading fare I needed. I have no belief in the human soul, but I didn't want my absence of a soul stretched that far this early. I quickly dressed to go inside, feeling some of the melancholy I do when I hear *Petrouchka,* or the Bach Partitas. Maybe I should start at the beginning, I thought, and avoid the surprise of lurid dreams and dead wives. It was difficult to imagine actually living through that period on a first-hand, intimate basis, as did Northridge: from the end of the Civil War to the massacre at Wounded Knee in 1890, the Great Plains were in a state of historical convulsion. It seems that governments have never evinced any particular talent or inclination for keeping the citizenry alive. Perhaps life itself was the remotest of preoccupations in Washington, D.C. I stood in the middle of the yard trying to stop myself. The grass was the deepest green and the geese were the whitest white. A psychiatrist once told me to try to concentrate on the physical world when my brain became a frazzled whirl. My wife divorced me because I couldn't stop. Period. I have to avoid novels and the cinema because they set me off. I have learned to guard my sympathies in order to minimize the range of my disappointments. The psychiatrist prescribed lithium but I was unable to complete my dissertation under the soporific influence of this drug. My marriage effectively ended on a two-day car trip up to Seattle to visit her parents. I had been reading an old text called *Extraordinary Popular Delusions and Madnesses of Crowds,* and talked about it nonstop while she drove. My jaw ached but I couldn't stop. I continued talking after she got out of the car with our daughter in Seattle. I remember turning on the radio so I would have someone to talk to! I think of myself as ninety-nine percent cured, though the use of alcohol as a sedative is occasionally counterproductive. I have to stop. I decided to chase the geese to watch them fly, but evidently they weren't the flying sort of geese. Several of them turned on me and I got my shins nipped while backpedaling. The largest—a male, I presumed—followed me right up to the pump-shed back door of the house. I hoped I hadn't started a permanent war, what with having to travel to and from the bunkhouse.

In the kitchen I opened the fridge to inspect the imported goodies, but then closed it immediately. I had just finished breakfast and wanted to wait until I was hungry to get the full impact of the food. I went into the den and looked at a shelf of books, picking out Thomas Carlyle's translation of Dante; it was a first edition and there was a dried flower marking a page with a passage underlined—"I wailed not so of stone I grew within; they wailed." In the first Northridge's hand was the note "The Sioux!" Fuck this melancholy, I thought. I went upstairs to Dalva's room on a snooping expedition, but my skin began to crawl, so I only stayed a moment. There were a number of photographs, including old ones of the succession of the three J. W. Northridges, plus Paul as a young man leaning on a shovel. I was drawn to a peculiar-looking young man on a pale horse who reminded me of Rimbaud on the cover of the Varese New Directions translation. There was a photo of Dalva and another handsome young woman taken in what looked like Montmartre, and another of Dalva and a striking though greasy-looking polo player in Rio. She gets around. The phone rang in her room and I rushed downstairs to the kitchen in order not to be caught red-handed. It was my daughter, who was thrilled that Dalva had written to invite her out for July and August, and had included an open round-trip plane ticket. We chatted about Dalva's offer to teach her to ride horses, and any number of things including her mother's rather happy remarriage to a Seattle stockbroker who was actually footing the bill for the private school she didn't want to go to. I was somehow pleased that she wanted to stay with me in San Francisco, however inconvenient it might be.

My next move was my most daring. I opened the door to the cellar but couldn't find any light switch. There were a number of kerosene railroad lanterns and several flashlights on a shelf. I took the largest flashlight and proceeded nervously down the steps, reminding myself that it was 1986 and there was nothing to fear but fear itself. The cellar was a huge, dry room, with only the large timbers that supported the house interrupting the airiness of the space. It was neat as a pin and had a varnished plank floor, which seemed curious. I had no intention of moving beyond the bottom step but from this vantage point I could see stacked steamer trunks, furniture, huge wooden shipping cases, an office-sized dehumidifier. To my right was a sturdy wire cage some fifteen feet square containing bins of wine. There was a combination lock on the door of the wine cage. I let out a small shriek when I heard a voice say, "You can't get at the wine." It was a gnome at the top of the stairs.

○

Old Lundquist proved to be inimitable; that is to say, there is no reason why another human should achieve his unique confirmation. I won't attempt to render the Swede accent that persisted despite the fact that he spent the entirety of his eighty-seven years in Minnesota and Nebraska. The accent was absurdly singsongy, with the end of a sentence or comment lifting upward but declining in volume, as if he were running out of breath. When I walked up the stairs and into the kitchen he repeated the comment about the wine several times, each time more woefully. Then he reached in the refrigerator, grabbed a can of beer, and quickly chugged it while backing away, as if I were bent on stopping him. It was at this odd moment that I mentally bet that Northridge had returned to the Swede settler's encampment and married the girl he had seen bathing, and that perhaps Lundquist was a relative— rather, a descendant. His nose seemed his largest feature, and he wore a soiled denim jacket buttoned to his Adam's apple despite the June warmth. On the way out through the pump shed he helped me on with a pair of coveralls, as if I were a child, or as if he had accurately estimated my incompetency. I had never worn farmer's coveralls before and they made me feel like a son of the soil.

So off to town we went in his 1947 Studebaker pickup, the best vehicle ever built in America, or so he said. Between us on the seat his ancient small terrier growled and humped at a pile of oily rags as if I were competing for the rags' affections. Lundquist drove painfully slow, his pale-blue eyes never leaving the vacant road, his arms stiff at the wheel. He said with an air of sternness that Dalva had told him I was a "drinker" and there was to be no stopping today at the tavern. Normally his daughter, Frieda, gave him two dollars, which allowed him two bottled beers or three drafts on Saturday afternoon, or one bottled beer and two schnapps—he went on with the permutations, but the upshot was that there were to be no treats because I was along. He saddened me, so I showed him the two twenty-dollar bills I had in my pocket. His face brightened, but then he said no, that my health was at stake.

To change the groggy subject, I began to interview Lundquist on his employer's family history. By experience I know these rural types insist on beginning at the virtual dawn of creation; in this case, the murder of his own grandfather during the Sioux uprising near New Ulm, Minnesota, in 1862. Lundquist had decided, for reasons he didn't care to explain, that all Indians were members of a "lost tribe of Israel," and our mistreatment of them would bring our eventual doom. I attempted to divert him from this gibberish back to actuality, with mixed luck. I damned myself for not having brought along my small dictaphone-recorder. After all, the man was eighty-seven and liable to drop dead at any moment. He began working for Dalva's grandfather in 1919, and thus had been a family employee for an astonishing total of sixty-seven years. I was tempted to inquire after his wages, but then he said he had received his own farm in a will when Dalva's grandfather had died in 1957. Lundquist had never expected to own anything—under the system of primogeniture the family farm had always gone to the oldest son. Immigrant families tended to perpetuate this European custom, creating the class of disaffected hired hands made up of younger sons, which helped fuel the Populist Revolt. I was brought up abruptly then by his statement that he would say nothing about the family without Dalva's permission. His deceased wife had mentioned a secret to a preacher and had been banished from the household the last year of "Mr. John W's" life. If he talked to me maybe his farm would be somehow taken back, and then what would happen to his daughter, Frieda, who had always been too big to find a husband? I attempted to get him rewarmed by directing him back to the Indians. He said Indians were ignored because they were bothersome. They were bothersome because they were a different kind of "animal" compared to us, wolves as opposed to foxes, horses compared to cows. This was peculiar enough to me to be interesting. We in the academic world like to think we are bathing the country in logic and right reason, when all you have to do is stop at a service station or read a newspaper to find out otherwise. There is a spine of goofiness in America that has never been deterred by literacy. It's not that we are in a genetic sump but that literacy, the educative system, barely scratches the surface of the ordinary consciousness. Just as we hit a bump on the gravel road and were choking on the road dust filtering up through the floorboards, Lundquist announced that once a Sioux boy had worked for the family. This boy had "secret powers," could beat up the toughest men, ride his horse at night while standing on it, and talk with wild animals. Everyone in the family and in town was happy when this boy disappeared. I made a note to question Dalva on the wonder boy. On the outskirts of town Lundquist looked at me with a trace of scorn and said that Dalva should have married the president of the United States, or at least the governor. He left me feeling like small potatoes when he stopped at a butcher shop, returning quickly with a single frankfurter for his dog. The terrier held the wiener in his mouth during a few moments of frantic growling, then closed his eyes and ate it with grim pleasure.

The upshot of the day was navy-blue shame, memory loss, minor recriminations, and what a scholar (the fabled Weisinger) called "the paradox of the fortunate fall," which (in short) means that if the hero (me) doesn't fall from grace because of his "hubris," there can be no reaffirmation of the common good. The bottom line was a little mayhem and public drunkenness. The downfall began with the miniature fiddle Lundquist kept under the seat of the pickup. Our intentions were still good at the grain elevator and feed store where I passed for white, was generally ignored and invisible like any bumpkin in bib overalls. We loaded up with bags of horse feed, then looked at each other and up and down the summery main street, which was crowded with farm families doing their Saturday shopping. There was an unworded agreement that it was a shame to leave this festive scene for a quick turnaround back home.

Our first stop was at the Swede Hall, where several dozen extremely old men were playing pinochle and drinking beer and schnapps. Lundquist went to the head of a big room and rapped on a table. Everyone stood with a certain irritation, which changed to applause and bows when I was introduced as a professor from "the coast of the Pacific" writing a history of the Northridge family. The room was acrid with the smell of cow manure, chewing tobacco, and kerosene. We made our way from table to table back toward the entrance, accepting gracefully little "snoots" and "snits" from bottles of low-grade whiskey such as Guckenheimer, which I had never seen outside of a steeltown.

Back on the street Lundquist rubbed his tummy and offered that he sure would like a hamburger to cut the raw whiskey if he had the money. I suggested the biggest steak in town but he said he couldn't chew steak, a hamburger would be fine. Off we went to the Lazy Daze Tavern for a massive burger with fried onions and a few cold beers. This bar was full of the largest men I had ever seen assembled in one place short of the San Francisco 49ers I had once studied at the airport lounge. Several of the men turned out to be from the posse that had rescued me, including the man who had hoisted me aboard the horse. He bought me a shot and said he hoped I had "got my bearings." A drunken wag insisted that Lundquist fetch his fiddle, which met with general agreement in the form of table-thumping.

It was an extraordinary performance, and I would not have traded the experience, though I would gladly have given the hangover to a television evangelist. Lundquist began with the Swedish national anthem (*Du gamla du fria, du fjällhöga Nord,*" etc.) with a few of the old men from his club who had filtered in joining him. It was really quite touching the way these codgers sang about a motherland they probably had never seen, looking upward at an invisible flag or vision with moist eyes. Lundquist continued with songs I hadn't heard since the Steelworkers Union picnics of my childhood: the "Battle Hymn of the Republic" (the whole room rowdy), "Red River Valley," "Drink to Me Only with Thine Eyes" (ironically), "Juanita" ("Soft o'er the fountain, ling'ring falls the southern moon," etc., with everyone coming in on the chorus, "Nita! Juanita! Lean thou on my heart," etc.), and others. I'm not by nature sentimental but became quite moved by it all, the way Lundquist would crane his prunish neck, his wavery voice being joined by all those farmers in their longing, as we all feel, for an imaginary Juanita. Then, as a sign-off, Lundquist played a few jigs, with several spry octogenarians dancing in unison, after which they all collapsed, quite parched, in a booth, where they resumed their pinochle game.

Up at the bar I was introduced to a younger man, about thirty, an outsider like myself, who was referred to with good humor as "Nature Boy." I am aware enough of bar etiquette to know that "Nature Boy" would normally be an overt term of ridicule, but exceptions could be made: every village in America owns a huge oaf named Tiny. In this particular case the sobriquet was used in a light, jocular way, because the man in question, though only a little over average height, was well muscled and had an air about him of the bounty hunter or soldier of fortune. We played several games of eight ball and I found out he was doing a survey on a large piece of federal land north of town on the effect that surrounding farming practices had on the flora and fauna. He mentioned his sponsor, one of a dozen nonprofit environmental groups, the activities of which have confused me for years. My ex-wife was forever trying to save, from a distance, everything from mountains and whales to rivers and baby seals. In my conversation with Nature Boy there was a little of the embarrassment of being the only two educated men in the tavern, though he seemed oblivious to this.

Our pool game was interrupted by a tussle between two behemoths over one selling another a group of calves with something called "shipping fever." They were bent on squeezing each other to death and knocked the heavy pool table against the wall. Everyone in the area tried to stop them by piling on when they hit the floor, and it reminded one of those nasty incidents in a professional football game where control is only tentatively reestablished by referees. The ozone of violence pushed me to drink a little quickly, and I was forced to doze in a booth with Lundquist and the odorous pinochle players. After I don't know how long, Lundquist actually yelled "Yumpin' Yiminy" and we were out of there in a trice. It was getting late—twilight, to be exact—and Frieda would be angry if he was late for dinner. Drunk, he drove twice as fast as sober, and halfway home we caromed off into a soggy ditch. I remember we argued about the next course of action and apparently agreed on falling asleep. At some point we were located by two sheriff's deputies, Dalva, Naomi, Frieda, a wrecker, and various concerned folk. I was taken home and put to bed without supper in the bunkhouse, waking in hysterics in the middle of the night because I was being chased by an Indian who resembled a minotaur in Ghirardelli Square. I wrapped myself in a sheet and stumbled out into the serene moonlight, curling up on the ground, where I discovered myself in the morning covered by flies and surrounded by geese feet.

○

This woeful experience kept me on the straight and narrow for several weeks. I worked like a demon for days from dawn to dusk, as if I were trying to save my life and good name, which was the point. My first few days in Nebraska, I realized, had been a bit trying, to myself and others. Dalva, by never uttering a word of criticism, allowed me to stew in the juices of self-knowledge. For instance, under my white sheet tent, and guarded by geese, I was trying to think of a way to put a good face on a top-ten hangover when Dalva arrived with ice water, aspirin, a wet washcloth, a glass of fresh orange juice, and a thermos of coffee. She was dressed prettily and on her way to church with Naomi. Rather than saying, "Michael, Michael, Michael," then lacing into me as my ex-wife would have done, Dalva merely said, "I hoped you weren't dead," wiped my face with the washcloth, helped with the water and aspirins, poured the first cup of coffee. I could see under her skirt, which bore the same infantile excitement as seeing up the teacher's dress at school. Oh, to be a groundhog, burrowing there, searching for health. She did say Lundquist had walked over early that morning to apologize for letting me drink. It was a seven-mile round trip on foot, and sometimes he had to carry the dog, who tended to lose interest in walking. Frieda was denying him use of his pickup for the day. The dog, out of sympathy, had kept the geese away from my sleeping body, and had even fetched me a stick to play with if I ever awoke. She handed me the stick and drove off for church. In my own friendly circle of louts and abrasive intellects I didn't know anyone who went to church. I could see her singing hymns in her white underpants. There's a sexual pathology in severe hangovers that I never quite understood; booze in large quantities acts as a shock treatment, and the unlived sexual life hits you pretty hard in the morning. My ex-wife, who was a truly horny soul, tended to take advantage of my Sunday-morning illnesses. Now I became meditative, as if the white sheet were the Himalayas—I reminded myself to call a Jungian I knew and ask him where the redskin minotaur came from.

When I threw off the sheet the second time Dalva was home from church and busy digging out the barnyard spring that led into the creek. The day had become hot and she was wearing shorts, halter, and knee-high rubber boots, an incitement for me to help out. I chugged the thermos of coffee, went to the bunkhouse and put on my coveralls and boots, and joined her. I was a little dizzy but dug vigorously by her side, waiting for her to say something complimentary about my efforts. Instead she prattled about the humor in the sermon—in these Last Days we are all hostages to our doom, whether in Beirut or Omaha—so I dug even harder until suddenly the sky darkened and I pitched backward into the cold creek, which just as quickly revived me. She stood over me with more than a trace of concern, and, looking up at her from this vantage, she reminded one of an S&M Valkyrie. She said I probably had forgotten my high-blood-pressure pills, and also needed something to eat. I admitted it had been twenty-four hours since my hamburger. I rolled over and used my hands to drag myself into the shallow current and wash off the mud, a fully clothed fish, possibly a carp.

After lunch and back at the desk, I began to brood about the nature of time and how it is involved with the private struggle, usually in silence, with public life. Memoirs, especially those that attempt to sum up an entire life, tend to gloss over this struggle: the utterly wrong turns, paths, marriages, decisions, time as a flood of vertigo sweeping all of us over the edge of being, time, which never forgave anyone a single second. A little girl I loved, who used to proudly make me snow angels on January hillsides in the sooty Ohio Valley, drowns in suspicious circumstances, after three marriages, in tropical waters. I see her long hair floating, her body tumbling in the tidal rush.

At lunch I had asked Dalva about the Indian wonder boy Lundquist had mentioned. And that's what I mean. It was thirty years ago but she bridled, reddened, became cross.

"There's no such thing as an Indian. You know that, for Christ's sake. There are Sioux, Hopi, Cheyenne, Apache. . . ."

"What about this magic Sioux boy Lundquist talked about?" I repeated.

"What did he say?" Her back was turned at the stove.

"Nothing much. He rode horses at night and talked to animals and scared people. That's all."

"I barely knew him. He was just another sorry cowboy who stopped by for a few months of work."

"There's a few months missing in the 1860s," I said, sensing that a change of subject was in order. She relaxed and continued making one of my favorite hangover remedies (linguine in a sauce made of fresh peas, julienned prosciutto, a mixture of fontina and asiago cheeses).

"When you read on you see that after he delivered a letter to a widow in Sault Sainte Marie in Michigan, he boarded a schooner for Duluth that wrecked in a storm between Grand Marais and Munising. He seemed pleased that the rest of the widow letters were lost at sea."

She poured my ration of wine as if nothing had happened the day before. Those not in the know vis-à-vis alcohol fail to understand that after a serious day of boozing the drinker can't simply quit, but must taper off and enter a temperate glide pattern. As she served lunch there was still a trace of flush on her face from my initial question. Of course I realized it was pointless to test the dimensions of her hospitality. Also I loved her. Also I was somewhat frightened of her.

"I've got a few days of horse business in Rapid City. I'm sure you can take care of yourself? Naomi will get you to your Rotary speech."

"I'll bury myself in my work. If you're going away perhaps we could have a date tonight."

"Perhaps." The phone rang and I looked at her remaining food, having finished my own. I had reached over to nail a forkful when she shrieked and I dropped my fork, feeling like an asshole.

It turned out that the caller was her uncle Paul and he had

managed, with the aid of the Mexican detective, to find the abused boy. Despite her joy on the phone she noticed my discomfort and gestured to me to finish her lunch. She began speaking in rapid Spanish to the boy, then back in English with Paul. When she hung up the phone I gave her a hug, smelling the sunlight absorbed by her neck. Then she returned to the phone to call her brother-in-law, Ted, and his employee Andrew, and I went out the door and back to work.

What I mean with time: it is more the phone call that doesn't come than the one that did. The rage for order doesn't create a concomitant space in which order might occur. As Angus Fletcher quips in his powerful piece on Coleridge, "Time in our world displays an instantaneity so perfect in its slippery transit—its slither from one temporal fix to another—that there is nothing to mark, let alone measure, its being, its at-homeness." And this, of course, is why some folks expire from dread. Coleridge is described as "a solitary haunted by vast conceptions in which he cannot participate." He is a hero of consciousness, always standing at the threshold, an edge at which participation in the sacred and the profane are always simultaneous, always possible. This is not less poignant for the fact that the knowledge drove Coleridge batty, though the definition of "batty" has recently been redefined by a hyperthyroid Englishman named Laing.

To bring all of this down to earth, old Northridge devotes twenty-five years, from 1865 to 1890, trying to help the defeated native population adapt to an agrarian existence, but the native population is being driven hither and yon by the government and has never had a good piece of land that hasn't been removed from them instantly. And the effect of the Dawes Act in 1887 was, intentional or not, to further the swindle, so that within thirty years one hundred million acres of their initial one hundred twenty-five had been taken from them. To be sure, much of it was "purchased," as if these nomads were cagey M.B.A.'s striking a tough bargain.

But this all is on the record, though largely ignored, and Northridge isn't. We academics are known for creating artificial questions to which we give artificial answers, thus ensuring our continuing employment. Northridge is interesting because of his consciousness and his conscience, just as Schindler alone is fascinating while millions of Germans who didn't give a fuck are lost to history. . . .

○

Jesus Christ! There is a face peering in the window above my desk! It is Lundquist and I slide open the window, closed because I've been using the air conditioning. He is sweating but still wears the jacket buttoned to the neck. He wonders if I might have a beer for him? I ask him in but he doesn't want to be discovered by anyone. I pass a beer through the window and a small chunk of salami for the dog. Lundquist finishes the beer in a moment, then scurries off through the burdocks with the terrier backward over his shoulder giving a farewell bark. That means the old fool will be covering altogether fourteen miles on a hot June day. I caution myself against pitying the man—he is a full fifty years older than I am and it is apparent he is enjoying life, a matter at which I haven't proved myself. I mentally dismiss the idea that I could get family secrets from Lundquist by bribing him with booze. There are ethical considerations. Or are there?

**December 26, 1865, Chicago**
**I have been here two weeks now and in the morning will set off for La Crosse, Wisconsin to learn more of my mission about which I have the gravest doubts. Chicago is a prison though a great deal less onerous than Andersonville. Traveling over five months I have avoided cities from Georgia to Sault Ste Marie at the nether end of Michigan, where there were snowflakes in early October, though when the sun came through roiling clouds there were the deciduous golds and reds of New England autumn. I wished to see the shoreline so I bought a ticket on a trading schooner that would stop at various ports rather than a steamer that would traverse Lake Superior directly from the Soo to Duluth. The schooner, Ashtabula by name, was manned by drunken fools, and the Captain, Ballard by name, the worst of a sad lot. This man would not be a third mate out of Boston. He brought the boat about suddenly & it broached, capsizing near the harbor mouth of Grand Marais, a trading post in a charmless swamp. All of us survived by God's grace & shallow water. It was**

there I lost two precious journals of my trip north, saving a small one in my pocket from prison and month afterwards. From Grand Marais I made a two-day walk some forty miles to Munising, and I should say the moment I was beyond reach of the despicable crew I entered country that has few equals on God's earth. I studied this land at Cornell through the work of the great Scientist of Harvard Agassiz who made an expedition here many years ago. The Boston poet Longfellow wrote of this land in Hiawatha though I am unaware if he travelled there, poets out of tradition being of tall imagination and little good sense. Since the War I have lost my taste for Emerson but the good man should have walked here in country beside which the woodlots of New England are pale. I saw great bears, heard wolves howling in chase through trees three men could not have encircled with their arms. Before I left the Soo and the ingenious locks for which many men died in cold and cholera, I met an Ojibway at the local mission of the unlikely name of Chief Bill Waiska, who stood a full six and a half feet and weighed a little short of three hundred, though there was no surplus flesh on him. He was witty, kind, and tolerated my questions with humor. It is certain that if given enough land these vigorous people will endure and thrive despite living in the foulest climate in the United States. The Chief told me that two hundred years ago just west of here his people battled an Iroquois war party and in total a thousand warriors died. He is a reader and said with a twinkle that poor Indians could not match the magnificent numbers of Antietam, Gettysburg, Vicksburg. These people understand us with a clarity no one has supposed.

My host in Chicago, Samuel _____, for he wishes anonymity, is a prominent merchant of this city and a Quaker. He said I would have enjoyed the city more had there been fewer people in mourning from the War. Everywhere on the street one sees the dazed faces of survivors, many of whom have lost limbs, the faculties of reason and the will to work. It is this merchant who journeyed to Ithaca to visit his son at Cornell and struck the bargain with me & thus I ransomed body & soul, taking his son's call to conscription. His son was headstrong, impetuous, and a drinker, and has disappeared West, not wanting to be a merchant. His parents are overwhelmed with sadness, nevertheless they fulfilled their obligations to me. This merchant will oversee my business until it is well established, hopefully by spring when I will return before my trip West. During sleepless nights, or when I wake from nightmares of prison, I wonder if my beloved and deceased mother in Heaven can see my shame, the sins of pride and greed that led me to gamble my life. I could not bear to spend my life designing & constructing gardens for rich men who often cannot tell a rhododendron from a pear tree. One is neither guest nor servant, but in between the two, and at close hand there is a preposterous laziness. I pushed both wives & daughters, cousins and guests from my bed. It is said in the Old Testament in Amos 3:15 "And I will smite the winter house with the summer house; and the houses of ivory shall perish, and the great houses shall have an end, saith the Lord."

I noticed a rather grudging return to religion, so looked in the chest for the small notebook that included the passage on his departure from Andersonville. The notebook was evidently the survivor of the shipwreck. The dates meant that there were four months of missing material from Michigan, but, then, the history of that state at that time was the race between competing lumber barons to cut down every tree enclosed by Lake Michigan and Lake Huron. In my youth at a summer camp sponsored by my dad's union up in Michigan I saw the few dozen remaining virgin trees, and they looked lonely indeed. The girls at a neighboring camp were not allowed to socialize with us poor union brats. These girls paddled the lake in swift green canoes, while we rowed heavy, shabby rowboats. They all seemed to be blond and one of them "mooned" us with her bare bottom when we rowed past their beach. It was an attractive insult and represented all that is unattainable about wealth. It suddenly occurred to me that Dalva's horse business in Rapid City might be seen as a euphemism for visiting a gentleman friend, perhaps a rancher of wealth and power. The cuckold again.

### June 1865. Georgia
I do not know the day, and none in my vermin-ridden pack of men knows the day. We are together for safety. Mother always abjured me to look daily after the condition of my soul, but yesterday I saw a man shot for a dead dog another man wanted for supper.

In the land of dog eaters no one has a soul. I surprised our pack by snaring a deer near a swamp with a snare common to the Iroquois. I traded the heart and liver of the deer at a parsonage in Rome, Georgia, for the coat and collar of an Episcopalian cleric, and was again able to travel alone. It is unthinkable that the gov't let General Sherman burn & pillage Georgia, and now wishes to starve the survivors. Have noted many non-indigenous plants: camellia, oleander, gardenia, tea roses, azaleas, kalmias. Have enjoyed some hospitality with Georgians with my new collar, also my knowledge of botany & gardening.

June. Solstice. 1865. Tennessee
Along the road I met a thin young woman who wished to sell herself for something to eat. I had caught some catfish in the Tennessee River & smoked them bathed in salt over green hickory, and traded one of the fish for a loaf. I shared this supper with her, and she was nonplussed by my refusal to bed with her. My confinement was short and I am now in good health so I brooded in the night about the sin of fornication. I turned with desire to her at first light, but she had slipped away, taking with her the remaining smoked fish. I was forced to laugh at this incident. Talked to old black witch about local medicinal plants—snake root, ginseng, carolina pink, angelica, senna, anise and spikenard. She shared with me her dinner, a stew of opossum and a squirrel and flavored by hot peppers she grew, also delicious wild-cherry wine. I impulsively gave her a silver locket of my mother's. We prayed together though her prayers were more African than Christian. Her daughter, a high-spirited girl who was pregnant, came by the log hut and finished the pot of stew and joined us in wine drinking. I confess I slept with this black girl who smelled of woodsmoke and sassafras & was uncommonly happy in my sin. . . ."

This combination of the sacraments of food and sex drove me to the house. It was almost five in the afternoon anyway, and my belly burbled its need for a bite and a drink. I was pleased to see that Naomi had come over and we were to have a Sunday-evening picnic on the front lawn. Dalva went in the house to mix a pitcher of martinis. I pretended to be bored with the idea but my hair roots tingled at the prospect. While

Dalva was off on her mission Naomi rather shyly said that an ex-student of hers was an intern on the county newspaper for the summer before she went off to college, and would like to interview me tomorrow, on Monday. Was this possible? I affected a little strain and agreed to do so during my lunch break. Dalva was coming down the porch steps and knew of the request.

"If you touch her you'll doubtless get your ass shot off. I went to school with her father."

"Dalva, he's old enough to be her father," Naomi said, not without merry irony.

My hands were sweating for the martini, but I looked off at the blooming lilacs of the family graveyard as if offended. "I think I'm capable of regarding beauty without leaping at it like a flying squirrel. In all my years of teaching I've never taken advantage of a student, even when it was thrust at me."

"Oh, bullshit." She handed me a cold glass and gave me a peck on the cheek. "I saw Karen in town yesterday and I assure you no one will ever take advantage of her—technically, that is. I'm just saying a deer rifle leaves a big hole in a deer."

"If you like, I'll come over and chaperone," Naomi offered.

"I accepted an interview before I was aware of all of this. Now I'm a fucking deer with his guts blasted out. You forget I'm a father. In my wildest fantasies I haven't poked anything under twenty since I was under twenty."

They grew tired of teasing me and began discussing the possibility of a family reunion in July. I felt a little like a discarded trinket and edged toward the picnic table and the pitcher of martinis. Their base accusations had made me nervously gulp my first drink. My curiosity urged me to walk into their lilac-surrounded family graveyard but I hesitated—two years ago I had visited my father's grave with my mother and I had hyperventilated, bawling like a baby. This was quite a shock, since I think I live readily under the assumption that I know myself, and understand others with some accuracy, despite the number of times I catch myself off balance. Most of life is lived, perforce, simplemindedly; to think of Spinoza when you're taking a pee is to risk missing the bowl.

Naomi sensed my martini nervousness and refilled my

glass half full. While Dalva sliced a ham, Naomi told me about her two days spent with a visiting naturalist, Nelse, talking about her bird-count records since the forties. From her description of the man I figured out he was the nature boy I met in the Lazy Daze Tavern. She made him Sunday breakfast; then he was off to Minneapolis to feed his data into a computer. Naomi said there weren't as many songbirds or hawks anymore due to an amazing assortment of causes: high-tension wires, huge TV-transmitting aerials, auto traffic, pesticides, destruction of migratory habitats in Louisiana and Mexico, destruction of all hedgerows in modern farm practices, which reduced nesting possibilities. As I ate I admitted to myself that it never occurred to me that birds had living conditions.

I subscribe to a half-dozen food magazines that are blithely unaware how certain people eat at home: this afternoon it was a ham that the noble Lundquist had smoked and aged, tiny fresh new potatoes, the year's first spinach in a salad; even the horseradish had been pureed from a root in the garden and mixed with heavy cream from a neighbor's herd. It was possible to resent the amount that Dalva could eat because she was so active. She and Naomi were talking about some disturbing aspects of the farm problem. Two more local farms and their families were going under, and there was the barely mentioned undercurrent that there might not be enough students to merit opening the country school, leaving Dalva adrift. Naomi was, surprisingly enough, on the board at the only local bank, and was upset with the misunderstanding spread by the national press: most rural banks are farmer-owned and -operated, so in essence they are borrowing from each other, rather than from some abstract banking community. It's hard to blame the banker when the "banker" works the neighboring farm. Two men in the adjoining county had recently taken their lives—one a hired hand who had to be let go after thirty years of work. I wanted to say something incisive about money and credit in inexperienced hands but held my tongue. Instead, I told them that circa 1887 a half-million farmers were basically starved out of this longitude and to the west of here, because they had been lied to about the amount of rainfall, even though it could have been checked in an atlas or almanac.

"If it's been raining for three years it's been raining forever," Dalva said. "Then the fourth year it didn't rain at all."

I tended to forget that she had read all the journals during her nervous collapse. I reminded myself to try to pry out of her the reasons, because she seemed the unlikeliest candidate I ever met for mental problems.

"Back then the first John Wesley went around buying up abandoned land for a dollar or so an acre," Naomi said. "He tried to resettle some Lakota Sioux families but the government stopped him. My grandparents knew him and after I married into the Northridge family I was told that John Wesley was the bogeyman they used to make children behave. All that land and money, and this was a grand house to be built in those days, when everyone else was scraping by." Naomi poured me the rest of the wine, for which I was grateful. "I was frightened of Dalva's grandfather, but the old folks said he was nothing compared with his father." Naomi got up from the table then, saying she was tired. She had checked out a prairie-falcon nest with Nelse at daylight and wasn't getting any younger. She tousled my thin hair and said she was proud I had the courage to camp outdoors the night before. She laughed very hard at her own joke. So did Dalva, and so did I. "Teddy Roosevelt said you don't know a man until you've camped with him and that includes yourself." I offered this lame *non sequitur,* which further amused them. I began to understand that the main way of criticizing someone in rural areas is to make a joke at his or her expense. Despite the heaviness of the intent the joke was liable to be breezy. Dalva had said that when she looked out her bedroom window in the morning she was pleased to see her first mummy in the barnyard, and the geese were there as a temple guard.

When Naomi left we sat there listening to the gravel ping off the underside of her car. I made Dalva stay seated while I cleared the table and carried the leftovers and dishes indoors. Inside, I drank the rest of the martini pitcher, but it was mostly melted ice. Back on the front porch, I saw her in the far corner of the yard, pushing an empty tire swing as if it held an imaginary child. I am thought to be insensitive in such matters, but there was something poignant in the way she pushed the empty swing back and forth, a solemn rhythm in the twilight. For the first time in weeks I thought of her lost son and my rash offer to find him. She turned and walked toward me slowly, still dressed in her riding jeans. We embraced in the middle of the yard and I felt that rare feeling of being more than myself, that my human failings were being absorbed by the leaves in the trees above us, and perhaps the darkening sky above the trees was helping out. I felt an evanescent fatherliness, a wish to take any pain away with an embrace, something I had felt many times with my daughter. She whispered something in Spanish about wishing "to sleep the dream of apples," which made me smell appleness. She kissed me with an open mouth and I'll be goddamned if it didn't dizzy me. For some not so incoherent reason the kiss drew me back to when I was a busboy at the country club and all lovely girls, near and far but mostly far, smelled of horses. There was clover and lilac in the air, and the yellowish light of the rising moon. I sensed all my ironical urges as a poisonous weight in a corner of my heart. In the small of her back I felt a strength I could never have, and wasn't sure I would want. Way back there Northridge had said that if God has made us strong, then weakness is blasphemy.

We thought we'd make a run on the motel way down the road (over forty miles on the interstate), but my mouth opened to its carnival barker's options the moment we got in her car. "We are all most lovely not making love but just before," a poet friend had said, and if we had simply flopped on the lawn and made love the evening would have been perfect.

"This is fucking absurd. I mean driving this far, the same distance as San Francisco to Sonoma, Chicago halfway to Madison. Why don't you and Naomi have a motel built down the road for entertaining your houseguests?"

She had started the car, but turned it off as if waiting for me to complete my thought. She gave me a look of complete incomprehension, and I tried to get out of the hole I was digging. There was always the chance I could lose her if I couldn't become a little more than myself.

"For God's sake, don't just sit there looking at me. Start the fucking car. I'm sorry. I guess my nerves are a little frayed. I beg your forgiveness."

"I really think you should go alone," she said, handing me

the keys. "I'll see you in a few days. Be careful." Then she got out of the car and walked toward the house. I sat there a full ten minutes examining all the dimensions of self-loathing. A few tears actually fell. I held up my hands before my face in the gathering dark and I didn't like them. I heard a whippoor-will from over by the ditch and I craved a soul as serene as a bird's. The light came on in Dalva's bedroom and that yellow square made me unfathomably lonely. I went into the house and located a bottle of vodka. I wanted to leave a note but could only come up with "Have a good trip. I'm sorry. Love, Michael." I stood there, wishing her down the stairs in a night-gown, all smiles with light step and heart. I have no secret powers, I thought.

Out in the bunkhouse I set the vodka on my desk, made a pot of coffee, and turned on the radio. I meant to work all night, like some Great Plains Faustus, or, to be less dramatic, like a penniless graduate student. I took a pull from the bottle and imagined myself in the Nebraska night to be on the verge of a discovery, a historical equivalent of DNA. I picked a Northridge journal at random, too excitable to continue the methodical beginning-to-end routine. I flicked the radio dial to a PBS station out of Lincoln that was broadcasting one of those "music from many lands" programs. You can only care so much; then you bury yourself in your work. At least this is what a nitwit says to himself after he's created the kind of emotional shitstorm that drives the beloved away. The radio played a song by the Jamaican Bob Marley with a lyric that said "brutal-ize me with music." My ex-wife danced to this very song for exercise while I sat at the kitchen table writing witty lecture notes. I'd plot a usually successful beery leap at her when she emerged from the shower. I held a journal in my hands, feeling unworthy, and tried to remember a small Latin prayer that a Jesuit professor of mine always uttered at the beginning of our Shakespeare class. I suppose I don't feel unworthy often enough to remember such a prayer.

**March 7, 1874**
**Summoned by a messenger from He Dog who says the little daughter of Crazy Horse, They Are Afraid of Her, is ill with the same cough as the trader's children. I am useless against this**

whooping cough which is often survived by white children but almost never by the Sioux. I pack up my herbs and medicines, and all the dried meat I have left which scarcely fills one saddle-bag. Only last October I gave this little girl several apples I had grown and she laughed seeing the shadow of her reflection on the polished fruit. I headed out on the two-day ride seeing everywhere the dire effects of the worst winter in memory. In one draw there were the carcases of dead deer, really only the skins after the ravens and coyotes had fed, as if the deer had decided to die together. Those who have stopped by my cabin say that both Sioux and settlers are alike near starvation. And with buffalo so sparse there is little fuel provided by their dried dung. If my pack horse had not died I could have brought potatoes, carrots, cabbages, and turnips I have grown.

March 8, 1874
I have made camp unsure of how to proceed. I am a few hours from the Tongue River where I was told to go. I am so disturbed I cannot help but weep. A few hours ago I was surveying the country with my ship captain's telescope and saw movement on a far hill. Imagining I had found game I tethered my horse, and took my rifle to stalk the hilltop slowly. I crawled along a low rock abutment then sighted with my telescope again. The movement had been on a small burial platform and Crazy Horse sat beside the small, red-wrapped bundle that must be his daughter, They Are Afraid of Her. I was too late. He touched her playthings that hung on one of the posts, an antelope-hoof rattle, and a painted willow hoop. He lay down beside her and took her still body in his arms.

Back to my horse I made camp though lit no fire. I prayed for her soul so that my heart twisted painfully in my chest. I wrapped myself in my buffalo robe and had no will but to watch the sky grow dark and the cold wind blow the colder stars around the sky, as my thoughts were those of a crazed man. I heard wolves and the beauty of their chorus I imagined welcomed the little girl into a better heaven than my own. I saw her again hold the shiny apple to her lips & heard her laughter when she first bit the crisp fruit. She gave the core to her pup, and her mother Black Shawl held her before the fire until she slept. My heart could not imagine her dead, and in the night I prayed that this greatest of all Sioux men would bring his daughter back to life with his embrace, as Jesus did to Lazurus.

March 9, 10, 11, 1874
There is a trace of early spring today so I sit in a niche of rock like an Italianate statue feeling some warmth out of the wind. My dreams were too troubled to note & in the light of morning I think of my professor at Cornell who knew the myths of the Norse & Greeks. I wonder if our Lord is only the Lord of the Mediterranean area and something else is afoot in this sere landscape. Crazy Horse nodded to me the day after I brought the fruit last fall, but we have never otherwise spoken. He Dog said they were all troubled of late when three warriors found him sitting among a herd of buffalo speaking to the beasts who were not disturbed. My predilection for science leads me to cynicism about such tales, though there is something to the man of the god on earth as in the myths I have read. In former times before Christ came to earth gods & men were said to be confused in their identities.

I am here another night. I could not help but stalk the platform within a half-mile and saw he still lay there with the body of his daughter. I wondered at his thoughts and whether he would make war again on us who brought this pestilence to his country. The Sioux commonly think we purposefully infected the trouble-some Mandans with smallpox so as not to have the bother of hanging them as we did 39 Santees up in Mankato. Ate a thin sage hen I snared and am sleepless before the small fire.

A cold stormy day, and a night when the constellations seemed to draw too close until I was frightened.

This morning I made my way to the encampment but stopped a good distance away as I heard wails of mourning. He Dog rode out to greet me and I made him the gift of the dried meat. He said he watched me sit in the hole in the rock during two days but did not approach me as this is a place where men go to understand the world. At that moment he looked over my shoulder & saw Crazy Horse riding toward the encampment. I bade He Dog goodbye, not wanting to intrude. As I rode off toward home I became so lost in my thoughts I did not direct my horse which carried me within a hundred yards passing the platform. I looked up from my mind & saw the small red bundle and the ravens encircling it far overhead. This loosened my tears so I rode hard into the cold wind.

On my second day riding & within an hour of my cabin I encountered a detachment of Cavalry headed by Lieut. _____ whom I despise enough to shoot if I could do so with impunity. Once near the Dismal River he wished to question me on Sioux movements but I would only answer in Latin which disgusted him & his men. They would drive me from the West were not the Methodists such a fearsome political power, a fact that holds some humor. On this day I rode on as if the detachment did not exist & the Lieut. shot in the air as a joke to startle me but I did not swerve. They are still angry as before Christmas in Yankton several years ago I thrashed two drunken soldiers who rode me down in the street, thus spilling a 100 lbs. of flour I was carrying into the mud, and no charges were brought against me. This was witnessed by several Sioux who were amused and spread the tale. General Miles questioned the head of our Mission in Omaha about the nature of my religious and agricultural activities among the Sioux. The head of Missions is a sanctimonious fop but knows I am by comparison wealthy & defers to me as religious leaders do to Mammon. General Miles does not understand I have no pact with the Sioux or any other tribe but that my preoccupation with trees, plants & herbs, rather than Jesus is thought among them to be a sacred calling. I am also a student of their language & dialects and on long winter days & nights I speak to myself in Sioux. He Dog, however, was once troubled by my graftings, slips & plant breeding, wondering if I had abrogated the proper work of the Earth.

A red bundle & antelope-hoof rattle. I poured another drink and went outside. It was well after midnight but the moon was bright and, though ignorant of the stars, I studied them, wondering if they were the same ones to be seen on a March night so long ago. I had made a note to buy a general horticulture text, since half the journals were full of that sort of material and it was as distant to me as trigonometry. Sensing a presence, my skin tingled, but it was the horses staring at me from the corral. The Sioux were weak on taxonomy and at one time thought of them as "sacred dogs." I begin to speak to the horses in a low, even voice, repeating nonsense syllables, bits of poetry ("what can ail thee, wretched wight"), snatches of commercials, all the while shuffling closer to them. They stayed there until we were almost nose to nose over the top slat of the corral; then one shied away. Maybe he smelled the booze and had been beaten by a drinker as a child! The others stayed, but I didn't attempt to pet them. I accepted it as a small triumph that I didn't piss them off. Tomorrow I might try to extend my luck with the geese. Then I heard a distant coyote and turned for the comfort of the bunkhouse, the guitar music of Soria I could hear through the screen.

I read and skimmed all night, avoiding passages that held any violent emotional impact. Frankly, I found some of the Northridge passages too extreme for my disposition, tending to scramble and fray my nerve ends. When my daughter, Laurel, was a very little girl and was either sick or had bad dreams, I would hold her and dance slowly around the living room to the radio. She had a bright-red terrycloth robe she wore until it was tatters, and then she still slept with the shreds. It finally doesn't matter that fathers are misunderstood. I went over in the corner and stooped before a bookcase holding volumes that had been there when I arrived, including a complete set of Zane Grey. On the flyleaf of *Riders of the Purple Sage,* I read, "This book owned by Duane Stone Horse from Parmelee S. Dakota 1956," whoever that was. I heard a crowing that Dalva had said was a cock pheasant. Like roosters, they announced day—it is rather like a male to announce the obvious. I headed for my bed, being reasonably sure that the ghosts that might bother me had fled back into the ground. Out here the spirits required more than a light bulb to keep them away.

○

A rapping. "Are you in there, sir?" More rapping. "Should I come back some other day?"

I hustled to the screen door, forgetting I was naked, and my confused morning wiener was pointing forty-five degrees upward at a dream. It was a girl of incomparable loveliness. She held up my ravaged breakfast tray and spoke in a whispery voice, politely averting her eyes.

"I'm afraid the geese ate your breakfast. Shall I come back later?"

"Not at all. Of course not. Just a second." I turned and scrambled for my robe. There was no way I was going to let her out of my sight. I tapped my dick against the desk to bring it to its senses.

She brought in my coffee thermos and two notes. "I'm Karen Olafson. I'm just floored to meet a man who has written books. Naomi said you were just the smartest man she ever met."

She was tall, probably five nine, with darkish blond hair, green eyes, in a beige summer skirt, sandals, a white sleeveless blouse. She rounded her shoulders slightly to misannounce the size of her breasts. She was blushing and toyed at a large class ring hanging from a silver chain around her neck. I stared at it, pretending ignorance—for a while my daughter wore the ring of a pimply oaf who delivered rather good pizzas.

"Does it look stupid? I suppose it does. Really, if I'm in your way . . ." She glanced at the messy desk and half-empty vodka bottle. I sat her down, poured myself coffee, and took my two notes into the bathroom. The first was Dalva's and a reflection of the sad ending to our evening—"I can't help liking you even though you're an asshole." What a way with words. The other note read, "Dear Mister Lazy Bones. We brought your car over. Please call if you get lost or drunk. Your servant, Frieda Lundquist." Out the bathroom window I could see Dalva's muddy Subaru. I hadn't quite got a fix on Big Frieda. In the kitchen she kept a stack of the sort of romantic, bodice-ripping novels my mother still read in her sixties. In the shower I thought of the tall, virginal, blushing Karen, her tanned calves and knees disappearing upward, presumably into thighs. I could always push her over a goose for a peek at the legs.

As it turned out the goose ploy wasn't necessary. No, I didn't tup the heifer, though the call was heart-drummingly close. When I got out of the shower there was a frantic second when she wasn't there, but through the window I could see her in the corral petting two of the horses. Dalva must have taken the other two to her Rapid City assignation, a long way to avoid my company. While I dressed in my neatest best I plotted a campaign like Rommel about to enter Egypt, Timoshenko before his maps of war.

To keep the upper hand I had Karen conduct the interview in the den. I sat behind the immense Northridge desk, and placed her on the deep leather couch, the better to see her limbs. She was utterly flabbergasted to be in the house, shy to stiffness, holding her hands and steno pad behind her back. She said she had been in the barnyard years before when her father had come to shoe the horses, but never in the house.

"This is quite the day. Here I am interviewing a famous man in a mansion." She actually said this and I had to think she was putting me on, but the questions that followed said no. How did I get my start? How old was I when I started writing? What were the names of my books? Was there a message for today's youth? Was education the ticket to the future? Did a girl have an equal chance in today's troubled world? What was the future for Nebraska? What is the main lesson of history? Should today's farmer rely on the government? In a nutshell, was there hope for the future of the world?

Holy shit, but my hair roots began to sweat a few minutes into this mudbath. If she hadn't been a beauty I would have sent her packing. As a long-term teacher I have developed a subtle bedside manner. I answered all the questions with just a sliver of a British accent, affecting a Noël Coward weariness but an actor's intensity. I acted worldly, troubled, morose, so sophisticated that my answers tended to streak off into airy tangents. My bedside manner slowly rose to the surface as I began to turn the tables by asking her questions about her hopes and fears. She adjusted her skirt, flattered and nonplussed that I cared. With a millisecond glimpse of thigh my worm turned. I got up and poured us each an ample glass of cold white wine, not so much as a trick but to break the ice. I said the wine must be confidential, since I wasn't sure she was of drinking age. She blushed again and said they had had a dilly of a graduation party the week before, and a lot of kids drank so much they "blew lunch," a puzzling new euphemism, it seems, for puking. Now that I had tilted her off balance a little, I had to finish the job. I stared into her eyes long and hard without speaking—actually I was thinking about lunch. When she was sufficiently nervous I began to speak in the tone used on the horses.

"Karen, to be frank, I sense that you aren't very happy. You're an attractive young woman on the verge of going out into the world, but you are restless, fearful, unsure of yourself. I sense you need something more than this town or even the university in Lincoln can offer. You are trembling on the lip of self-knowledge, but it frightens you, just as some people are afraid of war, death, the never-ending dark. You've been told you have a bright future, but on this warm summer day you feel like you're sleepwalking. You crave direction, guidance, you're sick of the dread that greets you every morning. Am I correct?"

"I just don't know where to turn," she began, with moist eyes and clenched hands. It occurred to me I needed something with anchovies for lunch as her words began to pour out. "I might just be hearing a different drummer like I read in school. My home life is not too good and I don't have any privacy. It would be better if Dad had stuck to horseshoeing but he got into farming and now he thinks the bank is going to repo the new tractor. I want to give him my college savings but I also want to get out of town. My brother got drunk and joined the navy, so he's no help. My mother's got nervous problems, so she can't work. All she worries about is whether I am doing it with my boyfriend. It's my dream to pledge either Pi Beta Phi or Kappa Kappa Gamma if they'll have me. When I visited college this winter both sororities liked me and thought I might have a chance of being homecoming queen some day. Two weeks ago when we went to Chicago on our senior trip this guy that worked at the desk of the hotel said I should be a model and make big bucks. He wanted to take my picture and all the girls thought I should because it might be my big break but our teacher chaperone got wind of it and said no. I just couldn't help but cry."

Now she began to cry. I got up and refreshed her wine-glass, wanting to give her a pat but knowing this gesture was premature. She hadn't stewed in her banal juices quite long enough. I went to the window and looked out, lost in thought. Maybe a frittata with anchovies, eggs, shallots, fontina . . .

"Maybe, just maybe . . ." I finally said, turning with dramatic slowness from the window, my brow creased with worry. I walked over and stooped so that our eyes were level. "Maybe, maybe, maybe . . ."

"Maybe what?" she sniffled.

"I was just thinking about the modeling business," I said, standing and walking away with careless diffidence. "I've known a lot of models in L. A., San Francisco, New York City, catalogue models, superthin high-fashion models, bathing-suit models. There's a slight, outside chance you could cut the mustard as a bathing-suit model." I mentioned the name of a famous model, the wife of a rock star, I had met very briefly emerging from Ted's house. This elicited an excited "Oooo" from Karen, who I had guessed read the gossip rags. I sensed it was time to try to close the deal.

"Stand up and walk around. Try to relax. Pretend you're on the beach at Waikiki in a bikini. Imagine that a group of lifeguards are watching you and you just don't care because you're a pro and you're damned proud of your body."

She did a number of nimble but altogether nervous turns around the den, then gave me a shy but beseeching look.

"I just can't tell. Maybe this is all hopeless. I don't want to offer false encouragement but I just can't tell with all of your . . . you know." I waved at her clothes with distaste.

Ambitious girl that she was, she quickly slipped out of her skirt and blouse, paused a moment, then kicked off her sandals, and repeated the turns around the den. I frowned, put my hands on her shoulders to straighten them, and tilted up her chin. Holy Toledo, I thought, moving around behind her and trying to rattle my brain for some anatomical terms. I kept my touch light as if helping to correct minor defects.

"Good mylofrisis, latimus, fine clavicles." I knelt down until my nose was an inch from the white undies that were drawn up a bit into the crack of her buttocks, a bottom without equal in my experience. This was a critical point, as it were, and it took great force of will to contain myself. I made calipers out of my thumbs and forefingers and ran them from her ankles up her legs, watching the goose bumps spring to the surface of her skin. "Marvelous metatarsals, fair knee backs, good gluteus maximus." I kneaded the buttocks a bit as if searching for hidden problems, then scrambled around to her front, not wanting to lose this particular angle of vision. I had, sadly, used up all my terms, being short on the sciences, so muttered a few cooking and food terms in French. "Fine *ris de veau*," I said, a flick of the tongue away from the pubis; "*bagner de Bourgogne*" to her belly button, and "*tête de veau*" to her ample titties. At that point I had to turn away in unrestrained anguish. I was overrevving like a runaway diesel. Where would this lead? I thought. "I just might have to call my friend Ted in Los Angeles. He's a major figure in show business, you might say, a real coastal tycoon. But maybe first I should see some flexation. Suppleness is a major consideration." My mouth had dried out to an absurd degree but I didn't want to lose concentration by getting more wine. "Perhaps you could do a few exercises lying down, you know, sit-ups, knee and ankle grabs, anything."

She quickly got to the floor in front of me and drew her knees back, then shot her feet out so her toes grazed my shirt. My wiener had become a wisdom-tooth ache, and there was a roaring in my ears. Karen heard the roaring too, and jumped up. It was Frieda roaring into the yard in her big RAM. The spell was broken.

"Jeezo!" Karen said, grabbing at her clothes. I whipped out of the den, through the foyer, and into the kitchen. I caught Frieda at the pump-house door and gave her a lazy smile, but blocked her entry.

"I'm doing an interview. Everything's fine."

"I'm feeding the geese and horses," she said, pushing past me. "Naomi said Karen's over here. She's my third cousin."

I followed Frieda in with a prayer and a hot flash. I wanted to put my boot in her ass so far it would take a tow truck to pull it out. To my relief Karen was at the kitchen table adjusting her notes, cool as a bell pepper.

"Hi, Frieda. I just did the neatest interview. It's so fun to talk to a big brain." She gathered her tablet and breezed out, with a thank-you nod to me on the way. I found myself trotting out into the yard after her. She sat in her shabby little compact, her hands gripping the wheel, and staring straight ahead.

"Are you going to call that guy Ted?" There was a relentless set to her chin.

"Of course. This afternoon. Why don't you stop by about ten this evening? Bring some photos I can send Ted, preferably candid."

"I don't think I'll be able to. I've got a date."

"I'm sure you'll manage." I turned away to avoid any lame excuses.

As she drove off I glanced at Frieda at the kitchen window, then to the barnyard and the fields. Just after I had met Dalva and broached the subject of the papers, she had said that her great-grandfather had a peculiar sense of the order and balance in his life, caused by his difficult youth and months at Andersonville. Looking out at the clearing, which Dalva said was about thirty acres, I remembered a map of the prison camp I had seen in a graduate course on the Civil War. Andersonville and this clearing were the same size, and both had creeks running through the center. The former held as many as seventeen thousand prisoners, with not all that many survivors. This made me eager to check the journals from 1891, when the main house was built, though the land had been owned since the collapse of 1887. There was the abrupt, burning vision of Karen on the floor and a stomach growl. Saved by Frieda from mischief. The obvious mixture of lust and relief— my local track record really wasn't good enough for this sort of gamble. I idly hoped that she'd go on her date and forget this tired professor.

Back in the kitchen there was the heavy odor of my favorite flavor, garlic. It turned out that Frieda had made me a Basque lamb stew the evening before and was warming it up. It was gorgeous, with fresh baked bread and a smallish glass of cabernet she had unfortunately tested in a tin measuring cup. She told me that when she was nineteen she had run off with a Basque sheepherder who had been shearing in the area. He had kept her captive in the Ruby Mountains of northern Nevada and that year had given her all the sex she wanted in life. Mr. Northridge and her father had tracked her down and retrieved her from Basquaise clutches. The upshot was that she still liked the cooking her "crude" lover had taught her. I was pleased with this stew, but then she grabbed my hand and looked at me soulfully.

"You be careful with Karen. She's too fast for a school-teacher like you. Word around here is, last November she was frigging these pheasant-hunting doctors from Minneapolis. If her dad found out those docs would be hamburger."

"You don't say!" I croaked. "I would swear she had to be a virgin." The word "frigging" had a nautical air about it. Karen in the pirate doctor's rigging.

"You've got your poor head in books. You don't know a hot little slut from a worthwhile woman. That's for sure. She's as wild as Dalva used to be." Frieda bounced up and flicked on the radio. She never missed listening to Paul Harvey.

"How wild was Dalva?" I asked, I thought, innocently.

"None of your beeswax, mister. Don't try to pry into family affairs." Her umbrage was so grand I skipped up to Dalva's room to use the phone. Dalva had told me that any call I made in Frieda's presence would lose its confidentiality.

Ted turned out to be amused and alarmed by the idea that I had discovered a great model. He warned me rather sternly that local customs hadn't kept stride with California, and that he'd heard that a gay barber had been tarred and feathered in the fifties. I was somewhat surprised that he knew about my getting lost, also my drunken day with Lundquist. "You're making a real hit out there. You got a bullet." He, nevertheless, assured me that he would pass Karen's photos around if I sent them. I remembered then that I had promised to call a friend in the rare-book business and describe the journals. This man had wiped a felony from my record when I was caught trying to swipe a book from a rare-book room at Notre Dame. I was a penniless student at the time and frequented his shop on trips to Chicago. The theft was actually an assignment, and he had anonymously secured an expensive lawyer to get me off the hook. On the phone he was thrilled to hear about my discoveries and begged for a Xerox of certain portions. He had a collector in Westchester and one in Liechtenstein who would pay a fortune for a few journals. I told him in no uncertain terms that this was out of the question.

Back at my desk I was troubled again by the notion of symmetry in the farm clearing and Andersonville. I had packed along Shelby Foote's hypnotic volumes on the Civil War but didn't want to pursue a possibly false lead. The recurrent temptation in my profession was to draw the strings too tight, to cut off the horse's legs to fit him in a stall. Unlike my mother, the discipline of history does not suggest that in the long run things have turned out the best and the neatest: you can collate research material until your hair is gray and your face blue and arrive at false conclusions that have been repeated a thousand times by other fools. The recent, infantile excavation of the Custer battlefield will reveal nothing of the nature of the men that fought there, the ultimate valid intent of an inquiry. But, then, I had to disallow myself this sort of grandness: I hoped I had all of Northridge before me and would stamp him into a book. I could not begin to diagram the sentence in history that is Crazy Horse, but I could certainly gloss Northridge's understanding of the Sioux. Ambition turns sane men into hysterics. I gave up Melville because the hanging of Billy Budd, not to speak of the whiteness of the whale, was a subject that would have caused me to end my life under psychiatric care.

I spent most of the afternoon trying to figure out Northridge's stay in La Crosse, Wisconsin, in the winter of 1866. It was full of relatively colorless botanical and theological ramblings. He was forever climbing the immense hill that abuts the city to the east and looking off across the Mississippi to the west. His mind was addled with his attempt to recapture his faith, and thus the journals were chock-full of pithy quotes from the King James version, musings about the obvious causes of the cholera that was afflicting the westward movement. I jumped forward to the late spring, which found him in the northwest part of Nebraska territory.

**May, the week of the 22nd, 1866**
**Camped here ten days along a stream I take to be Warbonnet Creek. I am now more alone than I thought possible and am well shut of the filth along the Oregon Trail, and pioneers so enfeebled by illness and stupidity that they are marching toward their own Antietam. I have been warned overmuch since La Crosse and the**

journey across Nebraska territory to keep clear of this area and its dangers. Men tell wild tales to excuse their cowardice & this is always true of soldiers & missionaries. If I lacked courage now I might better pack myself back to Barrytown and become a dainty gentleman. Perhaps I have some of my unseen father's blood. . . .

Jesus, he's supposed to be a bastard, illegitimate, but obviously knows who his father was. Ask Dalva.

. . . I have been planting my root stock along the creek bed well up from possible flooding. There is a northwest-southwest flow of air to help with frost at budding time. The tender root hairs [?] did not fare well on the journey and I have no high hopes for my first orchard. As I move to higher elevation I am digging deeper holes to examine the striations of soil, most ill-suited thus far for fruit trees. I continue an hour daily with my largest hole near a cottonwood tree to examine its tap-root. After a winter's ease except for hiking it is good to bury my hands in the soil. *Machaeranthera canescens* today! Pubescence roughish; stem purple, sparingly branched; leaves lanceolate, repand, mucronate.

The last sentence here is what I mean about the field notes—botany for the botanists!

My hobbled horses were nervous and fitful in the night and at dawn I found the tracks of the great bear, the grizzly, in the mud along the creek bank. I resolve to keep my fire better tended as it would be ironical for a man to survive the War only to provide a meal for this wild creature. The bears of the Adirondacks are often quite curious and range wide for food in Spring & perhaps these are the same, though the fierceness of these is said to be undisputed in the animal domain. Have dug too long today I suppose as when I poked my head from the hole I thought I saw a wolf on a hill stand upright and run away on its hind-legs. When I had my dinner of prairie chicken it occurred to me this was possibly a Sioux in disguise. I have craved to see my first Indian, wild & untainted by any settlement, not begging & trading their valuables for liquor which does not suit them. In Boston & New York it is said the Italians may drink wine, but liquor makes them violent and they are often arrested without clothing. The Chaplain at Cornell said only the Chosen People, the Jews, can contain their vices & should be our example.

At first light a Sioux boy was looking at my horses but fled up creek into a thicket. I yelled after him in his language "Stay a while and speak with me" but he did not return. It is a solace to me if I am murdered there are no relatives to mourn me unless my father left other bastards on the Continent.

A melancholy Sabbath, or so I think as I may have forgotten to check a day on my calendar. In the night there was violent thunder & lightning, and my crude shelter leaked, so hastily built in fair weather. I bathe in the creek and try to spend the day with my Bible but it reads less well in the wilderness. In college I debated a quite brilliant Atheist on whether the savages needed our religion. In private I think they would not have needed it had we not disturbed their peace. We are too much a mystery to them, and they to us. When I sit here on this rock too long my mind ceases its activity and I seem to understand nothing or everything.

In the late afternoon I give up on bibles & sabbaths and take a long walk, after which I wish for two reasons I had taken one of my two horses, for the one was stolen in my absence, or perhaps the hobbles loosened, and the other would have saved me from danger. I climbed a hill two miles distant from my camp seeing on the way a lazuli finch & olive-backed thrush. From the hill through the telescope I surveyed the immense grasslands to the west & was puzzled by an enormous dark mass as if the darkest thunder clouds had dropped to earth. My skin pricked & tingled when I saw the mass was moving toward me and making a noise as of distant thunder. It was the buffalo, *Bos americanus,* and there could not have been a more awesome sight in God's creation. Over them was a red sun in the western sky and it burnished this sea of moving beasts. Still miles away but closing toward me their thunder increased as if they were trampling the life from earth herself. All manner of songbirds & hawks, sage hens & sharp-tailed grouse flushed before them and began to sail past me, and when the buffalo were within a mile or so I felt tremors in the ground. It was then it occurred to me I was in their path on this treeless hill, so I tucked my telescope and sprinted for my camp, much startled when I was passed by deer & antelope in their fright. O to have a safe hole in the ground like the badger, gopher or ferret. I flew to the camp and somehow climbed the cottonwood as a tropical monkey would. From the tree I could see out over the ridge of the creek bed & the buffalo swelled over my hill then veered to the south, taking a full half-hour to pass completely. I will add I built a large fire & filled my tin cup with the whiskey I kept for illness. I smoked my pipe and sang many hymns to keep myself company. I felt I was being watched but was tired & resigned to my fate as a freezing drunkard in the snowbanks of Maine.

A fair morning with many cups of tea & cold water. Back in my large hole before breakfast as a penitent. I laugh to think the buffalo would have forced Saint Paul into more than a little wine. I remember I should search for my missing horse but they will not go far from their own company. The hole is too muddy to dig well and as I begin to clamber out I smell leather and the copper-ish smell of blood. There are three warriors, a boy, and a garishly painted old man who stoops before my drying plant specimens dressed in animal skins. I am startled to breathlessness but say in Sioux "Welcome to my camp. I am pleased to see you." The boy shys backwards but the warriors move forward staring at me closely. Their arms are covered with dried blood and I suppose they have been hunting. Two of the warriors are large & muscular and have rifles though they are not pointed at me. The third has a large belly and is unarmed except for a hatchet & club at his waist. I say to him in Sioux "It is good to see you on this lovely day. I have been digging in the earth to look at the roots of trees. I'm afraid I'm a little muddy. May I make you a cup of tea?" The painted old man approached & I take him to be a medicine man. Now the warrior with the large belly and no rifle smiled at me. "The boy said there was a white man who ate earth and burrowed as a badger in the ground. He took little trees from a blanket and planted them in the ground." Then he gestured to one of the warriors. "Last night he saw you smoking a pipe and singing songs. We are very angry with white men now. I am wondering now if I should kill you. What have you to say to that?" I said that the Holy Spirit told me to come here several years ago but first I had to fight in the Civil War where I was captured. Now that I am here, if the Holy Spirit wishes me dead that is His affair. Big Belly answered that he had seen and heard of missionaries and that they were all liars and cowards. I said that if I were a coward why would I be here alone? I am a different sort of missionary. I rapidly named the wild fruits and berries his people ate and said that I was planting new fruits, not white men's fruits, but fruits from the whole world. The medicine man stared in my left eye and said to Big Belly that he had never heard of a missionary covered with mud. He led me over and we discussed my drying herbs & specimens, and also looked at my root stock I had hilled up. At this time we walked back over to my large hole near the cottonwood. I jumped in and explained quickly the nature of the tree's root system. The three warriors stepped off out of earshot and discussed the situation. I put on a pot of water to boil for tea & then showed the medicine man some dried apples, pears, and peaches, putting a handful of each in another pot with water to cook. I got out a pound of good tobacco as a gift and looked over to read Big Belly's face as he approached. "You are a confusing man and we don't know what to do with you. Why haven't you asked about your stolen horse?" I offered a silent prayer as I knew I was teetering between life and death as if I were walking a narrow beam way up in a barn. I said that I wished to give my extra horse to the boy who had brought us together on this fine day. The boy heard this and jumped in the air. Now Big Belly took a private consultation with the medicine man, and when they returned to the fire where I was stirring the pot of tea & the pot of fruit, Big Belly said "You are too strange to kill. The old man says it would be bad luck to kill you." They all laughed at this so I joined them though a bit weakly. Contrary to popular opinion, I'm told, Indians are full of wit, jokes & laughter. We sat down for tea, and stewed fruit, which they pronounced delicious. The boy was sent up the creek bed to fetch something & returned quickly with a bloody buffalo heart which was cut in chunks & roasted over the fire. The heart was very good indeed. . . .

I turned to see Naomi driving in the yard. It was five in the afternoon and typical of her to wait until she thought my workday was at an end. By the time I reached her, she was holding up a dead cock pheasant, and looking very sad. The pheasant had flushed from a ditch and had run into the side of her car, breaking its neck. Cars haven't been around long enough for creatures to have made a genetic adaptation, she said. She handed me the bird and told me to cook it for my dinner. I cringed a bit at the warmth I still felt in its breast. Most of us successfully ignore the fact that what we eat was once as alive as we are. She was quick to note my queasiness, took the bird back, and began to pluck it as we spoke.

"Karen called me and said you were going to help her become a model. Is this so?"

I glanced up at an imaginary cloud for a moment. "She's beautiful, so I simply called Ted to check it out. He offered to help."

"I'm not being critical, I simply want you to be careful. Girls here are very matter-of-fact and gullible. She's willful and doesn't quite have both oars in the water. She's also been teasing men around here since she was thirteen. I don't want you to complicate your life with an errant suggestion."

"I need a drink," I said, walking toward the house. It was as if my mother had caught me red-handed toying with my noodle.

I was sitting at the kitchen table with five fingers of vodka when Naomi came in with the plucked pheasant. She patted me on the head and took a sip of my drink.

"Don't get flustered. I'm more worried for you than Karen. The high-school coach was fired over her but Dalva told me on the phone the same man had bothered her thirty years before. But enough of this. Look at the long spur here. It's an older bird, which means you can't simply roast it or it would be too tough." She showed me the bony spurs on the pheasant's legs, saying that they are used as defense, or in arguments over hen pheasants.

We talked as she browned the pheasant in a small Dutch oven, added chopped leeks, white wine, and a few sprigs of thyme and rosemary from the kitchen window box. I could put it in when I wanted to eat in an hour. She couldn't stay for dinner because a friend belonged to a movie club and had gotten a cassette in the mail of *The Misfits* with Montgomery Clift, Clark Gable, and Marilyn Monroe. It was her favorite movie, and she and two other widows regularly watched classic movies and had dinner together. I suddenly asked her if Dalva had a gentleman friend in Rapid City. Jealousy rose in my gorge when I thought of Arthur Miller putting up with Marilyn's shenanigans. If you're cuckolded by the president you can scarcely slap his face. Naomi laughed at my question, saying, "You'll never know and neither will I," and that Dalva had a cabin over in the Black Hills she used as a retreat. An old Sioux woman lived there and took care of the place. Then I asked what she knew about the building of the house. She said Northridge had made the design and brought out a group of Swedish craftsmen from Galesburg, Illinois. Dalva's grandfather would have been five at the time. We went into the den and Naomi, innocently enough, showed me a hidden panel that concealed a half-dozen or so English shotguns that I recognized to be quite valuable. There was also a wall safe that aroused my curiosity. She said that between 1890 and the turn of the century there was a great deal of animosity in Nebraska toward Northridge because he was thought to have harbored Sioux and Cheyenne leaders who were fugitives from the government, in the manner of the earlier Underground Railway. In effect, he had been on the wrong side of the war, though he had enough political power—his property in Chicago had been sold for a large sum—that no one tried to bother him. I asked her why she hadn't read the journals.

"They remind me too much of my husband's voice," she said, kissing me goodbye.

After she left I stood in the yard altogether too long. I felt a level of anxiety that I had been taught during the period of my treatment to regard as a warning signal. I refuse to flip in this foreign land, I thought, before an audience of geese and horses. I need some noise. The woman's husband was dead in Korea nearly forty years ago, in 1950. There is the question of whether life is long enough to get over anything. I sat down on the ground to avoid tipping over from the enormity of it all. Here comes the pictograph as if I'm in an airplane. I should be in the Mitchell Brothers porn palace in San Francisco watching Jap tourists go crazy over naked girls while drinking seven-dollar weak Scotches. This loneliness at supper hour. I had studied war and reparations. The Japs and Germans did very

well, while the Indians were too incomprehensible. What can
you do if the fuckers won't learn to grow potatoes? Sitting
down was also vertiginous, so I got up and walked purposefully
over to the lilac grove that contained the family cemetery. It
was overgrown by design, and the only inexplicable marker
was for someone named Duane Stone Horse, who died in 1971.
I remembered that he was the one who had read Zane Grey's
*Riders of the Purple Sage.* I'd ask Dalva, if she ever returned
from her Rapid City lover. To what degree were these people
actually dead? Who the fuck were Indians? I made a tight-
assed trot out of the graveyard as if pursued. Why am I curious
about anything beyond the professional level, or am I? I didn't
dare have another drink in this state. I had read the inconclusive information on the possible origins of Indians, all bleached
with supposition and speculation. The Bible wisely settles for
Adam and Eve. A lovely, frazzled lady in the No Name bar in
Sausalito told me the Indians had arrived by spaceship in Peru
and made their way north, which was as viable as Lundquist's
lost tribe of the Children of Israel. Back home I relied on
television news, especially Ted Koppel, to settle this sort of
mental indigestion. A twenty-inch screen was the requisite
glue. If it weren't for the waiting pheasant I could very well
go into the barn (which frightened me), set the barn afire, and
go up in smoke along with it. I tried to approach the geese over
by the creek, but they were more cynical than the horses. I got
in Dalva's Subaru, started it, and turned on the radio, but the
smell of her gave me a lump in the throat. I listened carefully
to a local county agent talking about grain and livestock prices,
which helped. Then he began a dirge about farm foreclosures
and I flicked the dial, pausing at a country station with its
freight of unendurable sentiment. I settled for PBS and a dose
of soporific Brahms, and began to repeat aloud certain things
I liked, a nostrum from the psychiatrist: the first year of my
marriage, my daughter, certain birds, garlic, Bordeaux, exotic
dancers, the ocean when it's not rough, Gary Cooper movies,
John Ford movies, John Huston movies, Victoria's Secret cata-
logs, cassoulet, Stravinsky, ZZ Top videos (where the girl gets
out of the old car), New York City on Saturday afternoons,
fresh copies of the *American Scholar* and *American History* in
the mailbox, the river Liffey at dawn, Patrick Kavanaugh, the

Tate Gallery, Cheyne Walk. . . . There, I went back to work, forgetting dinner for the time being. I want a pet whippoor-will!

**Oct. 21, 1890**
**They painted us white & we danced day and night until we could no longer move & then we rested, got up and danced again though the day turned dark with high winds and sleet. . . ."**

Not what I need now: Northridge during the decline of the Ghost Dance movement. I will save this for a bright, clear morning, not a lonely evening. I put away the journals and read in two supplementary texts—Carlson's *Indians, Bureau-crats, and Land* and D. S. Otis's *The Dawes Act and the Allot-ment of Indian Lands.*

At nine, when it began to get dark, I went back in the house and put the pheasant in the oven. I thought it was safe to have a drink, though the first sip made me wonder whether or not Karen was going to show up. The girl was a toss-up—they say a hard dick has no conscience, but a scholar's dick is a shy item full of question marks, guilt, ironies. My attempts to keep a distance from my material were losing ground. There is a reason why scholars work in libraries. A number of studies of the Holocaust have clearly illustrated that it constituted the most repellent series of events in human history. I doubt, though, if any of the writers and scholars of the studies had set up shop in Buchenwald, Belsen, or Treblinka to compose. Here, I was too much in the thick of it. I envisioned an apart-ment above a friendly pub in Dublin, the two trunks of journals safely under the bed, or, barring that, two trunks of Xeroxes of the material, if that were permissible. Of course, the prob-lem was, what I had read so far made me timid; it was too stark and poignant and I could foresee how the bad parts were going to scan. If the Nazis had won the war the Holocaust, finally, would have been set to music, just as our victorious and bloody trek west is accompanied on film by thousands of violins and kettle drums.

I had just begun some interior pissing and moaning about the locked up Bordeaux in the cellar when Karen's car swerved in under the yard light. I went to the pump-shed door with a flock of butterflies and a thumping heart. From the shadows she said she didn't want to come in, but could we go to the bunkhouse? She seemed flitty and skittish, and I couldn't quite keep her pace across the barnyard. As I opened the door I could smell schnapps and the singed furze of marijuana. Under the light she was wet, and wore a skirt over a leotard-type bathing suit. She somehow looked taller, her eyes glittering, her speech a little slurred. She handed me an envelope with a pealing giggle.

"My friend Carla took these with her dad's Polaroid camera. We had to have some drinks first, and now we're swimming, so I have to hurry, because my boyfriend's going to meet me and I don't want him to think I'm off in a car with someone else. . . ."

The photos were a cattle prod to the nape nerve, a masturbative fantasia, candid candy: clumsy but explosive pics of Karen in bra and panties, in several bathing suits, also three total nudes. She was looking over my shoulder and continuing the prattle: ". . . so I hope these are OK though they aren't too professional." I flipped them on the desk and turned to her. "Actually, this is a bathing suit. . . ." She dropped the skirt and adjusted the wet suit around her crotch and bottom. She paused, then smiled a bit crudely at my hopeless look. "I almost thought you were going to go down on me today in the den. Jeez, I thought, this guy is serious. I'm straight with my boyfriend but maybe it wouldn't hurt to do the other thing." She pulled the straps down her shoulders and peeled out of the wet suit. "Don't try to put it in, buster." She came nakedly into my arms, dropping a hand and unzipping my fly. I undid my belt and button and my trousers dropped. "Boy are you ever ready!" I stumbled with her toward the bed, where she sat on the edge and engulfed as much of me as she could with a wide-open mouth. I collapsed beside her, and she threw a leg and thigh over my face, smacking her parts with energy directly into my face. I did my best in the short time allotted me, noting the way the cooling effect left by the wet bathing suit quickly dissipated. Then I was a violent goner. She quickly jumped up and daintily wiped her mouth and chin with my pillow, putting the pillow back down on my wobbling red wiener. "You guys always look silly," she said, as she hastily dressed. "Sorry I can't stay. See you later. Let me know." And she was gone.

Some call it sex. A twinge of angina, and a blur in the vision. Her car starts and a rattle of gravel, the ears and their blood tympani. Even at thirty-nine I'm getting on in years for this sort of thing. Why not throw myself under a moving car? I felt like my face had been slapped, which was technically correct. I lay there until the ceiling focused itself, waiting for some oxygen flow and postlapsarian wisdom. I was lonely for Dalva but I did not think she was lonely for me, wherever she was. I reached up overhead and grabbed a journal from the pile, thinking, "I came to Carthage, where a cauldron of un-holy loves boiled round about me." Poor Saint Augustine. Who would guess, or bother to guess, that the average scholar is as full of self-drama as those dipshit bliss ninny actors on after-noon soap operas?

## Month of February, 1871

Have been shut in by weather for three days now, a fearsome blizzard so that heaven and earth alike are a solid, blinding white. I am without visitors since early January when He Dog stopped with a haunch of elk. At the time we discussed how each of his people is guided to some extent by their dreams. We spoke of this several days & I told him that in my own experience I have observed that I dream more actively in the waxing rather than the waning moon. He thought this was true but said he would consult the medicine man who helped preserve my life over five years ago & who asked me last summer why I walked so much in the middle of the night. I knew it was unlikely I was observed and so was discomfited by his statement. I then asked him how I might rid myself of my re-current nightmares of the war, especially one that came from being near horses when they were blown apart & I was covered with coils of their entrails. I was deafened for a week but could still hear in my deafness the screaming of horses. When this nightmare came I would awake and force myself to sing a song. He said I must dig a small hole and put a fire in it. I was then to sleep by the hole until the bad dream came which would happen quickly. When I awoke I was to "chase" the night-mare into the hole where it would burn, then smother the fire and dream with dirt, and it would never come to me again. I pondered this advice for several weeks, wondering if it should be considered unchristian. It was August then and on the waxing moon & I was again covered with the guts of horses & wept for the creatures. I prayed to no avail and was afraid to sleep again. Then I did as he advised in defiance of science & my religion and the nightmare was gone & the horses in my dreams were transfigured into the most beautiful of creatures.

I have not a single apple or a convert to show for myself in five years. He Dog and some of his friends will listen to the Bible but they prefer passages of war. They say above all they prefer to hunt, dance, fight, make love & feast. They also love to hear this passage from Nahum:

> Woe to the bloody city all full of lies & booty no end to plunder!
> The crack of whip, the rumble of wheel, galloping horse and bounding chariot!
> Horsemen charging, flashing sword and glittering spear, hosts of slain, heaps of corpses, dead bodies without end— they stumble over the bodies.

One of He Dog's friends, a dour warrior named Seven Knives, sings me the song of a battle I know to be the Fetterman Massacre of December 1866, when Crazy Horse used the tactics of decoy to lure 80 soldiers from Fort Phil Kearny to their deaths. I have been shown scalps from this battle & have inspected them politely, fearful to offend.

My Winter Count is much doubt repeating itself. With the Sioux I may have chosen the wrong tribe to aid. An old missionary I spoke with last summer in Omaha says the Arikara who once were in Nebraska and driven out by the Sioux were splendid farmers. These Arikara by actual count had developed 14 varieties of corn, and many of beans, and tapped elder trees for liquid sugar as maples are tapped in the East. At this meeting of missionaries we were addressed by a Reverend Dillsworth who has spent years in Arizona and northern Mexico. He suggested that our Sioux may be as hopeless as the Apache in terms of conversion to Christ. I do not care for this man so am not much discouraged by his suggestions. He did make an intelligent discussion of the progress of the papist Jesuits with many Indian tribes of the Southwest. These Jesuits do not so much convert, he said, but add another coat of Catholic paint to what is already there. This is thought by us to be dishonest but I am not sure. It is indeed difficult to convince the Sioux of the uniqueness of the Sabbath when in his beliefs every day of the week is Sabbath. He Dog teased me saying if I would fast three days and three nights on a mountain top he knows in the Black Hills I would give up my Sabbath notions. His humor is often coarse and he said if I would not make love to a woman on the Sabbath she would run to someone else.

I have ordered 10,000 root grafts of fruit trees from Monroe, Michigan for ten cents apiece. My trees will survive by the force of their numbers! I shall have a busy spring & now when my door shudders from the force of the storm I long to put my hands in the warm earth.

It was nearly midnight when I remembered my braised pheasant, which meant the bird had been cooking nearly three times as long as it should have. This newest disaster was a less pleasant slap in the face than the last one. A brisk run to the house might save a minute from the overcooking time. I stood up, stretched, and tried to pretend I didn't notice the stack of a dozen or so photos, the top one an aperture-to-aperture face-off. There was a nudge to the joint. Like many literary men, I've read widely on the vagaries of lust, a course of inquiry as confused as the history of Italy. It is an experience not to be learned from, like death, only far more comic. I had noted the attempts in Ireland to ignore or drown the problem. On a side a good deal brighter than sex or pheasant was the notion that the journals were going to bring me fame as a historian—surely not the "fame" bandied about by the media, but a solidly marked trail that might very well result in an Endowed Chair by the time I hit forty-five.

In the kitchen my sense of well-being was doubly renewed. Dalva called from her cabin in Buffalo Gap, sounding rather merry and bright-eyed for so late an hour. Had Frieda told me about the surprise bottle of Bordeaux left for me in the breadbox? Nope, as they say out here, of course not. Things would go better for me if I tried to be a little charming with Frieda. I spoke about the progress of my work with excitement, which pleased her. She was glad that I had "settled in," then asked about how Karen's interview had gone. I breathed deeply to keep my voice from pinching into a tight little shriek of guilt. "Neither here nor there," I said, "not enough energy in the situation to make it enervating."

"I talked to Naomi and I heard you're going to become a model's agent. Is that lateral or a move up?"

"Oh, fuck you, darling." I felt too good to bother defending myself. Her laughter was soft and rich.

"I'll be back in a day or so. Just remember you won't hear the bullet that hits you. I miss you."

"I miss you too." When I heard her receiver click I began to reflect on the heartiness of frontier humor: those folkloric tales of life in our early raw. "Well, then Tad put the boot to the blackguard's head till he was spitting teeth, and we all ponied up to the bar glad to see the day well ended and justice done. The man had learned not to put a burr under the saddle of a cowboy from the Two Dot outfit." That sort of thing.

The second thrill was that the pheasant wasn't really ruined, and the breadbox Bordeaux was a '49 Latour, an outstanding wine, the gift of which moistened my unworthy eyes. This is the kind of farming I could get used to. The wine made me a little sorry I would not be permitted to look into the grandfather's papers, as he was apparently a great deal less austere than his own father. This home and wine revealed the spender I would wish to be. The bird itself was overly loosened, falling apart as I took it from the Dutch oven, but the juices had an excruciating flavor, and I picked the thing down to its bones. I am not by nature a hunter, but I meant to ask old Lundquist to snare me a few of these critters. I stretched out the bottle of Latour through a pointless but happy reverie about my first year of marriage. In reaction to me and a number of difficult years, she had managed to develop a well-oiled survival mechanism, and I had to be discarded like a vestigial appendage.

○

Just before dawn there was a terrible commotion among the geese, a fury of honking and flapping. I very nearly went outside to check but didn't have a flashlight, and my imaginings wouldn't permit a foray without one. I was confused by what had been a wonderful dream at the beginning, where Dalva and my daughter, Laurel, were riding through the pasture on splendid gold-tinged horses, but when I went out to meet them their faces were of old Indian women and looked like shucked pecans. If my daughter is that old, then I must be dead, I thought, when the geese woke me. It didn't occur to me to turn on the light, so I lay there another half an hour until I could see the room clearly. I looked out the back window to the west and there, on a mound of earth surrounded by burdocks, was a coyote feeding on a goose, his muzzle red with blood. He (or she) saw my movement at the window and dashed off through the weeds with the remains of the goose. Sad and startling though it was, I hoped the dead one was the pesky goose leader. At that moment Frieda pulled in the yard and went into the house to make my breakfast. I pulled on my trousers to inspect the morning, and any additional goose carnage. I counted thirteen but the number was meaningless, since I didn't know how many there were in the first place. I was pleased to see the geese were a good deal more friendly. The arrogant leader had survived, and he led the flock to me, with all of them apparently trying to explain the terrible thing that had happened. I was a little touched and felt called upon to make my first speech to geese, wherein I told them I would build a shelter, a sleeping bungalow they could enter in the evening, and sleep sound and safe from predators. I bowed and made the sign of benediction. I meant to check out the unvisited barn for cage materials. It was impossible not to be pleased with my progress with animals. I gave a hearty hello to the horses and went to the house.

"You walk barefoot around here, you'll sure as hell get lockjaw," Frieda greeted me from the stove. I saw she was making me a low-calorie, low-cholesterol breakfast of thick bacon, fried new potatoes, and a giant omelet. I also saw her eyes were red, as if from weeping. I secretly hoped to get through breakfast without an explanation for recent sorrow. I pretended to listen attentively to Paul Harvey's first word for the day, glad tidings from a town in Iowa where welfare layabouts were put to work sweeping the streets and washing all the cars in the courthouse parking lot.

"Come and get it if you want it hot," she bellowed, though I was only a few feet away. It was easy to see she was being brave. I reached for the Tabasco and got the usual "That stuff's going to eat out your guts."

"You might have noticed my dad is a little goofy?" she began.

"In a pleasant way." I wanted to slow her down, for I saw tremors in her full face.

"I'm fifty-seven and I'm not getting any younger. My boyfriend, Gus, wants to marry me but he's not sure he can put up with my old dad around the house. Gus has always been a hired hand, and in the back of my mind I'm thinking he might want our farm more than me. I just don't think I could bear to put Dad in the county farm. . . ." The poor soul put her face in her hands. Her big shoulders began to shake as I allowed a fly to land on my last bite of omelet.

"Does Gus come from a good family?" I was buying time with this stupid question.

"He's just a working stiff. He plays the banjo on Saturday nights. He's sixty-two but he looks a lot younger. When Dad goes I don't want to be lonely. I need someone to look after."

"Deal from your strength, dear. Tell Gus it's your farm and his conditions are unacceptable. If he won't accept old Dad, tell Gus to take a fucking hike."

She wiped her tears on my napkin. My advice seemed to stiffen her spine. "That's what Dalva said. The son of a bitch is getting pushy. He already owes me thirty-five bucks. He might just be on probation with me!" She rushed to the phone and I made my escape.

I felt strong at my desk and resolved to locate the wife Northridge had mentioned, thinking it might be Aase, from the Swedish family he had helped find a homestead. I mur-

mured a verbless prayer to the gods of scholarship not to confuse myself with my work, and after an hour of shuffling I discovered I was right!

## May 20, 1876

I have been in bad humor as I was forced to ride five days southwest to Scotts Bluff to meet with the new Director of Missions, a porcine Reverend from Cincinnati who cannot mount a horse and finds carriages not to his liking, so is never found more than a block from the railroad. Our meeting is a short half-hour. He tells me of rumors that I have "gone over" to the Indians by my refusal to build the simplest church. I answer that I must teach them to grow food before I presume to build a church when lumber is in such short supply. I say that the Sioux are anyway nomads & it would be difficult to locate a church. He said he has it on good word from the government that in the coming year the Sioux will be moved to the southern part of the Dakota Territory & there to be confined. This news shocked me a good deal as it is in defiance of all previous treaties. He is of the opinion that the Sioux are dying of our diseases so quickly (including hunger) that I should busy myself with saving souls rather than with agriculture. He then advises me that I am the last of the church in free concourse with the worst of the Sioux, and the brethren all pray for my safety with little confidence. I thank him for his prayers & make a retreat to escape the heaviness of his talcum.

I find myself in the dry-goods store buying gifts, slow to admit my intentions other than to leave this foul place with Godspeed. I remember the man Jensen, his wife, two sons and a daughter by the name of Aase. Riding two days out of my way I hope to find them where I helped settle them last year at this time. At my first night's camp I am embarrassed by the sight of the bundle of gifts as it seems not in my character, though I have made numberless exchanges with the Sioux. What if they are not there, having moved East or West out of despair and hunger? I sip a little whiskey after my evening prayers, and admit my heart wishes to see the girl again. I smile to think it is Spring and I am an aging swain of thirty-three & riding across the prairie to see a young lady with whom I exchanged but few words. It occurs to me I am carrying no mirror and am unsure of my appearance. He Dog said the medicine man told him that mirrors are bad as others should see us & we are not meant to spend time looking at ourselves.

I use my telescope to watch the Jensens far off in the afternoon. The father and sons are in a field with a team of oxen picking up the large stones & putting them on a stone boat. I have asked my friends among the Sioux to not harm these people or steal their animals. The mother is working in a garden. I see a cow and chickens. The small house is made of sod and timbers & the farm is altogether extraordinary, having been put together in one year. I stare until my eye waters but I do not see the girl. Perhaps she has married another, as seventeen is considered a marriageable age among these immigrant settlers.

The father is pleased to see me, also confused and embarrassed. He thanked me for registering his acreage and wondered how I managed to add two sections in the names of his sons. I told him the gov't agent was a good fellow and I had bought him a fine dinner. Land this far from the rail head is considered worthless for speculation, and speculators are ignorant of the presence of springs here. Jensen looks away and tells me they used the gold nugget for a team of oxen, chickens, pigs, and food supplies. A great bear came in the last October and took the pigs. Jensen said he knew the gift was intended for the daughter but I shushed him. I said I was also in business and would bring him fruit root stock. I do not say I have no family and only a few acquaintances outside the Sioux.

We stand by the garden, the father & mother, two sons and myself. I am looking at new flowers from seeds brought from Sweden, but my mind and heart are wondering if the girl is still here. I look up from the flowers and Aase is standing by the doorway looking away from me & holding her hands at her waist. I am unsure how to proceed but the others seem to know more than I why I have stopped for a visit. I gather my courage and walk over to her, take off my hat and bow. I offer my hand & she takes it and curtsies. I tell her how good it is to see her and that she had been often in my thoughts. She says the same thing to me and we smile. We walk further away from the others to a spring in the cottonwoods. She is of surpassing loveliness but does not look in good health. I ask her if she is well and she shakes her head no. She says she has studied English all winter and now I have come to talk to her, so we speak of everything far from the subject of illness. My hopes are well founded & I find my heart drawn to her & finally I kiss her hand.

We have a fine dinner outside as these makeshift sod houses are badly lit. All settlers long for the time they will afford to build a frame house. They are quite taken aback by my gifts, but I learn the next day that my behavior constitutes a proposal of marriage in their country. I take a bottle of good whiskey from my saddle-bag, and Aase, her mother & two brothers go in the house. I look off in the twilit distance with Jensen for a long time. Finally he speaks and it is to give me the reasons why I may not marry his daughter. He says in his country gentlemen do not marry peasant girls. I answer that we are not in his country but in the United States where men and women may marry whom they wish. He then says his beloved daughter is very ill and will not live long. He has difficulty pronouncing "tuberculosis" and begins to weep. I feel that I have fallen from a horse but say I know she is ill & that I could help by taking her to doctors in Omaha or Chicago. He composes himself & asks me to spend a day with her to be sure & then a few weeks away to think it over. He could not bear her unhappiness if I should marry her and change my mind and leave. I said I would build a place a few hours away on the Loup River so that she would not be far from her family. We spoke no more but drank another whiskey & then washed at the spring for bed. In the house they had made me a pallet next to Aase's bed as is their country's custom I supposed. When the last candle was blown out she reached out and entwined her hand in mine.

I am not bold to say the next day was the finest of my life & that I do not dare hope for another to equal it. We left early on a lovely day with a picnic her mother had packed us & walked slowly, I should say strolled, along the creek northwards. The first few hours I acted the school teacher, giving the names of birds and flowers. She knew the habits of the birds but not their names. We found a badger's den and she gave me the Swedish name for the badger. She said in the winter her brother had shot a deer & two Sioux happened upon him. Her brother was frightened but the Sioux showed him how to skin the beast and helped to carry it back on their horses. One of the Indians was especially kind & was missing an ear & spoke English. I said that was young Sam Creekmouth who was the first wild Sioux I had ever met & the old horse he rode was one I had given him ten years ago. Over the years when we met I taught him some English. He had lost an ear in a fight with a full grown Cheyenne when he was still quite young. I told her that he is much favored by the great chief Crazy Horse. She tired easily so we put down the cloth & picnic by the creek in a grove of box elder & cottonwoods. She fell asleep then and I looked at her intently for a hour. When she began to stir I pretended I was asleep & then it was she kissed me. I put my arm around her & we lay there wordlessly for a long time merely watching the sun dapple down through the pale green leaves of the trees. It was near noon and all the birds on earth were still & our music was our hearts and breath.

I looked up at a noise to see Lundquist driving in the yard in his old truck. It was only fifteen minutes after Frieda had left, so I presumed he was lurking down the road, hidden in a grove of trees and waiting to cadge a beer. Frankly, I didn't mind the interruption from Northridge and Aase, for the obvious reason that I knew how the story ended. Lundquist, meanwhile, was standing there staring at the missing goose. How would he have noticed such a thing, I wondered, because I had forgotten to mention it to Frieda? He glanced at the bunkhouse rather hopefully. I knew if he found me dead he would have a cold beer before he reported it. The renowned terrier, Roscoe, was scratching at my door. I let him in and cut him a chunk of Manganaro Genoa salami, which he lunged at, growling at me in thanks. It was nearly eleven in the morning, not an indecent time of day for a beer, so I grabbed two and went out to meet my wise friend, who was wearing the identical soiled denim outfit buttoned to the neck.

"It was Precious," he said, gravely taking the beer. "She was the mother of all of them. She was the oldest goose in the county." He showed me the coyote tracks in the moist earth along the creek, at which Roscoe made a wild display of anger. I decided at this point not to admit that I had heard the attack and failed to act out of cowardice.

"I think we should build a cage for the geese to sleep in," I offered.

"Not unless Miss Dalva tells us to." Now he was clearly imitating a black TV servant.

"Oh, bullshit. I'll take full responsibility. Should more geese die because she's off in the bloody mountains with a boyfriend? I say no in thunder, goddamnit. The geese shall not die!" Lundquist was a gulper and had already finished his beer. "I'll set up the grill and we'll have us a little barbecue we can tend while we work, get it? To be on the safe side we'll have a beer only every half-hour."

"Starting when? Does this one count?" he asked sagely, waving the empty can.

I became a little mean then, pausing in fake consternation, wondering if I might trade a few beers for some information I thought critical.

"Who is Duane Stone Horse? I saw the marker over in the graveyard?"

"He was a goddamned redskin who dropped dead on the front porch one day. We had to bury him somewheres. If I was you, I wouldn't go in a family's graveyard. It's not a goddamned picture show. What kind of people do you come from?" Lundquist scurried away toward his truck in total umbrage, and I went through the indignity of chasing him down. I had been making the mistake of thinking that simple country people were actually simple.

We labored hard for an hour building the cage and drank not all that many beers. Lundquist was vastly inventive with the materials found in the barn and I mostly watched him while tending to our chicken on the barbecue. I had second thoughts about whether he would like the chicken, but I devised my sauce of "lust and violence" that is famous among my friends for renewing vigor on Saturdays after a dreary week in the classrooms. Before we ate, though, we had a rather tense time trying to convince the geese that we had their best interests in mind—they refused to be herded into our cage and, in fact, became combative, though not with Lundquist. He finally lay down in the cage with a heap of ground corn on his chest, and began cooing, clucking, and humming through his nose, which the geese couldn't resist. He smiled a smile of triumph at me through the close-meshed wire fence.

We ate the chicken straight off the grill and weren't disturbed when Frieda rammed in the yard—we were working folk and not subject to criticism. Lundquist explained the death of the mother goose, to which Frieda responded, "Precious wasn't getting any younger." Frieda snagged herself a well-sauced thigh from the grill—I was glad I had cooked two chickens—and pronounced it "good black stuff." On questioning, she explained that after her unfortunate year with the Basque she had joined the WACs and had been stationed in El Paso, Texas, where they weren't afraid of hot sauce. She then thanked me for my advice on how to handle Gus.

"That shitsucker got on the high horse until I gave him the bottom line," she said.

"Frieda never swore until she got home from the service. She lost her religion in the service but she learned how to stand on her own two feet. That's what her mother said. Gus was always a good boy, but he spent his money on clothes and cars, and now he don't own an acre," Lundquist explained.

Frieda left after inhaling another thigh and half a breast. She told her daddy to be home for a nap pretty soon and kissed him on the top of the head. She pulled Roscoe's ear and the dog growled menacingly, guarding his cache of chicken bones.

"Duane was as good a shovel man as Paul was. In Paul's time we had a team of shires that were brought all the way from England, and a ditcher, but Paul wanted to dig by hand. I won the State Fair horse pull with the shires in 1938. I shook the governor's hand, if you can believe that. Duane made up stories. He told me he was born in a cave in Arizona and his father shot Kit Carson in the brain. Could this be true?"

I nodded yes to encourage any further revelations. We were sprawled under the tailgate of his old Studebaker truck to get out of the sun. I didn't dare chance another question.

"Duane was quite a bit like Dalva's father. That boy was tough. Those football boys learned not to bother Duane. He was built like pictures of Billy Conn. Both of them were. I'm going to show you a place, if you keep your mouth shut."

I agreed and followed Lundquist out into the barn. He found the light switch and we climbed a ladder up into the enormous mow, which held a number of carriages and sleighs, also a large assortment of harness hanging from the rafters. Lundquist said none of the harness had been used since 1950 but he kept it in shape because "you never can tell." In a corner farthest from light there was a big square stack of hay bales propped up with timbers. I was inattentive, watching the swallows swoop around overhead, and Lundquist disappeared. It was a perplexing joke and I waited a few minutes before calling out. His reply was muffled, apparently coming from inside the hay bales. Then he pushed out a piece of burlap to which a mat of hay had been glued. I went inside with a little trepidation, as if on the verge of a likely practical joke. It was pitch dark, with the cracks between the slots of the barn having evidently been caulked or battened. I heard Lundquist fumbling with a hinge or a latch; then the brilliant light of the sun was on us. I glanced up, shouted, and ducked. I thought a white boulder was falling on me, but the boulder turned out to be a huge white buffalo skull suspended from the rafter. I reached up and spun it around, then sat down on the milk stool that was the only other object in the enclosure. It was a fine view to the west, though the bright sun on the skull was a bit much for my taste.

"One winter day J. W. says to me, Find Duane, and he was nowhere to be found. So the dog Sonia leads me to the ladder. Still nothing. So I carry her up the ladder and she brings me over here and scoots in. Duane makes some ghost noises and scares the shit out of me. This was Duane's mumbo-jumbo place for the dead of winter. He had other places for other times but this was the place for the bad months."

"Did he call it his mumbo-jumbo place?"

"That's what I just told you. Seems to me I got a schnapps coming."

Lundquist waited outside the screen door of the bunkhouse, not wanting to enter, for unexplained reasons. I passed him a triple schnapps, plus a wedge of salami for Roscoe, who had returned from a mission of burying chicken bones covered with filth.

After they left I took a shower and set about my work. I

hastily shoved the photos of Karen in a manila envelope and wrote a short note to Ted. On second thought, I kept one of the photos as a memento of a strategic but not altogether pleasant campaign in foreign territory—the photo was unsuitable for anyone but a young man bent on a path of self-abuse: a rear shot standing against a bed post, leaning over slightly, facing a poster of the musician Sting. The bottom of bottoms, said Bottom. Enough of this, and to be hidden between the pages of John D. Hicks's seminal *The Populist Revolt.*

I picked out the three volumes from 1874 in hopes of not taking a walk with love and death. Love might set me off on one of my spells and certainly death will. *Timor mortis conturbat me.* In that Northridge didn't maintain any scholarly distance, his redskins had also begun to get to me. I felt a distant envy for a friend who had busied himself the past ten years writing an uneventful history of the United Nations' efforts in the Caribbean. He was always tanned.

## July 19–25, 1874

I have made a long journey up near the Belle Fourche River so as to escape a great plague of grasshoppers & the smoke of prairie fires. My thoughts have been troubled by loss of faith & the doom of the Sioux brought about by the extermination of the buffalo. I have written the President, many Senators, also General Terry on this matter but none have deigned to answer in a year's time. With few exceptions I have learned that politicians are to be purchased. Said Matthew "For they bind heavy burdens and grievous to be borne, and lay them on men's shoulders; but they themselves will not move them with one of their fingers. . . . Woe unto you, scribes and Pharisees, hypocrites! For ye compass sea and land to make one proselyte, and when he is made, ye make him twofold more the child of hell than yourselves."

That written I had to wrap my book in oilskin as the sky fairly opened with rain & thunder bellowed. I had made a tarpaulin shelter from the sun & thus sat there pleased with the great power of the storm & eating wild strawberries I had picked in the morning. I was somewhat alarmed to see an Indian sitting on a large rock upstream a hundred yards away. He had either just arrived or I had previously confused him with a rock as I had been looking in that direction. At dawn I had heard an elk bugling upstream and hoped the rain had washed my scent away so this grand creature might make an appearance. I waved at the Indian & he approached at a gait unhurried by the storm. I stretched out a saddle blanket, made him a cup of tea & offered him strawberries. He was impressive in his bearing rather than in size, or fierce mien. He said he had watched me the day before and had told the white men he was guiding & they wished to invite me to dinner. I replied I knew they had been coming for days as Short Bull had told me. He nodded pleased to hear of Short Bull who is the younger brother of Crazy Horse. I then added that Sitting Bull was encamped near Bear Butte with five thousand warriors and it would be wise to avoid the area. He was aware of this but nonetheless seemed unimpressed & pleasant. His name is One Stab, a solitary chief, who has lost nearly all his people to the illnesses we have brought them.

When the storm abated about four in the afternoon we rode an hour north to a large encampment. There were a full seven companies of Cavalry under the command of the reknowned G. A. Custer. One Stab brought me to the tent of Capt. William Ludlow who is chief of Engineers for the U. S. Army, an educated gentleman from Cornwall, England. Also there to be met was the geographer Prof. N. H. Winchell, and the scholar of Indians Geo. Bird Grinnell. In the beginning I felt shy with this august company as I had not spoken with men of this quality of intellect since I had left Cornell twelve years before. Their questioning was relentless & intense but civil. We had whiskies and a fine dinner including pies made of gooseberries, wild cherries & blueberries. Mr. Grinnell wished to know why he had discovered row upon row of garishly painted buffalo skulls. I replied that certain Sioux medicine men wish to bring the buffalo back from the dead. I assured Mr. Grinnell that I would send him some interesting fossil specimens as the progress of their march is too rapid to permit proper scientific inquiry. Lieut.-Colonel Custer stopped by to greet us though he seemed not altogether pleased by my presence, as if my being in the Black Hills decreased the drama of his expedition. This man is something of a mystery. There is something missing in him, but also something more than in other men. I was reminded of a brilliant Thespian who performed the role of Othello at Cornell. The Sioux are unequivocal in their respect for him. He stopped barely short of calling me a meddler & also asked of Sioux movements. I repeated what I had told the guide, that Sitting Bull was near Bear Butte with five thousand warriors and the mood among the Sioux was such that an encounter should be avoided. Custer asked me if I was sure & certain of this information & I said I was not in the habit of invention. He stalked off and when out of earshot Ludlow, Winchell & Grinnell had a good laugh over this comedy of manners. I was fatigued & a little angry by it all, so Ludlow poured some more whiskey before bed. He is of the opinion, and will say so in his report to the Gov't., that the Black Hills must remain the exclusive province of the Sioux, who have been driven so relentlessly hither and yon. To bid goodnight on a pleasant note Ludlow told me of a view. "Harney's Peak was visible from the top of a high, bare hill, and the sun having just set, we were in a few minutes well rewarded for the ride of five miles. The moon was rising just over the southern shoulder of Harney, and masked by heavy clouds. A patch of bright blood-red flame was first seen, looking like a brilliant fire, and soon after another so far from the first that it was difficult to connect the two. A portion of the moon's disk became presently visible, and the origin of the flame was apparent. While it lasted the sight was superb. The moon's mass looked enormous & blood-red, with only portions of its surface visible, while the clouds just above and to the left, colored by the flame, resembled smoke drifting from an immense conflagration. The moon soon buried herself completely in the clouds, and under a rapidly darkening sky we returned to camp.

A Wagner opera of the prairies! I had to dash off an immediate note to my chairman, who was a scholar of military movements of the time. I would give him a copy of this portion of the journal—a new and unknown description of Custer would be a feather in his hat!

I jumped in fright, hearing a voice at the door. It was Naomi and I hadn't heard her drive in. She looked at me oddly and told me to check the mirror: I was sunburned from the goose-cage barbecue, and my habit of tweaking my own nose while working made it raw where it wasn't stained by ink.

While I washed up for our martini she gave me an assortment of news. Dalva would be back in the morning. Did I remember I was speaking at Rotary tomorrow? (I didn't.) Could she help me make some dinner? Her young friend the naturalist had called from Minneapolis to say that he had received more funding and wondered if she would be willing to be his paid assistant. I darted out of the bathroom to give her a hug, because I could hear the pleasure in her voice over the job. I had to say that she had only been retired two weeks and a new job was pushing it. Then out of the blue I asked her why Northridge would marry Aase if she were dying of tuberculosis.

"I told you I can't read those journals, but I know about that part because Aase's brother Jon, the one who killed the deer the Sioux helped with, is my grandfather. Dalva's grandfather made John Wesley and Paul read the journals when they were young men. So one day in late October John Wesley was in our area pheasant-hunting and he pulled into our yard in a new Ford convertible with three English setters. It was a bright, clear Indian-summer Sunday. You know, it was the tail end of the Depression and we were just surviving, even though we had never taken any bank loans. My parents and John Wesley, who was twenty at the time, sat and talked of what was known about the old days. I was seventeen and in my last year of high school and very shy. He said it was strange but there had been no contact between the families in sixty years. Then my dad was embarrassed, because he said he followed the Northridges in the newspapers, but John Wesley laughed. The year before his dad had slugged a U. S. senator at an Omaha dinner party when the senator insulted his own wife in public. Then John Wesley asked my parents if he could take me for a ride in his car, and they said yes. I barely said a word, and when he dropped me off I never thought I'd see him again. He told me he had had one year at Cornell but hated college because he wanted to be a farmer. He certainly didn't remind me of any farmer I had ever seen, and this puzzled me. A few days later a package came with an inlaid-ivory hand mirror. A note said he wished at this moment to be the mirror looking back at me. I remember it so clearly because the weather had changed and the first snow was falling. I was sitting at the kitchen table with my parents, listening to Gabriel Heatter on the radio. We were all shocked by the gift. Every few days another present and note would come. And that's how it began."

Naomi abruptly walked outside, a bit overcome. I wanted her to continue but she refused, even under the urging of the extra-strong martinis I fixed when we went in for dinner. We decided it was still too hot in the early evening for much food, so I whipped up an antipasto from the air-freight goodies. I was feeling virtuous about this light eating until I recalled I had polished off an entire chicken for lunch.

"You remember everything that ever happened to you as if it was yesterday, don't you?"

She began to answer, then stopped short for a minute or so, smiled, and started to name every student she had taught since 1948. She also admitted she could name all the over four hundred birds on her life list.

"It's pleasant to meet someone without blockages. I bet you've never been to a shrink."

"Just once, a number of years ago, down in Lincoln. I talk to my husband a little while every day."

"I'm sure it's harmless as long as he doesn't talk back."

"He does. The psychiatrist said it was OK if I kept it strictly limited and it doesn't interfere with the rest of my life, so every evening just before dark I sit on the porch swing and we have a chat."

"Even in winter?" I was aghast at this bit of news.

"I bundle up. John Wesley was always discreet. For instance, he would never tell me who was the father of Dalva's baby son. He said the dead don't know everything. I still don't believe him. I think he knows." She noticed the discomfort this was causing me and laughed. "Let's go for a ride," she said.

We drove north on the gravel road to the same place Dalva had gone swimming. We walked a mile or so along the riverbank, stopping when she pointed out a huge nest in a pine tree. She handed me the binoculars, saying it was a blue heron sitting on its eggs. It was dark when we got back to the car. The water made the air smell lovely, though the evening was still overwarm.

"You suit yourself, but I'm going to have a little swim."

The moon hadn't come up and I was fearful, but on a whim disrobed and followed her into the river. We held hands against the light current, sitting on the sandy bottom with the water up to our breasts.

"What does he say death is like?" I couldn't help asking the obvious question.

"He won't be specific but said it was a pleasant surprise. We all get what we deserve."

"I don't think that would be a pleasant surprise," I said, a little morosely.

"You're really not a bad sort." She put an arm around my shoulder and gave me a squeeze. When her breast nudged my shoulder I became instantly erect. Oh my God, she's old enough to be my mother, I thought. Then she said it was time to go, and we helped each other up. I couldn't help embracing her. She lingered just a second, feeling me against her tummy. "It wouldn't be right. Dalva will be home tomorrow." She moved away and I loved the sound of her high, clear laughter in the dark.

○

After Naomi dropped me off and I went back to work I felt a little confused and mysterious, the latter being normally beyond my ken. It was the very rare feeling that life was indeed larger and much more awesome than I presumed it to be. I knew this feeling would disappear by morning, and I meant to relish it as long as possible. It was a perfect time to check on the progress of my lovers, Northridge and the fair Aase.

**May 27–June 7, 1876**
**I have been far too busy for my journal until this rainy day has given us respite. Leaving the Jensens I rode back to Scotts Bluff which had much improved in appearance with my new happiness. I engaged a Norwegian and his three helpers at an exorbitant price to come with me and build a good cabin in a short time. I bought house furnishings and food to live on, also many items for a wedding feast, and on impulse a white wedding gown for my Aase. I spoke to my gov't agent friend, Spaeth, who promised to be beside me at the wedding, and also found an old Lutheran**

preacher willing to make the trip for a goodly price. Spaeth tells me that after my wedding he will move back to Kansas to make himself some money & to be in a place, Lawrence, where he can find good books to read. I post a letter and a telegraph message to my Quaker merchant partner in Chicago to find the best doctors possible as we will arrive in a few weeks' time on our wedding trip. We are all ready to leave the next morning when I remember I need a suit of clothes & must further bribe a tailor to measure & find someone to deliver.

Back on the north fork of the Loup. I am pleased to see the Norwegian and his crew up at daylight and working hard. I ride off to find my Sioux friends at their summer camp to invite them to my wedding & am dismayed to find only a few of the very old, and three crippled children in their care. One of the old is the medicine man I have known ten years & whose name I am not permitted to write down. He says all my friends have gone off to war in the West: White Tree, He Dog, Short Bull, Sam Creekmouth, and thousands of others led by Crazy Horse. They hope to engage with other groups of Sioux (Tetons, Lakota, Minneconjou), General Custer and any others who may wish to fight in Wyoming & Montana. I spent the day and night with the old man who is quite palsied & his joints are swollen. He tells me that this is his eighty-sixth summer which means he was born around 1790. He speaks long and slowly about the glory & decline of the Sioux & insists his observations & dreams tell him the end is near for his people. In honor of my name he gives me a necklace of badger claws, advising me to keep it on my body as in the coming years I will be in the gravest danger because of my efforts to help the Sioux.

I bid him adieu at first light and ride off in a state of melancholy despite the fine weather. I question my accomplishments which are few. I ride everywhere to tend my trees in dozens of locations & have tried to offer by word & example the Gospel to the Sioux. I tell them that all white men are not evil & they seem to know this though nearly all of their land has been stolen. The Sioux also know that I am thought to be a lunatic by the white men at various Forts, by soldiery and civilians alike. They are not disturbed by this though there is humor on the matter, having a different notion of what constitutes a lunatic. White Tree told me that I had been around long enough now to begin having dreams & visions. I have tried to tell them I will only have the vision Christ has given me, but they say they have already heard that from all manner of thieves & swindlers. I am recently of the opinion that the Antichrist is Greed.

At the cabin my spirits lift when the Norwegians say they will finish four days earlier than promised. I am desperate to see Aase & bury myself in the hard work of the cabin to exhaust myself. On the afternoon the Norwegians are packing to leave, Aase's brother Jon rides up & tells me that I am to come tomorrow if I will. His sister is not feeling well and Jensen has relented on our waiting time. Jon helps me put the furnishings in the house & we pack up the wagon and are off for the wedding.

It was past midnight and I was not up to a wedding, especially in regard to the uncertain results. I poured a nightcap and craved for something less high-minded to occupy myself with—a magazine, television, a trip to the bar. The car was there but I doubted I could figure out how to get to town or, if I got there, whether or not the Lazy Daze would still be open. I dismissed the urge to look at my single photo of Karen. There was plenty of time in the morning, before Naomi picked me up, to prepare notes for my address to the Rotary. In any event, I had planned tidbits, piths, gists, and witticisms from American History 102. There was the temptation to knock them off their seats with the story-behind-the-story. A note of caution was the idea that the burghers might be lying in wait for another of my pratfalls, and I didn't want to oblige them.

There was a single goose honk and I rushed outside without thinking. The geese were huddled together against the cage but not inside, and were staring off in the dark in a single direction, where their doom apparently lurked, watching us. I rushed to the pump shed to look for their food but couldn't find it. I filched a sack from Frieda's hidden cache of corn chips in the kitchen, rushed back out, poured the contents in the cage, and managed to shove and cajole them to safety. The last one in leaned against my leg for a moment in possible thanksgiving. The fine feeling this poor bird gave me substituted for another nightcap, and I fell asleep thinking about blessed nothing. I had almost yelled "Fuck you, coyote" into the dark, but thought better of it.

○

At eleven in the morning I am dressed in my suit of lights, an anti-bullfighter in gray flannel trousers, brogans, Harris-tweed jacket, my only J. Press shirt. The day is cool and dark with rain and a strong northerly wind. The change in weather is exhilarating, reminding me as it does of my home in the Bay Area. I sort through some notes, waiting for Naomi to pick me up. I had been a bit miffed when Frieda hadn't showed up, then remembered Wednesday was her day off. It occurred to me then that I had completed my first full week in Nebraska and had settled in quite nicely.

Earlier, when I made my coffee (after releasing my grateful geese), I sat at the big Northridge desk and got out the Edward Curtis portfolio for breakfast reading. When I untied the first folio there was a note—"Dalva & Ruth. Wash your hands. I love you. Grandpa." A simple old note, brittle with age, but I was momentarily overcome with loneliness for her; at the same time, though, I knew in a deeper sense that I was totally out of the running. In the long and short of it, love is a more difficult subject than sex. Or history. I began to flip through the photos: Bear's Belly, the Arakira chief, stared back at me in his grizzly robe, an image of such singular magnificence that I took my coffee to the window to watch the rain. These folks used to wander around in this area, I thought, watching the wind push against the empty tire swing. When Dalva returned I would become noble. Maybe I'm like the sun, who doth allow the base, contagious clouds to cover up his beauty. Or not.

I returned to Bear's Belly and thought my father's eyes had some of the same quality. Maybe it was the insistence of physical strength got from forty years in a steel mill, or of time spent in the Truck Islands and Guadalcanal in World War II. I flipped through the prints, stopping at the Crow chief Two Whistles with a crow perched on his head. I had done my senior thesis at Notre Dame on Edward Curtis and never found out why this man had a crow perched on his head. Curtis probably never found out either, because after thirty-three years in the field taking photos of the Indians he went crazy and was placed in an asylum. When they let him go he went down to old Mexico and looked for gold, with a diffidence in recovery that characterized the behavior of many great men—let's go the edge and jump off again.

○

Naomi fetched me promptly from the enchanted forest. She was slightly irritated with Dalva, who had driven the old convertible and had thus been delayed by the rain. I had noticed among my relatives that a woman can be sixty and her mother eighty, and the sixty-year-old will still be treated very much like a daughter.

"I don't for the life of me understand why you consented to do this," she laughed, hitting the big puddles on the gravel road with abandon.

"I felt it was an obligation. I mean, Dalva implied it was an honor." The puddles brought the idea of a mudbath to mind. There was the same flutter in my guts as when someone tells you that you don't look all that well.

"That girl is never beyond a practical joke. She's not mean about it, though. I'd say you were in for it. Those boys at the Rotary can give an outsider a hard time. They like to probe but they're not vicious."

"I'm tempted to ask you to stop the car, but, then, I can handle anything short of a lynch mob. I presume they serve drinks."

"Wrong. No one drinks around here at lunch." She let the import of this push me to panic, then reached into her purse for two small, airline bottles of booze. "One now, and one for a trip to the bathroom later."

"I owe you a million bucks."

"It only lasts an hour. About the same time as a tooth extraction." She flashed a smile.

I had no idea what they actually did in these organizations, for which there are often little signposts on the road entering small towns: Rotary, Kiwanis, Chamber of Commerce, Knights of Columbus, Masons, Lions, American Legion, VFW, Moose, Eagles, and the Elks. That's all I could think of. Why weren't there Bears?

○

Afterward, at the Lazy Daze, I felt the hour had been the equivalent of a fifteen-round fight. The big back room of Lena's Café was stuffed to the rafters. I had guessed, which proved correct, that getting lost, public drunkenness, the little wreck with Lundquist, all by an ostensibly prominent person, would help build a crowd. It had also become clear that the Northridges represented a unique fiefdom in the area, and everyone is perennially curious about the rich.

The first shock was seeing Karen as the waitress for the head table. I wasn't really seeing all that well because of nerves, but there she was, clear as day, and giving me a wink. The sea of faces at long tables were an even mixture of reddish and pale, those whose work took them out of doors, and those who manned the stores and offices. The master of ceremonies was a big, jovial soul, a farm-implement dealer named Bill. He slapped me on the back and whispered, "You Easterners always give us a lot of guff." I told him I was a Westerner, which didn't seem to record. Here is a skit of this homely movie:

All stood and sang "America the Beautiful." Followed by "Rotary."

"R-O-T-A-R-Y That spells Rotary;
R-O-T-A-R-Y is known on land and sea;" etc.

I was given a songbook but my heart wasn't in it. I noticed that, other than Lena and the waitresses, Naomi was the only woman in attendance. It was a stag club, and back in feminist San Francisco the ladies would have torn these guys a new asshole. I must admit I felt a great deal of inscrutable good will, although there was the overlying sense that one better not break the rules, written or unwritten, of the locale.

I didn't listen to my introduction, because I was watching Karen pass out bowls of iceberg lettuce covered by pinkish dressing. She attracted a lot of shifty-eyed, admiring looks. I had "telephoned her stomach," as the witty French say. Sud-

denly the whole room rose and bellowed "HELLO, MICHAEL!"
It was thunderous and my bowels loosened a bit. They all sat
down and stared at me, amused at my confusion. Good ole Bill
gestured for me to begin.

I began with a witticism that history hopes to create reasons for what we've already done. No reaction. I went on to
talk about the Turner Thesis, Charles Beard, Bernard De Voto,
Henry Adams, Brooks Adams, Toynbee's adversary theory,
and so on. No reaction. Sweat trickled down my chest and
thighs. Holy shit, I thought, I better get dramatic. My first real
salvo was that the entire westward movement between the
Civil War and the turn of the century was a nasty pyramid
scheme concocted by the robber barons of the railroads and a
vastly corrupt U. S. Congress. The audience becomes perky,
which encourages me to go too far. The Civil War was so
vicious because the frontier was dead and all the yokels,
hopped on murderous adrenaline, were stewing for a fight.
Murmurs in the crowd. The settlers came out and swindled
and swiped the land treatied to the Indians, protected by a
government drunk on power, money, and booze. When the
settlers needed more fuel for their greed they used Christianity, and the idea that the Indians weren't using the land. If your
neighbor leaves his land fallow, grab it. I saw Naomi frown at
the back of the room but there was nowhere to go at this point.
History judges us by how we behave in victory. I added a lot
of apocalyptic blather on how we have extended this general
swinishness into our current foreign policy, then sat down to
generous but polite applause. The lectern was still in reach, so
I poured my second miniature booze into my glass of water
and gulped it down. MC Bill caught this and twinkled. Everyone else had begun eating, and I poked at my traditional
chicken à la king. Bill asked me if I was willing to "field" some
questions, so I got back to my sweating feet. A goofy fellow in
a pale-blue suit raised his hand. "One thing I don't like about
history is that it doesn't deal with the future. . . ." There were
moans at this *non sequitur* and he became flustered. "What I
don't get is, where was all those immigrants supposed to go?"
I admitted this was a good question but I was describing what
happened, rather than what was supposed to happen. A rather
smartly dressed man (the only lawyer in town, also the prose-

cutor) tried to catch me with a question about the farm problem in 1887. I said when a Nebraska farmer sells a bushel of
wheat for twenty-five cents minus freight, and the middleman
in Chicago or New York gets a dollar and a half, it proves that
times never change. This brought pleasant applause. There
were a number of inane questions before the mood darkened
with a question about Jimmy Carter, whom I tried to defend,
then a baiting query about Central America, Nicaragua in particular. I replied, Why should we be worried about a country
with only five elevators? This brought mass confusion. Only
five elevators in the whole country? Was I sure? Yes, I had been
there. Of course this was a lie—I had actually got my information from a copy of my daughter's *Rolling Stone.* Didn't the
president say these communists were only a day's drive from
Texas? I replied that how was a standing army of thirty thousand commies going to get by three million Texas deer-hunters
armed to the teeth? This brought hearty applause. The last
question was idiotically poignant, and asked by the oldest man
in the audience. "A lot of our parents felt that old Northridge
was on the wrong side of the Indian Wars. What do you say to
that? With apologies to Naomi here, who is anyway a Jensen,
some folks think that the first Northridge was a bona-fide lunatic. And if you think these drunken Sioux are so wonderful,
why don't you go up to Pine Ridge and try living with them?
Anyway, you can't fight history." There was a moderate
amount of cheering, and a tender sense that "drunken Sioux"
was a slight against my own behavior in the locale.

I pulled a rhetorical trick and turned my back to the
crowd to collect my thoughts. The vision of a hamburger with
fried onions and a cold beer passed before my eyes. I stayed
with my back turned until I felt their sharpening nervousness,
somewhat in the manner in which the great Nijinsky had become a human statue.

"Of course you can't fight history, but men of conscience
occasionally help make it. You certainly don't fight or make
history patting each other's asses at business lunches, or by the
time-honored practice of buying cheap and selling dear. But,
then, didn't Northridge become what all you folks really want?
I mean rich, quite rich, crazy rich. How would you behave if
you and your relatives had spent the last hundred years in a

rural slum, an arid concentration camp? I never said the Sioux were weeping-Jesus white Christians. I'm saying that history teaches us that your forefathers behaved like hundreds of thousands of pack-rat little Nazis sweeping across Europe. That's all. You won the war. Don't sweat it. I've never been to Pine Ridge. I'll go if you drive. I'll buy a case of whiskey and we'll have a party and you can give them a sermon on how they're behaving like so many redskin Leon Spinkses. . . ." I was just getting cranked up but MC Bill quickly adjourned the meeting as a response to a wave of moans and gasps. The upshot was that my last questioner, the old man, was a retired Methodist minister, a leading citizen, a town father, that sort of thing. Naomi led me out as swiftly as possible, not without some sparse handshakes and merriment by several of the younger men. There were also a few older types who slapped my back and guffawed as if I were a great stand-up comedian.

I made a beeline to the Lazy Daze, followed by Naomi and the owner-editor of the newspaper, who wanted to clarify some details from my interview with Karen. On my sweat-soaked way out of Lena's Café, Karen had been standing with several other waitresses and had given me another winning wink. For some reason I thought of Gene Pitney's song "Town Without Pity." The lassie could make for a real afternoon mood change if it were only possible. Instead, my solace was to be an immediate double Scotch and beer chaser. Naomi and the editor entered laughing. The thought that Dalva had set me up for the whole thing was a spear in my side.

"You're the biggest news since we were runner-up in state basketball three years ago," the editor said.

I glanced over his shoulder at the passel of burghers gathered on the sidewalk outside of Lena's, looking across the street at the bar with a specific envy. Back to the cash registers, dipshits! I thought. But, then, curiously, there had been enough smiles to tell me that the frontier amusement with a real mess was intact. Naomi said a curious thing—in forty years of living near this community she had never been in the bar! It was frowned on for schoolteachers. If they wished to drink in public there was a lounge-restaurant in a town forty miles to the east. The editor, who was a younger fellow educated in Lincoln, said that carloads of teachers would go over on Friday afternoons, get drunk, and eat two-pound steaks. It was an attractive idea.

"Karen told me you're going to help her become a model," the editor said, with a ludicrous wink, and an elbow in my ribs.

○

Back to the safety of Sherwood Forest, or some such, though Dalva is a closer reach to Maid Marian than I am to Robin Hood, I suppose. When we came in she was standing by the kitchen table next to a bowl of half-eaten cereal, of all things, staring out the window. I went to her for the embrace I craved and felt I deserved, and couldn't stop my momentum when she turned, looking utterly fatigued and haggard.

"Jesus, you look like you've been shacked up with a detachment of U. S. Cavalry."

"Please shut up, Michael." She avoided my embrace and went to her mother. "Rachel died. She said on the phone that she was sick but not that she was dying." Now she was weeping and Naomi was attempting to comfort her. My face burned with embarrassment. She came over to where I was trying to slide out the door, took my arm, and bussed my cheek. "I need to sleep for a while." I said I was sorry Rachel had died and left.

Out in the emotional safety of the bunkhouse it occurred to me that I didn't know who Rachel was. I remembered a Northridge passage wherein a group of young Sioux warriors were practicing a game or rite they had learned from a "crazy society" among the Cheyenne. The warriors stood in a circle and fired hunting arrows straight up in the air, then waited fearlessly to see if anyone would be injured or die from the behavior, which was ostensibly religious in nature. I took off my damp and sorry professorial clothes and went into the shower to cleanse myself of my last two arrows, my Rotary speech and then my comment to Dalva.

Out of the shower, I put on my farmer costume in obeisance to an actor's impulse to feel different. I glanced at my notes on a word and page count and figured I had looked at about ten percent of the journals from 1865 to 1877. I had not touched the trunk in the bank vault, which carried on from there. I picked up the second and last volume of 1877—a sparse year for the journals—and saw my marker on a place where Northridge described his dream of dead Aase, and the beating death of his friend White Tree.

**Aug. 28, 1877**
**It is curious that my dream of Aase wherein she entered my body has relieved me of so much of the suffering of mourning this past week. One dream wakes one from another & it is as if I can see the world further and in more detail. I am not sure what has occurred here. I deduce that each mourner of a beloved is buried in thoughts of his uniqueness. This thought reminds me of the wild goose I shot for dinner one day up on the Missouri not far from Fort Pierre. The mate of the goose circled the area for two days & I moved my camp to rid myself of this melancholy sight. Sam Creekmouth assured me that this phenomenon is also true of wolves. I have spent a year where my soul was buried with her body & I was of no use to the people whom I came to help in the time of their great peril. Though it has been twelve years now the memory of our own war is still violent & fresh enough that I wished in my grief to keep my distance from their own. . . .**

Northridge is referring at this time to the extraordinary last six months of "freedom" for the Sioux and other tribes of the Great Plains: they won against Reynolds on the Powder River, won again under Crazy Horse at Rosebud Creek, and against Custer on the Little Big Horn; after which came the horror of defeat at Slim Buttes, Bull Knife, the Battle of Lame Deer, and the murder of Sioux chiefs at Fort Keogh. These six months allowed the warriors to relive their glory, also the doom their leaders had foreseen for so many years. Not much more remained for them after the surrender of the last remaining band of Oglalas under Crazy Horse, another six months later, at Fort Robinson.

**Aug. 29–Sept. 5, 1877**
**I awake well before daylight at last conscious of my obligation to my dead brother White Tree—he had seen a birch tree in a dream but never in reality. I must look after his widow who is called Small or Shy Bird—her name in Sioux means a bird who sits**

rather deliberately on a branch & regards all the activities of man with suspicion and amusement.

I am packed by mid-morning & say my prayers under the oak tree where she died a year ago. Kneeling as I knelt then I see her on the cot I made where she wished to spend her days out of doors, wrapped in a blanket despite the heat of the sun. We talked and I read to her from the Bible & the Sonnets of Shakespeare which she preferred. On that day I was disturbed as she saw a large bird I could not see so at last I admitted I saw it to relieve her concern. She said the bird was bringing the thunder. There were no clouds & I went down to the spring for a fresh pitcher of cold water. When I came back she reached out for me & we embraced & I felt her last breath against my ear. I sat there with her until early evening when indeed the lightning & thunder arrived. I let the rain fall on us, the first rain in a month, until we were wet & baptized anew & then I carried her body into the cabin.

I make the ride to Fort Robinson which is normally three days in less than two. For reasons that are not clear to me I feel panic & have strapped a pistol to my leg I purchased from a fearful man I met on the trail who is headed back to the East. He says there is a sense of ugliness & despair at Fort Robinson as all the Sioux are to be moved from Nebraska up to the Missouri where they do not wish to go. He expects a great battle and I assure him there are no more free Sioux to do battle. He says he sent his family to North Platte from his cabin & ranch near Buffalo Gap in June not wanting them scalped by the savages. I say I know the area well & there is a glint in his eye as he offers to sell me his section of land for a hundred dollars. He shows me the deed & I make the purchase & he is off at a gallop as if I intended to change my mind.

At Fort Robinson the Sioux are encamped a few miles to the south of headquarters on the creek, but I am told I am not allowed to visit them. When I remonstrate I am arrested and taken to the small stockade and jail. By great and incomprehensible coincidence the Lieutenant in charge there is my friend from long ago at Cornell whose Quaker father last summer told me was soldiering in the West. He dismisses the men who arrested me & we walk outside. He begs me not to tell that he did not serve his country in the Civil War. I look at him as if he were daft, saying that I am ashamed to have accepted gold to take his place & the secret is safe with me. I explain my obligation to White Tree's widow & he sends two men for her. He tells me he is without sympathy for my efforts among the Sioux whom he will continue to help destroy, but feels somewhat bound by our past friendship. Small Bird is brought still soiled with the ashes of mourning & we are sent on our way after I have extracted a letter of safe passage from him. Since there are others in view he does not shake my hand when we depart.

Sept. 8, 1877

I have taken Small Bird on a two-day ride up to Buffalo Gap where I have purchased the cabin & property which is in reasonable repair. She had begged me to return to Fort Robinson to retrieve her mother who is not well. I would rather not do so but the memory of my own mother when she was ill spurs me toward my duty.

My classmate the Lieutenant is not pleased to see me again & smells of whiskey. The jail is hot & full of flies. He looks at papers & says Small Bird's mother is recently dead of cholera. I do not believe him but have no recourse. He points to a large darkened spot on the floor covered with flies & says it is there that Crazy Horse died the evening before after trying to escape. On orders he was bayoneted by another Indian. He wears a smile as he offers his condolences. My head grows dizzy & I kneel and touch the blood-moistened floor. I say a prayer & he tells me to get out. Two guards escort me out & to my horse. Far off a mile or so to the South I see the Sioux encampment and ride toward there though there are shouts & gunfire, whether directly at me or into the air I do not know. I look for faces I know among the mourners & Sam Creekmouth tells me that it is true. I see Worm, Black Shawl, He Dog, and Touch the Clouds but do not approach them. All the Sioux are to be moved to the Missouri immediately. Two boys run up to us to warn me that the detachment is mounting near the stockade perhaps to come arrest me. I mount & ride through the Sioux camp to the South at all possible speed & thankful that I am on my best horse & the day is darkening. I circle to the West, then North toward Warbonnet Creek, discovering their pursuit to be short-lived. At nightfall I feel the coward in my heart for not drawing the pistol and shooting the man. Before I sleep I find I cannot ask forgiveness for this impulse so opposed as it is to my waning faith.

I find myself staring at the ceiling as if in momentary regret that I can read. It had been so long since I had read Sandoz and others that it was an effort to remember who Touch the Clouds was. I checked a reference text and discovered that this man with the curious name was the medicine man in whose arms Crazy Horse died. He Dog was allowed to visit his friend during the last few moments of his life. I turned from the desk, sensing I was being watched, to find the geese at the screen door waiting for dinner. Perhaps they were hoping for another bag of Frieda's corn chips. My wife and daughter had shared the affections of a nasty little toy poodle who preferred fried chicken livers. This mutt had shit in my shoe and I fed it a teaspoon of Tabasco in punishment. The dog had done a precise little aerial flip and begged for more hot sauce.

I walked toward the house, trailed by geese, just as Dalva came out the door with a pail of feed. The birds rushed her with their peculiar wobble-trot. How could I understand the past when I couldn't comprehend geese? I thought. Dalva looked rested and spiffy in a pale-blue summer dress and sandals.

"Can I do it? I'm trying to make contact with terrestrial creatures." She handed me the pail and I flung handfuls of grain around the barnyard with a light heart.

"I hope you had a fine time at the luncheon club. Naomi said it went well though you got a little irascible." She said this almost shyly and with inappropriate gravity, then began to shake with suppressed laughter. I threw myself on the ground in an imitation of a girl who had a bad time at the prom, kicking my legs and shrieking. The geese fed on, being accustomed to my behavior. Dalva continued laughing, then leaned against the grape arbor for support. I crawled over and bit her foot.

"Some day at some time somewhere in the fucking world I'm getting even," I spoke to her toes.

She served me a drink in the den, a big person's drink, having decided that I was working too hard. She was amazed I hadn't been to town except with Lundquist on Saturday, and with Naomi this noon. She said she was taking me to a horse affair at the fairgrounds the next day. I admitted that I'd thought of going to town but didn't know the way, which had her stopped. If you drive north you hit the river, she said, and if you go south you reach town, because that's the only place the roads go around here. This was an amazing piece of information. I became a bit manic then, describing my afternoon's work, and wondering if I should go on immediately to the second trunk of journals to get perspective.

"They were going to ship Crazy Horse to the Dry Tortugas," she said. "It's an old prison in a fort about seventy miles off Key West, in the Gulf of Mexico. It's hard to imagine a Sioux warrior at sea." She became a little morose and sent me off to get ready for dinner. Naomi's nature boy, Nelse, had rearrived and she wanted us to come to dinner, but Dalva wasn't up to an evening with someone new. We were driving to the next town for a steak and hopefully the motel, but I wasn't pushing my luck by bringing up the subject. While I dressed I began to think of Crazy Horse in the tropics, then pushed the subject from my mind with a cheapish look at Karen's photo.

We drove in a car with a top—Dalva's Subaru—listening to a merry tape of Bob Wills and the Texas Playboys. I loathe country music but what Dalva called "Texas swing" seemed different and put us in a light mood. Most of this part of Nebraska is distinctly Western, and we paused by the side of the road to watch four cowboys herding cattle down a gravel road—two of the men were on horses, and two on small motorcycles. Cowboys have taken to wearing baseball-type caps, though in the evening they return to the Stetson shape. I was so bloody hungry that I asked Dalva to describe the menu. She answered in an affected Sand Hills drawl.

"You have your basic beef in many shapes, and your basic varieties of Jell-o, and the foil-wrapped potato that just might be yesterday's, and those great big ole drinks you favor."

"How about wine?"

"Only the sugar-added variety!"

It was only eight in the evening and still light outside, but sturdy folks were already dancing to Leon Tadulsky and the Riverboat Seven. Some of the band wore straw boaters while the others had on cowboy hats. We asked for a table as far as possible from the band and ordered Whopping Big drinks. Several people waved at Dalva but none approached our table. I doubt if she was ever thought to be chatty. The Tadulsky band was playing an odd mixture of Glenn Miller swing, polkas, and country-Western. Couples would take a few bites, then get up and dance, return to their food, and repeat the process. Everyone in the barnlike room was eating steak or roast beef on hot metal platters. This was definitely not Santa Monica. There was a long table of cowboys with their wives or girlfriends, and the men kept their hats on whether they were dancing or eating. The ranchers and business types wore leisure wear, but you could tell them apart, because the ranchers had sunburned or browned arms and faces. We were seated fairly near the salad bar, with its ubiquitous Plexiglas sneeze shield—I noted bowls of Jell-o of every color of the rainbow, cottage cheese, pickles, three-bean salad, all of which were being ignored by the crowd. Dalva ordered the Princess Cut of butt steak while I chose the forty-ounce King's Cut of porterhouse, designed for the man who really "believes in beef." I really didn't but, then, a wag had once said that the best sauce is hunger. Dalva noticed that I was tapping my fingers and mouthing the words to the band playing "Beer Barrel Polka" ("In heaven there is no beer, that's why we drink it here"). She thought this was amusing, and I replied that if you grow up in an Ohio Valley steeltown this is the music of your people. She grabbed my arm and we were out on the floor in a trice, cutting a rug that astounded the locals. The band played several polkas in a row to keep us going, and though I feared for my wildly thumping heart I was pleased to do something that was so widely admired. We continued on until midnight, mixed with eating and drinking, and I confess I've never felt so much like a real American since the Boy Scouts. The last dance of the evening was a rendition of the Mills Brothers' "Mood Indigo," which I danced with the leftovers of my porterhouse in my jacket. At the end of the song we dipped, then shamelessly kissed.

Outside, the night air was wonderful, because we were

soaked with sweat. In the car we kissed again and I got a hard-on like a toothache, which she gave a couple of squeezes on the hundred-yard drive to the motel. We made love for the first time with our clothes half on and without benefit of a shower. When she went into the bathroom I checked out the TV and was astounded to find a fuck-movie channel sponsored by the motel. I was chewing my steak and shouted for Dalva, who came nakedly from the shower. "Oh my God," she said.

We fell asleep to this not altogether fortunate test pattern, both waking at 3:00 A.M. dry-mouthed. I turned off the TV while Dalva let the water run cold; then we struggled with the usual plastic-wrapped plastic glasses, which their inventor should be forced to eat in quantity. We looked absurd enough in the mirror to maintain the good mood, making ugly faces at each other and spilling the aspirin on the floor. I stepped on the steak bone getting into bed, and then we made love again.

○

This was a day I should have "stood" in bed, as they used to say, in the safety of that distant motel. The random violence of America struck home, and without the slightest premonition on my part. It was cloudy and cool when she dragged me from bed, handing me a large Styrofoam cup of coffee, a fresh shirt, and undies from her suitcase. She had planned it all. Neither the shirt nor the undies were my own, but they were of unquestioned quality.

We were off for the hometown horse show, horse sale, whatever it was I'm unsure. There were enough horses at the rainy fairgrounds to last a lifetime. Dalva pointed out a refreshment stand where I might drink myself senseless on coffee, then abandoned me to look at horses with an eye for a purchase. Aren't four horses enough? I asked no one in particular. At the refreshment stand I ordered coffee and noted with satisfaction that they were putting beer down on ice. These folks are the Mongols or Cossacks of the Great Plains, I thought, constantly avoiding wheeling, backing, lunging, and prancing horses. A number of men greeted me with "Good morning, Professor," which made me feel I belonged there.

I never really saw it coming. An extremely large man

approached whom I recognized as the posse fellow who lifted me onto the horse the day I was lost, and who bought me a drink on my Saturday in town with Lundquist. I was struggling for his name when he marched right up, glared down at me, and showed me a nude photo of Karen.

"Pretty, isn't she?" I said, wondering what the big oaf was doing with the picture.

"My little Karen!" he yelled, grabbing my arm and wrenching it. The arm made a dreadful popping sound and seemed detached from my body, just hanging there by itself. Then he slapped me a mighty blow to the side of the face and I fell on my bottom. Jesus, will this never end? I thought, seeing his boot poised to kick me. Then men started shouting and several cowpokes bore him to the ground. The world was turning reddish and there was a nasty grating sound when I moved my jaw. The world turned darker red, with men stooping around me. Dalva came to me and held me. "Oh, Jesus, Michael, what have you done now?" Then I passed out into a painful dream as colorful as all of the Jell-os in Nebraska.

# BOOK III

# GOING HOME

# DALVA

## *June 15, 1986—Nebraska*

There was a peculiar moment, quite eerie in fact, in the waiting area of the emergency room. Immediately after Michael had been whisked away Naomi turned to me and I looked down at the floor feeling quite faint. She took my arm and we quickly walked out a back door of the hospital. It was an utterly oppressive sense of *déjà-vu*—the last time we had been in a hospital together was when I gave birth to my son in Tucson thirty years before. It was beyond discussing so we simply stood there a few minutes trying to allow our world to regain its proper shape. Finally we were able to make some plans and went back in so I could call a cab. Naomi would stay at the hospital for the time being while I went off to the lawyer's to discuss the situation, both dismal alternatives on a late afternoon in June. I peevishly thought I had missed buying the mare I had been after.

We had flown to Omaha in a Medi-Vac plane after a long ambulance ride down to North Platte where it was determined that Michael's jaw would require the attention of a specialist. His left arm was both broken and dislocated but the nature of the injury was minor compared with the mandibular fracture.

Right after the battle of the fairgrounds the sheriff and

prosecutor met me at the doctor's office where Michael was laid out on a table looking not all that good. The doctor was being careful to check for complications beyond broken bones. I discussed the tentative legalities with the sheriff and prosecutor who had taken a statement from Pete Olafson, Karen's father, at the jail. Would I object if he was released because it was Friday and no judge would be available until Monday? I said I had no objection because I had gone to school with Pete and it wasn't the sort of crime that would be repeated. There were other thorny problems: Karen was a week short of eighteen and was legally a minor. She would not admit to sleeping with Michael and said he hadn't taken the photo her mother had found in her room, though the photo had been taken at his request. Their sympathies were understandably with the local man despite the severity of Michael's injuries. The prosecutor showed me the photo in question which looked particularly banal in a doctor's office. They were acting on the verge of condescension when I told them I was sure the expenses involved in repairing Michael would bankrupt the guilty party. They gave each other a Mutt & Jeff look and the sheriff said "Maybe he had it coming." I said that he wasn't in a position to decide, and added that they wouldn't want to trade away Olafson's farm for some ill-considered charges against my houseguest. This veiled threat wasn't a gamble on my part, but a small plot to buy time. Not very far in the back of my mind I remembered a tenured English professor while I was at the University of Minnesota who had been dismissed for "moral turpitude" (truly underage girls). I naturally wanted to make sure that the news of Michael's latest adventure didn't reach his employer in California.

In the cab on the way to the lawyer's I reconsidered my involvement with the miserable son of a bitch. He simply in some classic sense didn't know any better. The idea that a man or a woman could be incisively brilliant in one area, and a grotesque fuck-up in another, was scarcely limited to the academic profession. Most of the bright and energetic people I had known in my life had closeted away secrets that were far too vivid to be referred to as skeletons.

At the lawyer's office I was startled to see how old the senior partners had become—all those who greeted me and had known my grandfather, father, Paul, and the rest of us looked near retirement. They put me in the care of an abrasive young man, assuring me that he handled "difficult" problems for the firm. He certainly was prepared: Pete Olafson had been arrested for assault three times in twenty-five years, though the charges were always dropped. Michael had been charged with grand theft (rare books) while at Notre Dame with the charges dropped, three drunk-driving convictions while in graduate school in Wisconsin, and was institutionalized under psychiatric care in Seattle for six weeks, the details of which were not available. The lawyer said he would come up on Monday morning and recommended a compromise whereby any and all possible charges against either party would be dropped. He had been on the phone and the girl in question had admitted to the prosecutor an hour ago that she and Michael had gone "sixty-nine," which, of course, was a criminal act, especially since she was short of eighteen. This in itself was meaningless, because the girl also had an established reputation for promiscuity, which could be proved in court. This lawyer meant to establish that Michael had "fallen from a horse," and his insurance would take care of most of the medical expenses. Was I agreeable to the plan? If not, we could get Mr. Olafson at least a year in jail, but some sort of charge would stick against Michael, and possibly interfere with his employment. Quite naturally I agreed to the compromise, and assured him that Michael would sign anything to that effect.

At the hotel it occurred to me that there was nothing quite like an hour spent at a law firm to make you want a shower and a drink, both of which I accomplished. While I was having my drink Naomi called from the hospital to say that they were going to do the surgery in the evening, which was closing in. There was some concern over Michael's high blood pressure, evidence of chain-smoking and minor damage in the blood profile caused by alcohol. The surgeon, however, was optimistic, and told Naomi that the patient would be fine except for the inconvenience of having his mouth wired shut for two months. Michael would be out of the hospital in ten days to two weeks and would survive nicely on a readily available liquid diet. Despite the nastiness of the situation there was something quite amusing about the wired mouth and the diet. Naomi would be at the hotel in an hour. To avoid complications she had airily assured the staff she was Michael's ex-wife and had signed all the necessary papers and had written a check on the account of the NRA Travel Fund, which she thought was funny. His insurance was adequate—the extra check was for an especially "lovely" sort of room that modern hospitals make available for those who can afford them. I told Naomi on the phone that the shitheel deserved the basement.

That evening over dinner Naomi asked why I had turned against Michael when, given my experience, I must have understood his failings from the beginning. And why had I chosen him for the papers when it couldn't have simply been out of sympathy? I said I didn't want a boring scholar who would only produce a boring work of scholarship. The first question was harder; he was exhausting me and, though the recent incident was horrible I felt a guilty sense of relief to not have to deal with him for a few weeks. She said she would be traveling back and forth a good deal with the young man on the project, and why not move Michael to her place for his convalescence and have Frieda take care of him?

At this point an actual tear fell into my white wine and I couldn't finish my dinner. I ordered an enormous brandy, reached over and put my hand on Naomi's. "Are you sure?"

"I've always been a bit lonely, and I've always enjoyed a little bad behavior. You've seen so much and I've seen so little. I'm sure he would have amused your father."

"Are you going to tell him?" I had known for a long time that she had imaginary talks with my father.

"Of course. I've never hidden anything from him. I had a few boyfriends over the years and I never kept anything from him."

"I always thought you believed he could see us?"

"No, that would be too ordinary. The dead just sense and understand our feelings. At least that's what I've come to believe. They are infinitely broad-minded."

I looked at her directly a long time, as if I no longer understood the term "mother," much less "daughter." "Do you think my son is alive?" I had to ask this though there was an instant pang of regret.

"I think you do," she said rather briskly. "I can tell you're thinking of looking for him too, though you probably won't admit it to me. I won't tell you it's wrong, but I believe it's up to him to look for you if he so desires. Along with your father, it is the other tragedy that came into our life. You weren't ready to be a mother even if there had been a father to be found. I finally knew who the father was when you put up a gravestone for Duane in 1972, and I wept for you for weeks and I couldn't say anything to you. I thought, My poor lovely Dalva, her only husband a crazy Sioux boy dead like my own. I'm sure you didn't know this but I was proud of your courage in wanting his gravestone next to your own father's, because it meant you must have loved him so."

We were both crying by then, and I'm sure that others in the hotel dining room were a little disturbed by us. When we got up to leave the maître d' rushed over and in a thick accent said the surgeon had called to say the operation had gone well and "everyone" was alive. His pronunciation of "everyone" was so dramatic that we had to laugh, which added to the confusion.

○

Early in the morning, on the way to the airport, we stopped at the hospital. A friend of my mother's, a farm-implement dealer named Bill Mercer, was flying down to pick us up in his small Cessna. I looked forward to the trip because I loved flying close to the ground. Michael's quarters turned out to resemble a pleasant enough suburban bedroom though overdosed on paisley. He had a fresh newspaper in front of his face and didn't hear us enter. His left arm was in a light cast from his palm to his shoulder. I said "Hello" and we gasped with shock when he dropped the paper. His face looked like an overripe plum and one eye was completely closed. He quickly wrote a note—"These hot shots do the knife work from the inside to avoid marring my beauty. Was there ever a plum so fair?" I picked up his free hand and involuntarily kissed it. He closed his good eye, then handed me a prepared note with a list of things and books he needed, adding that for "God's sake" put the journals back in the bank vault for the time being. At the bottom of the note it said "I'm terribly sorry. Save me the embarrassment and leave me alone, though don't forget to pick me up in two weeks. Before you go, tell me you forgive me, if possible." I handed the note to Naomi and kissed his forehead. Naomi kissed him, and then a rather pretty nurse entered with a smile. It was impossible not to see her as his probable victim of one thing or another. She placed a plastic straw and a small paper cup to his lips. She said it was a liquid tranquilizer to compensate for lack of such items as solid food, nicotine, and alcohol. He gave us the peace sign and we left.

We flew northwest into the morning with the sun behind us, and once well outside Omaha and past Columbus, we descended and followed the North Loup. Naomi was up in front with Bill and as soon as it was polite to do so, I took off my earphones and mike, not wanting to talk or be talked to. Bill had been full of gossip about the great event, including the irony of Karen's interview with Michael in the weekly newspaper yesterday. Town opinion was split but many felt the punishment was too great for "you know what," which seemed to be public knowledge. There was his nervous laugh on the earphones over their euphemism for what men in jocular moments call "eating pussy" and "sucking dick." Then Bill began to tease Naomi about her new job, which included camping trips with a young man. It was at this point that I had had enough sexual innuendo at three thousand feet.

What I craved was loneliness, and could see there were plenty of possibilities down on the green and verdant earth. I felt a giggle in my stomach remembering a visiting poet in college who quoted Charles Olson's "I take space to be the central fact of America" in an oracular baritone. At a gathering after his reading this poet had spent more than an hour verbally seducing me when I had already decided to make love to him. He was led off by an assistant professor's wife when his speech to me got too loud. He was similar to Michael, only more so, and I wondered if this penchant for eccentric men came from being raised in the horse latitudes of Nebraska. The poet appeared the next morning at the apartment I shared with Charlene and began his speech again, and I hurriedly took him off to my bedroom. Charlene was involved with a Minneapolis businessman at the time. Years later I had seen this poet weaving around a Greenwich Village bar, pathetically bloated with alcohol and whatever was being ingested at the time. I didn't approach him.

When we landed I said goodbye to Naomi who was headed off to Sheridan County with Nelse. I hadn't met him yet but was without curiosity about anyone for the time being. On the drive back to the farm I began to wonder if my life was winding down or merely adjusting itself. If two more children left the school district I would be without a job in September.

In the mail was an enormous bill for the repair of Michael's car in Denver. I wrote a check with no irritation whatsoever. Another letter, without a return address, was a clumsy note of apology from Pete Olafson. His lawyer would disapprove, but, then, he likely didn't have a lawyer—that was reason enough to compromise. "So in closing I say, I did not mean to slap your friend that hard. I just grabbed his arm and saw red. I thought who is this man who wants to see naked pictures of little girls. One more money setback and we will go bottom up, that's for sure. My life is in your hands. Usually if you hit a guy he rolls with the punches and no one gets hurt. If you see fit to be understanding I will shoe your horses free of charge for 10 years. I should never have left the business. My wife is crying day and night. Yr. friend Pete O."

Fathers are habitually a half-decade behind their daughters' actual age. Pete had always been a bully and a lout, but a first-class farrier. His wife, who was in Ruth's class, was a devious neurotic, the sort of woman who gives Scandinavians an undeservedly bad name for looniness. How hopeless, I thought. It was too easy to be confused by the idea of personality, so I looked through a tack chest in the pump shed for the saddlebags that I had made for me in San Antonio years before. The view of the North Loup from the plane had reminded me of a swale near the Niobrara I hadn't seen since I was a girl, and I meant to ride there in the afternoon. First, though, I had the obligation to write Paul and tell him that Rachel had died, sending along a photo she wanted him to have of the two of them together so long ago in Buffalo Gap. There was the sense in the photo of my father's unseen presence, and I quickly slid it into the envelope, wondering if it was he or Grandfather who took the picture. Rachel was lovely but Paul never looked comfortable in a cowboy hat, and even with a shovel in his hand he was melancholy and studious. He told me that after his mother died in Omaha in early May he came to the farm, started digging irrigation ditches, and didn't stop until September when it was time to go back to school. Grandfather and Wesley would ride out to see him but he wouldn't talk to them. He made his own meals on a hot plate in the bunkhouse.

By midafternoon I was saddled and headed for the swale. At the last moment I had packed a ground cloth and a summer bag in case I wanted to spend the night. After a half-hour or so the world I was tired of had disappeared, and the only thing I was missing was a dog or two. Naomi had mentioned that a friend over in Ainsworth had a litter of Labrador-Airedale crosses which would make an ideal ranch dog. I told her I would think it over but I wanted to make sure that the school was going to open in September.

I was riding Peach, a mare, on a trail on the south side of the Niobrara. She loved water and I let her swim a few minutes, soaking me to the upper thighs. This didn't do the job so I tethered her and took off the saddle and my bags, then took off my clothes. We found a deeper stretch—there was still plenty of water in June—and we floundered around together having a wonderful time. She was alarmed by minnows and stared at them with her ears perked as a puppy would. Bathing with horses; I let my mind slip back to the best parts of the afternoon in the Keys, the glittering blue creek in the mangroves, swimming with Duane and the buckskin in the tidal thrust, the whiteness of the scar tissue around the healed shrapnel and bullet wounds as if the insides had sucked themselves away from the incursion of metal.

I let myself sun-dry while Peach rolled in a sunken, dusty area that must have been an old buffalo wallow. After my conversation with Naomi in the hotel dining room I had considered trying to talk to Duane as she did Father but I didn't dare. I thought of Michael's agitation over the idea of Crazy Horse's being sent to the Dry Tortugas—Michael spent a lot of time trying unsuccessfully to avoid the human dimension, affecting the emotional distance of a surgeon. I wondered how he would hold up against the insanity of some of the volumes in the second chest, but then there was a vast difference between being involved in the Ghost Dance movement and writing about it. Perhaps it was too peculiar and embarrassing, too unique to be imagined. There was a trace of obverse pride in Michael's actually not knowing an Indian, other than the day spent with the Nez Percé student, but then his sense of himself needed an improbable amount of protection. When I mentioned a particular novel or movie I enjoyed he would reject the idea because "it would set me off."

I dressed and remounted Peach, riding as hard as she would allow for an hour only to discover the swale was no longer there. It had been drained, filled, and contoured for what remained of a cornfield—unplanted this year because the country had twice as much corn as it needed. Sometimes they needed help at it but farmers had always been pretty good at cutting their own throats. Hanging invisibly in the air, just above the ground, was the delightful hummock of cottonwoods, osier, and wild cherry, the clouds of birds that mated and nested there.

I doubled back and crossed the river, headed for the small box canyon favored by Grandfather, Paul, Duane, and myself. There was more than a little fear in my heart but the miniature canyon was intact; if anything the trees and bushes were more dense and the groundwater yielded up a fuller spring. I sat on the flat rock, ate a half-sandwich, and drank iced tea from a thermos. It was so curious to close my eyes and realize the sandwich tasted like Bleecker Street and Washington Square in the late sixties. If you wanted a sandwich you had to go to New York City or send for supplies.

I felt a mental tremor as I sat on the rock, as if I were being revisited by the emotions I had felt there the summer after the baby, both good and bad. Naomi had been canning tomatoes. I left it where it was, large breasts and all. New places and old bring on unstudied emotions. At one time I made a study of all of them. Grandfather wouldn't go beyond his volume of William James and that was the book that got me started. During an advanced graduate course in abnormal psychology at Minnesota five of us had gone on a week-long field trip of state hospitals with our brash young professor from New York. At one of the institutions we had met an inmate, a middle-aged Chippewa from the Red Lake Reservation up in Rainy River

County. The hospital guide assured us that the Chippewa was
an incurable schizophrenic but when we were left alone with
him the professor, who was passionate and quite Jewish, determined the Chippewa was a shaman who had been institutionalized through the efforts of the usual malevolent nitwits from
the Bureau of Indian Affairs. The shaman had been caught in
the act of being trees and stones for a year and had been sent
away. The first few years in the hospital he had answered his
confinement by becoming a river. We were all sitting out on
a lawn beside some flower beds. He told us to watch closely as
he lay down and put on his "suit of running water." The professor said later it was a specific type of group hypnosis, but the
Chippewa did seem to become water. It disturbed us all a great
deal except the professor who thought it was interesting. After
a year of concerted effort he got the Chippewa released under
the guise of further study. You're not legitimately schizophrenic if you can turn it off at will and return to consensual
reality. The shaman, however, was quite unhappy in Minneapolis and disappeared. Later, when I saw the professor at
a coffee house, he told me that the man had adopted a group
of crows that fed out on the ice of the frozen Mississippi, and
had probably gone off with them. Neither of us seemed sure
if he was serious.

Peach stared, trembled, then shied away from a rock for-
mation just beyond me at the head of the canyon. I was sure
it was a rattlesnake but didn't bother getting up to check. At
the Omaha airport in the morning the weatherman had said
a cool front was headed down from Alberta in the early evening, which meant rattlesnakes would take cover and the canyon would be fine for sleeping. I brushed Peach down and gave
her some oats from the saddlebags. She didn't need to be
hobbled since I had trained her from a filly a few summers ago
and she liked to stick close to the nearest human, not really a
peculiarity. She also liked Lundquist's dog Roscoe and the two
of them played tag. She followed me down the canyon to the
river flats where I gathered firewood, studying all of my movements. I made several trips because I had pretty much decided
to stay the night. I followed the eyes of Peach off to an enormous cottonwood by the river where a group of crows had
gathered and were obviously discussing our presence.

○

When I awoke from my night in the desert two weeks ago I
made a pot of coffee and drank it sitting cross-legged on the
cot. The dawn was radiant with the sun coming up over the
Sauceda Mountains, and there was the question why I didn't
do this more often though I had enjoyed hundreds of such
solitary dawns in my life. It was hot within an hour and I drove
across the Papago Reservation, then south toward Sasabe, cutting off at Arivaca Canyon Road to Nogales, to Patagonia, and
down to the San Rafael Valley where Paul now spent much of
his time. My thoughts the entire day were subsumed in the
aftermath of Duane's suicide fifteen years before, not in a
grotesque way but there was something in the mood that made
the memories of the night before continue their natural
course.

I had driven back to my room at the Pier House and
throughout the day I sat there being visited by the police, an
armed-services representative (the benefits), the coroner who
doubted the body would be found, an officer from the Coast
Guard who doubted the body would ever be found, an obtuse
reporter from the local Key West *Citizen,* and an intelligent
young man from the Miami *Herald* who had also been in
Vietnam. A Sioux on horseback committing suicide at sea was
thought to be newsworthy—I was never able to read this arti-
cle which was called "Requiem for a Warrior." The reporter
from the *Herald* was missing his left arm, at which sight I
finally wept. It was as if with this missing arm I knew that
Duane was gone from the earth and buried in the endless
prairie of the ocean. It was the only day of my life I was to be
addressed as Mrs. Stone Horse. I had been trying every half-
hour or so to get through to Paul because I didn't want to
worry Naomi. When I succeeded and told Paul the story he
said to sit tight and he would come for me. Perhaps it is pretentious and doesn't matter but I have put in my will that "Dalva
Stone Horse" is to be on my gravestone, and that my ashes are
to be cast into the ocean in the Gulf Stream off Big Pine Key.
I shall join him in the great ocean river.

Rather than take me to the Arizona ranch Paul had de-

cided that his cottage near Loreto, down on the Baja Peninsula, was a better idea. He told me later that he didn't feel the
death of a husband should be survived in the same area the son
was lost. Loreto had the same features of otherworldliness for
me at thirty that southern Arizona had had for me at an over-
plump fifteen so long ago.

Now in my canyon it occurred to me that I had reached
Paul's ranch two weeks ago to this very hour. He had expanded
the stucco house, the horse barn, and the kennels since my last
visit a year before. Emilia was there, also a younger woman
named Luisa with a daughter about five, an older woman
named Margaret, perhaps in her mid-sixties, about Paul's age.
She was a retired anthropologist from the University of Louisiana. At dinner she and Paul explained that they had met in
Florence in 1949, and had an affair despite her art-historian
husband who was hard at work at the Uffizi. I had the not
altogether comfortable feeling that I was in the presence of
three generations of his lovers. His gentleness and humor were
so disarming that no one seemed to mind, and at one point all
three of the women were discussing their current husbands. I
was road-weary and had several drinks, but stayed up late to
listen and ask questions. Paul went to bed first, after telling us
that we couldn't talk about him in his absence which meant,
of course, that we would. Margaret wanted to know about my
grandfather because Paul never talked much about the way he
grew up, except to say that a hundred years of intensive farming had made Nebraska a charmless place, the vast prairie
utterly desiccated. I somewhat agree but then what state, including Arizona and Louisiana, hadn't tried to squeeze itself
plug-ugly to make a final dollar? I said that until his late twenties or so Paul's father had aimed to be a painter but his will
toward art hadn't survived World War I. Paul's notion was that
his father had worked desperately to be an artist, then was
rejected for the Armory Show in 1913, went to war out of
depression, and returned understandably coarsened. In his
postwar state of fatigue and depression he felt morally and
artistically bankrupt and never picked up a brush again. All the
energies he had given to his art were directed to horses and
making money by buying, trading, and selling large landhold-
ings, also commercial real estate in Chicago, Omaha, Lincoln,

and Rapid City. Paul felt that his parents were utterly unsuited for each other, and after the birth of his two sons, his father avoided Omaha, spending his time at the farm or in Texas and Arizona. With the death of Wesley he simply withdrew, though Paul felt that most of his motive was to try to act the father for Ruth and myself.

I felt this brief explanation was enough and resisted further probings by Margaret on the subject of money, except to say that I scarcely felt responsible for either the talents or the shortcomings of my forebears. When the three of them became insistently curious on the subject of why I hadn't married it was humorous. If you're cross at the time the easiest way to put a stop to this is by saying that you're a lesbian. It creates a wonderful aura of instant embarrassment and backpedaling. Instead I used Michael's idea that people completely change every seven years and the adaptation process was too much of a strain. Only Paul and Rachel knew I had been married less than a day, except for Bobby and his Bahamian wife, Grace.

Paul woke me at dawn with a cup of coffee to go for a ride. Out the window I could see two saddled horses, plus a group of dogs whirling around in excitement. I hurriedly got out of bed forgetting I was naked. Paul winked as he slid out the door, saying he hoped I wasn't keeping all that to myself. I answered that I was trying not to, but success in this area was difficult to measure.

An hour into our ride my horse drew up lame from a stone bruise on the "frog" of its hoof. Paul whistled in the English setters to adjust their range to our new slow pace as we headed toward home on foot. We were in the foothills between Mowry Wash and Cherry Creek, on the edge of Meadow Valley Flat. Paul knew two young naturalists from the University of Arizona who had been in the area for quite some time checking out reports and looking for the Mexican gray wolf, or lobo. Paul had been searching for three months himself and had one sighting at twilight down near Lochiel on the border. South of there in Sonora the country was enormous and capable of nurturing a resurgence of the mammal. To the southwest we could see the sun coming up over the Huachucas, the vision of which was spoiled a little by the immense Defense installation there, including a cave that held God knows what. At least the

Huachucas were diminished for me, that is: Paul's impenetrable private religion didn't allow ordinary fixtures like the Defense Department to disturb him. Even his inability to sleep more than a few hours a day had long been beyond his concern. As far as I had ever been able to determine the central aspects of his ethic were rather stern notions of generosity and accountability. You were accountable in the strictest sense for every moment you were alive, though it was never clear to me who you were accountable *to;* I had certainly never seen his records but knew he supported and educated young people, mostly orphans, in Loreto, Agua Prieta, Tucson, Mulege, and other places I didn't know about. If you were rich you were to give of your money and yourself—if poor, your "self" would do fine. He was the most deeply idiosyncratic and solitary man I had ever known. Part of his beliefs included not taking credit for anything or drawing conclusions. I asked him once about the largish number of books of a religious nature in his library, most of which were dated in the flyleafs from the late forties. He said that that was when he discovered he was sterile and needed a bit of what he called "consolation." He felt his grandfather had been "nearly" a great man until he became murderous. He was rather pleased that the Northridge name would die out because they had done quite enough "for and against" the world, and a name was anyway a patrilineal artificiality. He spent a great deal of time alone—or "standing by the fire" as he called it—or otherwise he would be of no use to anyone. He wished to offer his clarity, not his confusion. These were mostly my own conclusions for he was far too modest to be doctrinal. Years before when I was an ardent graduate student I had accused him of being, in turn, a Sufi, a Taoist, a Zen Buddhist, a Christian, and possibly a sexual compulsive-obsessive. He had only complimented me on my reading, and asked about Charlene whom I had once brought down on vacation, though he later said that he didn't think anyone was anything except to the extent they thought they were. I had suspected Charlene of sneaking off to his bedroom but never asked her. Paul had given her what he called a "scholarship" to go to Paris after she graduated from the University of Minnesota.

The walk home took nearly three hours, well into the heat of the morning. We detoured up an arroyo to reach a rock pool

that still held water in May. The rock pool was fed by a mere
trickle of a spring, really just a seep, but enough to make the
area densely green. There were javelina tracks everywhere
and a covey of Gambel's quail flushed out not fifty feet away,
their crisp wingbeats echoing up the canyon walls. We both
were very hungry and made a pact not to talk about food as
we watched the horses drink, then the dogs drink and take
turns wallowing in a small patch of mud.

Paul had been trying to find Ruth a suitable man—they
had had dinner twice in the past week, and Ruth was coming
down in the evening. He had met the grocer and thought it an
impossible match because they were too similar—quiet, rather
melancholy twins. Paul's neighbor was an intelligent though
bumbling and unsuccessful rancher and Paul had high hopes
for the intended introduction. His reasoning was that Ruth had
plenty of money, and in his divorce from a wealthy woman the
man had been given a ranch he couldn't afford to maintain.
The man was a first-rate amateur archaeologist, among a number of other wild enthusiasms. He and Paul had made several
trips down into the Baranca del Cobre and everywhere in
Tarahumara country together.

"What about me?" I said. "He sounds pretty good."

"I'll get him in the house and you ladies can work it out.
He has two rather awful teenagers the mother ignores, though
they're away at school."

The rest of the way home from the spring we talked about
a penchant toward manic-depressive tendencies, however
subdued, that ran in the family and which he viewed as distinctly genetic. He felt that an insistence on an intense level
of consciousness carried with it a susceptibility to odd forms of
mental disease. Paul thought that Ted and Ruth's son, Bradley,
who was at the Air Force Academy, was due some day for a
serious crack-up. Paul was the only member of the family that
Bradley cared for—even gracious Naomi was viewed as just
another "weak sister."

After lunch and a short siesta I went out to Paul's study to
look at the diary we had kept together during the month in
Baja after Duane's suicide. I had never read it before and for
some reason this was the first time I felt fully capable of looking
at it. I was addled by the idea of asking either Paul or Ruth to

check out Tucson birth records for me but dismissed it. Perhaps mistakenly I felt confident that Michael would know how to proceed.

The diaries turned out to be a surprise and a delight, though a few portions were a little frightening. The only therapeutic aspects were implicit rather than explicit: long walks at daylight before the fullness of heat arrived, and in the evening when it subsided; comments on the progress of the free English lessons I gave (Paul volunteered my services) to a couple of dozen locals every afternoon at three; my efforts to become a really good cook under the tutelage of Paul's cook, a fragile, tiny woman named Epiphania who couldn't have weighed more than seventy pounds; and, finally, the comments of the grief-stricken insomniac. All of the passages except the latter were written during the hour before dinner while we were having drinks, which were fruit-and-rum or -tequila concoctions.

PAUL

On the third day she can see all the way across the room. This morning she lifted her eyes from her feet more frequently while we walked. I gave an ambulatory lecture on Cortez—his namesake sea beside us as we walked— which would have been futile yesterday. History allows but few men to figuratively rape and kill a million virgins, revive and rape them again and again, all in the name of God and Spain.

DALVA

Somewhere my son is fifteen. I began teaching English today to a motley group whose actual ages run from seven, a street urchin, to a retired fishing-boat captain of seventy-three, with the unlikely name of Felipe Sullivan. This has long been an unsuccessful project of Paul's and I have a weathered stack of paperback texts put out by the University of Michigan for the teaching of English as a foreign language. Their plan involves the repetition teaching of specific phrases under the supposition that the language, given the comprehension of enough phrases, will all fall together, though perhaps not in this lifetime.

Late at night: I think I hear Duane breathing outside the window. The music from the cantina down the beach stopped an hour ago. An old man kept singing a ranchero song in a raspy voice with a refrain that went "two friends, two horses, two guns." The song does not end happily. Someone, perhaps a sentimental murderer, must have been paying the man to repeat the song. I thought the breathing I heard was a prowler, though I can't imagine anyone getting past Paul's mongrels. I whisper, "Duane, is that you?" The sound of the breathing increases. I repeat the question in Sioux and the breathing grows louder. I began to cry, and then go out to the front porch which is bright with moonlight. Paul is sitting there watching an enormous pod of dolphin not fifty yards off the beach, swimming slowly on the surface and breathing deeply. It is all so grand I begin to shiver. After a half-hour or so they swim out to sea, crisscrossing in the sheen of moonlight on the water. We go back to bed without speaking.

PAUL

C. S. Sherrington said, "The brain is an enchanted loom, weaving a dissolving pattern, always a meaningful pattern, though never an abiding one, a shifting harmony of subpatterns." This seems written by someone who lived in the water! On her sixth day here Dalva states that her beloved could not have done otherwise and that she couldn't imagine him connected to life-support systems in a VA hospital. She is writing a letter to a woman in Los Angeles for Captain Felipe Sullivan. I haven't told her that I have written a dozen or so of these letters for Felipe since he met the woman with her husband on his charter boat in 1956. She has never answered and he had finally told me that my words lack the necessary romantic touch though I quote him directly. "Oh, return to me, beloved flower of the north," etc. Dalva and Felipe are sitting at a card table on the porch struggling with his feelings as the sun sets behind the Sierra de la Gigante. She is still in her brief bathing suit and his old goat's eyes flicker to her legs, then back into the hacienda, fearful that I am watching him. Now she is laughing, and loudly repeats an appropriate line: "We men of the sea are whales of love who dive deeply, roosterfish who caress the shore in the spring, beautiful sharks who never tire of the struggles of love," etc. She now sees the locals as individuals and is learning their names. She no longer stops in mid-sentence and has begun to ask what particular mountains are called, also what kind of fish she is eating, what kind of mixes the mongrel are, and who is my current girlfriend.

DALVA

I found a snorkel and fins in a closet but discovered I could not use them, thinking as I did that the bottom of the sea was a repository of bodies. I never had him for my own, and when I did it was only the afternoon and part of an evening, plus that short time so long ago. I have read enough about suicide to know that in certain cases the conditions of life have become untenable. If he had come back to Nebraska or South Dakota he would have called me and we would have married at his insistence for his benefits; then he would have ridden far out on the prairie at night on his old buckskin and have done the same thing. I find myself hoping that Capt. Sullivan will get an answer. He admitted to me today he has not received one in sixteen years. This love of his was based on a single kiss in the galley while the husband was fighting a grouper, which makes me reflect on the depth of the irrationality involved in love. Because I am an outsider and speak Spanish I have been sought out for advice by several young girls of thirteen years or so. Their problems are love problems. I spoke to the boyfriend of one—a cowboy from the interior who was so nasty, preening, feral, also filthy, that I wondered at the craziness that would make her want to give herself to him. Curious about the medical details of the actual "heartache" that diminishes a little in its intensity each day.

PAUL

Dalva said something on our hike this morning that reminded me of the character of longing. The mist was thickish and we could hear sea lions bellowing and she supposed they were calling out to absent partners, a hollowish roar sweeping out over the water, a noise so grand you wanted to bow to it. I remembered the only truly wonderful trip Father took us on. John Wesley and I were in our early teens, and mother was still pretty healthy but showing the first signs of disintegration by drugs and alcohol—a combination that has nothing new about it. Dad had decided we should have an outing in order to see the Konza, the last remaining tall-grass prairie down in Kansas. It was June and I remember the dense, sweeping purple of the pasqueflower mixed with the yellow of the goldenrod. It was the middle of the Great Depression and I was somewhat embarrassed by our Packard, though Dad and John Wesley didn't seem to mind. I saw Dad give some money to a man and his big family with a broken-down truck at a gas station. Wesley asked him why he did it, and he gruffly said "Only an asshole won't give away money." It is often forgotten that some of us went through the Depression untouched. We didn't camp very well without Lundquist to pick up the ample slack. Dad got drunk with some horse people in Great Bend and John Wesley and I talked to an actual prostitute outside the hotel. The next day was hot and Dad slept in the backseat, letting us do the driving, though we barely knew how and were heavy on the gas. When we reached the virgin, tall-grass prairie with its shorter blue grama, and the blue-stem, which grew up to fourteen feet high, Dad plunged right in with us in tow. In short order we were lost, and remained lost for a couple of hours. Dad and Wesley finally lifted me up to Dad's shoulders and I saw a distant farm truck. When we finally made it out we drank and took a swim in a cold clear stock tank, and Dad began to laugh. We joined in, rolling and kicking on the ground in our wet underpants. He later said that he had wondered how settlers got lost on the prairie and now he knew. When things began to go bad I thought of this day with great longing. I would read Dickens to my very sick mother on hot summer afternoons in Omaha while Dad and John Wesley were hundreds of miles to the northwest on the farm. It was as if we had chosen up sides and there was nothing to be done about it.

I had barely finished this passage when Paul came out to his study. It was five in the afternoon and he was bringing me a cold margarita in a big brandy snifter. We talked about the last few days in Loreto and the school picnic for my students that Paul had hosted, an all-afternoon-and-evening-and-half-the-night affair with a ragtag band, beer, tequila, shrimp and spiny lobster, piglets and *cabrito,* a barrel of *menudo* for the end of it all. Paul said that when he's in Loreto the locals speak to him of the party fourteen years later.

Paul looked through a file cabinet, found an envelope, and handed it to me, saying that it wasn't too important but he had meant to send it to me while I was in Brazil in the mid-seventies. He and his friend Douglas had written it so I would remember the Loreto area as it was during my recovery, not what had become of the the area in recent years. Douglas had introduced me to the Cabeza Prieta and I asked how he was doing. Paul said that he was busy shocking normal folks and had just headed north with his family to spend the summer with grizzly bears. Douglas was another living fatality of our last war but, unlike Duane, had the sort of functional and literate intelligence that gave him the perspective to stay alive.

Ruth arrived at the last minute before dinner, running late because she had been reading a book called *Arctic Dreams* and had been carried away—the book must have been fascinating because Ruth was one of those overly punctual souls who arrived everywhere quite early. When we were girls she'd suggest we go riding at eight-fifteen in the morning and she meant eight-fifteen on the dot. I suppose I'm the opposite—dates and numbers have always been an abstraction to me.

It turned out she rather liked Paul's neighbor, Fred, the divorced rancher. I felt noncommittal about him after a half-hour's chat; he wore slightly too much cologne, his informal ranch clothes were too precisely tailored and didn't seem quite comfortable, the sort of clothes a CEO would wear at a chuck-wagon outing at a Phoenix convention. He was terribly bright and knowledgeable, but lacked the "indentations," the unique character traits I look for in men. I imagined that he ate donuts with a fork and folded his underpants. This trace of bitchiness in me reminded me of what my Santa Monica gynecologist friend had told me—that I was too "autolelic," i.e., I only did things for and of themselves and lacked an overall "game plan." At least with Fred there were no edges against which one could bruise—he had taken care of himself so well he'd likely grow old and die in a single minute when the time was appropriate. In contrast to these observations, which mostly meant I was overdue in getting out of southern California, Paul and Fred were having an engrossing discussion about the Apache wars wherein it finally took five thousand U. S. Army troops to capture the last seven Apaches. Then Fred began a semi-speech, I guessed for Ruth's benefit, about "the freedom and the heraldic mysteries of the desert," and how "the heritage of freedom represented by this wild country must be preserved." Paul became a little irritable, perhaps not noticeably to anyone else, but I could tell by the peculiar way his eyes began to shine. His voice remained soft which always served to make people more attentive.

"You can't make the desert represent a freedom you should have organized for yourself in your bedroom or living room. That's what is so otiose about nearly all nature writing. People naturally shed their petty and inordinate grievances in the natural world, then resume them when the sheer novelty dissipates. We always destroy wilderness when we make it represent something else, because that something else can always fall out of fashion. Freedom to the all-terrain-vehicle addict, the mining and oil and timber companies, has always meant the absolute license to do as they wish, while 'heritage' is a word brought up by politicians to recall a virtue they can't quite remember. The only traceable heritage related to our use of the land is to exhaust it."

"You're trying to tell me you feel as free on the crapper as we did down in the Baranca del Cobre?" There was a trace of pink in Fred's earlobes that he hoped to diminish by a witticism.

"I feel as free—which is your word, not mine—though naturally not as exhilarated. When you first come to the desert, and I suspect it's true of any wild area, it's just a desert, an accretion of all the bits and pieces of information and opinion you've picked up along the way about deserts. Then you study and walk and camp in the desert for years, as we both have, and it becomes, as you say, heraldic, mysterious, stupefying, full of auras and ghosts, with the voices of those who lived there speaking from every petroglyph and pottery shard. At this point you must let the desert go back to being the desert or you'll gradually become quite blind to it. Of course, on a metaphoric level the desert is an unfathomably intricate prison, and you may understandably wish to play with this fact, comparing it to your own life. By not letting places be themselves we show our contempt for them. We bury them in sentiment, then suffocate them to death in one way or another. I can ruin both the desert and the Museum of Modern Art in New York by carrying to them an insufferable load of distinctions that disallows actually seeing the flora and fauna or the paintings. Children are usually better at finding mushrooms and arrowheads because they are either ignorant of or unwilling to carry the load." He paused, slightly embarrassed, then bustled out into the kitchen to get another bottle of wine. I felt a specific admiration for Fred because he acted as though he had just heard something fascinating, which I thought we all had. Paul was genuinely apologetic about his speech.

"This Burgundy is a little fancy for Henry's *carne seca,* but then I rarely get to see my nieces at the same time. Maybe I'm getting Alzheimer's. I sat down on a rock up Sycamore Creek last week and lost track of five hours. If Daisy here hadn't started barking from hunger I might still be there." He patted the yellow Labrador beside his chair and fed it a tidbit of meat.

"Maybe one of your abandoned ghosts kept you there," I said.

"Probably. When you're old you tend to stick to a place if you like it. I saw a girl in the museum in Nogales the other day and that upset me. She was very beautiful and I was sure I had seen her in Tucson in 1949. Ruth, will you play something morose and sentimental?"

Ruth gave Fred a friendly pat, got up, and went to the piano with an untypically crazy smile. She began with a harpsichord imitation, lapsed into a polka, then slid into the Debussy she knew Paul favored. In turn he laughed, closed his eyes, then smiled. When I looked at him I couldn't help wondering what sort of man my father would have become.

○

I slept badly and got up just before daylight to leave for Nebraska. In my dreams I had been chased around the desert,
finally escaping to the high country near Paul's ranch, where
my invisible pursuers had trapped me at the spring I had
visited with Paul the day before. I was relieved when the
sound of the first rooster drove them away.

A small stovelight was on and coffee was made. In the first
bit of light I could see the outline of Paul at a table out on the
small veranda that adjoined the kitchen. The birds had become very loud and the roosters down the valley sounded as
if they were trying to fight the wild birds with sheer noise. It
is out of fashion now but there is something endearing and
absurd about the way a rooster behaves, the comic indomita-
bility of his walk.

We had a pleasant half-hour and then said goodbye. He
thought he might drive up for a visit in late July or August,
partly to give Michael a hand. He laughed softly when he
mentioned Michael's name, saying there was something of
Petrouchka in his character. Paul wanted to show me a few
things in the basement of the farmhouse and wondered if I
knew they were there. I said I did but Grandfather had asked
me to wait until this summer to take a look. Paul had wanted
to make sure in case he "kicked off" because they were so well
hidden they wouldn't otherwise be found.

○

My drive north was wonderful because I had taken the trip
many times and was anticipating favorite places with pleasure.
I cut off at Lordsburg for Silver City and the Caballo exit on
Route 25, making Socorro by evening and checking into the
same dreary but favorite motel. I drove a few miles south
to the village of San Antonio for dinner at a café that I had discovered with Charlene twenty-five years before. It was near
the Basque del Apache bird refuge that Naomi loved so
much. Over dinner I took out the envelope from Paul and
Douglas.

Dear Woman of the World,

Here are a few notes from two thoroughly irresponsible men who study things that won't buy you a drink. Come back, little Sheba!

## LORETO AREA

Standing on the coarse sand beach of Loreto, even when heading north, the eye is drawn south along the increasingly rugged coast and out to the midrift islands, past Isla Carmen to turtle-shaped Monserato and beyond to Isla Catalina. In the calm of daybreak the islands and headlands shift in the sea, mirages, making the actual landscape impossible to tell even half a mile off shore. The colors run a wider spectrum than the Pacific, rose and mauve of dawn turning royal purple then more shades of gold and crimson at dusk. Along the south coast the Sierra de la Gigante dominates the landscape; there are desert bighorn sheep and deer and lion in these rugged mountains and mysterious rock paintings in hematitic ocher splashed by ancient Indians on an overhang of granite fifteen to twenty feet overhead of life-sized and bigger figures and animals as if slapped on with pole-sized Matisse brushes by giants.

If the mountains are an intimidation (a wall of rotten barren rock rising along an escarpment 1,500 feet high perhaps totally without water) the islands to the east are inviting; it's hard to resist checking them out by sea. Not so much Carmen, the biggest; Monserato though low has rocky coasts and pirate gold buried somewhere among the bursera (elephant trees), torote, cholla, and barrel cactus. By midday the early calm is replaced by mild breeze and choppy water. Even if out of your way you want to head for Catalina, best known for a species of rattleless rattlesnake found nowhere else. The truth is that everything living on each of these islands is a bit unique having evolved on volcanic peaks sinking in the waters filling the San Andreas Fault, which slipped violently, creating the Sea of Cortez some 15 million years ago. South of here melanism has prevailed in a species of jackrabbit living among gray andesties and scabrous vegetation—also unique. On Catalina, barrel cactus reach ten feet and nothing is like anything else. The only things familiar are feral goats released by 19th-century whalers in hope of future fresh meat.

Everywhere are birds, gulls of three species and terns and boobies, particularly around seamounts and dolphin-slashing schools of herring, which you can see dive-bombing the baitfish a mile distant. Along the coasts brown pelicans and cormorants perch on rocks and headlands.

In these open waters you see manta rays, the biggest maybe fifteen feet, leaping perhaps to dislodge parasites and hammerheads checking out the boat. Finback whales are resident and before the sea grows rough dolphinfish cruise by. Sometimes you see roosterfish, yellowtail, or bonito ripping into balls of baitfish the size of baseball diamonds accompanied by the diving birds which turn the ocean surface greasy.

Underwater the mass of critter life boggles the mind. The upwellings teem with plankton making the sea a bit cloudier than the crystalline Caribbean. Swimming along any of these islands you see triggerfish, parrotfish, needlefish, grouper of several kinds; close up scorpion fish, blowfish, and gobies, and rafts of smaller fishes everywhere. Ten feet off a cliff of Catalina you see a school of yellowtail in April beyond the 4-inch spines of sea urchin covering the rock you cling to in the surf. To eat there are cabrilla and black sea bass. Cruising the sandy bays you see 5-foot-wide eagle rays so numerous in four feet of water you can barely find standing room in between; deeper are brown electric rays with a spot on their back and smaller rays closer to shore. Garden eels wave like grasses growing out of the sandy ocean bottom. Among the rocks there are moray eels, some spotted, who look frightening when caught in the open. Three miles south of the yellowtail is the best shallow-water spiny-lobster area in the gulf.

At night you burn driftwood, which often flames green and red or orange from trace elemental metals, because the local bursera and paloverde make poor firewood. During the long nights of winter's new moons you might learn the constellations as never before, beginning with the great square of Pegasus and waking every three hours to identify the new ones swinging in on the celestial clock from the east until Sagittarius fades in the light of dawn. In a tiny cave on the side of a wash 4-inch black scorpions by the dozens mate combatively by flashlight. The unique species of rattlesnake is aggressive by Arizona standards and shakes his rattleless tail under a huge native fig tree whose big green leaves seem out of character next to the jungle of sweet-and-sour pitahaya cactus overgrown with a thick cobweb of dried vine on the slopes above; close up the live strands of vine lacing the spines of a pitahaya dulce have tiny bell-shaped white flowers.

Heading north of Loreto the coast is gentle with coves separated by headlands and small rocky islands. There are palmas in the larger washes and an occasional rancheria. Sometimes you see wild burros on the beach and in protected coves and on secure wave-cut benches sleep herds of sea lions whose racket can keep you awake two miles away during the full moon. You find clams and mussels most anywhere though especially in the mangroves rich in shellfish and red snapper, *huachinango al mojo de ajo* broiled over root of saltbrush which is fished by green and black-crowned night herons and egrets; the call of the mangrove warbler is distinct once you see one chipping; fortunately the more distant males do the singing. Oysters are not as abundant as they once were though the beaches are covered with winged oyster shells fished out by 19th-century pearlers.

Reaching the mouth of Bahía Concepción the same is true of butter clams and Pacific crayfish. This intertidal zone was once known for powderhorn-shaped pinshells whose hinge muscle eaten raw with a *picante* sauce of tomato is a treat. From earlier trips you might notice the depletion of large sailfish, marlin, and tortuava though the gulf still feels like Nebraska maybe did in 1870—there were still so many of them.

The ocean can be rough, sometimes for days in winter and spring, though the big *chubascos* are in summer. Except for rare mornings there is always a breeze, important in summer when clouds of gnats and mosquitoes hover along beaches and mangroves.

Walking the beaches, you see grunion in spring or late winter a few days before those big tides of the full moon and roosterfish-slashing baitfish in the breaking waves only a few feet from shore. Tiny gastropods, clams of several species, and shells of cowries require worm-eye viewing. Some beaches are covered with pink murax shells. On calm March mornings a thin line of krill might lie at the high-tide mark. Larger relatives, six-inch Pacific-type shrimp, swim along the boat in deep water and hide under piers. At night you can always see dinoflagelates phosphoresce in the surf, seasonally blooming as red tides. On the rocky shores and islands the easiest way to travel is often at low tide on the wave-cut benches below the cliffs and headlands, being careful not to get caught below sheer cliffs with rising tides. . . .

○

Peach nuzzles me. Thunder in elongated cracks. I am swimming on hard ground. I reach up into the rain and touch her soaked muzzle. Jesus, but I'm a wet girl. The rain just came because the fire still hisses. "To Know Him Is to Love Him," they sang long ago. *"Tunkasila, mato pehin wan!"* "Oh, grandfather bear, here is some of your hair!" That was from a childhood game and the last thing she said. Rachel took the "Wanagi Canku," the Ghost Road. Will I drive that far to feed her ghost? she asked. Of course. Then she'll stay around for a year. My dog ran away and was eaten by coyotes so I knew I was going to die, she said. I called you and here you are. Could you bring my old sister Blue Earth Woman? So I drove to Pine Ridge and picked her up, then a doctor who was young and pleasant and said nothing was terribly wrong, she was just dying. He had seen it before. The thunder so loud I sat up which made Peach happy. Rachel said Duane's spirit had become part horse and part fish, a fish that breathed through its back. What a fine thing to call it, the Ghost Road.

The fire had withered too far to make coffee. I was startled to see the railroad watch in the saddlebag said ten in the morning. I had stayed up thinking until I heard the first bird. The violent part of the storm was passing and hard rain set in, so hard I couldn't see the river. I packed in an ankle-deep puddle, feeding Peach a few handfuls of oats. She wanted the hell out of here. I always wondered what horses and dogs thought thunder was. Barn cats, as ever, pretend they are bored. I tucked my chin down and let Peach trot me the hour home, wondering what day it was. Before Paul had kissed me goodbye he bet that Fred would call Ruth in Tucson by noon. He hadn't meant to chide Fred the night before, but it seemed to him that you never detected the spirit or soul of a landscape by purposely looking for it as if it were a Grail to be acquired and coveted. That sort of spiritual greed seemed to produce life as a linear nightmare: I acquire, then move on, and acquire more. After you learned what was actually in any landscape, including cities, you might finally perceive the character of the soul life of the area. He was not prepared to mock human effort by saying that the Sonoran wilderness had more virtue than Florence. I remembered reading that Geronimo hadn't cared for the New York World's Fair but then he was a captive visitor, summoned as he was in chains.

○

I have spent the last three days in bed with a slight fever and a bad cold, and haven't minded it a bit. This has happened before—a modest illness becomes a welcome relief, tempered a little in this case by another semi-legal problem: Frieda's boyfriend, Gus, has slugged her and she can't make up her mind whether or not to press charges. She is embarrassed to appear in public with a black eye and will miss the last two evenings of the pinochle tournament. She has sent Lundquist over with a pot of the best chicken soup in the world, with the possible exception of that made for a mogul aquaintance of Ted's who has a private club in Hollywood. You can eat anything you wish at this club and drink the finest wines, but it is peculiar how soothing this chicken soup can be in Los Angeles.

This morning I watched Lundquist feed the geese under the watchful eye of his dog Roscoe. I have a Kennedy rocker drawn up to the window and wear my favorite twenty-year-old robe. Roscoe becomes a little irritable when Lundquist sits down, as he always does, to pet the geese. When he entered the kitchen with the mail I called down for him to come up for a chat. He is always a little formal, beginning with the same question ever since I can remember: "And how is my little girl doing today, heh?" He hands me a thickish letter from Michael, about whom he is deeply grieved, along with the recent situation with Gus and Frieda. Lundquist feels that if only Michael and Frieda would read the teachings of Swedenborg they wouldn't be susceptible to the "fruits of the devil" as personified by Karen and Gus. Lundquist points out that when he was sixteen Karen's grandmother tried to seduce him after an all-night threshing party "not three miles from where we sit." The fact that this happened seventy years ago does not disturb his notion that lust probably runs in that family.

All the dominant events in Lundquist's life could have happened earlier this morning so vivid are they to him. Grandfather, John Wesley, and his own wife are merely absent rather than dead. Seven years ago or so this July I had him drive up to Livingston, Montana, with a horse trailer. I flew in from Los Angeles and bought a filly out of a famous stud, King Benjamin, who was standing at a ranch up Deep Creek Road. There were two fillies for sale and it took all afternoon for me to make up my mind. I was having iced tea with the owner and his lovely wife in the ranch house which was full of books, the walls covered with impressive landscapes. We heard a voice through a screened window and discovered Lundquist talking to their three ranch dogs about Nebraska, as if to explain why he was there. The owner and his wife were impressed because the dogs were rarely manageable and now they were sitting in an attentive row listening to a stranger. On the two-day trip back to Nebraska I asked him about this and he said it was a common courtesy since he could tell the dogs were very curious about what we were doing there. I decided to let the problem of language go for the time being, but he continued by saying he had never met an animal that didn't know if your heart was in the right place. Humans could develop this ability with each other if they would only study the works of Emanuel Swedenborg.

Before Lundquist left I could see that he was anxious about the contents of the letter from Michael so I opened it, and fibbed by saying that Michael was fine and wanted to be remembered to him. I also said that he could have a bottle of beer on the way out which brought a beam to his face that must be described as radiant.

"A single bottle of beer can bring on a flow of great thoughts," he said, without irony, as he waved goodbye.

Michael's letter kept me rocking at the window for quite some time. There was a tinge of longing in me to be back in Santa Monica working with disturbed young people. Back in the sixties and early seventies it was faddish to say that certain people were troublesome but "worth the trip." His letter was boldly titled "The Conditions of Life During the Plague Years," and the handwriting was uncharacteristically even and readable, which I attributed to his unintended detoxification.

Dearest D.,

We all know the end but where is the middle? It occurred to me this morning that this mess I've been try-ing to extricate myself from all these years is actually my life! A circadian sump where every day is Monday morn-ing. The time of spring floods when my dad and I would spend half the night bailing the muddy water out of the basement until a better-heeled uncle made us the gift of a Briggs-Stratton motorized pump. Your kiss of forgive-ness technically meant the world to me two days later, on Monday, when I really woke up. It was evening and I was hungry, thirsty, and in pain. I reached over to the buzzer, then hesitated, trying to remember if I had felt all three before simultaneously—hunger, thirst, and pain—not counting self-imposed hangovers. This acute gestalt of sensations opened a tiny door to the world, like the little door of a cuckoo clock, with me shooting out and seeing the briefest of glimpses of the world. I thought of Northridge, Aase, the Sioux, the pathetic settlers lost in the sea of grass. I thought of their hunger, thirst, pain. I thought of Crazy Horse on the burial platform, his arms around his daughter on a bitterly cold and windy March night. I thought of Aase burning with fever on a cot beneath the tree at noon & Northridge sitting beside her body in the rain. The incredible, physical bitterness of it all. I still held off from the buzzer on the pillow. I remembered my father coming home from the night shift at the steel mill just as I was getting up for school. I would sit there toying with my bowl of cereal while he drank a quart of beer and ate an enormous meal, the vulgarity of which offended me. I was an aesthete, a young fan of James Joyce and Scott Fitzgerald, and resented having to go off to the eleventh grade smelling like sauerkraut and pork, or whatever gargantuan pile of low-class slop he was eating. One morning his eyebrows and hair were singed and one hand was heavily bandaged. He wasn't eating but there was a bottle of whiskey on the table and he was weeping. Mother sat next to him and rubbed his head and arms. A furnace had blown, killing two of his friends—I knew the men from watching their horseshoe games on Saturdays, and sometimes they came over with their wives to play euchre. I went into the bathroom, looked at myself in the mirror, and tried to figure out what my emotions should be. I hated the oilcloth on the table, the linoleum on the floor, the coal-company calendar on the wall, the Christmas trip to our relatives down in Mullens, West Virginia, who were even poorer than we were. I hated the stories from World War II that I had loved when younger. I suppose that part of the problem was that we lived on the border of the school district and I was a poor kid at the rich high school, rather than being with the mill kids where I belonged. I was amazed when I went to dinner at a friend's house and his parents ate fried chicken with knife and fork! Anyway, I was a contemptible, whining little snot, and perhaps I still am in some respects.

I finally pressed the buzzer and got my water, Demerol, and liquid diet. Coffee is not too interesting through a glass straw. The cuckoo went back into his hermetic clock and watched five hours of news on the twenty-four-hour news channel, but the door didn't close properly and I remained uncommonly conscious of the hunger, thirst, and pain I was watching. I was stoned as a monkey but I still sensed the world of hunger, thirst, and pain. A bureaucratic wag in a rep tie thought that a hundred million people might die worldwide from AIDS in the next ten years. I thought of my daughter, Laurel, and her generation trying to be Keatsian romantics while totally sheathed in preventive rubber. I saw extensive items on spouse abuse, child abuse, widespread starvation, the epidemic of teenage suicide. There were frequent news updates on everything awful that was happening in the world—this is the first time in history that we get to know all of the world's bad news at once.

The upshot of all of this is that I knew the beginning and end and this was apparently the unvarnished middle. I forgot nuclear proliferation, where an arms expert said within ten years every country in the world equaling or exceeding the budget of the state of Arkansas will have nuclear capability. *Nel mezzo del camin de nostra vita,* etc. Probably misquoted. I absolutely seethe to get at the second trunk of Northridge's journals, because all of the above leads me to think it is the first meaningful work of my life.

To be continued: love, Michael

P.S. The nurses are pleasant but dense. I have learned to make my notes to them simple. Nurse Sally wondered how I hurt myself and I wrote, "I let my wiener, like a baton, rule the orchestra," which took a lot of explanation!

This letter slipped involuntarily from my weakened hand. I wanted to see a group of polled Herefords out the window

simply eating, then pausing to look at each other as cattle do.
I was touched by his comments about the journals and his
father but it was a little tiring to see a man of thirty-nine
discover human suffering other than his own. That was the
biggest problem when breaking in a newly hired social
worker—suffering seems to have more dimension than the
compensatory pleasures. I picked up a slip of paper Naomi had
given me with the phone number of the owner of the puppies
for sale. He was the brother of one of her friends with the
somehow familiar name of Sam Creekmouth. After a few minutes I remembered that it was the name of one of Northridge's
Oglala friends. The West was full of people that were a bit of
this and a bit of that, and the man was likely no more Sioux
than my own one-eighth. There is no such thing as "part Indian"—you either are or aren't out of a combination of some
blood and a predilection. I made the call before I understood
what I was doing but got no answer—ranchers don't hang
around the house in the afternoon in mid-June. Then I impulsively called Andrew at Ted's house and begged him to take
a few days off, go to Tucson, and start tracing my son. He heard
the congestion and panic in my voice and after some dead
pleasantries he agreed. If I felt like it, goddamnit, I'd drive way
over to someplace and buy some bona-fide cattle, registered or
not, or some cutting steers, a few dogs, some families with
children to move into the area so I could teach school, a lover
I was crazy about, a car that flew, a plane ticket, or whatever.
I meant to do something besides rock at the window with a
cold.

I tried to calm down with a shower and a drink, which hit
my empty stomach rather hard but failed as a soporific. I fried
a steak that was streaked with delicious but purportedly unhealthy fat. I went out and hoof-picked and groomed the
horses, then shooed the geese back into their pen which had
required two chickens and a case of beer to build. On an
unspecific level Michael, Lundquist, and Roscoe formed a perfect trio.

My head and heart stopped thumping in the bunkhouse
when I sat down at the desk and gazed out at the rich green
grass and burdock covering the ancient manure pile. The window had been left open and the papers and books were still

damp from the rainstorm during my night in the canyon. The journals were intact in their trunk and I slid it to the door to remember to take it back to the bank. The effect of the second trunk was problematical, but then I hadn't signed on as a historian. The summer after Loreto I had busied myself June, July, and the first half of August putting the papers in order, then drove around the state and parts of South Dakota visiting many of the first Northridge sites. Rachel spent a week riding with me—she loved the old convertible because it was more like a horse. She used an Oglala word, "Hanblecheyapi," a rite of "lament," to describe a period where you expressed all your anguish, then received a new vision of life to keep you going.

I shuffled the dampest of Michael's papers to dry them out and came upon a photo of Karen, a nude shot from the rear with her head turning in a totally silly grin. I laughed out loud, thinking of her mother's shock. She certainly was splendidly put together, and my critical attitude toward Michael was tempered somewhat by the memory of a boy at the University of Minnesota who was an athlete, a swimmer, I had made love to simply because he was beautiful. I had been startled to discover that his legs and chest were shaved to lessen drag and increase speed in the water. I put the photo in an envelope and sealed it in case Frieda began snooping as she cleaned.

Karen's photo made me look at my hands which, unsurprisingly, were getting older. Naomi had said her address book was filling up with dead people, an attitude so laconic as to be admirable. I had been around New York and Los Angeles enough to know that Karen could easily be a bathing-suit or lingerie model, a not unrealistic option to becoming another of the hundreds of thousands of B.A.'s in the liberal arts. That sort of attractiveness is undemocratic but then so are an astronomical IQ, innate athletic ability, and possibly creative talent. Naomi had spoken to a friend, the county agricultural agent, about a job opening in case they closed the country school. She thought I'd be ideal for the job which was to be funded by the federal government: mental counseling for bankrupt farmers and their families. Holy Jesus, I had said, and she laughed. I had always worked because nothing whatsoever in my background had prepared me to act like a rich person, a notorious non-

profession, the dregs of which everyone has witnessed in life,
or in magazines and on television. I had also been taught that
rancorous self-judgment was a Protestant vice that never did
anyone any good. You did your best and made do. One of those
whirring, semi-fatuous rehearsals passed through my mind
after I remembered the last job evaluation by my superior—
"an intense, effective, and affable worker with no particular
leadership abilities." How correct! What is thought of as leadership involves an ability to deal with thoroughly compromised situations, while I am hopelessly addicted to primary
colors, and the direct approach. The necessary adumbrations
involved in telling people what to do require a particular gift.
I worked three summers in college and graduate school as a
seasonal employee of the Department of the Interior on a
lamprey control project, which was an annual three-month
camping trip on the feeder streams entering Lake Superior
and Lake Michigan; Naomi's cousin, Warren, with whom I had
stayed when pregnant, got me the job. With my not very
valuable master's degree I worked at a famous clinic for rich
alcohol and drug abusers in Minneapolis as an ineffective coun-
selor—I was too young to understand how deep wounds can be
and I was basically unsympathetic to the problems of the rich
because it was the late sixties. I moved to New York, a city I
loved, but not my job with a lower-echelon fashion magazine
which served to make me permanently bored with elaborate
clothing. After that were two years with a documentary-film
maker which ended, as I mentioned, with my trip to Key West.
After recovery I tried the East again and through the influence
of a friend of Naomi, a U. S. representative, I became an "assistant assistant" liaison for the Organization of American States,
really an errand girl between New York and Washington. I
seemed to have a genetic aversion to politics but then our
influence in Central and South America has never been pretty.
At a party at the Costa Rican Embassy I met and became
infatuated with a Brazilian diplomat twice my age. He said he
wanted to marry me and invited me down for Carnival. After
enduring frequent absences in a lavish hotel on Ipanema I
spotted him with his wife at a party I had come to with an
American actor I met at the hotel. At the confrontation we

both acted very badly but no one seemed to mind, including his wife. After this sophisticated mud bath I returned home for another summer, then took a job as a social worker in Escanaba, Michigan. Two years of the Upper Peninsula were more than enough, and I moved to Santa Monica at the suggestion of the actor I had met in Brazil. We spent an expensive month doing cocaine, then parted company. After a week of eating a great deal, insomnia, and exercise, I recovered and took the job working with teenagers who had problems with alcohol, drugs, and/or were suicidal. They didn't have the language and necessary set of perceptions to deal with the world we had made for them. It was a harder language to teach than the English I taught to the poor folks of Loreto or Baja. All of this adds up to a wonderfully undistinguished career, but an interesting enough life. Regrettably few women have careers but then most men have jobs that they don't like.

○

I toted and dragged the trunk to the house for safekeeping because it was late in the afternoon and the bank was closed. It was an absurd gesture in a remote and crime-free area (except for wife-beating, sodomy, occasional embezzlement) but I had promised Michael. I got Sam Creekmouth on the phone about the pups and agreed to arrive at noon because I otherwise wouldn't be able to find him on the ranch. He would be out back in the foreman's trailer, he said, in a Sand Hills drawl that reminded me of Duane's. The dog meant I might stay here, job or not. Then I called Ruth who had been spending time with Fred, either in Tucson or down on his ranch near Patagonia. I asked her if he folded his underpants before they made love and there was a long pause before she said yes, then began to giggle. She added that he was "somewhat metronomic" and I guessed that Paul was failing as a matchmaker. She said she had received a sweet, placatory letter from her priest in Costa Rica who begged her to come down for a visit. She wondered why the idea "stimulated" her and I admitted I had never begun to figure out that question. Maybe it all depended on a cluster or assortment of sexual "signals" that none of us ever perceived on a conscious level. I did know that never in my life had I been seduced, though of course I had pretended to the man that I had been "swept off my feet," as they say.

I went outside and sat in the tire swing, smelling the rotting scent of the last of this year's lilacs. As a child the graveyard hidden within them was one of my secret places, especially when the flowers were loud with bees, which my dad had told me were tiny birds. There was a lightheadedness in the moment, almost as if I could feel my father's hands at my back pushing me higher on a summer evening. Naomi would be leading Ruth around on her pony during that happy time after the war. Now I heard crickets, frogs from the creek, a whippoorwill, the plaintive good night of the white-throated sparrow.

On our trip in the convertible Rachel had worn a faded pink scarf to keep her hair out of the wind. We were up near Kadoka drinking coffee from a thermos and on our way to the Badlands to see a place she knew as a child. I asked her if she had ever known the medicine man Black Elk because I had recently reread Neihardt's book for the first time since college. She corrected me, saying that "medicine man" was *pejuta wicasa,* a Sioux version of "doctor," "herbalist," one who tended to the sick and wounded. Black Elk, whom she had known slightly, was *wichasa wakan,* a holy man who got his first vision at age nine. She hadn't seen him again after going off to Denver and becoming a whore during wartime, though she had heard that when Black Elk was well into his eighties he and other Sioux made a little money picking potatoes in Nebraska. At the time I couldn't believe this great man was allowed to end his life in a Nebraska potato field but I later checked Rachel's information and found it to be true. As I drifted back and forth in the tire swing I thought this fact would be hard to stomach for certain lovers of redskin lore, fans of Indian exotica, collectors of artifacts, and wearers of immense turquoise necklaces, but then I was sure Black Elk was above any annoyance over picking potatoes. It was a job.

○

I stayed in the swing until I couldn't see across the yard. Just because you've been a student of all the permutations of brain chemistry and their behavioral effects, doesn't exclude you from being a victim, albeit a knowledgeable victim. There was a hollow, quivering sensation, while I admitted I had come home and was going to stay there. I turned and looked at the light left on in the kitchen—a yellow square that shone out on the honeysuckle bushes that bordered the porch. It was my house. I was no longer a visitor. I would travel wherever I wished but this house that I couldn't help but think of as "Grandfather's" had passed into my being thirty years after his death, when it was mine by title only.

I went inside to tentatively consider changes, though I knew they would be slight, involving only the kitchen and a little painting to lighten an atmosphere that could tend toward gloom. I opened the door and turned on the cellar light with the intention of looking into the concealed storage area. Over the years I had received a fair amount of inquiry from dealers and museum curators about what had happened to Grandfather's collection. I forwarded these to the law firm which responded to the effect that the collection had been sold to a private party who wished to remain anonymous. It was a little stupid for Paul and myself to keep this secret to ourselves, but then the storage area supposedly held additional things. It seemed curious that Grandfather has asked me to wait until the age of forty-five with the implication that the contents were not altogether pleasant, which I knew from the journals. I turned and looked at the paintings, thinking that in New York, Chicago, Los Angeles, perhaps a few other cities, they would certainly require a security system. A Nebraska thief might swipe a Remington, or a Charley Russell out of sentiment, but Sheeler, Marin, Burchfield, even Sargent would be beyond his ken. Paul said he hadn't known precisely what was there until he came home for my father's funeral. There was anyway something inconsolable in the decline and death of the Sioux civilization as Northridge had known it. I thought of

Rachel's pink dime-store scarf, then turned out the cellar light and closed the door. The phone startled me from my reverie— it was Naomi full of bird and beast news. She was happy to hear I was buying a dog.

○

The night wasn't kind to me. The breeze had come around to the south, and the darkness was warmer than the day had been. The horses were restless and I went out twice in the night to check them. The geese were upset and I guessed the coyote had made a pass through the barnyard. It was one of those nights when your perceptions are much grander than you want to indulge; instead of having a succession of idle thoughts ending in sleep you are unbalanced, nearly punished, by images with all the logic of snow flurries in the mind. The last moments before sleep went like this: At the fairgrounds when I stooped beside Michael, his jaw made an audible, grating sound. "What did I do?" he asked, and his jaw caught on "what" so that the question was slurred before his eyes fluttered and closed. My lover in Brazil masturbated me with a handful of flowers. I could see the reflection of the sea in a mirror at the end of the room. The ambulance passed a large gray building on the outskirts of town owned by my family that at one time was the Grange Hall. Farmers in their hopeless fight in the 1880s and 1890s against the power of the railroads. So the Chamber of Commerce determined the town could only support a motel with two rooms which no one wanted to build. The school system used the first floor of the Grange building for storage. Upstairs was full of old office furniture and odds and ends from buildings Grandfather had owned in town by default during the Depression. We thought we had the only key to the upstairs, but last summer we were looking for a marble end table and a box of old photographs by Butcher, and we discovered someone had set up a trysting place in an interior room. We hadn't been up there in years. The window was boarded in this room, and there was a bed with a nice bedspread, a radio, some magazines and paperbacks on a night table, three towels, an ashtray with lipstick on a few of the butts. Naomi and I were startled, then amused, then we didn't quite know what to think. Who could the lovers be? A *McCall's* magazine, a Barbara Cartland romance, and two Elmore Leonards were on the floor. There was a palpable sense of the lovers in the room, and though it was our building we felt we were invading their privacy. The pillowcases were fresh and ironed. We were silent for a minute or two listening to the wind against the tin roof. The woman's scent was nearly undetectable lavender.

○

In the morning I lingered for an extra half-hour waiting for a smallish thunderstorm to pass. I was pleased at its direction because it meant I could follow it over toward Ainsworth—there was something wonderful about following a squall with the sun at your back in the early morning, shining off the roiling cumulus and stratocumulus clouds.

In the first half-hour on the wet, glistening blacktop I passed only one car, and another coming toward me. I slowed down a bit when I began to come too close to the storm, entering an area of gusty winds that revealed the pale underleafs of the windbreaks and shelterbelt trees: I was at the precise back edge of the storm so when I let up on the gas the world became still, and every bird was emerging noiselessly from the quiet aftermath. I listened to a very glum stock-and-grain report, and one of those equally glum and whining "citybilly" songs that had been taking over country music. I punched in a Patsy Cline tape that quickly erased the bad taste of the other, just as I turned onto the road, Route 20, that I had driven on when Grandfather had retrieved me from Chadron after my search for Duane. I felt a thickening of sentiment beneath my breastbone so changed the tape for chamber music by the Pro Musica Antiqua. I was amused by this small battle against sentiment and by something Lundquist had said to the effect that it was a good thing we had time and clocks or everything might happen at once.

At Ainsworth I caught up with the storm again, and stopped for gas, coffee, and more precise directions. I was helped by two teenage boys in very wet FFA (Future Farmers of America) jackets. When I was getting back in the car in the blustery wind and rain, and they thought I was out of earshot, I heard one say something naughty but complimentary about my body—"What a great ass. I sure would like to fuck that." There was an errant impulse to march over and tell them I was more than old enough to be their mother, but then that never was part of the game. Some wise soul said that grownups are only deteriorated children.

○

The entry gate of the ranch was new and ludicrously impressive, but there was also a very large and fresh "For Sale" sign, the listing by a national realtor. These were both indications of a tax shelter gone amiss, probably for someone in the oil business, since they seemed to be the only ones who bought large ranches these days. Scarcely any big ranches had been put together since World War II, and most of them were based on railroad grants before the turn of the century, or in the surge of prosperity during World War I.

I drove a full mile up a blacktop driveway—another absurdity—along a creek, the air sweet with cottonwoods. The house had once been an ordinary Nebraska farmhouse but was now elaborately remodeled and empty: the outbuildings were uniformly painted, and there was a pond with a sunken rowboat still tethered to a dock. The ample number of corrals without cattle chutes showed it had been an expensive horse operation. I circled the pond on a two-track that led to a mobile home perched nakedly against the side of a hill, with a three-quarter-ton pickup parked beside it. I was met by a large, grizzled male Airedale, and a bitch black Labrador who waggled out from under the trailer's steps. The Airedale bounced up with his paws on my open window to stare at me. I waited for his eyes to soften to get out, wanting to let him do his job. I walked around the side of the trailer where Sam Creekmouth was replacing a tire on a horse trailer. There was a small corral holding three fine-looking quarter horses, two mares, and a gelding. The Airedale barked at Sam to tell him I was there which he doubtless knew, but was either shy, or the sort of man that wanted to finish the job before he chatted, or both. When he stood and I offered my hand I thought he could be anywhere between thirty-five and fifty but I guessed about my age. He was a little over six feet, slender but large-chested, with arms that seemed elongated by too much hard work. His nose was crooked as if badly set after a fracture, his hair coal-black under a feed-store cap, his eyes remote but almost friendly. He was uncommonly dark and beaten by the weather and there was an edge of anger in his gestures.

"I was down at that horse sale. How's your friend doing?"

"It looked bad at first but he's OK. They had to wire his jaw together."

"That Pete always was a bully. I saw him get his butt kicked down in Broken Bow last fall." He paused and looked off at the ranch house with resignation. If he had been talking to another man he would have said "ass kicked" but the few cowboys left retain an air of the courtly. "Strange to say but me and my brother calf-roped against you and that Injun boy years ago. He had that fine buckskin."

"I remember. It was too hot. You guys won and we took third." I flushed at the memory, and followed his eyes off to the empty ranch house.

"Next year you and that other gal won the polka contest at the fair. I remember that. What happened to the Injun boy? He was quite the cowboy."

"Died in the war. Or after the war from wounds."

"Not surprised. I was over there a year myself and I'll be goddamned if I still know what it was about. Your momma called my sister late last night and says I got to force this dog on you."

"She wants me to stay home. I've been gone a long time."

"You don't look more than half Nebraska to me. If you'd stayed here you'd be a whole lot bigger. These ladies are feeders."

"I'm hoping that's a compliment."

"Guess it is."

I followed him into the trailer. He said he had to keep the pup inside while he worked, but would be sad to see him go. Naomi had said I wanted a bitch but this was the last pup and he was a male of ten weeks. The pup was under the formica kitchen table enclosed by chicken wire. He was dark but I knew the Airedale in him would lighten the stomach; his head was large with a terrier's grizzled hair and reserved eyes. When the wire was loosened he shot out of Sam's grasp, scooting through the trailer at top speed, and caroming off the furniture, pausing a moment to pee on the couch.

"He's not too smart but he sure is enthused," Sam said, cornering the pup on an easy chair.

"What can I give you for him?" This was not an easy question out here.

"About one dime. He's not the kind of animal you can sell like a horse. Besides, Naomi and my sister figured out we're seventh cousins by marriage, you know, distant relatives."

The phone rang and he handed me the pup which growled and struggled furiously, then abruptly went to sleep on my lap. It was said that except for newcomers (since World War II) everyone that ranched in the western two-thirds of Nebraska either knew or knew about each other, but then this didn't entail all that many people. They had been drawn together by the common concerns of cattle, wheat, and horses, and I suspected it was equally true of any of the sparsely populated Western states. Naomi had advised me to offer a bottle of whiskey which I had packed along. She said Sam had had a run of hard luck, some of the bad credit ramifications of which I was hearing on the phone. He finished with "All I can say is I'm sorry it happened." I didn't say anything because his face had tightened and his eyes squinted out the small, dirty back window. He stalked out and I waited a few minutes before I put the pup away and followed. I was wondering what an expensive Questar telescope was doing on the kitchen counter but I wasn't going to ask.

He was saddling the gelding and a mare and when he gestured I adjusted the stirrups on the gelding for myself. The Airedale and Lab were spinning and chasing each other in excitement over the outing. I wanted to ask him why he didn't have a blue-heeler, the normal cowboy dog, but I didn't think he was ready for conversation. He mounted in the single, fluid movement that is admired in people who live with horses.

We rode wordlessly a full hour before stopping for a rest, and that was when he noted that the Lab bitch, who had not regained her shape from whelping, was overwinded. It was a breathtaking ranch, and from the way the fences ran I guessed we were on the northeast border. Some of the native grasses had returned from disuse and the coulees and the creek bottom were full of wildflowers. It was deceptively lush, verdant, in June, the graceful prelude to the dry spell that always came. I had to imagine Northridge, and then the Sioux who had owned it all without thinking about the word "own."

Sam got off the mare and wound up a stretch of rusty barbed wire and hung it on a cottonwood branch. I tethered the gelding and walked over to the creek bank, where the Airedale was excavating a big hole for unknown reasons. The Lab was sprawled in the creek on her tummy, cooling the teats which were still enlarged from nursing. I scuffed off my boots and socks and stuck my feet in the cool, muddy water. Without the recent rain there wouldn't have been more than a trickle.

"Not bad country, is it?" He stood beside me staring down at my feet.

"If I didn't have a place I'd want to buy it." I knew it was the wrong thing to say before it was out of my mouth.

"It must be nice to be able to say that." His voice was soft enough but the hammer was there.

"I didn't mean it that way. I was only saying it was beautiful." This was so lame that it deepened the mess.

"Years ago I had a wife who wanted a ranch so bad she ran off with a rancher. By that time we were pretty tired of each other anyway. She was one of those rodeo queens and I was on the circuit doing everything but best at saddle bronc. Now I hear she's got her own tennis court and twenty pairs of Lucchese boots."

I couldn't think of anything to say. It's rare that a cowboy gets a ranch of his own, even when he becomes a top hand or foreman. This was a fact of life. I found myself so upset that I couldn't draw a clear breath which meant I liked him a great deal and I didn't want to say the wrong thing.

"Where you going next?" I was the most innocent question I could think of.

"I got a good offer in Texas but if I see another oilman I might shoot the son of a bitch. I got a brother with a cow-calf operation over near Hardin, Montana, and I might go over there."

I asked enough right questions to get rid of his anger for

the time being. Since I had never grown up with an angry father it was one thing I didn't know how to handle or react to in men. He had started three different horse operations for rich people after he quit the rodeo circuit: the first two took four years apiece, and the last five. They all had ended up with a loss of interest, auctions, and a general, inconclusive mess that he was expected to stay behind and clean up before collecting the doubtful severance pay. I suspected he knew more about tax problems, depreciation schedules, and the decline in oil prices than he allowed to, but then those weren't subjects that bore speaking about along a lovely creek bottom on a June afternoon. The situation eased when we talked of breeding lines, and he told me the story of his trip to Lexington, Kentucky, where his last boss had taken him to investigate the thoroughbred business. By now he was stretched out beside me, leaning on an elbow and chewing on a piece of grass. I asked him about his expensive Questar telescope and he said the owner's wife had given it to him but with no directions. I said I would show him how to operate it which pleased him. Just before he got up he put his hand on mine for a moment.

"Let's ride back and work on that bottle of whiskey," he said. " 'Course you don't have to help but I'm in a five-drink mood."

○

Early the next afternoon, when I drove out the gate, I said to the pup who was chewing on a piece of harness, "Well, I think I've got myself a boyfriend." I had a bourbon headache and was bone tired but otherwise relaxed and happy. The dirty joke about being "rode hard and put away wet" came to mind. When we got back from the ride the trailer was very hot and we both were quite nervous and overly polite. While he made drinks I rinsed my hands and face in the sink and the flies against the window seemed to be buzzing in my ears. We were standing at the counter and I began to explain the telescope in a jittery voice, saying that after dark we could put it on the car hood for stability and look at the stars. I blushed and looked away because that meant I was offering to stay the night before he asked. He understood this and tried to get me off the hook with a joke.

"Sounds good to me. I'm not real up-to-date on the universe. It's a long ways from feed bills."

We clicked our overfull glasses and I drank as deeply as possible. "Here's to horses and dogs," I said, then traced a finger along two zigzag scars on his hand. "You're supposed to turn a hay-baler off before you fix it," he said. We stared out the window at the horses as if they were something new and we hadn't just been riding them. His face shone with sweat and I felt sweat trickling down between my breasts. The obvious thing was to go outside and catch the breeze. He put a hand on my waist and that was finally all it took. We embraced as if to bruise our ribs, then kissed, and I dropped my drink on the floor. We banged against the table getting our clothes off and making our way to the sofa. The pup was disturbed from its sleep and began yiping and howling, but that didn't slow us down one bit. The lovemaking on the sofa was awkward and quick, and then we lay there with our hearts pounding hard trying to catch our breath, listening to the pup. "That dog music's a real mood swinger," he said. He got up naked, fetched the pup and took it outside where I heard the horse-trailer door close. When he came back in he looked at me on the couch, smiled, and we started laughing as he tried to draw a picture on the sweat on his chest. Then we walked down to the pond and had a cooling swim, talked for a while and made love on our small towels, and went swimming again. Sam remembered the pup and ran up the hill to let it go. We sat on the dock and watched it hunt frogs with its parents. The Lab ate the frogs the Airedale caught. Now it was late afternoon so we dressed and went off to a roadhouse twenty miles down the road. It was blessedly air-conditioned, and we danced to the jukebox, played pool, ate dinner, and danced again. When we got back we simply fell asleep with a fan moaning at the window and made love with hangovers in the first light, then slept again until midmorning.

It was at breakfast that I became quite upset. He was frying bacon at the stove in jeans with no shirt and I was

admiring all the muscles in his back which were functional
rather than those got from exercise. There was a pale half-
moon scar on his shoulder that he said came from an operation
when he was thrown against a fence at the rodeo in Big Timber. My breath shortened and I looked around the trailer
thinking, My God, am I with Duane? The similarity might have
dawned on me by then but perhaps I didn't want it to. I walked
outside feeling nude in my bra and jeans trying to catch my
breath. I thought, I'll be goddamned if I'll let this stop me. I
won't let this stop me because I like this man. I deserve this
man for however long. I don't give a good goddamn if he is like
Duane and lives in a fucking trailer and smells like a horse. I
heard him come outside and turned to where he stood on the
porch.

"You OK, darling?" he asked softly.

"I'm fine. I just thought of something, that's all." I walked
up the porch steps and he gave me a hug. He tried to tease me
into a smile.

"You know it's funny but way back there at the fair when
you were dancing in that short dress I was up front and thought
about doing this. And now here I am."

"I saw all you assholes from Ainsworth standing over there
but I must say I didn't plan this."

So driving home was pleasant, though the pup was a problem until I stopped by a big, unfenced field and chased him
around, and then we were both tired. Then he slept and I
sorted out my plans, which was simple, because we had agreed
that we would meet in a week. Despite our ages there had
been the usual uneasiness of new lovers about what to do next,
if anything. You can sit there and let time sort it out but time
can do a bad job. I had convinced him without too much effort
to spend some time at the cabin in Buffalo Gap while he
figured out whether to take a job in Texas or go to Montana.
I frankly hoped for neither, but I cautioned myself not to look
that far ahead. At forty-five we all fear death by suffocation. I
tried to remember without success a line by Rilke that I had
read in college: how lovers try to swallow each other until
there is nothing left of either of them except a peculiar kind
of emotional disease.

I took a detour down toward Elsmere and Purdum where the road would cross the North Loup. It wasn't far from this juncture that Northridge and Aase had spent her last days. I had visited the site that summer after Duane died when the location and the thought of Aase meant a good deal to me. I read and reread the journal passages concerning her and her unimaginable will toward life, or so it seemed to me at the time:

She is so thin now that deep in the night with my arms around her it is as if I feel her retreating into the little girl she once was. Her energies in the early morning are cheerful and if the weather is coolish we sit by the fire with our cups of tea and the dictionary, though it now seems doubtful we shall proceed beyond the "a's". Yesterday out on her cot she discovered my ruse as I wished to pass over "agony" and she said in her slight, bell-clear voice, "Agony is the struggle before death. I read it when you fetched the water." Her faith & belief in God & His Son are so direct as to embarrass the theologian in me. To Aase, God is tangible as the sky above & the earth below, the full red moon we saw rising as if burnt by a prairie fire. She is similar to devout Sioux who speak so directly to the Spirits they are doubtless heard. This morning before daylight she was delirious & vomited forth blood & when I lit a candle she touched the blood with a forefinger and held it to the light as if she were studying life itself. I gave her opium, stirred the fire & added wood, then rocked her in my lap before the fire until dawn. She always wakes when the birds begin their singing though it is probable that one morning soon she will not awake. Her favorite is the flutelike sound of the meadowlark & she was quite enthused when I told her these birds are said to migrate to South America with the coming of fall. She fancies that at death her spirit will be allowed to migrate over all the earth so that she may see those places to which her curiosity has become attached. I have assured her that God is just & this will be so. In the trunk she has brought along with our marriage there is a doll she has kept from her childhood & for which she embroidered many small & beautiful dresses. She wishes me to marry again and give this doll to my child as her greatest pain has been not to bear us children. When light entered the cabin & the birds

**began her pale-blue eyes opened and looked into mine saying all that remains voiceless within us & she touched the tear on my cheek with the finger with the dried blood upon it.**

○

Within an hour of my arrival Lundquist had rigged a gate between the kitchen and the dining room so I could toilet-train the pup in the kitchen with newspapers. Frieda sat across the table from me as I read my mail, more than a little disgusted at the idea of a puppy "pooping" all over her kitchen. I told her to take a few days off by which time she would be taking care of Michael over at Naomi's. The core of her gossip was that this morning a "Jap" photographer and a big tall woman in a purple dress had shown up and taken about a thousand "pitchers" of Karen Olafson and the whole town was "abuzz."

"Poor Professor Michael, getting his head broke trying to help that slut. She gets famous and he gets a headache. He ought to sue her for a cold million. Maybe she'll be a bunny for God's sake."

While she prattled I sorted out the bills from letters from Michael, Paul, and a postcard from Naomi postmarked Chadron. I was waiting to call Andrew until Frieda and Lundquist left—he was sitting in the corner on the floor, admiring his gate with the pup on his lap, while Roscoe watched through the porch window. Roscoe had decided the pup was his and didn't want the rest of us near his new possession. When I didn't rise to the Karen bait Frieda began to talk about the Cornhuskers, the University of Nebraska football team, which is the state's central passion. One of her Christmas presents from our family had always been two season tickets for prime seats secured by the Omaha law firm. Only God knows what she and her girl-friend Marge did on these football weekends in Lincoln. I was never around in the fall but Naomi said that Frieda and Marge would return on Sunday much the worse for wear. Frieda felt that nature's worst joke was that most men were shrimps and not like the "big ole Cornhuskers."

The phone rang and Frieda answered it with the usual "I'll just see if she wants to talk to you." It was Sam so I took the call upstairs. I could immediately sense the cold feet in his voice but overrode it by pretending I didn't. He felt he couldn't stay at my cabin unless he did something for his keep, so I said I would get some lumber delivered and he could expand and repair the corral. That satisfied him and his voice warmed to say "I miss you." Late at night when we had had far too much to drink he had said he always wanted to go to New York City because when he was a kid his parents had taken him to see *A Tree Grows In Brooklyn* over in O'Neill. I had thought this funny but he was terribly serious, admitting that he had never been east of Lexington, Kentucky. He didn't care for hot dogs and his mother had told him that according to the *Reader's Digest* they eat three million hot dogs a day in New York. I assured him that they were a better quality than those red-dyed ones at rodeos, which seemed to bring a boozy relief.

Naomi had added two more birds to her life list and Nelse had taken photos to prove it. They would return in ten days or so. Paul wrote to ask if mid-July was an appropriate time for a visit from him and Luiz since they would be looking at two schools in Colorado. Included was a thank-you note from Luiz for "saving" him from a life which he detailed briefly. I was embarrassed by his thanks, partly because I knew he was one out of a thousand to be retrieved, and I had spent too many years just beyond the edge of sadness—barely, in fact—to equate retrieval with cure.

Michael's note was a mercifully short response to a letter I had written. He agreed that a convalescence at Naomi's under Frieda's care was a good idea if I promised to visit. He would also agree to any capitulation of principles to avoid a court case and trial over Karen and his fractured jaw. He had been feeling well but rather "empty" what with the loss of his habits, and the depended-upon short circuits that were a source of energy. All in all, though, the experience had given him an "intimation of mortality" that had dropped him into a void; it was as if the world had grown not only too quiet, but too large. A rather pretty staff psychologist had told him that this was a "splendid opportunity" to quit drinking. She had quoted someone, he couldn't remember who, as saying "You can't do something you don't know if you keep doing what you do know." Michael was sharp on the subject of our comtemporary infatuation with repellent psychologisms and wondered if this qualified? In anticipation of his daughter Laurel's visit he had written her to say he had fallen from a horse. He thanked me for sending two books, Luchetti & Olwell's *Women of the West* and Carter's *Solomon D. Butcher: Photographing the American Dream.* Both books would have been unbearable to read, he said, on the usual hangover, and had extended his sympathies somewhat beyond the Indians to all those involved in the financial hoax of the westward movement. It was the unimaginable bleakness of being stranded in Cheyenne County during the drought of 1887 with a wife and children, the deaths by exhaustion and malnutrition. He closed by admitting an infatuation with a plumpish nurse who thus far had refused to get him a bottle of whiskey, though he had upped his offer to a hundred dollars.

Frieda called up the stairs to say goodbye. I watched out the window as she left, then went back down to the kitchen. Lundquist still sat in the corner with the pup in his lap.

"This child is related to Sonia. I can tell by the eyes." He was referring to an Airedale Grandfather owned that was my favorite. It seemed implausible, but could be true since some of Sonia's pups went up to the Ainsworth area. I poured Lundquist a shot of whiskey and gave him a bottle of beer from the refrigerator. Both were gone in a minute. He had been letting the pup chew his denim coat and it was difficult to get the little dog to let go.

The moment Lundquist left I felt dry-mouthed and fluttery. I pretended to be interested in the idea that it was the summer solstice which was normally the most dramatic day of the year to me, far more than Christmas and New Year's. It was time to call Andrew and my deepest, unvoiced fear was that my son was dead. Most people would think it a little pretentious for me to say "my son" when all I did is make love, carry him, and give birth, and all the actual mothering was done by someone else. But then I knew I was far beyond rationality, above or below it, and I had involuntarily thought so much about the subject that it had reduced itself to a knot, a lump of coal beneath my breastbone. I rinsed my face in cold water, then dialed Andrew as quickly as possible. Thankfully, he didn't dally around.

"Omaha. He grew up in Omaha. The father is dead, the mother living. She was quite shocked but willing to talk to you, though only in the most general terms and in person. He's alive. I know that's your biggest fear."

"How did you find out?" I had to repeat myself because I was unable to raise my voice above a whisper.

"I called your uncle Paul. Your grandfather arranged it, and Paul handled the legalities in Tucson. The adoptive father was a member of a law firm your grandfather dealt with in Omaha. I suppose he wanted to keep track but then he died. Paul would have told you if you asked but he hoped he wouldn't have to."

"I'm not sure what you mean." My heart was pounding to the point of dizziness.

"These sorts of things usually don't work out well. He could have been dead, maimed, crazy, or resentful. He's not dead or maimed, but I don't know about the others. She thinks I'm a private detective and won't say much. You can see her tomorrow or wait two weeks because she's going to Maryland to see her daughter. I can set it up."

"Please do . . . thanks." That was as much as I could say. I couldn't draw a clear breath and my stomach began to cramp. I curled up and stared out the window at the tops of the sugar maples moving slightly in the breeze. I began to breathe with the pattern of a cicada I singled out from the rest and that helped. Lying there I wondered what he looked like, where he was at this very moment, and if we ever met, would he dislike me for giving him up, no matter that it was not my choice? I stopped these thoughts just short of screaming by running cold water in the upstairs bathroom sink and putting my face in it. There was an unbearable sense of density and congestion.

I closed the pup in the kitchen, went outside, and saddled up Peach. She was overready and wheeled around, scattering the geese. I headed west, letting the horse warm before I allowed her to break into the gallop I sensed she wanted. We skirted the alfalfa fields and followed the old tractor and game trails between the alfalfa and the windbreaks. We were going fast enough that I squinted my eyes and the bugs that hit my face stung. In a clear quarter-mile stretch I let her go and when I pulled her up to a canter I discovered I had been yelling along with the wind in my ears. Goddamn the world who gives me no father and no son. No husband. It was much more, I hope, than self-pity, and when I continued to yell the eyes of Peach rolled backward to see if it was her fault. I leaned forward until my face was along her mane. I suppose I was yelling at God, not claiming a uniqueness in sorrow, but claiming what I was. The ache still came upward from my stomach to my heart to my throat and into my head and back down for another circle. Larks and kildeer skittered above the grass before us, and I slowed us down, running my fingers through the mare's sweating flanks. We picked our way through the last windbreak before the slough. Now the cattails were thick along the trail and red-winged blackbirds were perched bobbing on the cattail heads. What kind of fucking world is this? I asked them. Peach trembled as she smelled the water, and when we reached the creek and swimming hole I loosened the reins and let her go for it, which she did in a breathtaking leap and plunge. There was the creek bottom Charlene drew me up from when I wanted to stay there. We made a circle; then we were up the far bank near Duane's tipi ring and hanging white deer skull. I jumped off and unsaddled Peach so she could roll in her beloved dust. The late-afternoon sun was warm so I shed my clothes, squeezed and wrung out water, and hung them over a bush. I shivered a bit; then for no reason I rolled in the sand and dust. I stood up laughing as Peach watched me, then I got back down and rolled in the sand again. It was so wonderful I wondered why I had never done it before. I rolled over and over and down the bank and back into the water. Peach ran up and down the bank, then made a marvelous leap into the creek. We're quite the girls today, I thought.

When I lay stretched out on the damp and smelly horse blanket I realized that my stomachache was gone and with it the pain beneath my breastbone and in my throat and head. I rolled over on my belly and stared at ants. A number of times in my life I'd been told, or overheard, how much men had paid for whores, prostitutes, call girls, whatever, and I mentally

toted up the amount I'd pay to have Sam there. As the auction-
eers say, it would be "top dollar."

With my eyes just above ground level I looked above the
stones outside the tipi ring to the burial mounds in the thicket.
An ornithologist had asked Naomi if he might bring in an
archaeologist friend with the idea of clearing and excavating
the mounds. She said no: enough mounds had been dug up.
When she was way up Canyon de Chelly a Navajo told her that
some college folks had dug up his grandmother who had only
been dead a few years. The mounds weren't Sioux, who had
come to the area around the time of Columbus, driven westward by the forest people, the Ojibway. When my father
showed them to me I rode a smallish bay mare and he rode a
large black gelding. I must have been almost eight. Just before
he left, with a witch-hazel smell on his chin. He said it was the
best camping spot in the world and when he and Naomi were
first married they camped there on summer nights and
watched shooting stars: There's one. There's another one over
there. He frightened Naomi before they slept by saying Sioux
words to the mounds in the thicket, pretending he was asking
the dead warriors about their great buffalo hunts. Duane had
that skull in the barn. He'd let Sonia in there among the hay
bales with him. I can see him looking out to the west wondering what his life would be like; then like all of us he found out.
I lifted my eyes and there was a bird I didn't recognize on the
antler. I memorized its black-and-yellow markings knowing it
was so small and fragile it had to be a warbler. It looked at me.
I was a fellow creature, I thought. Peach napped standing up.
I dozed until I heard the first mosquito of the evening, then
dressed in damp clothes, saddled Peach, and made my way
home.

○

I remembered the entrance gate of the Happy Hollow Country Club from somewhere in my childhood, perhaps right after
World War II, on my first trip to Omaha with my parents; the
landscaping was formed with hedges like trimmed 4-H sheep
at a fair, and there was the feeling, absurd name and all, that
one was transported back to Connecticut or Bucks County.

The people who tended to make the money in the westward movement were Yankee in origin.

I felt uncomfortably fragile, and the sensation was as foreign to me as the onset of flu or food poisoning. It was similar to my illness in the Marquette hospital before the trip to Arizona—since waking before dawn I had tried everything to rid myself of the giddiness which was only a form of helplessness. The unvoiced prayer that was to be answered today—that I find out what happened to my son—enlarged itself and seemed to fill all the cells of my being. I even looked into a classic text on anxiety I had studied in graduate school but the words muddied themselves, blurred, and became senseless. Just after first light I rode Peach for an hour but rather than preventing the sweep of memory the ride abetted it; I turned around after emerging from a gully behind the country Methodist church, which only served to remind me of the lecture on sin I had received the summer after the baby. There was the temptation to become a foxhole Christian, throw myself before the altar in supplication as countless millions of women have done over their children but I knew that the church was locked. Besides, what I remembered in the Bible was the central lesson of the terrifying fragility of life.

The only thing, finally, that helped kill the hours before my departure for Omaha was to sit on a cottonwood stump in a grove of flowering crab behind the barn. It was near the creek and the geese followed me, nestling to doze in the green grass like huge white eggs. I began by breathing slowly and gave myself up to my thoughts rather than quarrel with them, which helped make them drift away: "He is not what is left of Duane. I hope he does not look like my father. It is altogether possible that he won't care for me, given the conditions of his life. Perhaps his adoptive mother will tell me nothing this afternoon. This doesn't mean I will ever see him, only that I'll learn something of him. It has to be enough that he is not dead and that I learn he is not unhappy. Perhaps it would be better if he never knew I existed but I don't want that to be so. Oh God he is the only child I ever had but so is my father the only father I will ever have. Oh Father wherever you are. Grandfather. I am strong enough but not for this. Life has gone by please let me know. Grandfather said the year he was born in

1886 it was the hottest summer to be followed by the coldest winter ever so that the sheep in the west died and the starving cattle ate the wool off the sheep and died beside them. He said in the car, Take courage, the earth is all that lasts. That is true but I am a woman sitting on a stump. I want to love my son or at least touch his arm and greet him."

○

She was backlit by a window in the lounge so that when I came in from the sunlight I couldn't see her features clearly. She stood and waved and a waiter took me to her. Her hand was thin to boniness when I took it, and so was her voice, which was also lightly slurred.

"My goodness, but I would have recognized you anywhere. You must not come to Omaha often. I thought I saw you at the hospital last week when I was visiting a friend. Were you there? I said it must be you, though it all was thirty years ago."

I nodded yes, unable to find my voice. She was extremely thin, beautifully dressed, and I guessed in her early sixties. It was apparent she had done some drinking in her life but her eyes were kind.

"I'm having a Manhattan, because this is a bit nerve-racking. May I order one for you? I'm puzzled, confused. I don't hear from him often, perhaps once or twice a year, but he said he'd seen you in Santa Monica, also in Nebraska last summer. He said during his Christmas call he would be seeing you again this summer. So when that man called for you I didn't know what to think. He was always a bit of a fibber, but he described what you looked like."

My breath was shallow and I could barely speak. "He never introduced himself if he saw me. Do you have a photo?" This immediately seemed the wrong thing to say.

"Oh my God, no. I went to a therapist this morning who helped me when my husband died. The therapist said it's the young man's decision. Of course, now that you know his last name you could obviously find him with your resources, but it wouldn't be right. Or so they say."

"I wouldn't do that. I understand that. It's natural for me to wonder what he looks like."

"Of course. Let me think it over. There's no way to prepare for this, is there? Your grandfather was a very intimidating man. We were fearful of him even though the adoption was legal. My husband was only a junior member of the firm. Your grandfather asked that the boy be named John. We agreed and that's his legal name, though we resented it and never used the name. We saw your grandfather once more and that was during the August before he died. It was at a dinner given by a senior partner to which we had been summoned and instructed to bring the baby. My husband nearly resigned over the issue, but that evening he got along famously with your grandfather. My husband was from a poor family up in Moorhead, Minnesota, and very probably worked himself to death. Your grandfather came into a bedroom to see the baby and kissed its forehead. He said something to the baby in a foreign language; I suspect it was Indian, because I was told your grandfather was part Indian. Within a few weeks my husband was made the youngest full partner. I don't know why I'm saying this, because what you want to hear is about the boy. We were in our early thirties and thought we were infertile, but after the adoption we had two daughters of our own. One lives here in Omaha and one lives in Maryland. I guess this sometimes happens. So it was all quite wonderful for us. To be frank, the boy was always quite contrary and only infrequently a good student. He was a better student in college. But he was kind to his sisters and was a superb athlete, which meant a lot to his dad and means a lot around here, perhaps too much. During his last two years of high school we let him work on a dude ranch in Wyoming, and we never had any real control of him after that. We had told him he was adopted, because you're supposed to, but I'm not sure that's right. Your grandfather didn't help by leaving him a modest income for when he turned eighteen. The daughters were so easy, and he tended to be out of our control. But I guess so many sons are like that." She stopped and waved away an acquaintance who was approaching, pointing to her watch. She appeared to be waiting for me to ask questions.

"I know I don't have any rights in this matter. The most I dared expect is to find out what happened to him." Now I felt as if someone had driven a spike in my skull. A fresh drink had arrived but I knew it wouldn't help.

"Well, when that man called, at first I refused to talk about it, but then he said it was the only child you ever had. That brought back the hospital to me and how when I looked in your room you looked so lovely, and I thought, How can we take this girl's baby from her? Later I understood no one owns a child, you just raise it. Everyone owns themselves. I keep wondering why he said he knew you. Many of our friends always thought he was arrogant and brash but he was quite shy in matters he really cared about. Maybe after he looked for you and found you he was just too shy to say anything. That must be it."

"When he calls again will you tell him I want desperately to meet him?" I had begun to cry now out of utter frustration.

"Of course I will. Oh my God, but he could be such a bastard. But not about this sort of thing. He probably thought you might not want to know him." Now she began to cry and gulped her drink. "How awful for you."

"Please tell me a little bit more about him. I'm very grateful." I dried my eyes and felt a specific relief, thinking, My God, he *was* looking for me, and he found me, though he didn't say anything. He said to himself, That is my mother.

"He went to several colleges. . . ." She tried to lighten her voice. "First he was going to be a veterinarian, then a biologist, then a rancher. After the dude ranch he began to care for horses, but not the equitation sort. He started at Macalester, his dad's school, then over in Lincoln, then to Michigan State to study cattle. It was hard to keep track. He got in trouble in Mexico for resisting arrest but his father got him out of that, though it was expensive. His father died five years ago, but just before that he used his political influence to get him into the Peace Corps in Guatemala. But he got kicked out of the Peace Corps, and I received a postcard from Alaska. The last time he called he was in Seattle. His father was very strict and orthodox with the girls, but he was never hard on John, though we never called him that. I was going to say, You'll have to meet him because I can't really describe him. It sounds funny but I know it isn't."

I began to phrase another question, but it became apparent there was nothing more I could ask that wouldn't make it harder for both of us. It was the kind of silence that hurts your ears. She reached across the table and put her hand on mine. Two of her knuckles were swollen with arthritis and she caught my glance.

"I used to be ladies' champion and now I can't hold a club but I'm teaching my granddaughter. Life is goddamned awful, isn't it? Everything that consoles us can be taken away, and how can I say this to you? He'll call me again some day and I'll beg him, I'll force him to come see you. I'll say, Go see her or I'll shoot myself. I promise that. But now you must tell me who the father was. I've always wondered that."

"He was a half-breed Sioux boy named Duane Stone Horse. I loved him but he died a long time ago."

We both drew in as much breath as we could and said goodbye.

○

I was a full hundred miles out of Omaha on my five-hour drive home before I remembered that I hadn't stopped to see Michael. I had driven quite near the University of Nebraska Medical Center and he simply hadn't occurred to me. I absolved myself of neglect by remembering he said he wanted no visitors and, anyway, Frieda was going to retrieve him in two days.

The last hour of the trip home was in the dark. I was drowsy and hungry with all of the anguish of the day dissipated and replaced by the not very well-founded faith that I would see him some day. I even drove more slowly than usual as if I were being more cautious in my wait for the day to come. The adoptive mother was not the sort of person I would have liked on any immediate, social basis—I might have judged her as brittle and snotty—but by the end of our meeting she seemed rather grand. She had said nothing of herself other than that she was a lawyer's wife and the mother of three, but then I hadn't talked about myself either. It made me curious about her background. My thoughts drifted off to my gynecologist friend who told me his first wife had been a call girl. She had helped him through medical school and his internship and the unfortunate marriage had been his idea.

Back home I cleaned up after and played with the pup, made a drink, and called Sam at the cabin in Buffalo Gap. It was reassuring at this late hour to find his voice light and playful. He said that Naomi and her young scientist friend, Nelse, had stopped by and they had had dinner together. Naomi was going to come home for a few days but Nelse, who had "cowboyed" a little, was going to stay and help him build a set of corrals, also recaulk and varnish the cabin. I found myself almost begging him to stay there for a while and promising I'd be up within a few days after getting Michael settled. He said not to worry, that he liked the place so well he'd stay for a few weeks or as long as he could earn his "keep."

I lay down on the couch in the den too tired to eat and looked at the mail. There was a letter from Michael and I hoped it wouldn't further addle me, though the chances were remote that I could be reached in any meaningful sense after the day I had spent. I had been thinking of the words of a song that had been on the radio when I turned into the drive. It was a Neil Young and was something about being a "miner for a Heart of Gold." I had heard the song a dozen times over the years and it had always made me uncomfortable. It didn't occur to me until I drove into the yard that it was the song that they kept playing on my first night in Key West. The music was so imponderably plaintive that it was understandable that I forced it from my mind.

Dearest D.,

They tell me I am repairing well, though more in body than in mind. Brain repairs are inappropriate at this time. The senescence of quasi–mental health might deter my total immersion in the insanity of history. Thus I have a purpose, unlike when I lost my beloved wife because I was simply too stupid to seek help, afraid to lose the personal drama of a craziness that was, all in all, rather literary compared with that of history.

It is barely daylight and I've been remembering an evening when we sat on your balcony in Santa Monica. You had been telling me how your grandfather had been born in a tipi near Harney Peak in South Dakota in 1886 and that his own father had gone basically insane at about that time and until the winter of 1891, when he moved his family to where you live now. You said it was the Dawes Act that pushed him over the edge. I've been reading *The Dawes Act and the Allotment of Indian Lands* by D. S. Otis, which was reedited by Prucha. I won't bore you with details but wanted you to know some of my thinking on the matter.

Northridge was a witness to the twilight of the gods, beside which the Wagnerian constructs are pissant silliness. He was right there when it became dark, absolutely dark. He lived among people who talked to God and who thought "God" talked back to them through the mouthpiece of earth herself. There is no need, of course, to romanticize the Sioux or any other tribe. In the prism of history it is apparent that they all were destroyed because they were "bad for business." Naturally we were and are Americans to ourselves, but to them we were perfect "Germans" and they obviously felt much the same way that the Poles and French later felt before the Teutonic conquering horde. The Indians were rather decorative at war. Maybe it was the somewhat Newtonian principle that a nation at war tends to remain at war, and after our "Civil" pursuit the Indians fell victim to a mopping-up operation, the sort of thing we tried later in Korea and Vietnam, and are presently aiming at in Central America. All the machinery was there, left over from the Civil War, so why not use it? This is truly the fatalism of a primitive species.

I didn't intend the dourness of this note. To be honest, I have been unfaithful to you with a nurse called, inelegantly, Debbie. She's from Iowa and brought me (from my recipe) a quart of homemade beef broth with plenty of garlic in it, certainly the best thing that ever passed through a hospital straw. My belly has so subsided that for the first time in memory I can see my wienie while standing up! It remains unattractive though useful. Did anyone ever tell you that you were rather scary? I'm not saying you can't be nice or pleasant, but you've always frightened me a bit, and I suspect all your other men friends have felt it. I'm saying this because without alcohol I'm dreaming a great deal and you always appear as somewhat feral and predatory in my dreams. The culture doesn't prepare us for lionesses! See you soon, my love.

Michael

P.S. Greet the geese for me.

The last paragraph amused me. Way back in college Charlene and I concocted something that started as a game. One Saturday afternoon we began refusing to act as litmus paper for the moods of the men we encountered, and kept a journal for several months of their reactions. We were thought of as "twin bitches" for a while, and the pickings were slim indeed, mostly the shy, bookish, and somewhat masochistic errand-boy types. Then, though we were only sophomores, we begun hanging out with painters and writers who were graduate students and who didn't find our behavior offensive. I suspect that neither of us ever totally abandoned this parlor game and that was what Michael was referring to. Charlene enjoyed playing the queen bee while I was more interested in the notion that the protective coloring girls are taught to adapt seemed to work to their disadvantage. We both felt like pioneers, and though we had no artistic talent we thought we were in the avant-garde of new emotions.

○

Frieda called at 6:00 A.M. to say she couldn't come to work. Last evening Lundquist had been taken to the local clinic, a five-bed affair for minor illnesses that had been half underwritten by our family. He had a urinary infection and after being catheterized and put to bed he had disappeared. She had been up most of the night looking for him with the deputies and he had been discovered sleeping with Roscoe in the doghouse, which was a marvelous, ample structure with a weathervane and a birdhouse on the roof. Fearing death, Lundquist had walked the fifteen miles home cross-country at night. He had proved to the deputies and the doctor that he could pee, which had been the problem. Would I mind keeping an eye on him this evening because she needed to leave for Omaha to check Michael out of the hospital the following morning? Of course not, I said, looking forward to time spent in private with the old man.

When I got out of bed my muscles were sore as if I had spent the previous day hiking or putting in fence, or had been thrown from a horse. It was barely after six and the morning was cool and clear. Peach was staring up at my window from the corral and I called out to her, which sent her wheeling in a circle, upsetting the geese. I put on jeans and a sweater and went downstairs to the yodeling of the wakened pup, whom I put outside and watched scooting to the goose cage, where he sat down in puzzlement. I turned on the coffee maker and wished that Naomi were there to talk about yesterday. I went outside and walked through the dewy grass in my bare feet, wondering if my son had driven into the barnyard when I wasn't there, or had seen me on the street in town, in the grocery store, walking on the beach in Santa Monica. Or in the British Pub between Ocean Avenue and Second Street. I caught myself short when I hoped in retrospect I had behaved well while being watched.

I put the pup—to be called Ted, I had decided—in the old kennel beside the barn, then rode Peach up and down the half-mile-long driveway bareback, regretting the lack of a saddle when she shied at a flushing pheasant. My ex-brother-in-law loved to point out that you could pay ten grand for a horse, go for a ride, and if an empty ten-cent potato-chip bag blew across the path, you could die. I told him—admitting that it was true—that people, cats, and horses liked to imagine threats and react to imaginary dangers. I reminded myself as the cock pheasant rattled off through the brush and I was clinging to Peach that I meant to stay alive. I would be more alert and less foolhardy.

I drove in to Lena's Café and went in through the back door to find her in the kitchen. She embraced me when she heard the news that there was a chance I might see my son, or my "child" as she put it. After she said "child" we looked at each other for a moment and began to laugh. We continued to talk as she managed a dozen breakfast orders at once at the stove. She began her day at four in the morning, then closed after lunch. There was no transient business and people ate supper at home barring a special occasion that justified a long drive. Charlene wanted her to retire but to Lena the café was her life and now in her mid-sixties she still had an eye out for the perfect boyfriend. She liked to point to a framed award signed by a former governor that named hers the best chicken-fried steak in the great state of Nebraska. In the grand area between New York and California people are inordinately fond of giving each other trophies and awards.

Karen came into the kitchen in a prim blue uniform to pick up an order. She was startled to see me and blushed deeply. She looked up at the fan above the stove with a studied curiosity. Lena was kind enough to take Karen's order out into the café.

"I guess all I can say is I'm sorry it happened," she said.

"You're not even ten percent at fault. He should know better but he doesn't."

"Is he OK? Dad has this bad temper. I told him I never did it with him. . . ."

I shushed her and told her I hoped it would work out well. I turned over a pile of fried potatoes that looked like they might burn, feeling the wooden handle of the big spatula that had worn to Lena's grip. Karen said she was on "pins and needles" because she would hear that afternoon if the agency was flying her out to L. A. for more test photos or perhaps a contract. Looking at her I suspected the answer would be yes. I told her to let me know and I would alert Ted to keep an eye out for her. It was a neighborly gesture; she couldn't really be protected but I sensed a streak of her father's meanness that would help. All Ted could do would be to determine the level at which she was initially taken advantage of—models tended to prefer the easy confidence of rock musicians and drug wholesalers. Karen thanked me and Lena returned to say that the sheriff needed to talk to me. He had seen my car in the alley—I had forgotten that in a small town every auto bears its owner's signature.

The sheriff and a deputy stood when I approached. They both looked tired from the Lundquist escapade. The deputy felt that Lundquist had missed his calling and could have made a "mint" building doghouses for rich folks. His food was nearly hidden by catsup. The sheriff gave me some papers for Michael to sign, saying he was glad the affair was over without anyone's getting really hurt, a euphemism I decided not to respond to. All the silverware in the room had stopped clinking and I couldn't help flashing a smile at the business folk pausing above their grits.

I stood a full ten minutes in front of the bank waiting for it to open, wishing I had eaten some fried food at Lena's. In the cool morning air I could still smell the kitchen on my sweater. I was on the sunny west side and stared at the Edward Hopper shadows on the east side of the street. I waved at an old man opening the hardware store, remembering him in his early middle age when he helped Grandfather train bird dogs on pen-raised quail. Each year the life on the street was sparser and all the storefronts needed a little paint and repairs. There hadn't been a truly good year for farmers since the grain embargo seven years before, and the beef business was a victim of change in eating habits and bad foreign-trade policies. It occurred to me that I might see it become a virtual ghost town in my lifetime but then there had been bad times before. There were very few new cars around and even the water tower needed a coat of paint. Lena said that of the eighteen graduating seniors only two were staying in town, and one of those was semi-retarded. The UPS had an opening in the county and there were three hundred applicants. There was work for the capable way over in Omaha or Lincoln but it was hard for people to accept that their land, or their houses in town, had sunk to half the previous value.

The bank opened and I fetched the second trunk with an air of busyness to avoid the socializing that would bring about a discussion of hard times. I no longer knew any local people well enough to be asked for a loan, but I was aware Naomi had somewhat extended herself in this direction. I suspect rich people tend to live with each other in community compounds to avoid these unsecured loans, and the bruised consciences of seeing friends and acquaintances making the slow trek into insolvency. In farm communities people often carry each other well past hopelessness. I had noticed repeatedly there were fewer children playing on the streets than there used to be, and when I drove past the ball diamond on the way out of town there weren't enough boys to make two teams so they settled for some girls.

○

A few hours later, on Naomi's porch swing I realized the degree to which I had been knocked off balance by the event in Omaha. My skin began to prickle and my mouth grew dry. Nothing would be the same again but then I hadn't wanted it to be, as if nothing could be preserved past that point unless it was vital. Only myths last, my professor had said, because myths are vital. I hadn't thought much about that. What did it mean that I was forty-five and barren two-thirds of my life? I talked to Paul about it in Mexico but knew that after that first was lost I wouldn't have borne another anyway. At the diamond the boy hit the ball into the air and it stayed in the air ever since they began playing the game. There is always the first horse, usually a pony. The first dog. The first lover, real or mostly imagined. Now on the porch it was as if there was too much oxygen in the green air of June, and the son had doubtless driven down this road, perhaps glanced through the porch screen to see Naomi sitting here talking to the dead in the evening. It was too large to be understood, it was not meant to be understood except to sense how large it was as if we were particles of our own universe, each of us a part of a more intimate constellation. The reach from the porch to three crows sleeping in a dead cottonwood down the road was infinite. So were father, mother, son and daughter, lover, horse and dog. I was on the porch on a hot afternoon in June, and before me on hundreds of June afternoons Sioux girls looked for birds' eggs here, buffalo whelped, prairie wolves roamed, and far before that—in prehistory we're told—condors with wingspreads of thirty feet coasted on dense thermals in the hills along the Niobrara.

Back inside I rechecked the music room and Frieda's rather elaborate arrangements for Michael's new study, with everything moved over from the bunkhouse, including Karen's nude photo stuck in a Gideon Bible in the middle of the desk. I didn't disturb her little joke, mostly because it was quite funny. In the kitchen Frieda had stocked the refrigerator, and there were recipes for broths and purees on the counter, plus a case of an adult version of baby formula.

I thought of opening the second trunk of journals but sat on it instead. I had had my turn years ago and now it was Michael's job. I felt a little sorry for him. All the suffering had leavened my own at the time, and had helped explain my family's character to me. The images fluttered in my mind, focusing for a split second then passing on to others: the Bible, fruit trees, buffalo, Aase, He Dog and Crazy Horse, Sam Creek-mouth missing one ear, a field of gathered buffalo bones; all full of earnestness, a journal of work, love, and grief, becoming a journal of madness and starvation, becoming a journal of madness partly drug-induced, because by the time of the Ghost Dance peyote had made its way up, from tribe to tribe, to the Lakota. After Wounded Knee Northridge had seen far beyond and through what we at present call, with an air of banality, the "back wall." Our world is so drowned in suffering I suppose it meant more that it was a blood relation, an ancestor.

I borrowed a barnyard pullet from Naomi's freezer and drove home. I was a little desperate to do something as ordinary as to cook old Lundquist dinner. There was also the temptation, since my life had become inadvertently bold, to visit the room below the basement and get it over with. From the journals and Paul I pretty much knew what it held but I also realized it was terribly important to resolve the whole thing by actually seeing it.

○

When I drove in the yard Lundquist was sitting on a milkstool in the shadowed, open door of the barn with the pup on his lap and Roscoe at his feet. I got out of the car and approached quietly since he and the pup were asleep, though ever-watchful Roscoe bared his teeth, then growled softly in recognition of his master's snooze. The pup awoke and wriggled off Lundquist's lap which startled the old man.

"Frieda brought me over. I baby-sat for you girls once and I took you swimming. That's the last time I went swimming. You remember? Ruth wanted me to catch a muskrat and bring it home. I says you can't make a pet out of a muskrat. They stroll along the bottom of the water eating weeds. I could use a beer because I walked home last night. You probably know that. Everyone I know who died, they die at the hospital so it made sense to get home. I got turned around in Swanson's big cornfield because the clouds came and I didn't have stars to point the way. Frieda locks the door so I went to sleep with Roscoe. And that's why I could use a beer."

I readily agreed and turned toward the house but first he wanted to show me how he had trained the pup not to bother the geese, and vice versa. He put the pup down next to a goose and they instantly turned in opposite directions. I asked him how in God's name he'd accomplished it so quickly.

"I gave them both a pinch and then had them think about each other at close range." He wobbled off toward the house as if this explanation covered everything, waiting for me at the pump-shed door with a bow. He put a finger to his tongue. "Dry as a bone," he said, staring at the half-frozen chicken in my hands as if he recognized it without the feathers. Perhaps he did because it came from his flock.

After his shot and beer I tried to make him lie down on the couch in the den while I made dinner but he refused. It offended his notion of propriety, what with the sense of my grandfather's so fresh in his memory. He took the pup's pillow from the corner of the kitchen, then went out in the front yard where he nestled beneath the tree and tire swing, whistling for the dogs to join him. Watching him out the kitchen window I wanted him to live forever. Naomi had told me that the old gossip was that Lundquist had been quite the ladies' man, a church-and-party tenor, and a fine dancer. As Grandfather's amanuensis he had trailered horses and dogs all over the country though never spoke to me of these trips for fear of violating Grandfather's confidence, no matter that he was long dead. There was a photo in a family album from Kansas City in the thirties with Lundquist holding the leads of three polo ponies and being admired by a young woman who looked like a blond version of Joan Crawford. In the photo he was natty and muscular in riding breeches, and staring now at his fragile heap under the tree, with both the dogs on his chest and stomach, I very much admired the way he had grown old.

I served him his chicken and biscuits in the dining room

with candlelight and white wine. He said a rather long grace in Swedish in which I recognized my name three times though he resisted my questioning about it. It is eerie when you know someone is praying for you. He examined the white Bordeaux and said he had drunk the same kind of wine in the Brown Palace in Denver with Grandfather "way back when." The Glenn Miller orchestra had played and they had all danced very late.

"Who were the ladies?" I mostly asked for the reaction.

"I won't tell you!" He coughed into his napkin, tried to look stern, but there was merriment in his eyes. "They were fine young women but I won't say they were churchgoers." He always topped my glass off before he filled his own. "The week after Mister J. W. died my wife threw away my traveling clothes. She says, 'Your fancy days are over, big shot.' I didn't care one bit. She got crazy over this snoopy religion but I never let her aggravate me. On her deathbed she said she was sorry she limited our affections to the first Saturday every month." He blushed at this admission. "Wine loosens the mouth more than beer." He paused and became grave. "I've been thinking this over and I think I should tell you. I'm pretty sure I saw Duane in the bar a few Saturdays ago. He should have been older though when I thought it over."

"It had to be my son. You know about my son. I was told he was looking for me."

He nodded as if in agreement. "There was someone here right after the professor came. Roscoe and me tracked him halfway down the drive and through the trees to the house and bunkhouse, then back out to the road. I didn't say anything because I thought you might have had an extra gentleman friend."

"If you see him again will you tell him to come see me?"

"Of course I will. I'll bring him right out in the god-damned Studebaker. You waited long enough."

I could see he was wondering if I wanted the last of the wine so I poured it in his glass, then suggested we take a look in the basement. He was calm enough, saying he would go along as far as the door out of the root cellar. That's as far as he had gone with Grandfather when they had packed away all the Indian artifacts in 1950 after Father had died. He wouldn't go further than that because he was Christian and the place frightened him.

"Maybe we should have a brandy first," I thought aloud. He smiled at me as if I had read his thoughts. He got up and lit two Coleman lanterns from the stairwell. When I poured the brandy my hand shook a little which he noticed. I could see he was alarmed by what we intended to do. He glanced over at the window where a fresh breeze lifted the curtains and there was the sound of thunder from the east. Over the years I had noticed that the quality of his grammar varied depending on the formality of the occasion. It improved in situations that might recall my grandfather who loved what he thought of as the King's English. If your language was bad, then so was your thinking. Just underneath my thoughts on language, which were evasive, was a slogan of Ted's, bastardized from Montaigne and translated into Latin—he used it as a personal and business slogan and, though I couldn't remember the Latin, the intent was clear—"The world is staggering in natural drunkenness."

"I hope you don't mind blacksnakes. They live in the root cellar and eat all the field mice that come into the basement in November when it becomes cold. I don't know what they eat the rest of the year. Frieda says they eat their babies. I think they go out and in up near the pump shed. Do you think they eat their baby snakes to keep going?"

I recognized from the sound that the car coming into the barnyard was Naomi's. Lundquist looked at me with a relief that I shared.

"This is a thing you should do at noon. The bogeyman never gets anyone at noon." He scurried out into the kitchen to calm the pup and Roscoe who were setting up a racket over Naomi as she entered.

"I tried to call. Look at this." Naomi held up both the pup and the well-chewed phone cord. I had unplugged the upstairs phone after Frieda's call at daylight. Naomi was deeply tanned and weathered, thinner, but quite nervous. She heated up some leftovers as she talked of the progress of the research with Nelse, which included the suitability of certain properties for purchase by the Nature Conservancy. Nelse was going back to Minneapolis for a week and then they would resume the project. She had spent the last two days at Buffalo Gap sorting data while he helped Sam with my corral. She watched my reaction to the mention of Sam—she had been friends with his oldest sister, also a schoolteacher, for years. She glanced at the dining-room table where Lundquist sat before the lighted lanterns.

"One of the geese is missing. We were going to look for it," I lied.

"Is it true blacksnakes sometimes eat their babies?" Lundquist asked, snuffing the lantern and oblivious to my fib.

"I don't know but I can easily find out. You folks have been drinking." She laughed and gave him a pat as he made his way out the door followed by Roscoe and the pup. We watched him from the kitchen window under the yard light until he reached the bunkhouse. She began to talk about the plans she had made years before to build a little one-room cabin back near the baptismal pool on the creek. At the time she had said she hoped I wouldn't mind the cabin being on "my land." I liked to tease her about this ownership thing, also that the cabin would enable her to watch birds twenty-four hours a day because I was going to buy her an army nightscope which used the light of the stars and the phosphorescence in the air. That way she could watch sleeping birds. She reminded me of when I returned from my sophomore year at the University of Minnesota with a quote from William Blake, "How do you know but that every bird that cuts the airy way is an immense world of delight closed to our senses five." This idea had utterly thrilled her, and still does, she said. I distantly wondered if she were having a flirtation with her young friend, because she was acting ever so vaguely out of character. It was in the quickness of her gestures and so subtle that only a husband or a daughter would have noticed.

○

After she left I went into the den and opened the safe and took out the envelope. I sat on the couch with the envelope on my lap staring up at the John Marin seascape that Lundquist liked so much because he had never seen the ocean and the painting resembled what the ocean looked like in his mind. The note was terse, and mostly an admonition.

May 15, 1956

Dearest Dalva,

I am putting my affairs in order, and that is why you have this short letter from a dead man. I don't intend to tip over tomorrow but I sense this will be my last summer. Unless we are insensitive we know our own weather.

It should be 1986 now—what a foreign ring that has to me! Because you are curious, and because I have asked Paul to urge you to do so, you have probably read my father's journals, so the contents of the subbasement are no mystery to you. It is, however, a bit of a visual shock. My father's intent and my own was to preserve these artifacts from the graverobbers, the trinket vendors, and assorted filth who swindled my mother's people out of their physical sacraments. Think of a Buddhist home in the Orient where vestments, rosaries, and altar pieces are hanging on the walls, the owners recently slaughtered. The other "things" are self-evident.

I don't want this to pose a real burden to you, so at some point you may wish to give the whole lot to a museum with a protective covenant that none of it be sold. There are three labeled medicine bags that should go back to the tribes that are the rightful owners, assuming that you may find souls who are in the rightful mind to receive them. You may wish to bury what remains of the bodies by yourself, or with Paul, or with your son. I assume you will look for each other some day. If I owned my father's faith I would pray that to be so. Along with my sons, perhaps more so, you were the grace note of my life. Now I am so far down the ghost road I can't see you, but I still send you back a kiss and my embrace. We loved each other so.

Grandfather

○

I went to bed reassuring myself that I would handle the problem of the following noon, amused by the idea that I was taking Lundquist's recommendation for a proper time. I sat in my rocker at the window with the lights out watching a tremendous thunderstorm not all that far to the west. It was a relief to see that the wind was wrong for it to come in this direction and that I could watch it sail ponderously to the north with its resplendent lightning striking the horizon in the shapes of tree roots, the arterial system, river deltas from the air, the blue light shimmering off my bare stomach. It was so fearsome that I turned away, got in bed, and faced the far wall where the reflected light was like an artillery bombardment in a war movie. An unpleasant memory came I hadn't remembered in years: Dad swatted my bottom because I chased Ruth with a blacksnake I held which coiled around my arm. It is a bracelet, I said, and I'm wearing this black bracelet to Sunday school and I'm putting it in your piano so watch out. So I was spanked because he said the world is frightening enough without scaring someone on purpose. She will be afraid of snakes forever— only she isn't as a matter of fact. The tears were the same as the hospital when I woke up and I was torn by the baby and they pushed more liquid out. The smell was chloroform or iodine, the salt in tears in the throat like salt water. In and out of sleep and dreams, perhaps nightmares, the dreams remembering and rehearsing other nightmares: The dead wolf I lifted into the pickup on a gravel road near Baudette in Minnesota came back in my sleep and went into my mouth so it filled my body. I rode a huge crow to the river with silver reins. He drank from a sandbar. When they came for me feathers came out of my body which jerked and I flew away and could see them below. The old Sam Creekmouth, not this one—and he had no ear and his cheek was like tattered leather—was teaching me to be a creek mouth like that one when I was young beside the cooking-iron pot on the Missouri. I was a soft old marsh hawk caught between buildings in NYC and the doctor helped me out. In the desert the coyote and cobra went into my spine to be part of my spine and skull. That's too many animals for one body. The old man was trying to give me wisdom but I fucked him instead. All this chemical weeping somewhere near my heart. Who's in there weeping?

Someone is calling dalva dalva dalva up and into the window. It is daylight and raining lightly. It is Lundquist who turns away from looking up at my bare breasts which are hard and

I'm wet for some reason. You were yelling, he said. It was a dream, I said, the pup and Roscoe jumping against the house. Can I go home? I said yes and he put the pup in the shed. He shouldered Roscoe and I watched him walk off, still not quite awake.

In the shower I thought, Holy shit, the night is actually over. What would I say to a doctor and why would they recall each other, for the wolf had arrived more than ten years before. Making breakfast I remained groggy with dreams so decided to school Nick, my quarter-horse gelding, who had become a bit rank from neglect. He was fine in the beginning but then decided he would only do figure eights to the left, not the right. Michael had observed that Nick shied from the smell of alcohol but that isn't what I smelled like. I worked until he was lathered, then gave up. When I unsaddled him he nipped my ass and I hit him so hard my thumb felt sprained. Now I was sweating and yelling as I schooled him on a lunge line. He behaved perfectly then, looking at me as if he wondered what all the trouble had been about. I resaddled him but he still wouldn't do the figure eights to the right. I put him away thinking I'm not strong enough now to do the job. This isn't like me. I better get strong enough. What I have accomplished is a horse-teeth-bruised bite on my ass. I went inside and packed a bag.

○

Michael didn't look as good as he thought he did. He was bleached and flaccid, but gave me a bright smile when I came in the kitchen back door at Naomi's. He wore some of the clothes, freshly cleaned and pressed, I had bought him in San Francisco. The swelling had diminished but the bruise was still there, the left arm in a cast and sling. He stooped to greet the pup which had learned and imitated Roscoe's growl. Michael offered a bone left over from Naomi's stockpot which made them easy friends. He glanced at the door wishing to speak to me in private, but first helped Naomi pour some of the soup in the blender with a grimace of resignation. Naomi seemed sad and preoccupied so I kissed her cheek. She pointed at an open letter on the table from the county superintendent. I guessed that the country school would be closed, which proved true, but there was the fillip of the offer to counsel bankrupt farm families, working out of the office of the county agricultural agent. I impulsively went to the phone and accepted, partly to reassure Naomi, but mostly because I was goddamned sick of simple dangling. The fantasy of reactivating my farm might occur down the road but the present timing couldn't be more inappropriate. To do so now would be to place myself in Sam's category of "rich folk" playing at ornamental ranching, even though I had been born here. I waved to Naomi and went off to the music room with Michael in tow.

It turned out that Frieda had been able to check Michael out late the evening before and they had driven halfway home before stopping at a motel—with separate rooms at her insistence. He had been hard at work since midmorning and there were several open journals on the desk, plus a list of questions in handwriting that had become small and cramped. If I hadn't been trained in the area the hour we spent would have pushed me over the lip of daffiness. The minimum immediate recovery period for an alcoholic is at least six weeks and after ten days Michael verged on the delusional. Naomi's farm wasn't the place to recover but it was a decision I didn't intend to interfere with, one way or the other. His first written question made my skin itch and I spoke slowly as if to someone dull-witted.

"Northridge came for a few minutes to my hospital room in a dream. There was a bullet hole in his head. How did he die?"

"He died at home in bed in 1910 three days after his wife died."

"The journals stop a few days after the return to the farm in the February after Wounded Knee. Are there more?"

"There's one more I'll discuss with Paul when he comes here in July. You'll probably be able to see it when you reach the end of your week."

"That's not fair, goddamnit!" His forehead burst with sweat and I felt some empathy for his panic. We were a few feet away at the big desk but I could smell his sour odor.

"Calm down. I'm going away for a while, perhaps a week.

Maybe I can talk to Paul on the phone. It entails a great deal of money and I could be putting myself in physical jeopardy." This was a matter that in my confusion I hadn't been able to deal with. If I decided to give the materials to a museum I could simply excise the "other things" from the journal with a razor blade and dispose of them myself. Then Michael could finish his work. What wasn't needed now was the sort of grandmotherly compassion that indulges someone because they feel a childlike desperation.

"I can see you don't trust me!" Now he wrote in bolder strokes.

"Please stir your recent memory. You've been a tremendous pain in the ass. However, I admire the direction your conscience and intellect have been taking you. Just be patient."

"You look exhausted yourself. You're cold and distant. I don't get it."

"I've found out my son is alive and he's seen me several times though I don't know who he is. I'm waiting and it's very hard to wait after so long."

He was startled and reached over for my hand, pressed it to his forehead. Naomi came in to call us for lunch, and when we got to the table there was a small glass of wine at each place. Michael immediately drew his in through a glass straw, then stuck the straw in his pureed soup with a smile.

"May he have some more?" Naomi asked me, but Michael shook his head and made a writing notion to say he intended to work.

Out by the car Naomi told me that Ruth had tried to call me last night. She had flown to Costa Rica this morning and would stop for a visit on the way home next week. I thought Naomi was still acting a little strange but her humor returned and so did mine when we talked about Ruth, who was meeting her priest at an expensive seaside resort under the notion that it would be unlikely that anyone he knew would stop by.

"Is she going to try to get pregnant?"

"I don't think so. She's been spending a lot of time with Paul and she's agreed to take on some of his orphan projects when he passes on. I like the ambition you girls show. All those years in the great world you come up with a priest and a cowboy." Now she began to laugh helplessly, leaning against the car for support. She didn't do it often but when she did it was infectious. We made so much noise Michael rushed out on the porch and watched us through the screen in bafflement.

"It's just a joke," I called out to him. It certainly could be looked at that way, I thought.

○

The trouble with western Nebraska is that there's only one way to get to most places. Any other route would have added hours to the trip to Buffalo Gap. This means you have to put up with what you thought about on the road on other trips, as if these previous thoughts were hanging on the phone poles and power lines—even sexual fantasies from the distant past can lie in wait along creek bottoms and ditches, the village limits of no longer occupied crossroads, the name announcing nothing but itself and the memory of what you were doing and thinking other times you passed this way. But the susceptibility depends on drift, and I had begun not to drift, aware that I had been acting out effects rather than causing anything new. It was as if I had made my decision, gradual as it was, to come home, and I was hoping that would supplant all other considerations, save my phone call to Andrew.

It also occurred to me I had known Michael well a bit more than two months, and the only resonance got from seeing him today was regret. I wondered at the power of my melancholy in Santa Monica which accepted the idea that this brilliant nitwit would find my son in exchange for our history. It felt silly enough for me to laugh at myself in the car, but of what value was it for me to see it as clearly as Paul? And perhaps unconsciously, I had chosen Michael to rid myself of it. The idea of a major mistake made me turn on the radio but it was news time and the world's anguish quickly became a confusing substitute for my own so I turned it off. The questions became more oblique, involving conscience and history, winnowing down to the pettiness of the thought of Northridge's becoming a mere feather in Michael's sorry academic hat.

In Chadron I opted for a longer route, driving over to Crawford, then north to 71 through the Oglala and Buffalo Gap National Grasslands. I congratulated myself on stopping short of a quick return visit to Fort Robinson—depending on your knowledge of history and conscience the area was the Sioux equivalent of the Warsaw Ghetto. My anger gave me a leaden foot and I passed three campers with Iowa licenses, swerving way off the left shoulder to avoid an oncoming car. The drivers all shook their fists and beeped at me before they continued on. I was partly mired in the ditch so put it in four-wheel drive and fishtailed along until I made it back up to the shoulder. My heart was racing and I couldn't catch my breath so I stopped and got out of the car. I walked as fast as I could manage out into the ocean of grass and sat down hidden from the road. All that had just happened disappeared into the density of green with abruptness: "What I am trying to do is trade in a dead lover for a live son. I'll throw in a dead father with the dead lover and their souls I have kept in the basement perhaps. Even if I don't get to see the son I have to let the others go. The world around me and the world of people looks immense and solid but it is more fragile than lark or pheasant eggs, women eggs, anyone's last heartbeat. I'm a crazy woman. Why didn't I do this long ago? I'm forty-five and there's still a weeping girl in my stomach. I'm still in the arms of dead men—first Father then Duane. I may as well have burned down the goddamned house. Whether I see the son he is at least a living obsession."

○

Sam stayed ten yards away with cold feet when I reached the cabin. He showed me the fine new corral with well-concealed pride, a laconic cowboy shyness I had been familiar with since I was a child. With the corral done he had started wire-brushing the flaked varnish off the logs of the cabin to prepare for a new coat. When the shyness continued through the two drinks before dinner I began to wonder.

"Is there something wrong?" I was impatient, having decided so much that afternoon, or at least approached an area so critical that my relief reminded me of patients I had worked with the day after they emerged from successful shock treatment.

"I guess I'd have to say something's wrong with you. You act like you been sick."

I bristled but didn't know where to go next. I poured myself a third drink and pushed the bottle toward him. He shrugged, then joined me. We entered the neutral territory of the condition of the cabin, horses, the price of hay as the summer was shaping up for drought. He said he'd never figured out why Omaha could get forty inches of rain while the western border turned brown with ten inches. The whiskey had begun to relax us when he blurted out that he hoped I would start feeling better. My stomach and joints began to loosen when he said both his mother and younger sister had always had "nervous problems" so he knew it was as real as breaking a leg. I still refused to let go when I gave him an explanation in an affected, even voice. I said I'd found out that the son that I'd been forced to give up for adoption was looking for me, which was something I'd been hoping for all these years.

"I'd say that would call for a celebration. You shouldn't be too hard to find for Christ's sake. This all happen since last week?"

I nodded and now tears were brimming in my eyes. He came around the table, lifted me up, and sat down with me on his lap. He said this was the kind of thing that made it worthwhile for me to have a boyfriend. I'm not the sort of person who sits on laps but it was OK at the moment. It was wonderfully ordinary, as if I had made human contact after a long absence. He didn't ask a single question—just sat there with me on his lap. Then we made love and cooked dinner. He told me a story that he tried to make funny. When he was a boy of nine someone stole his horse which had been pastured with a dozen others. It was a fine chestnut mare. Twenty years later when his dad was dying in a VA hospital he had said, "Sam, it's time to stop thinking about getting that mare back."

○

It took three days to varnish the cabin. It was the kind of repetitive, menial work, similar to vegetable gardening, that allowed the world in my mind to retrieve its shape. I did the ladder work since even minimal heights made Sam feel queasy, and anything higher than a horse was out of the question. He disliked admitting this but once he let his guard down a few other confessions came along, usually funny: while other soldiers on leave enjoyed the massage parlors of Saigon he played the tourist, having overheard one of his dad's World War II stories, how Japanese women could entrap a man so that they had to be surgically disconnected. Knowing my training he wondered about the background of this phobia. I said that in my experience I had noticed that men generally worry more about their dicks than their jobs. Looking down from the ladder I could see him blush under his tan.

Late on the third afternoon, while he was packing for his departure the next morning, we had a quarrel. He had spent a full hour in the hot sun laboriously cleaning the paintbrushes while I had been in favor of throwing them away. I didn't catch myself in time and the paintbrushes quickly became a matter of money. The degree of his resentment was understandable considering his experiences in the horse business but I wanted him to be able to see me in a different light. I was sitting on the same couch where Grandfather had napped while Rachel looked over him. Where did my father make love to her? Off in the hills someplace. Sam talked or argued with his back to me which, frankly, pissed me off ungovernably. Naomi had told me his family had lost their ranch to the bank during the Depression and I realized whatever else he was saying this was the overwhelming fact that fueled his anger, and had limited his life to that of a foreman.

"If you'd turn around you could see I'm not the bank or your creditors or any of the assholes you've worked for. If you want to see yourself as a victim that's your business, but I could tell you some stories about the real thing because I've spent the last seven years working with them."

His hand was on a chunk of quartz on the mantel. He suddenly turned and threw the heavy chunk as hard as he could the length of the cabin. It was a perfect strike on the Dutch oven full of chili on the stove, blasting contents all over the stove and wall. Now he was stricken, and covered his face when we walked over and looked at the damage.

"I'm dead broke. You're going to have to buy dinner," he said.

"I stuck some money in your wallet when you were in the shower. Also some in the glove compartment of your truck. I put fifty gallons of gas in your truck and in the auxiliary tank when I went to the store this morning."

"You buying me, is that it?" He put his arm around my shoulder and ran a finger through the spilled chili on the stove, tasting it and approving of the flavor.

"Not me. Actually, I'm just renting. Our hired hand Lundquist likes to say that every boy needs some change in his pocket."

"That's about it. If I start that shit again tell me to move on."

We drove over to Hot Springs for dinner, then north toward Harney Peak to see the moon rise. It was nearly full and some thunderheads in the east reminded me of a passage in Northridge's journals. I got out of the truck and walked away from the ticking of the motor heat, until I was several hundred yards up a meadow slope where the trees began. Way down the hill I could see Sam lighting a cigarette. Halfway up, Harney was bathed in moonlight and watching closely you could see the light slowly move down the mountain as the moon rose. My mind felt so clear it shivered inside. I had told Sam I was going to the Crow Festival in August and would meet him in Hardin or Billings, Montana. For the time being at least, seeing him every month or two was all the traffic would bear.

○

I left at dawn when he did. After I had driven off and lowered the visor against the rising sun, half the money I had given him fell down in my lap. "I'm not that expensive, love, Sam" was all it said. This was about as far as you could get from the fast lane, and in a single month Santa Monica had become an imprecise image of trees and the ocean.

Crossing Cherry County on its only lateral road I was stopped by a deputy for going seventy-five, and told to get

Nebraska plates if I was going to live there. I agreed and didn't get a ticket. He was very large and battle-scarred and I wondered how many drunken Sioux down from the Rosebud he had fought with.

○

I made the farm by noon, the appointed time. I walked around the barnyard, working the travel out of my limbs, then headed for the house and stairwell where I lit two lanterns. Inside the wine cage, I pulled hard, and the last long rack which was heavy rolled out revealing the bin door of the root cellar. I lifted this bin door up and attached it by a hook to the rafter. The root cellar was twenty feet long and perhaps four feet deep, designed to store potatoes, cabbage, turnips, and so on through the winter. The light of the two lanterns revealed the door on the west end, also a fine mess of blacksnakes, the largest of which lifted its head into the air and moved toward the source of light as if it was a guardian. I whispered to it and reached down and out letting it scent my hand. It paused, then turned away. I climbed in and the vibration of my feet on the cellar floor disturbed the snakes which now slid around frantically as I made my way to the door. I'm not frightened of snakes but this seemed to be pushing my bravery a bit. At the door the largest wrapped around my boot and it was difficult to unwrap him. I opened the door, quickly closing it after me so none could follow, and made my way down the cold stone steps to the other door. The fact that I pretty much knew what to expect, and was moving quickly, diminished what would be a normal fear of what I was doing. My only irrational feeling was that I was in some way by this act releasing the souls of Duane and my father.

The room was large, perhaps twenty by thirty feet, and surprisingly airy because it was vented straight up through the wall between the bedroom and the den, and out through the roof. The only clear space was a slab-oak table with two oil lamps—I lit them both, then stared: at the west end on the bench sat the lieutenant's skeleton, and those of the sergeant and private still in their cavalry uniforms, and with a large hole from Northridge's .44 in the lieutenant's forehead. Along the

north side on wood cots lay five warriors in full regalia, friends
of Northridge who in the diaspora wished to have their remains kept safe from graverobbers. With all of his compulsive
journal-keeping the identity of these warriors remained a secret though Paul said he was sure his father knew. The rest of
the room was full of tagged and labeled artifacts from tribes of
the Great Basin: braided sweet grass, otter-skin collars, fur
bands of mountain lions, badger skins—Northridge's clan,
Crow bustles of eagle and hawk feathers, painted buffalo
heads, kit-fox wrist loops, grizzly-claw necklaces, turtle rattles,
horned ermine bonnets, rolled ermine tails, coup sticks and
three medicine bags, painted buffalo hides, a full golden eagle
into which a Crow holy man's head had fit into the rib cage,
buffalo horn bonnets, ravens, otter-skin-wrapped lances, rat-
tlesnake-skin-wrapped ceremonial bows, mountain-lion sashes,
bearskin belts, dog skins, a grizzly-bear headdress with ears
and two claws, wolf and coyote skins, owl-feather headdresses,
weasel skins, a knife with a grizzly-jaw handle and incisor,
bone whistles, full bear dancer hides, huge buffalo-head masks,
wolf-hide headdresses with teeth, snake-effigy rattles, dew-
claw rattles. . . .

I sat there for a full hour in the state that perhaps approached a prayer without words, not thinking about anything
except what I was looking at. My father and Duane seemed to
be with me, then went away as did the weeping girl I had felt
in my chest. She went out an upstairs window where she had
sat watching the summer morning, the descent of the moon.
Then I heard a cry or a moan far off behind me. It was Lundquist calling Dalva, Dalva, Dalva. . . . I put out the oil lamps
and left with a tremor up my spine and through my ribs.

○

He had come over and was worried that I had been "swal-
lowed up" when he reached the bin door of the root cellar, and
the door to the subbasement was closed. He was breathing
rapidly and huddled against the corner of the wine rack, claiming that all the snakes in the root cellar had come to the bin
door to prevent his saving me. I closed everything up and
helped him upstairs where the sun shone strongly through the

kitchen window. Now I was shaking and could feel my body moisten with sweat. I could swear there was a hollowness in my chest where the weeping girl had been. The "reality" of the kitchen was sharper than ever and when I rinsed my face in the sink my hair was already wet with sweat. I got Lundquist a beer and we sat down at the kitchen table. He finished his beer so quickly I nodded at the refrigerator to give him permission to have another. He was so unlike the Lundquist of five evenings before that I marveled again at the costumes of personality. He began rambling slowly about the summer of 1930 when Paul and little John were seven or eight or so. John W. had three Sioux men and one woman come down from near Keyapaha and erect a big tipi in the front yard to show the boys where part of their blood had come from. Lundquist smiled when he said he was the only "pure-white" person there. He sidetracked telling how John W. used to tease him about an issue of *National Geographic* that showed Lundquist's ancestors wearing animal skins with big horns on their heads, though that was before they learned of Jesus. Anyway, when evening came Lundquist had gathered wood for the Sioux and they had started a big bonfire. John W. and two of the Sioux men came up from the basement and out the front door and danced dressed up like warriors for the boys. The other Sioux beat on a drum and the old woman explained to the boys what was happening. When they became sleepy she shook them awake.

As he finished his story Lundquist asked me if it was a secret he should have kept, and I said no. Then he remembered why he had been sent over in the first place—Professor Michael was feeling "low" and Frieda didn't know how to handle it. Naomi was gone and Frieda didn't know the number where I was. He got up abruptly and literally dashed away. By the time I looked out the window he was out in the pasture on the backway to Naomi's with Roscoe over his shoulder. My first impulse was to call but I knew she wouldn't be able to talk about the problem if he was in the kitchen when she answered the phone. I took a quick shower and dressed, noticing that all the photos on the dresser failed to cause any heaviness in my chest. They were men and smiling, all quite as dead as I would be some day.

Michael was sitting on the porch swing with the pup sleeping on his lap. He had his clipboard and legal pad beside him and he didn't turn when I walked out on the porch. In the kitchen an utterly exasperated Frieda had given me a speech with indications that it had been prepared.

"It starts when Naomi leaves yesterday to meet her friend in Lincoln to do library work. But he's already blue. He writes down he can't sleep so he works all night and wanders around in the yard with the pup all day though he's been sitting there three goddamn hours and won't eat his soup. He won't talk to me because I wouldn't drive him to Denver to pick up his car. I called the dealer for him and he was upset that what you paid to get the car fixed was an arm and a leg. I said that was no big deal to you. It's like with Gus—when you do something for these guys they act like you were squeezing their nuts too hard. So early this morning I hear him crying and I think, This has gone too far for me. I drag him over near the phone with his tablet and we call this doctor in Omaha because I think he sure as hell needs nerve medicine. The doctor agrees, and this is what it is." She gave me a slip of paper with the name of a rather radical tranquilizer. I immediately called a Grand Island pharmacist so he could put it on the afternoon bus. The pharmacist knew our family and my background so let the scrip go without a doctor's call.

Then I went out on the porch and sat beside him on the swing, thinking if he could just babble on as usual this depression might not have happened. I put my hand on the pup's head. He yawned and went back to sleep. Tears were coming down Michael's cheek so I stood and wiped them with my blouse. He tried to smile and I sat down and put my arm around him, and then he began weeping in earnest.

"Michael, perhaps you are trying to do too much at once and there's not an appropriate net. I think it's admirable you've tried to stop drinking but maybe you should wait until you can talk. You could go to a clinic for a week or so then because you've already proved you can do it. The pills will be here this evening and I want you to take them for a few days even though you might not be able to work. I'll take you for walks and rides and Ruth will be here this weekend. You said you like her. Remember when I told you that she said you were sexy in sort of a dirty, European way? I'll make you the best purees in the world. . . ." Now my shoulder and a breast were wet with his tears. "I have some sleeping pills around here that I want you to take now because you're too tired to think. When you wake up we'll talk again."

I guided him into the music room where a single bed had been set up beside his desk, as per his request. I went for the pills and water, and when I got back he was under the sheet with the pup beside his head on the pillow. He took the pills and pointed to a manuscript on the desk, gesturing for me to take it. I kissed his clammy forehead and he ran a hand up my thigh under my skirt in a show of spirit. His eyes were those of a frightened teenager.

Dearest Dalva,

My personality doesn't seem to be panning out as sober, but I've been thinking my personality doesn't really count at all, at least in the form I supposed it to have. It certainly is interfering with the work at hand, for both the work and the personality seem to want to change their dimensions, their peripheries, moment by moment. I have added considerably to my definition of "short circuit"—if I fall asleep at 3:00 A.M., I wake up at 3:15 A.M. eager for work. The span between my manic and depressive stages can be hours, minutes, seconds, milliseconds. I must agree with the great Russian that to be too acutely conscious is to be diseased. But not in the way I would have agreed in the old days (two weeks ago!) when I would awake brooding on matters of dark import and it was all mostly a distortion, the biochemical effects of drinking. Unlike yourself I'm not very Oriental, and there must be more to me than what I do and what I perceive. Right now I couldn't tell you just what it is at gunpoint. I think it was in the fourth grade, when we were studying science, that I told the teacher I hoped to discover brand-new birds and animals, and she said, "They've all been discovered. Just learn your lessons." A few minutes ago I dialed my ex-wife to hear her voice, then, of course, wept because I couldn't speak to her, though I've been legally enjoined from attempting to do so. After that I dialed my daughter, Laurel, who said, "Is that you, Bob? Get fucked! No one's here but me. Leave me alone, Bob," which offered a little comic relief.

To be honest, while you were away I found the journal you were keeping from me. I searched your house, which was admittedly shameless. At the last moment the journal, hidden as it was in your underwear drawer, was almost safe since the sight of those dainties swept me away. I won't ask for forgiveness because none can be given for my heinous curiosity, but to set you at rest, I won't mention any of the bodies (eight, I think) or artifacts in my study. I can handle Northridge's efforts at an "underground railway" for pursued warriors by merely saying he hid them in a root cellar. Naturally, with your permission I'd like to include the splendid yarn of the lieutenant and two subalterns, but I could say the bodies were pitched into the Niobrara. I am at your mercy in this matter. In any event, I reborrowed kind Frieda's Ram and returned the journal to its cotton nest. Naturally there was the temptation to go down to the basement with a crowbar but I stopped myself. Another consideration was my cast and that I am quite frightened of such things—as a child some proselytizing Catholic kids held me down and made me kiss the rosary and cross (like the Spanish did to the Indians of Central and South America!).

So I read the second trunk in a little more than seventy-two hours, almost straight through. I snuck a few of Frieda's diet pills out of her purse while she was in the bathroom. It was what the sports pages call a blistering pace, and I fear my mind was blistered in the process. What follows are some key passages with my gloss, to show you the nature of my current thinking on our project.

At this point I was interrupted in my reading by Frieda asking for the night off now that I was home. Gus wanted to take her to dinner for the first time in a year on the proceeds of an old coin he had found in a deserted farmhouse. He was a member of a club of mostly indigent, middle-aged goofies called the Fortune Finders who traveled around the county with their cheap metal-detectors. They wore Fortune Finder T-shirts that never quite covered their bellies and Olympia beer caps. I said yes to Frieda's request but asked her to see if Lena could run out with Michael's prescription and stay for dinner. Frieda was showing specific signs of wear. She told me that Naomi was fine because she didn't take Michael "personally," another tribute to Naomi's ability to handle anyone short of Charlie Starkweather. On her way out Frieda told me that Michael had asked for beef marrow for dinner because he had read in his "old-timey stuff" that it was good for you. The bones were in the fridge and ready for my attention.

When she roared out the driveway scattering the usual gravel across the lawn I went to the kitchen thinking of marrow and gold, the poached marrow the Sioux fed themselves and the French still do. The center of bones. After the Custer-Ludlow expedition the Black Hills were aswarm with rapacious gold-miners and the Sioux never again had a chance to own their Holy Land. If they would stop drinking maybe they could get the Israelis to help them. Gus and his Fortune Finders. His sort gave our country California in a hurry. But you must think of freedom and the peasants arriving on the boat, Aase's parents and all the generations before them, who never owned a single acre they lived on. Suddenly they were here and gave me my mother. And Aase. Without the Aases there is no grace on earth. And Northridge, who could not accept the simplest, defensible injustice on earth, most of all his own.

I poached the marrow, then pureed it with a little garlic, leeks, and a few reconstituted morel mushrooms. I tested it through Michael's glass hospital straw—it was good though not quite like eating, a first course and no more. I thawed two veal chops for Lena and myself. When I heard him call out from the music room I looked up at the wall clock in disbelief for only two hours had passed and the sleeping pills should have worked much longer than that.

He was staring at the ceiling with his clipboard on his chest, the pup's head on the pillow beside him chewing his arm cast. He held out the message with his free hand—"I sense our romance is over. Will you make love to me one more time?"

"Camille, what craw you have for God's sake." I didn't think he'd dare ask, but perhaps he wished the further drama of refusal, so I said "no" and left the room. The pup followed me out and we played in the yard for a while and I gave him a marrow bone; then I mixed a drink and went back to my reading.

## March 7, 1886

The clear air is blue with cold at daylight. We have no meat left in the larder, only dried apples, rutabagas, and softening potatoes, corn flower. Small Bird does not wish me to leave the cabin to hunt. She has dreamed I will leave her in the middle of the coming summer on a train though she has never seen a train. The cabin is her fort and the land around it. She says she is feeling older and wishes to mother a child. We have been speaking of this since the past November. I had refused to countenance the idea but now in March I have less will to resist. She tells me it is improper for me to live my life without becoming a father. Who will take care of us when we are old, she asks? When I attempt to explain that there is money in the bank in Chicago and other places I see the weakness of my argument. How could she understand or place any trust in the "banks" of white men, or that I "own" a great deal of land well to the East of us. Her command of English is weak but extremely forceful & she refuses to discuss this in Sioux as her position would be weakened. She tells me that unlike myself she does not accept the doom of the Sioux, and there is the story that many centuries before the Sioux were driven from the forests into the plains by the Chippewa. The Sioux survived to become the strongest of all peoples until the white man arrived. How can the Sioux become strong again if I refuse to be a father? What if my own father had refused to be a father?

## March 23

There is a dream of my father doubtless caused by her questioning. I have heard, though am unsure, that he was an Arkansas drover who came north to visit a brother, and thus conquered my mother. At some point well before the war he sickened of guiding settlers to the West thus moving to Montana territory and to the northwest of there, and was not seen again. It was said he became a solitary trapper in the mountains, but there was no specific knowledge of his movements. I wonder why he would wish to live his life in this manner but then all white men have to come to question my own life. I have brought neither Christ nor agriculture to the Sioux who desire neither.

I have awakened from the dream where my father rubs his grizzled forehead against my own to give me strength. He is dressed in seal fur of which I only saw one specimen at Cornell. I am awake on a pallet before the fire where I've been for months thinking she will cover me in my sleep. I put wood on the fire and when it flares I understand how weak I have become these past years. In October I rode south into Nebraska with two pack horses to fetch my apples only to see that ignorant settlers had cut down one orchard the winter before for firewood, not understanding that they were fruit trees. I did not turn them off the land which I owned as swindlers had "sold" it to them. They were too pathetic to thrash. I gave them some money because their children were quite thin. They will all fail in the area due to inadequate rainfall & thus the Sioux land was stolen for nought. Before the fire I feel an anger I have not felt in a sorry decade. I have written my many articles, traveled to Washington & have bribed Congressmen & Senators only to be betrayed. In the fire I see I must murder Senator Dawes. I howl into the fire until I begin to weep. I turn and there is Small Bird sitting on the bed watching me. She is naked and comes down to the floor and sits beside me. She sings me a war song that says I must go to war or my shame will devour me. We make love until we have exhausted ourselves because we haven't had sufficient nourishment for quite some time.

At daylight I leave with my rifle in bitter cold. She will follow later if she hears a shot. The crust of snow supports my weight and it is my prayer—to whom I do not know—that I shoot a deer or elk before the afternoon sun warms enough for me to break through the snow. I climb as far as I can up a wooded draw, following tracks that are difficult to determine as there is a fresh skein of snow. I know I should climb higher but am quickly exhausted as dried apples do not offer much to the body. The prospect of eating one of my beloved horses upsets me & I pray a Sioux prayer He Dog used when we hunted. I fall asleep sitting on a rock & awake shivering uncontrollably. I sense someone behind me & turn to whisper to Small Bird who I think has joined me but it is an elk.

**I turn slowly with the rifle expecting the elk to bolt away but it stands there so that I doubt my senses & think I am looking at a dream elk. I fire and it drops as if poleaxed & I remember to bow to the beast as He Dog does. I look up to see Small Bird running across the meadow where she had lain concealed. . . .**

Lena called to say she'd be out in an hour. I read on through a long historical gloss of Michael's which was an astute belaboring of the obvious—the quality of the umbrage was appropriate but a little beside the point. Northridge had finally been stripped of his Methodist affiliation but avoided being kicked out of the area through the political influence of Grinnell and Ludlow. This influence waned as Northridge came to be considered a menace by government Indian agents and the army. When he finally was ordered to return to Nebraska and make no further contact with the Sioux he went to Washington and used bribery, an easy convenience in the Reconstruction era. The irony of his malnutrition in Buffalo Gap with Small Bird was that his nursery business was thriving and widespread. On his way to Washington he had stopped in Chicago to "secure a carpetbag of money for the swine." Meanwhile he was kept busy in the hiatus between the death of Crazy Horse in 1877 and the enactment of the Dawes Act in 1887 in teaching, feeding, and clothing the maverick Sioux who were avoiding the newly created Dakota reservations. His mission became pathetically ordinary to him—how to convince people that turnips, cabbage, salt pork, and bad beef were a substitute for buffalo. He was also battling against the government's program of forbidding the Sioux to perform any and all ritual dances, or to meet in any but the smallest groups. The few Sioux who were attempting to learn farming tended to "squander" the harvest on feasting and giving away the crop to others. The point was if they couldn't be made Christians they must be forced to behave like provident imitations.

I noted that the Mohonk Conference was next in Michael's manuscript so I put it aside and went up to my bedroom for a few minutes. I wanted to change my mood before I made dinner and could usually accomplish this by looking through books of reproductions of my favorite artists, Hokusai and Caravaggio, an unlikely pair. This time, however, I was distracted by the James Dean poster, so old now the edges were crinkled and frayed. Duane had thought James Dean was wonderful and bought the same sort of red windbreaker Dean wore in *Rebel Without a Cause.* I adored him too despite the obvious and curious mixture of fatalism, bravery, arrogance, perhaps ignorance. I caught myself being drawn ceaselessly back into a past that I wished mightily to emerge from—I had come to know only recently that one *could* emerge without forgetting, and that to remember need not be to suffocate. It was unfair but funny to look at the poster and wonder what kind of asshole he would have been as a grownup. It was anyway a tonic to Northridge's coming madness, and I thought of a question a Cree had pointedly asked—"What do stories do when they are not being told?"

○

Dinner went well. Michael was affable if groggy and was resigned to the tranquilizers. He brought his clipboard to the table to ask us questions. He sipped his marrow and was fascinated by Lena's peculiar impressions of Europe and the life in Paris of her daughter Charlene. Michael reminded me of a graduate-student boyfriend years before who was startled on seeing Grandfather's collection of paintings and wondered if they legitimately belonged in a Nebraska farmhouse, though it was to Michael's credit that he enjoyed having his preconceptions destroyed.

After dinner Lena suggested we do some weeding in Naomi's garden so she wouldn't get too far behind. Michael helped by amusing the pup, taking it for a walk down the road. While we weeded Lena spoke of Charlene and it was nearly dark when she turned to me with a question.

"The girls were talking to this customer last week, a young man, and I went up to remind them to clean off the tables, and I could have sworn he looked like Duane. Do you think he could have been your boy?"

We washed up and made a nightcap, sitting out on the porch where Michael was drying the pup, having bathed it after it rolled in a road-killed rabbit. The sounds he made through his wired jaw must have reminded the pup of its mother. My efforts to soothe Lena were interrupted by the phone. It was Paul to say he and Luiz would come up with Ruth on Saturday. They would meet at Stapleton and Bill, the farm-implement dealer, would come down to get them in his plane. It seemed an awkward match but Bill and Paul were boyhood chums who had once planned to roam the Seven Seas together, as Bill called it. At his request Paul was enrolling Luiz in a military prep school in Colorado Springs for the coming fall. I nearly protested this choice but let it go in the good feeling of the impending visit. Later it occurred to me the choice was quite natural—if you had been hurt that badly a spiffy uniform and the rigors of military discipline would be a comforting posture of defense.

Lena left after making plans to take Michael to the movies the following evening. You would have thought he had been invited to the Inaugural Ball, which made me plan to wean him from the tranquilizers as soon as possible. There was this image of an ambulatory cabbage wearing a smile. I tucked him in bed as one would a child while he monkeyed with the old Zenith radio on the night table, tuning in a popular but contentious talk show where the evening's discussion was to be the Star Wars controversy. Before going upstairs to read myself to sleep I went outside to look at the uninterrupted stars themselves, the night a "deep throw of star" as some poet said, a silken and thickish Milky Way accompanied by the war of thousands of grass frogs calling out to one another, land miniatures of those Baja sea lions of long ago, a call to life so dense, so impenetrable, that it perhaps equaled the magnitude of the night sky.

**July 17, 1886**
I am quite abashed on my fifth morning in jail. The authorities are drawing up papers that when signed will insure my release, or so I am told. I am to be taken to the train in Albany, there to board a train going west, & am not to get off the train in the state of New York, or ever return there on pain of prison internment. I have failed thoroughly as John Brown with not a corpse to my credit, and my wife's dream will not be fulfilled, as I left her pregnant & wailing despite my assurances to the contrary. She had managed to never see a train though she had heard of one.

She is staying with He Dog & his band, who comforted her telling her that my mission was essential to the Sioux.

I was welcomed to the Mohonk Conference on the "Indian Question" with a great show of friendliness from my hosts, due to my efforts with Congress and my articles in *Harper's* and *McClure's*. By evening, though, the participants began to shy away from me, sensing I was utterly serious in my plan to create an entire Indian Nation out of the western Dakotas, the western parts of Nebraska, Kansas, and Oklahoma, the eastern portions of Montana, Wyoming, Colorado, northeastern Arizona, and northeastern New Mexico. No matter that it is just, this plan is viewed as madness by these folks who are said to be the conscience of our Nation, both religious and political. Dawes is not here and is said to be vacationing, perhaps from the rigors of chicanery. These are not landgrabbers but men, I am told, who wish to help the Indians by destroying their tribal organization in the Dawes Act. I am told that at Mohonk last year Dawes said, "When you have set the Indian upon his feet, instead of telling him to 'Root, hog, or die,' you take him by the hand and show him how to learn to earn his daily bread." This man I vainly hoped to shoot to stop this horror would give each Indian a small farm to till or sell! Without their tribal authority they will be swindled and die.

Despite my anger I am amused the second day to discover that only three of the eighty participants have actually lived among the Indians, an item that ascribes us no particular authority as we are said to be blinded by this contiguity. Of the other two men, one has worked as an agricultural missionary to the Apaches in Arizona and has witnessed the slaughter of ninety of them by a posse from Tucson in Arivapa Canyon. The other has been teaching the Cheyenne to grow crops, and being quite poor is dressed in buckskins which elicits amusement from the gathering. The three of us are asked after a lavish dinner to speak of the pleasures of lives spent "tenting in God's nature," but decline to do so. Here in the East, and elsewhere, I am told there is a great deal of aping of Indian outdoor customs.

My downfall came on the afternoon of the third day. It had become clear to me that I was not to be permitted to present my case, and was everywhere avoided and shunned except by my two colleagues who had taken to drink out of despair. At a luncheon on the grass we were to be entertained by groups of dancing Mohawks & Iroquois. At one time the latter would have been quite happy to roast and devour their hosts. I refused to witness this humiliation and took a walk in the woods along the lake, seeking a quiet spot to pray for guidance. My prayers, however, stuck in my craw and I returned for the afternoon guest address determined to seize the lectern. I listened attentively to Reverend Gates who was also the President of Amherst College, who said something of the following, "The Savior's teaching is full of illustrations of the right use of property. There is an immense moral training that comes from the use of property and the Indian has all of that to learn. We have, to begin with, the absolute need of awakening in the savage Indian broader desires and ampler wants. In his dull savagery he must be touched by the wings of the divine angel of discontent. The desire for property of his own may become an intense educating force. Discontent with the 'teepee' and the starving rations of the Indian camp in winter is needed to get the Indian out of the blanket and into trousers—and trousers with a pocket in them, and with a pocket that aches to be filled with dollars! . . ."

On hearing this blasphemy I found myself running to the front of the hall. I shook the fool and hurled him into the crowd & attempted to begin my speech but was restrained by many from doing so. It was determined I had caused some injuries and was ultimately cast in jail from which I now await my deliverance.

The house had been quiet except for the muffled sound of Michael's radio, but now a slight and distant thunderstorm was causing sharp static and the pup began to whimper. I went downstairs and turned off the radio, picked up the pup, and dimmed the light—Michael refused to sleep in the dark, for which he had offered me a dozen reasons, including if he awoke in the dark how would he know conclusively if he were alive? I rocked the pup back to sleep on the porch swing, feeling not so much that I was getting old but indeterminably older. It was an oddly pleasurable sensation, and up to that moment quite unique: at forty-five I had finally accepted my life, a matter that given my supposed intelligence I might have managed earlier but hadn't. Somehow you are trying when you don't even know that you are trying. It is peculiar how people who think they are helping others—in my own family, from Northridge to Paul to Naomi, to myself—often are so neglectful of the most ordinary realities that men like Grandfather would counter directly and with dispatch: Paul in his drifting after the most viable abstractions, Naomi sitting on this porch for more than thirty-five years talking to a dead husband though all the while giving youngsters her energetic literacy. I was a mixture of Paul and Naomi.

My ears popped from the low pressure in the air and the dense smell of corn and wheat was oppressive, so different from the alfalfa and varied trees at my own place just three miles away. I recalled this sort of weather before a violent storm when I was a child. The wind-driven rain and hail had demolished that year's crops. We went to the basement when Father saw it coming just before dark. It was a storm-cellar room they had prepared with two beds, a couch, a table, and oil lamps. Our dog Sam lay frightened and stiff on the floor and Ruth and I comforted him while my parents played gin rummy. Then Mother read to us from the *Book House* while the actual house creaked above us and the wind was a hollow roaring sound. When we all awoke in the total silence of daylight and went upstairs the trees were stripped of their leaves and the wheat and corn were flattened in the fields. Ruth and I ran around in the big pools of water in the lawn while Father comforted Naomi for her destroyed garden. The trees restored themselves but it was too late in June for the crops to recover. My parents had been amazed to discover that the storm had struck only a small portion of the county before sailing off to the northwest.

Northridge had returned home after paying a fine and damages which were ample when the authorities discovered the amount of money in his carpetbag. He had learned the desperate and not very attractive measure, passed on to his son, that when things become impossible you must try to buy the obstruction. It never seemed to work more than temporarily. When he went home he literally became an Indian, or a version thereof, started a headquarters in the Badlands, away from ranchers, as a small fiefdom supporting as many as fifty charges, including a miniature army of a dozen headed by He Dog and Sam Creekmouth. Other than several irritating visits by his officer nemesis and former friend from Cornell, the government ignored him, using the effective policy of benign neglect to combat a man who was anyway widely considered in the West to be a total lunatic.

Grandfather was born late that year in a tipi on December 11, 1886, on the verge of the worst weather in the history of the Republic, a fact he always relished as a closet romantic. The drought followed by this severe winter drove literally hundreds of thousands of farmers back east, abandoning much of western Kansas and Nebraska, though only for a short time, and freezing a million or so cattle on the hoof. The Dawes Act became effective in 1887 but due to the impoverished nature of the area it was a few years before the land grabbers took full advantage of Indian innocence in matters of property. Even William Tecumseh Sherman defined a reservation as "a worthless parcel of land surrounded by white thieves."

Michael's litany contained nothing new except the names of Kicking Bear's children, which enabled me to figure out that Rachel had been Kicking Bear's granddaughter. Kicking Bear had ridden alone out to Nevada where he met Wovovka, and consequently began the Ghost Dance movement among the Sioux, joined by Iron Hail and Ben American Horse and others. The great chief Sitting Bull was noncommittal on the Ghost Dance but was murdered as a direct result of the controversy. During this period the government sought greater control over the Sioux by banning the Sun Dance (the ban wasn't lifted until 1934) and forbidding the killing of wild game on reservations, a rule so eccentric it could only have emerged from Washington. But this is all a matter of public record, of well-documented history.

Northridge himself drowned as an Indian in his Badlands camp. He lost the checks and balances of his religion and education, though he continued his journal in the few but intermittent periods of lucidity. Were it not for his wife and the occasionally noted responsibility of his son he would have surely died from his foolhardiness. He had sold one of his tree nurseries located in Omaha to support his charges, buying cattle, grain, and whiskey.

June 1889
I have been drinking far too much in this heat and have been led
to fear for my mind. I have learned that so many years ago when
Crazy Horse was murdered my classmate the Lieutenant ordered
that his legs be broken in many places so he could be jammed
into a small wooden coffin. Perhaps God was telling me that day
to shoot this man and I did not listen to His voice, thus insuring
greater indignities.

My little son takes great joy in riding on the saddle with me &
weeps with rage when he is not allowed it. When the cattle are
killed he tugs at the guts with the rest of the children & I was a
little troubled. To some extent or range I have become what the
Sioux are in terms of custom and language. But I am also quite
different and I am not allowed by my soul to forget this. My love
for these people whom my gov't and religion have abandoned is
great, but I have begun to fear that becoming a Sioux is an
illusion I may not indulge. . . .

This was the first time in several years he had expressed
such doubts, which actually were perceptions of the limits of
how much he could do to help. In effect, he had become a
privately endowed Indian agent and the logistics were becoming impossible. When you are traveling west on Interstate 90
in South Dakota and look off to the left at the country between
Kadoka and Box Elder the term "badlands" becomes euphe-
mistic. Yet this group which grew smaller in the blistering heat
of summer stayed there as the location exhausted their options.
The oldest of them also knew that it was the secret burial spot
of Crazy Horse, a place so alien that his bones were safe there,
though there is some speculation that the bones were eventu-
ally moved.
    There is another consideration that took years to occur to
me though Michael noticed it immediately: the journals
tended to form Northridge's conscience which became a good
deal more idiosyncratic as the years passed. By 1890 he had
spent a full twenty-five years "in the field" as missionaries call
it, and his sense of accomplishment had become as brutalized
as the landscape itself. His secretive business dealings had always provided a semi-schizoid overtone, a restrained bet-

hedging, the orphan always mindful of his future nest. As an obvious instance, the business documents show that he met with his nursery agents who had been summoned to Rapid City in August of 1889. One of these, a Swede from Illinois, stayed on for three days with Northridge and received the design and instructions for the building of the current homestead. For reasons of his inherent secrecy the entire carpentry crew was secured in Galesburg, Illinois, and they worked with little or no contract with the local Nebraska population.

Still, the farm was there for more than a year before Northridge moved in with his wife and son and spent virtually the rest of his life, a little over twenty years, planting trees. Eighteen eighty-nine was the year the Great Sioux Reservation was further broken up through the efforts of General Crook and the most powerful of the area's land grabbers, with the loss of eleven million acres. Northridge saw that the twilight was quickly fading into dark. By the onset of winter in November he was back in Buffalo Gap alone with Small Bird and his son. He leased his pasture to a local rancher for two steers for the winter's meat. He kept separate from the far-flung ranching community by saying that he was doing a fresh translation of the New Testament into the Sioux language. He was regarded as peculiar rather than dangerous except by the lieutenant, now a lieutenant colonel under General Miles, who was aware—through his network of surveillance by the "metal breasts," Sioux police in the employ of the government—of the power Northridge held among the Sioux. Despite his sense of his own abysmal failure, the Sioux thought of Northridge as a holy man in his many roles as one who fed them, who taught them to grow things no matter that they despised it, and who had become a capable if amateur doctor over the years.

The beginning of the end was a visit from Kicking Bear in mid-January of 1890.

**Jan. 13, 1890**
**Kicking Bear made a not altogether pleasant visit this morning before daylight. I have met this great warrior several times over the years & have always found him friendly though somewhat frightening. In his presence Small Bird is nearly rigid with fear though she warmed for him last evening's stew & went out in the**

snow to feed his horse. He is said to have inherited the powers of Crazy Horse and wears around his neck a stone worn by that greatest of men. He is lonesome for his own children and holds my son on his knee & stares long and hard at Aase's doll as if it were a religious artifact similar to the Kachina dolls brought up by traders from the Southwest. He tells me of a vision that came to him on Jan. 1st when the sun was eclipsed. I draw him an involved picture of why the sun was eclipsed & he is not interested in this morsel of science. He is on his way to Nevada to see the renowned shaman, Wowavka, who has devised the Ghost Dance much talked about for years. Grinnell in a letter has given me a description of this & I attempt to dissuade Kicking Bear from his travels as the Dance appears a mishmash of heretical Christianity and Paiute beliefs. He is sure of himself & sleeps the day, leaving at dark as he has been forbidden to leave the reservation though the metal breasts are awed by him, and avoid contact.

○

Michael and Frieda wakened me by midmorning, neither of them wanting to do it by themselves. I had slept in my clothes in a sprawl of his manuscript, part of which had fallen on the floor and been stained by pup pee. This amused him as did the sight of the brandy bottle on the night table. I accepted the coffee tray from Frieda and shooed them away. She looked a bit bleary herself from her evening with Gus. I burned my mouth on a quick cup of coffee, stuffed the manuscript in my purse, and made my way out of the house without the civility of a goodbye.

Back at the homestead Lundquist was sitting on a milk stool in the open door of the barn saddle-soaping the draft-horse harness for the second time in a month. The geese were watching attentively and the fact that the harness had not been used in forty years, and very probably wouldn't be used again did not decrease the thoroughness of the job he was doing. He had prepared a little joke about Frieda's having spent the night with Gus in a motel and perhaps there should be a shotgun marriage. I agreed, noting that the distant motel I had stayed in with Michael was a synonym for sinfulness with the elders in the community. They all seemed to know about the "naked" movies and two friends of Naomi had gone so far as to actually see one at the motel. Before I could get away Lundquist wondered if his sore tooth might justify a cold beer.

It was a relief to be home and my energies returned despite my bedraggled sleep. I ignored the mail except for a postcard from Naomi saying she would be home by late Friday which was this evening, in order to get ready for the arrival of Paul and Ruth. She and her friend had been offered the possibility of a National Science Foundation grant for their work, which she was reticent about accepting.

Lundquist gulped his beer in a trice and went back to work, after requesting a pat of butter for Roscoe, the dog's favorite treat. I made a pot of coffee, and flopped on the den couch in order to finish Michael's manuscript, knowing that he was eager for a response. I was in a hurry because the day was pleasantly cool and I wanted to take Peach on a long ride.

Michael wrote well, if eccentrically, on the "threat of dance," and the irony that after all the years of the Indian Wars the settlers and government had now whipped themselves into a virtual frenzy over the fact that many tribes, but foremost the Sioux, were being allowed to perform this new Ghost Dance. The attitude can be best summarized by an editorial in the Chicago *Tribune* in the spring of 1890 that stated, "If the United States Army would kill a thousand or so of the dancing Indians there would be no more trouble." This presented the solution rather succinctly though it was difficult to get that many Sioux to stand still in one place to be shot. The most the government was able to manage were the three hundred or so Sioux men, women, and children, though two-thirds women and children, who were massacred at Wounded Knee later that year in December during the moon of the popping trees. But again this was a matter of the frequently ignored public record. One can imagine a Caucasian witness to hundreds, perhaps thousands of Sioux joining hands and dancing slowly in a circle for days on end, wildly painted but dancing without the accompaniment of drums, quietly with rain falling, then by late November with snow covering the perfect circle. Wovovka had assured them that if they continued to dance "the earth would shake like a rattle" and all dead warriors and ancestors would return to life, and the great herds of buffalo would sweep back across the prairie.

## April 3, 1890

Kicking Bear returned in the night from his trip to the Paiutes, rather gaunt & fatigued, though in haste after a few hours' rest to be on his way home. I dissuaded him from this as his health needs mending & in private Small Bird is angry as she sees him as a threat to our peace. I tell her she has become a mother first and a Sioux second, though the difficulties of her life justify this.

Late in the afternoon Kicking Bear prepares a jug of water & takes an elk-calf bag & we walk across a field and up the same draw where I shot an elk winters before. We sit on adjoining rocks & he draws from his bag a dozen small cacti which I recognize from my correspondence with Grinnell to be *Lophophora williamsii* or "peyote" as it is commonly called. We ate these bitter fruit as one would crabapples, then gathered wood for a fire. When we had a fair-sized heap of wood we both began to bitterly retch & flush ourselves with the jug of water. Soon enough the plant took over & I was inside the skull of my mother looking into the eyes of my father & out the back of his head into the prairie. I was the thoughts of my mother & father and through the evening and night I was a buffalo, a rattlesnake, a badger deep in his hole. I was the open sewer at Andersonville & the guts of horses, I was a woman in the city of Chicago, and then, alas, I was with my beloved Aase flying slowly over the continents & oceans looking down at whales & ice floes & great white bears. Intermixed with our visions we chanted before the fire, oftentimes new songs:

> *The world of the dead is returning,*
> *over the earth I see them coming,*
> *our dead drive before them*
> *elk and deer and herds of buffalo,*
> *as the Father has promised.*

Near dawn in my last vision I was with Crazy Horse and his daughter & we played with her toys on the burial platform & the sky was thick with birds. He told me not to take the cacti again which troubled me into consciousness. . . .

As a missionary of the Wesleyan Methodists, a sect that forbade dancing, Northridge now began seven months of dancing, and the ingestion of the cactus whenever his spirits flagged or whenever it was available, or so he wrote later—there are no journal entries until a month after Wounded Knee when he had traveled to the homestead with his wife and son. He had been brought to his senses by a grotesque event: When he arrived late on the scene of the massacre at Wounded Knee with Black Elk and twenty warriors, Black Elk had instructed him to stay well back from the gunfire. Northridge later reflected that Black Elk's sense of the appropriate never left him, and he wouldn't allow Northridge, who was ill with pneumonia, to offer himself up in this manner. Consequently, Northridge watched the cessation of rifle fire for a few minutes through his telescope, which then caught the dozen or so small children, none of them over five, emerging birdlike from a covert, thinking the battle was over. All of the children were sliced to ribbons by the resumption of fire, so light in their bodies that the bullets sent them rolling and tumbling down the hill toward their dead parents. After the "battle" Northridge was arrested by the army during his maddened efforts to bandage back together what was left of these children. He was incarcerated, then put under medical care, then released on orders by General Miles under the condition that he not return to the Dakotas or make further contact with the Sioux.

There are only the briefest entries throughout the winter and spring of 1891 and they are mostly agricultural in nature, though some of his tree-planting notations beginning in mid-March are transparent code for his other activities: the hiding of escaping chiefs and warriors including Kicking Bear (who was later "sentenced" to join Buffalo Bill's show for two years, including the humiliation of having a cast made of him at the Smithsonian as a perfect specimen of Indian); and the hiding of cherished artifacts from the collectors and the government which had proscribed all obvious signs of Indianness. The limited use of the subbasement as mausoleum came about because of the Sioux fear of indignities after death—after Sitting Bull's murder some businessman had offered the army a thousand dollars for his body in order to display it for profit.

Northridge's activities gradually came to the notice of his

Cornell classmate the lieutenant colonel, who now commanded the intelligence activities for the army in the region that included the Dakotas and Nebraska. It wasn't a question of active interest or pursuit by this man since all the primary escapees had been captured and there was no current law against storing artifacts. Army and newspaper records of the time show that the lieutenant colonel, accompanied by a sergeant and a private, was riding north toward the railhead at Valentine to intercept a rail carload of new horses destined for Fort Robinson, in order to select the best mounts. The homestead was only a day's ride off his route so the lieutenant made his way to Northridge's, perhaps to rub salt in his wounds. He demanded food and shelter which he was entitled to by law.

### June 21, 1891

The blessed event of the Solstice disturbed by the arrival of the Lieutenant and two men. He makes an elaborate show of friendliness as if the past is done & I attempt a feeling of Christian forbearance with his kind father in mind. When they gallop into the yard in the late afternoon my three Swede tree planters are frightened, having escaped conscription in their own land.

There is an ample stew in the pot in the fireplace and we sit at the table discussing horses & the weather which has been fair with good prospects for the crops. The Lieutenant drinks whiskey quickly and his mood becomes mean by the time he eats his dinner. He looks at Small Bird who tends the fire & says in half jest that we must acquire a license of marriage or she would be returned to the Reservation. I say we will do so. He then teases little John about the doll he carries around which was owned by Aase. John is abashed and puts the doll on the table. Small Bird senses the evil in the man's voice and takes little John away. The man becomes abusive to the embarrassment of his men whom he forces to join him in more drink. Finally he picks up the doll and with no reason tosses it in the fire. Just as quickly I draw out the .44 I have concealed under the table and shoot him in the head. The sergeant draws his weapon & I shoot him in the heart. The private runs to the door & I shoot him twice in the back. Small Bird returns from where I saw her peeking from the kitchen. She helps me drag the bodies down under the basement & then boils water to scrub the blood away. I go out into the barnyard and see the three Swedes standing in front of the bunk-house. We stare at each other until one says, "I hear only the birds this evening." I re-saddle their horses and my own mount and travel north across the Niobrara & turn their horses loose, praying for rain which is gathering in the sky to wipe away our trail. I return home.

It was several days before the army launched a search party and found the stray horses a hundred miles to the north in the possession of two petty criminals who were summarily executed for the murder of the three men. Except for twenty years of farming and planting trees the story of Northridge was ended.

○

I had a long and easy ride with Peach, traveling east toward the Lundquist farm to make sure he could come to the picnic tomorrow. He was whittling on the front porch and was de-lighted by my visit and made a pot of tea. He worked with his knife at a dog whistle, inaudible to the human ear, which was to be a present for me. Regular dog whistles, he said, tended to disturb every bird and animal in the area, while the silent whistle only mystified them. He blew tentatively at the whistle and Roscoe streaked across the yard, leaping at the chicken pen. He said he had been a bit melancholy because it had occurred to him he wouldn't reach the age of a hundred and two, which meant he would miss the Millennium and the Sec-ond Coming of Christ. I asked him if he was sure that was the date, and he answered "Nope" with a laugh. In any event, he looked forward to helping Michael with the barbecue.

When I remounted Peach and rode away I remembered the evening a few summers before when Lundquist had asked if he might be buried on the "edge" of the family cemetery, and I told him his plot could be plumb in the center next to his friend J. W.

I took the long way home to allow Peach a river swim since she kept wanting to turn in that direction anyway. I also let her run the length of the drive which was wonderful except that I was smacked in the forehead by a June bug. After I put her away I climbed up in the mow to watch the sunset from Duane's room. I allowed myself the sentiment of this act once a summer, and every Christmas vacation or so when the cold weather was sunny and the frozen sheen of snow caught the sparkling light and if there was a wind the loose snow moved in coils across the pasture. This evening it was pleasant to feel no weight in my heart while sitting there. There was enough haze in the air so that the sun set orangely behind the distant windbreak—as a small child I had thought that was where the sun lived—and enough breeze so that the white buffalo skull above me turned ever so slowly as if its ghost were looking for a better angle of vision.

I went in the house when it was pitch dark, warmed a frozen container of Frieda's chicken soup, and went to bed with a curious book about snow leopards in Tibet that I had already read several times because the book was filled with stillness. Then Naomi called to say she was home and wondering whether we should have the picnic at her house or mine. I left it up to her and she chose my place because it was more "private"—a matter of having no cars pass rather than the one or two neighbors that came down her road every day. She added that when she had arrived Michael and Frieda were drinking butterscotch schnapps and playing two-handed pinochle. Michael had fallen asleep in his chair and Frieda carried him to his bed.

○

I had one of those great sleeps, so that when you awake you are a part of the mattress and your limbs are heavy and soft, and everything you look at is lucid and sharp-edged. The world is full of primary colors as if the unlikely had happened and Gauguin had decided to paint this part of Nebraska. My dreams had been rich and varied and over coffee I looked in the Curtis folio for an image that had survived my dreams. When it wasn't there I was pleased that my brain in its sleep had created a brand-new Edward Curtis photograph.

At midmorning Frieda swerved in the yard with Michael and Lundquist. Through the window I could see the old man was wearing the usual denim jacket plus a pair of Sunday trousers that were robin's-egg blue, and his black work shoes were spit-polished. Michael and Frieda started in the house with cartons of groceries while Lundquist lifted a washtub full of ice and beer off the pickup, doubtless weighing over a hundred pounds. He glanced around, pocketed a beer, and headed for the barn, then turned back to lift Roscoe out of the cab of the truck.

Michael and Frieda were a bit red-eyed but chipper. Michael began making a secret barbecue sauce, the sort of thing men can be proud of though the results are often undistinguished. Frieda began peeling potatoes for potato salad, then unwrapped the halved chickens, looking at the neatly plucked birds critically.

"Thank Jesus Daddy got up early and butchered. I didn't have the stomach for it. This bung hole here"—she glared at Michael—"had Naomi lock up her liquor cabinet so we had to settle for a bottle of butterscotch schnapps Gus left in the truck. That shows how goddamn dumb we are."

I went to the stove and bit Michael's ear, watching his face redden. He sighed and burped, then dumped a small bottle of Tabasco into his sauce.

"He also cheats at pinochle," Frieda added.

I went outside and helped Lundquist drag Grandfather's old cast-iron grill out of the barn. Like the harness the grill had been kept in immaculate condition, and we were wrestling it out to the front yard when Naomi drove in with Paul, Ruth, and Luiz. Luiz was quite shy after so long but had already begun to carry himself with what he imagined was a military bearing. Paul was kind enough to tell me that country life had improved my appearance in a little more than a month. Then Paul and Lundquist took Luiz off for a tour of the farm and I went inside with Naomi and Ruth, who looked tired, having spent, she admitted, a week in the best hotel in Costa Rica with her priest.

In the kitchen we sampled Michael's sauce which was a scorcher. He pulled his long glass straw out of his pocket and went outside to have a beer. From the window I could see Lundquist talking intently to Luiz, no doubt telling him he was a member of a lost tribe of Israel. Ruth and I began snipping the tips off the ends of green beans while Naomi helped Frieda with the potato salad. Frieda overheard our talk at the sink and said she was surprised that Ruth got that much "action" what with being so thin. Ruth was kind enough to say her lover was a pervert for thin women. At that moment Naomi's young man came in the yard and she went out to greet him. He was driving a pickup as old as Lundquist's and there was a rather comic emblem of lightning on the door panel.

I asked Ruth what her plans were and she laughed and said she had none. She wondered if I was ready to immerse myself in human suffering again this fall, what with my new job counseling bankrupt farm families. Luiz ran in and asked if he could ride a horse, and I said yes, that Paul could saddle the bay mare for him. Luiz admitted he had only ridden a burro down in Sonora but he was sure he could manage a horse. At the school he was going to there was a whole course in riding and he wanted to get ready. He left and we continued talking and sampled the dressing for Frieda's potato salad. I turned and thought Ruth was looking at me strangely but I said nothing. I stared out the window and they were all standing by the corral. Lundquist carried a saddle out of the barn and Naomi's young man, Nelse, was in the corral checking the mare's hoofs. Then he led the mare out and reached for the saddle in Lundquist's arms. He stood still for a moment, calming the mare, and I became a little dizzy as if my heart were swollen and constricting my chest. I had never had a good look at him before and suddenly he reminded me of Duane standing there in the frozen barnyard looking wordlessly at the buckskin. I wiped my hands on a kitchen towel and looked down at the green beans floating in the cold water. Ruth touched my shoulder. I went outside and couldn't feel my feet on the grass. I stood there looking at them all and Naomi walked over to me. Nelse handed the reins to Paul and came slowly toward me, and I was wondering if he was Duane and myself in one single place.

"Dalva, this is your son," Naomi said.

I think I said, "I know it," and he and I turned and walked beside each other out toward the driveway. We walked up the small road between the trees for a quarter of a mile without saying anything. I didn't even look at him. Then I looked at the ground and said, "This is where I met your father." I turned to him and he averted his glance as if comprehending what I said.

"Looks like a better place than most," he said. He put his hand around my arm above the elbow and I thought, Jesus this is going to kill me, I hope not right now. What should we do?

"Why didn't you say something before?" I finally had the courage to ask. He was a little paler, his hair lighter, but he had Duane's eyes and his shoulders.

"You've just been home a month, and I wasn't sure you wanted to know me. Naomi figured it out a week or so ago when we were working. I tracked you down last year. So I called my mother, the other one, and she said you two had met."

He still held my arm so I hugged him a little stiffly, looking down at the dust where his father had sat one hot afternoon with a burlap bag full of all he owned on earth.

"Naomi said my father was quite the young man but not necessarily the kind you wanted in your living room." Now he smiled.

"She was trying to look out for me but I guess it didn't work."

Quite naturally he wanted to see a photo of his dad so we walked back to the house and went up to my bedroom. He looked at the pictures unsure of what to say except to admire the buckskin. I ran downstairs and then back up with a bottle of brandy. We toasted repeatedly straight from the bottle, and talked a half-hour until we heard music. We went to the window and looked down at the front yard: Michael was roasting the chickens, Frieda was setting the table, Paul was standing near the tire swing with Luiz, who was petting the mare, and Naomi and Ruth were sitting at the picnic table. Naomi looked up at us standing at the window. We waved and she covered her face with her hands. The music came from Lundquist who was wandering around in the groves of lilacs, among the gravestones, then back into the yard, playing his miniature violin, as if he were at the same time serenading the living and the dead. We went down to join them.